THE MONEY IS GREEN

OWEN SULLIVAN

The Money Is Green
By Owen Sullivan

1.   FIC000000 – Fiction / General
2.   FIC002000 – Fiction / Action & Adventure

ISBN-13: 978-0-692-51474-0

Cover design by
David Flanagan
Misfit Agency
1013 7th Street, Sacramento, CA 95814
916-290-9660
www.agencymisfit.com

Printed in the United States of America

To all the men and women in uniform who have served
or are currently serving our great country.

ACKNOWLEDGEMENTS

I would like to thank Andrea Hurst of Andrea Hurst & Associates as well as Jessica Schmitz and David Flanagan at Misfit Agency. A shout out is due to Edward McGowan for taking the time to read and give valuable suggestions. I also want to thank both Lori McCulley and Jolene Childers for their contribution.

ONE

Jason hurried up the aggregate walkway, a soft winter rain leaving small droplets on his overcoat, to a pair of ten-foot glass doors, yanked hard at the chrome handle, and let himself into the building. He paused for a moment, running his hand through his thick brown hair as his eyes focused on the shiny brass lettering on the wall behind the receptionist counter. The word "Soltech" jumped out at him. Its logo of Earth with bursting rays of light surrounding it hung directly below the company name. In neat script, following the curvature of the Earth, read the words, "Everything we do revolves around the Sun." On both sides of the logo hung vertical white banners with Chinese characters written in red.

Jason stepped toward a young receptionist with close-cropped, jet-black hair, who was busily reading from her computer screen. She looked up, gave him a quick smile, and then nodded her head to the left.

"Hi, Mr. Ballard," she said in a soft voice. "She's already started the meeting."

"Thanks, Sandy," Jason said. He walked swiftly past her, switched the briefcase he was carrying from his left to his right hand,

and glanced at his watch. "Shoot, I'm five minutes early to the meeting, and she started without me. I guess she figures being on time is late." He turned a corner and headed down a corridor. Through the glass windows he could see a group of people sitting around a large conference room table.

As quietly as possible, he opened the door slowly and moved to the first open chair he saw. The room was lit up with ten sets of high-efficiency LED lights hanging from the ceiling on thin metal tubes. Tuck-and-roll leather chairs with tall backs surrounded the oval-shaped, tinted glass table. Framed black and white pictures of construction projects in downtown Hong Kong hung from the light beige walls.

As always, his boss, Mei Chen, was attractively dressed. She sat ramrod straight at the head of the table wearing a grey business suit with a white blouse and black bowtie.

She held up her hand to a younger man who was addressing her, and he stopped speaking. "It's nice of you to join us, Jason," she said curtly.

"I'm sorry, Madam Mei Chen, but there was a wreck on the 880 and traffic was backed up."

Her dark, almond-shaped eyes stared out intently from the wireless glasses that sat perched on her nose. Her creamy smooth skin made her look many years younger than she was. She turned away and nodded to the man standing. "Continue."

After the man finished, he sat down and nervously arranged papers in front of him. Jason watched as she spewed question after question at his colleague, Peter, who had the unfortunate task of trying to explain why the Kaiser solar job, a very visible job right off of Interstate 80 in Fairfield, was behind schedule. Geeze, Mei, he thought, give the poor guy a break. The project is only behind by three days. Peter was obviously shaken by the intensity of the questioning and was stuttering out answers, which only made Mei more irritated.

He glanced around the table at the other eleven participants in the room, who all had their eyes glued on Mei. I'm just glad it's not me on the hot seat today, he thought. Mei thrives on keeping everyone on edge. Just like my daughter, Crystal, likes to do.

Jason's thoughts drifted to last Saturday when he was driving his daughter from her soccer tournament. Out of the blue she'd brought up the divorce and caught him off guard. He was about to rehash the conversation in his mind when he heard Mei call to him in a stern voice, yanking him back to the present.

"Give us an update on the Copper Mountain project, Jason," she barked. Before he could answer, she followed up with additional staccato questions. "Has the Power Purchase Agreement been signed between Nevada Power and Inter-Power? What rate did Nevada Power agree to pay for the new energy? Has Inter-Power accepted our proposal to furnish the photovoltaic panels for the job?"

Jason stole a quick glance around the room. Eleven sets of eyes, all of them at least ten years younger than his forty-three years, were focusing intently on him. He quickly regained his composure and fired back.

"Madam Mei Chen, the Power Purchase Agreement, or PPA, has not been signed, but it's my understanding that it's being routed around Nevada Power for the appropriate signatures. My sources at Inter-Power say there is a closing of the documents scheduled for next Friday."

He glanced down at the legal pad in front of him, checked his handwritten notes, then looked up and stared back at her. "As you know, the utilities are being forced by the federal government to receive thirty percent of their energy from renewable sources by 2013. Even though Nevada Power needs another three hundred fifty megawatts of power to reach that goal, they are still fighting to keep rates low."

He turned a page in his notebook, all the while keeping eye contact with Mei Chen. He continued in a steady voice, "As such,

3

Inter-Power believes the deal will be struck at nineteen cents a kilowatt hour for the first hundred megawatts produced. They also think the rates will go lower from there."

He placed his hands together under the table and rubbed his sweaty palms. Except for the soft sound of air conditioning coming out of two vents above the table, the room remained totally silent. Jason could feel his colleagues stare as he waited for Mei Chen to respond.

Mei threw a pen on the table in disgust. "Nineteen cents a kilowatt!" she yelled. "How is that supposed to pencil out? I thought these power companies were behind the green energy movement."

"They are behind the movement," Jason continued. "It's that they have to consider the everyday customers they pass the additional cost on to. It's a difficult balance. As for your question regarding whether our proposal for the panels has been accepted, Brian Thompson at Inter-Power told me that as soon as the PPA is signed, he'll let out the contract and we're in the first position."

Thank god Brian is such a great friend, Jason thought. He's given me more insight into what direction Inter-Power is going, and it's helped keep Soltech in the mix for the Copper Mountain job.

Mei crossed her arms and a slight smile crept across her face. "Inter-Power better purchase my solar panels. Mine are the cheapest and nobody can compete with me." Picking up her pen, she pointed it at Jason. "Do you know what other panel manufacturers are bidding on this job? It's going to run over three hundred million dollars, and there are only a few of us who can deliver that kind of volume."

Jason nodded. "I know that the American company, RayTech, is one of the bidders."

"Hah!" Mei yelled, causing half the room to jump. "Those are the fools who got the five-hundred-million-dollar loan from the United States to start up their company, and the first thing they did was build an overpriced, over-the-top facility in Fremont. They can't compete with me, and mark my words, I'll drive them out of business in two years. Who else?"

Jason straightened up in his chair and took a deep breath. "Well, there's Ying-Lee and TerraSol, the two Chinese companies that are our closest competitors."

Before he could continue, she stopped him. Looking slowly at each individual around the table, she spoke in a firm voice, "As you all are aware, Soltech has been in business for the last five years and has the backing of the Chinese government, which has poured in millions of dollars to ensure its success. There is a tremendous amount of national pride involved here. The United States Congress has set aside billions of dollars from the stimulus bill passed in 2009 for green energy projects like Copper Mountain. It is imperative for us to land that job, as billions of dollars are at stake—billions of dollars that have Soltech's name on it. I need everyone in this room to redouble your efforts and make this project happen."

Jason looked around the room at all the faces of his colleagues, which remained expressionless. These people are working twelve-hour days as it is. What more does she want out of them? They're all scared to death of her and will do what she wants, but how long will they last before they burn out?

Mei clapped her hands and stood up. "Okay, that's it for today. Everyone back to work, chop chop!"

Jason stood to leave when Mei called to him.

"Hold on, Jason. I want to speak to you."

He sat back down and waited for the room to empty. Mei let the last person out and shut the door. She came around the conference table and sat on the table next to Jason. He shifted nervously in his seat as he waited for her to speak.

"That was good information you presented today," she said in an even tone. "You're efficient and thorough and don't complain. These are good traits. You've been with Soltech for over a year, and I've observed the way you manage our affairs and like what I see."

"Thank you, Madam Mei Chen," Jason said.

She held up the palm of her hand. "Please, call me Mei. Where are you proposing we stage the solar panels, inverters, and the rest of the materials we're going to need for this job? This part is going to be crucial for us to get this project built in a timely manner."

"I've gotten us an option to lease a large warehouse at Steadman Airport outside of Reno." He pulled out a legal document and handed it to her. "This airport can handle jets the size that we'll be flying the panels in on. It's not heavily used and the warehouse is located at the back of the airport right off one the runways. The planes can park just outside, and we can easily unload them and get back in the air to China in a matter of hours."

Mei scanned the document for a moment and handed it back. "The planes will fly back to China empty? Do you think we might be able to find a company that might want to use our planes to ship cargo back to China at a reduced price? It would help offset our costs of getting the panels to Nevada."

Jason paused and pondered her question. "Other than the wooden boxes that the panels were shipped in, the planes would be empty. I hadn't thought about shipping goods back to Shanghai, but I can certainly make some inquiries. It might be tough to find a company that will be able to keep up with our schedule. Once we get started, those planes are going to be flying in there all day and all night."

"See what you can do," she said as she stood up, "as it would be a shame to fly those planes back empty. I want you to come with me to Shanghai to tour my solar panel production facility. I know we can't build our facility in California exactly like that one, nor can we use the labor here like over there, but I'd at least like you to see what we're doing."

How am I going to pull this one off? Jason thought, trying not to show any emotion.

Mei looked at him. "Does this create a problem for you? You will only be gone a week at the most."

He took a deep breath. "No, it's not so much a problem as it is the logistics with my daughter and getting her where she needs to be while I'm gone."

She knows I'm a single parent raising a fifteen-year-old girl, he thought as he looked into her eyes. It's not like I can lock Crystal in her room while I'm gone. Someone has to watch her and get her to all her activities. She probably thinks I have a fulltime babysitter for her.

Mei arched an eyebrow, folded her arms across her chest, and started pacing in front of him. "You're a smart man, Jason, and a resourceful person. I'm sure you can find a caretaker for your daughter for a short period of time."

Jason nodded, feeling a tinge of excitement and guilt. He really wanted to see Shanghai, but at the same time he hated being away from Crystal. This would be the first time he would leave her with someone since the divorce, when his wife Debbie had walked out on them two years ago. She'd moved out of state to North Dakota with her new boyfriend to chase oil leases and left him to raise Crystal alone. He had recently found love with Janine, his current girlfriend, but Crystal was not pleased with their relationship.

He hadn't noticed that Mei had stopped pacing and was staring at him. She rested against the conference table and asked, "Well, are you going to accompany me or not? I'll show you China like no one else will, I guarantee you that. I'll give you my key to my presidential suite at the Grand Hyatt and you can use it whenever you want. It's a great way to unwind."

Jason let a grin come across his face. "I appreciate your generosity, Mei. Just give me a little time to figure out everything and I'll be ready. I agree with you it would be important for me to see how your panels are made. I've never been to China or Hong Kong, so it ought to be an interesting trip."

Mei smiled a wiry smile. "I'll give you a day to iron out your personal issues, but I expect a positive reply. I'll be taking the corporate jet to Hong Kong for a few days before you leave and then

I'll meet up with you in Shanghai." She turned and left the conference room, leaving Jason by himself.

Oh boy, he thought. This is going to be tricky. I know Janine will help out with Crystal and stay at the apartment while I'm gone, but how will Crystal react? Fireworks probably.

♦

His daughter, Crystal, sat quietly at the kitchen table, making pencil marks on a paper as she went back and forth from the paper to the open math book in front of her. She wore a dirty yellow and green soccer jersey with black shorts, and her hair was pulled back in a ponytail with a ribbon tied in a bow. At her feet, a small dog lay outstretched across the linoleum floor. A stack of schoolbooks and a half-opened backpack sat on the corner of their small walnut-stained kitchen table. Absentmindedly, she reached into a small bowl of Cheerios and popped a couple into her mouth.

Jason watched her as he leaned against a small white stove, stirring a pan of spaghetti sauce as he waited for the noodles to boil. Two white plates sat on the light brown Formica countertop. He stopped stirring the sauce. "Do you need any help, Crystal? I know that algebra can be daunting sometimes."

Crystal looked up over her shoulder and smiled. "No thanks, Dad. I think I've got it so far. When will dinner be ready?"

"In about ten minutes." He wiped his hands on a towel, came over, and sat across from her. "How was soccer? Is your team ready for the Union City tourney?"

She put her pencil to her mouth. Jason couldn't help but look at her delicate face with her bright hazel eyes and think about how much she looked like her mother. Crystal was only six years younger than Debbie was when I first met her. That was a much happier time. He sighed.

"What are you staring at?" she asked. "I'm not a circus animal."

Jason smiled a weary smile. "No, you're not." He stood up and returned to the stove. A few minutes later, he served the steaming plates of spaghetti. She had moved her books and backpack to the side of the table and was hungrily diving into the meal. Jason cleared his throat. She looked up, a forkful of spaghetti in her mouth.

"Sometime in the next week or two, I've got to take a trip for work. It's a really important career trip for me." He swirled some noodles on his fork. She stared at him intently as he spoke. "It's going to take me away from you for at least a week."

"Where are you going?" she asked between bites.

Jason looked down at his plate and picked at his food. "I'm going to China to meet with my boss, Mei Chen. I've asked Janine to stay here with you and help you get to where you need to be while I'm gone, and she has graciously agreed to help us out."

Crystal flipped her fork onto her plate. "You've got to be kidding, right?" she asked, as she raised her voice. "No way! I don't want her to stay here and I don't want her taking me to school. How can you do this to me?" She stood up and put her hands on her hips. "Mom told me Janine was the reason you guys broke up."

"Crystal, please. We've been through this before. I didn't meet Janine until your mother had moved out on me. You can't blame our divorce on her; it's not true and it isn't fair." He looked into her eyes. "I need some help, Crystal, and Janine can do this. You can't blame her for something she didn't do."

"That's not what Mom says," she said, raising her chin. "She says if you hadn't been so busy chasing Janine around, your business wouldn't have failed and she wouldn't have left you."

Jason could feel the heat rising in his cheeks. "You know that isn't true. I've never laid a hand on another woman while I was with your mom. The reason my business failed was because of things I had no control over. I tried everything to save it. It happened to a lot of people who had construction businesses like mine. I'm sorry your mother left, more than you know. But it was not because of anything

9

that I did outside of our marriage. And Janine had nothing to do with it."

Crystal grabbed her books and backpack and stormed out of the kitchen, her bedroom door slamming a few seconds later.

Jason yelled after her, "You'd better get used to the idea of Janine, because whether you like it or not, you're going to be spending a lot of time together!"

He stared down at the floor for a second then walked over and opened the refrigerator door. He pulled a beer out of the door, opened it, and took a long swig. Oh, Janine, what have I signed you up for? I knew this wouldn't be easy, but I had hoped Crystal would have come around by now after all the time we've been dating. Janine has gone out of her way to be nice and get along. I hope when I get back from China they're both still talking to me.

Just as he was lifting his beer for a second sip, his phone rang. He recognized Brian Thompson's number. He answered. "Brian, what's up?"

"Jason," Brian said, a tone of seriousness in his voice. "I need to see you first thing in the morning at my office."

Jason swallowed hard. "Sure, Brian, I can be there right after I drop Crystal off, around 8:00. Can I ask what's going on?"

"There's been another accident at the Soltech solar panel plant in Shanghai. Three workers were killed. This isn't good PR for your firm."

Jason felt a knot growing in the pit of his stomach. "That isn't good. I'll see you in the morning." He hung up and slumped into his chair. Why didn't Mei Chen say something about this to me this afternoon? Is this why I'm going to Shanghai? What's going on over there?

Two

The sound of engines quietly humming could be heard above the din of voices coming from the front of the plane. A plush Persian carpet of intricately designed peacocks and tigers ran the length of the 747. Walnut paneling with thick crown molding covered the interior, and colorful watercolor paintings hung from the walls. Mei Chen relaxed in the spacious center room of the plane on a massive leather couch. In one hand she held a book, *The Art of the Deal,* by Donald Trump, and in the other a martini.

Small Bose speakers suspended from the ceiling emitted soft piano music. Mei set her drink down on the mahogany coffee table and closed her book. Pulling the curtain back from the small oval window, she looked down at the vast expanse of Pacific Ocean thirty-five thousand feet below her. She could barely make out the white caps of the waves, and looking closely, she could see a tiny dot that would be a cargo ship making its way to the orient.

A young woman in a traditional Mandarin gown came up to her and half-bowed. "May I get you another martini, Madam Chen?" she asked.

"Yes, that would be good, Xie Tung," she responded, handing the woman her empty glass. "How long until we reach Hong Kong?"

Without looking up, the woman answered in a wavering voice. "We have five hours until we're in Hong Kong, the last I checked. Would you like me to find out precisely when we will arrive?"

Mei waved her hand dismissively. "No, that will be all. Just bring me my drink." She leaned her head back and smiled. *That should give me plenty of time to get ready for the party at the Royal Plantation and Polo Club.* She looked forward to all the pomp and ceremony that the British put out. Not to mention the fact that David Wilson, the largest hotel owner in Hong Kong, would be attending.

She pulled a compact from her purse and checked her lipstick. *This will be our second meeting, and I left him wanting after our first. He doesn't know it yet, but I'm going to be his new partner in his hotel business. He won't be happy about it, but once I explain the alternative, he'll see things my way.*

Two minutes later, the young woman reappeared and set a fresh martini on the table next to Mei. She bowed in silence and left. Mei absently looked out the window again, observing the two massive Rolls Royce engines hanging from under the wing of the Boeing aircraft. The dull white color of the exterior was in sharp contrast to the lavish and lively interior of the plane. The plane was one of fifteen used by the upper members of the Communist Party and as such had to look as non-descript from the exterior as possible. But her husband had allowed Mei to redo the interior, and she'd spared no expense. The fact that she spent more money decorating the plane than whole villages in China made in two years did not bother her. Her family had paid its dues and it was good to reap the rewards.

Her father's image came into her head and with it the memories. *I know you were disappointed I was not a boy when I was born, Father. I did everything I could to prove to you I was worthy. Yet no matter what I did, Father, no matter how hard I tried to prove my worth, I would never be a boy. I out-studied everyone in my class and* graduated number one at the University. I worked harder at my government job than anyone else and was rewarded.

She knew if he had lived, he would be proud of what she had accomplished—both proud and appalled. He'd be proud that I am so elevated in the Party, but appalled at my desire for the material things of this world. Although she knew he would disapprove of her material interests, she couldn't forget the same dull gray outfits everyone wore as she grew up. She thought about all the meager things they'd had at home, when at the snap of a finger her father could have improved their lives immensely. Not anymore, she thought. She'd worked too hard, had sacrificed enough, and was going to enjoy the privilege her status gave her and take advantage of her power.

She picked up a memo sitting next to her that Jason had given her before she left. She studied it for a few minutes and then set it down. Jason is a great asset to my company. He's smart, loyal, and works hard. I like his ideas. She smiled to herself. And he's easy on the eyes. He could almost pass as George Clooney's younger brother. She licked the rim of her glass, thinking. If he didn't work for me, I would keep him for myself, to be my paramour. However, since he did work for her, it was out of the question. She envisioned him as being the face of Soltech and being in charge of the whole company.

Her thoughts were interrupted when the plane hit some turbulence and bounced a few feet in the air, causing her to fall forward, almost hitting her head on the table. The martini tumbled to the floor.

She yelled, and immediately a uniformed man appeared at the door.

"Yes, Madam Chen, can I help you?" he asked as he held onto the doorframe for support.

"You tell those two pilots to steer clear of bad air!" she screamed. "Tell them to fly this jet correctly, or I will have them both decommissioned and sent off to the North Korean border."

The man bowed. "Yes, ma'am, I will order them to fly the plane correctly. There is no excuse for this type of discomfort."

"Good, and get Xie Tung to clean up this mess and to bring me another martini!"

He bowed again. "Right away, ma'am."

Mei stared at the spilled liquid in disgust. I need to inform my husband of such poor flying. This type of performance should not be tolerated.

♦

Mei glided down the stairway, her colorful gown fluttering in the breeze. She walked ten steps and then slipped into a black stretch limo, accompanied by Xie Tung, her valet, and Cho Loy, her personal assistant. Before the doors were closed, she started dictating a letter, speaking so quickly Cho had to use stenography to get it all down. The limo left the tarmac led by two military jeeps in front and two in back. All of the jeeps were occupied with soldiers armed with automatic weapons raised straight up but at the ready. Traffic pulled aside as they approached to let the convoy through, and within twenty minutes Mei stepped out onto the porte-cochere of the Grand Hyatt.

She made her way to the elevator with Cho following close behind, and after a quick ride up, she was standing outside on the presidential suite balcony on the forty-fifth floor, where she gathered in the majestic view of Hong Kong. Inside the suite, a magnum of Dom Pérignon champagne sat in an ice-filled silver container on the granite counter next to an enormous bouquet of flowers. The note on the flowers read in Chinese, "The People of Hong Kong welcome Madam Mei Chen."

Cho, wearing a gray business suit and holding a legal pad, stood silently by Mei's side, ready to start scribbling should she begin to talk. She turned and looked at Cho. "You may go now. I need to get ready for the party, so instruct Xie Tung to draw my bath. Send that memo out right away."

Pushing her glasses back, Cho bowed and headed for the door, writing furiously as she walked and calling out for the personal valet. Mei followed her back into the suite and hurriedly threw off her clothes. This is going to be fun, she mused. I can't wait to see Mr. Wilson again.

♦

Mei stood at the landing on top of the marble stairway and slowly made her way down to the grand ballroom at the Royal Polo Club. The room was capable of holding over a thousand people at any one time, and this was one of those times. The light-stained parapet floors shined from the recent waxing. A large crystal chandelier hung from the ten-foot ceiling, which had twelve-inch white box beams set in a checkerboard pattern across the room. Large floor-to-ceiling windows surrounded two exterior walls overlooking a lush garden with a fountain and koi pond.

Mei paused halfway down the stairs as she took in the scene below her. It brought back memories of the days her father had brought her to Party events here. The difference was back then there was nothing ornate or special about the festivities. Everyone dressed the same and looked the same. There were very few decorations, other than Communist flags, which were hung everywhere around the room. She smiled and continued down the stairs, her head held high. Servers in black slacks, white blazers, and white gloves carried silver trays of salmon mousse, stuffed mushrooms, and enormous shrimp, along with other tasty appetizers from the club's world-famous kitchen. In all four corners, bartenders furiously tended to drink orders.

Mei took in the circular tables with white tablecloths, white rose centerpieces, and expensive bone china. The full orchestra, dressed in black tuxedos, on the stage in the center of the room, played music softly as directed by a balding conductor. Women in long flowing dresses with diamonds dripping off their necks and ears flitted from one group of tuxedoed men to the other, their laughter and conversation filling the room with merriment.

Mei stood at the entrance to the room and waited to be recognized. Her full-length white evening gown fit her curves neatly and showed enough cleavage to get attention, but not enough to be scandalous. Her diamond necklace sparkled as she moved, bouncing the light around the room.

Mei spotted David Wilson across the room talking to Blake Keel, the US Ambassador to Hong Kong, and his wife. She walked gracefully and deliberately towards them, stopping to greet the prominent citizens of Hong Kong as she came across them. Her conversation was light and carefree, her laughter controlled and deliberate. Eventually, she arrived at David's side and gently tugged at his arm.

"Ah, Mei, my favorite Communist," he said with a smile as he bent over and kissed her gloved hand. "You look splendid, as always. Do you know Ambassador Keel and his wife?" He held his arm out in the direction of the Ambassador.

Mei gave a slight curtsy. "Of course we have met, many times. Nice to see you, Blake, and you also, Loren."

The ambassador bowed and turned to David. "Excuse us, I just spotted Congressman Gordon, and I need to speak to him before he gets away. Nice to see you again, Mei. Say hello to your husband for me."

Mei forced a slight smile and watched them as they wandered off. She turned back to David and looked up at him. "How long will you be in Hong Kong? Will I be able to get the dinner you promised me?" She playfully pulled at his sleeve, pouting her lips. Her red lipstick glistened in the light.

"As a matter of fact, I'm going to be here for a week, so if you can find time in your busy schedule, I would love to take you to dinner.

Speaking of busy, how is the green energy business treating you?" He took a sip of champagne as he gazed into her eyes.

"It's going well. Now that the United States government has set aside billions for renewable energy projects, my factories are busy operating twenty-four hours a day to keep up with the demand. You watch, by this time next year Soltech will be the largest photovoltaic panel maker in the world!" Her eyes narrowed as she put her arm inside his. "Wouldn't you like to be part of that, David? I could make it happen."

"Really?" he responded in an amused voice. "Why would I want to get involved in a solar company when I have ten thousand hotel rooms to look after and another three thousand to build in the next two years?"

She looked over her shoulder and then spoke in a soft tone, barely enough to be heard above the noise from the orchestra and the crowd. "Because, I have reliable information and an inside track on some of the largest solar farms being built in the world. My company will make billions in the next few years while you'll be busting your fanny to make a few million." She leaned back, a smug look on her face. "That's why."

"Okay, I get that," he said, suddenly more interested. "But why do you want me to be part of this? You've got the Chinese government on your side, and from what I've heard, they're subsidizing your company so much that no one can compete with you. What would I bring to the table?"

"David, you're a successful real estate developer who builds multi-million-dollar resorts. You have the ability to navigate through complicated deals, and you know how to get things done." She winked at him and a wicked smile crept across her face. "Besides, real estate is a great way to hide lots of money."

She grabbed his elbow and guided him towards the other side of the room. "Come sit with me, David. There are many reasons I would like you to join up with me." As they walked, she acknowledged people as they passed. She slid into a booth toward the back of the room and patted the seat beside her. Once David got settled, she put her hand through his. "Let's see. Where was I? Oh yes. Because of my husband's high position in the government, the powers that be allow me to run my company as I see fit and take advantage of the subsidies the government makes available. But if my company is as successful as I know it will be, the government will never let me keep all the money. That's where you come in."

They came to a table where four other couples were already seated, and David held out a chair. Mei acknowledged the other couples and continued, speaking in a hushed tone. "I want to have a partner help me keep all of the money my company's going to make, preferably here in Hong Kong." She looked into his eyes and slid her hand down under the table to his lap, playfully giving him a squeeze. "Besides, there might be other benefits, too."

David let a smirk come across his face and then leaned in next to her ear. "I might be mistaken, but are you not already spoken for and is not your husband the third highest member of Communist China's government? I don't think playing in that shark tank would be healthy for one's longevity. I realize we went down this path once before, but I didn't think you or I wanted it to be a long-term affair. It would increase the chances of getting caught." He raised his eyebrows at her.

Mei batted her eyes at him with and waved her hand dismissively. "Oh, David, don't be such a wimp. Ho knows only one life and that is the Communist Party. Outside of the Party, he does what I tell him to and he knows that what I do with my life is none of his business." She reached for her glass of champagne and took a sip. "Think about my proposition. I know you're already wealthy, but you can never be too rich."

Picking up a dinner roll, David broke it in half. "I'll give it some thought and let you know." He patted her thigh under the table. "You're making me a tempting offer. I may find it hard to refuse."

THREE

Four cars sat ahead of Janine, their engines idling while their drivers waited for the school bell to ring and unload the students from the classrooms and out to the waiting parents. Janine, on her cellphone with her administrative assistant, watched the first door of the school building up the walkway twenty yards away.

"I like the concept, Kristin, but I'll need to see it when I get back to the office. Run it by Patrick and get his thoughts."

Suddenly, a loud bell rang, every door from the building burst open, and students with multi-colored backpacks poured out, yelling and laughing as they made their way toward the parking lot. Scanning the students, Janine searched nervously for Crystal, this being the first day of her father's trip and the first day of their week together.

"Kristin, I have to go. I'll see you in the morning." She set the phone down. I hope this goes well, she thought. Jason is depending on me, and Crystal is such a handful. I can't seem to get past her disdain for another female, other than her mother, in her father's life. Well, I guess this is as good of a time as any to get to know each other if we are ever going to bond.

She spotted Crystal walking and talking with another girl as they headed toward the car.

Should she honk the horn to get her attention? She started to press the horn, but just then Crystal looked up. She immediately slowed down. The cars in front of Janine had picked up their passengers and moved on, so she inched the car forward to the front. Crystal tossed her backpack in the back and jumped into the passenger seat. Janine put the car in gear and pulled out of the parking lot. "How was school today?" she asked nonchalantly. "Did you learn anything interesting?"

Crystal sat silently, her arms folded across her chest as she stared out the window. After a minute she answered. "Look, I know you don't want to be here anymore than I want you here. Let's not pretend we're friends or that you give a crap about me. The less said to each other the better."

So much for getting off to a good start, Janine thought. This is going to be tougher than I thought. Oh well, I get to drop her off at her soccer practice and then she can be on her own again for a while. Jason, you're going to owe me big time for this.

They drove in silence until they came up to a large park that doubled as a soccer field. Janine pulled up to the curb and Crystal jumped out, not saying a word.

"You're welcome, Crystal," Janine shouted at her.

Crystal turned, gave a blank stare, and then moved on toward a group of girls who were kicking balls back and forth in the middle of the field. Janine steered the car back on the street and headed to her workplace. Her cellphone rang and she attached the Bluetooth in the console to her ear. She recognized the number of her best friend Melany.

"Hey, Mel, what's up?" she answered as she moved onto the freeway onramp.

"Hey there, miss chauffeur," Melany's cheerful voice came through the headset. "How goes the babysitting? Are you two bonding like sisters?"

Janine signed and looked in the rearview mirror. "Not exactly, but we're going to give it the college try and hopefully this will be an uneventful week." She pulled into the fast lane and accelerated to keep up with the traffic. "I haven't been around a fifteen-year-old for a long time and it's going to take some adjustments on my part."

"Don't worry, you'll win her over, I know it," Melany said, a happy ring to her voice. "She'll warm up to you, just wait and see. Like I told you the other day: Be yourself. Don't try to bend over backward for her since she'll see it as a sign of weakness. Treat her as if she were any other teenager you know."

Janine laughed nervously. "That's easier said than done, and she's not just some random teenager. She's the daughter of the man I love and she's my responsibility while he's out of the country. I wouldn't put up with her attitude if she were my child."

Mel paused a second. "Speaking of Jason, how are things going with you two love birds? Has his absence made your heart grow fonder?"

Janine hit her blinker and headed toward the upcoming off ramp. "Of course I miss him. He and I are getting along great. I know he loves me and wants to be with me, but he's so scared of how his daughter is going to feel and act, and sometimes that puts me on the outside looking in. I think in time I can win Crystal over, but it's not going to be easy."

"Jason is a wonderful guy, Janine, and it sounds like you two are good for each other. Hang in there with him; it'll work out."

She eased the car into an open spot in front of the three-story office where she worked and shut off the engine. "Thanks for the encouraging words, Mel. I'll do my best to get to know Crystal, but I think it's going to get tougher before it gets easier."

♦

Two hours later, Janine stood by the kitchen counter of Jason's apartment. Reaching for the first of the dirty dishes that sat in the bottom of the stainless steel sink, she started the water and began scrubbing. After fifteen minutes she had finished and was wiping down the sink. Crystal sat at the breakfast table behind her, her face buried in her math textbook. Janine wiped her hands with a small towel, set it on the counter, and sat next to her.

"Crystal, can we talk for a minute?" she asked in a hushed voice.

Crystal shut the book, rolled her eyes, and placed her elbow on the table, resting her head in her hand.

"What?" she asked.

Janine rubbed her hands together under the table nervously. "I know you aren't happy that your dad is dating me and that we've become close. I realize I'm not your mother and have no intention of trying to step into her place." She looked at Crystal, who was staring at her with a glazed-over expression. "You're a big girl and I'm sure you think you can take care of yourself, but that's not your decision. While your dad is gone, I've been left to watch over you."

Crystal stood up, got a glass of water from the faucet, and plopped back down. "Can you get to the point? I've got a lot of homework to do."

Janine took a moment. "I'm not asking to be your new best friend, Crystal. I'm only asking that you treat me with respect and understand that I have a job to do. I'll try to make this as easy as possible and stay out of your way." She reached out to touch Crystal's hand "Can you at least try to meet me halfway and not make this week a miserable time for both of us?"

Crystal pulled her hands back and set them on her lap. She stared down at the table. "I didn't want you to watch me. You don't belong here. You ruined my parents' marriage and now you're trying to ruin my relationship with my father. I'll be counting the hours until you leave." She picked up her books, placed them in her backpack, and left for her room.

Janine followed her and stopped at the entrance to her bedroom. Crystal sat at the edge of her bed, her head down, staring at the cover of her schoolbook.

"I don't know what you've been told, Crystal, but here's the truth: I met your dad for the first time long after your mother had moved to North Dakota. I had nothing to do with their break-up. I have no reason to lie to you, Crystal. I just hope you will be fair and give me a chance."

Crystal looked up and nodded at the door. "I'll give that some thought. If you don't mind shutting the door behind you, I've got homework to do."

Janine shook her head and closed the door. She walked back to the kitchen table and sat down in silence, tears welling up in her eyes. She placed her head in her hands and wept softly.

FOUR

The older SUV bounced along the bumpy road leading to the outskirts of Shanghai. Dust from the vehicle left a large cloud behind them, rising up to join the already-dirty sky. On either side of the road, peasants carrying large bundles of wheat on their backs trudged methodically as they made their way to their given destinations. Once in a while one would look up blankly and watch as the vehicle passed them by. Every few miles Jason looked back to the skyline of the city, barely making it out due to the heavy concentration of smog. For the last two days his eyes itched and his throat felt scratchy, as if he had severe allergies. Unfortunately, he had found nothing in the drug store that could make them go away.

The driver of the SUV, a small Chinese man with two missing front teeth, pointed up ahead to two large smokestacks about five miles away spewing thick gray smoke into the atmosphere. "That's the plant over there, the place on the right. We'll be there in about fifteen minutes."

Jason squinted at the facility. "Really, fifteen minutes? It looks like it's just up the road."

The driver shook his head. "We have to weave our way through a residential section."

As they got closer to the plant, the road grew crowded with more peasants walking in both directions, carrying various foodstuffs and live poultry to and from the city. Hundreds of bicycles clogged the road, making travel by car hazardous. Jason noticed the homes along the road were not much more than cardboard shacks with corrugated tin roofs. Young children stared at them with quizzical faces from the front doors of the shacks as they passed.

He'd never really thought about poverty in China before. It was his impression that China's economy was expanding so fast that everyone was benefitting from it. He was obviously wrong.

They pulled up to a guard shack that protected the entry to the plant. A newer chain link fence with razor wire at the top surrounded it. A guard in a military uniform stepped out of a small shack and stopped them. He said a few words to the driver then quickly waved them through, and they drove down a long asphalt road to the front of the sprawling plant. From the street, the facility didn't look that large, but once they pulled up to the front of it, Jason could see that it had to be at least three football fields long and half as wide. The walls were a concrete tilt-up construction at least fourteen feet high with a few small windows up by the top and all covered by a flat composition-tiled roof. There was a large parking area around the building, but Jason saw mostly company trucks and very few personal autos. The site was devoid of any landscaping and almost looked like it had been dropped on this deserted spot.

The driver, now tour guide, motioned for Jason to follow him. He walked quickly through a pair of glass doors into a very modern office complex. Secretaries, managers, and other office staff hustled back and forth between offices and the building behind them. The sounds of shouting and yelling reverberated around the office, which to Jason seemed like organized chaos.

After a few introductions, he was handed a yellow hardhat and they walked through the office to the production facility of the photovoltaic panels. A blast of hot, stuffy air hit Jason as he stepped inside the building. He stood in awe just outside the doorway as he observed the massiveness of the plant. Dozens of forklifts whipped around the concrete floor, lifting hundreds of finished solar panels stacked on wooden pallets and placing them in one corner of the building.

Workers moved around like ants, some toiling over huge vats of silicone to make the back of the panels and then another group using large wooden oars to stir pools of aluminum that ultimately turned sunlight into electricity. Jason had never seen anything like it. So many activities going on at once made it hard to fathom them all. There is nothing like this in the US, primarily because it would never be allowed. The working conditions in here were atrocious, and it had to be at least one hundred degrees, with very little ventilation and no air conditioning.

Particles of thick dust flew around the air from the saws cutting the silicone into four-foot by three-foot panels. As hard as it was to breathe in the area around the city, Jason felt it was almost worse here.

Jason followed as they walked down the assembly line, which was lit up like a football field by large fluorescent lights hanging from the ceiling. He tried to listen to the explanation of the guide, who was almost yelling over the sounds of the forklifts, saws, and other machinery. The plant seemed like a beehive of activity, where everything was in constant motion.

He motioned the guide over to ask him a question regarding the panels and, when he couldn't hear the answer, motioned toward the office. The guide nodded his head and headed in that direction.

Soon they were standing behind a glass partition on the second floor above the offices. The sounds were still coming through the glass, but they were quieter now.

"Wow!"" Jason exclaimed as he watched the flurry of activity through the glass. "That's an incredible operation."

A manager with a microphone screamed something in Chinese at the workers in the factory, and they seemed to jump and move faster. Jason looked over at the man and asked the guide, "Who's that and what's he yelling?"

The guide leaned over and looked past Jason to see what he was referring to. "Oh, him. He's the production manager. He has a certain quota of solar panels to put out per day. In order for him to meet the quota, he has to check every fifteen minutes to see where they are. If they're falling behind, he implores workers to speed up production."

"What if they don't hit the daily quotas?" Jason asked. "They seem to be moving at full speed to me."

"If the quotas are not hit, the manager will fire every lead person and move someone else up." He pointed to a group of men in white coats walking up and down the plant. "Working here is an honor and it is a disgrace to be fired. There are thousands of people in Shanghai that are ready and willing to step in and get a job here."

Jason watched the men in white coats shout at the other workers along the assembly line. Man, the only things missing are the cat-o-nine tails to whip those poor slobs into pushing harder. It's almost hard to watch this. He turned to the guide. "Do you have any safety guidelines here? With all the equipment flying around and the men working as fast as they are, you've got to have accidents. How do you minimize that? Is there anyone here who's in charge of watching out for the workers' safety?"

The guide shrugged. "No, we have nothing in place for that, nor do we have anyone overseeing safety. This is not America. These workers are paid to put out a product in a specific timeframe and that is what they do. Sometimes accidents happen and we deal with them as they come. But the management does not spend a lot of time worrying about accidents."

Jason's eyes widened. "That would never fly in the US. This plant would be shut down in a minute with all the things that are going on."

A toothy smile spread across the guide's face. "That is true, and that is why we don't build that many panels in the US. What is the name of that solar panel manufacturer in the US, the one that got the five-hundred-million-dollar loan from the government to make solar panels?"

"RayTech," Jason answered.

"Ah yes, RayTech," he said, grinning. "They have to follow all the work rules and pay the high wages, which we don't. You can see there is no way they're going to make their panels cheaper than we will. We'll bury them."

Jason surveyed the plant as he listened. We might be making them cheaper and we might bury them, he thought, but at what human cost? He turned to the guide. "How do our panels hold up as far as warranty?" he asked. "Are we as good as the US manufacturers?"

"Of course we're as good. The good news is these panels don't have any moving parts that can break down. They only degenerate over time and have a lifespan of twenty to twenty-five years. Our panels are as good as any on the market."

The guide's cellphone rang and he answered it, speaking in quick, short bursts and then hanging up. As he slipped his phone into his pocket, he took a deep breath. "That was Madam Chen. She wants me to bring you back to the hotel and go over what you've seen. She requests your presence at dinner at seven o'clock tonight. Do you have any questions before we leave here?"

Jason shook his head. "No, but if I think of any, we can discuss them on our way out of here." He took another look around the facility and then followed the guide out the door and down the stairway back to their car. I'm glad I saw it with my own eyes since I wouldn't have believed it otherwise, he thought.

As they got in the car and drove off back the way they'd come, he started doing some mental calculations in his head. Finally he asked, "How many solar panels a day does that facility put out? I'm trying to do the math in my head and I can't grasp it."

"We do around thirty thousand panels a day out of there. One third of those go to Europe, primarily Spain and Germany, and the rest go to the United States."

Jason sat back in his seat. Thirty thousand panels a day! That's a huge amount of inventory they're generating. I know we're not selling anywhere near that number. What is Mei Chen not telling me?

♦

Jason sipped a glass of 2003 Silver Oak cabernet and waited for Mei to arrive. Waiters in dark slacks, white coats, and black bowties walked stiffly between tables at the Cherry Blossom restaurant, bringing crystal decanters of bottled water or refreshing drinks from the bar. The floor-to-ceiling windows gave an excellent view of the exotic gardens of the Shanghai Grand Terrace Hotel. Jason watched a flock of colorful peacocks strut along a walkway as brightly colored macaws and birds of paradise flitted from tree to tree. From the off-white-paneled walls and crown molding with the gold-gilded trim to the marble floors with individual Persian rugs under each rectangular table, it all smelled of money.

Without his asking, he was served a small dish of Black Sea sturgeon caviar with hard-boiled quail eggs and a cup of cream of mushroom soup with truffle oil. Out of curiosity, he tasted the caviar and found it rather good. The room was half-occupied with mostly Chinese men, a small number of Europeans and Americans amongst them, but even so, the noise coming from the staff and customers was quiet and muted except for an occasional clinking of glassware.

He heard a small commotion coming from his left and looked up to see Madam Chen striding purposefully through the restaurant. She wore a light blue business suit with a frilly white blouse and black pumps. The restaurant staff were frozen in place and every one of them bowed as she walked by. Many of the diners looked up from their meals and whispered to each other.

Mei held out her hand to shake before sitting next to Jason. A waiter immediately appeared to open her white cloth napkin and place it over her lap while another one poured her a glass of champagne. "I hope I didn't keep you waiting long," she said, smiling. "I was meeting with David Wilson. He owns this hotel, along with two dozen others around China." She leaned forward and whispered as though telling him a highly regarded secret. "He's a very smart and very rich man. He might be useful to us someday."

Jason nodded. "I've heard of him, but he's a hotel developer. Why would he be useful to us?"

"Be patient, Jason. I'll let you know what he can do in due time. So," she set her glass down and picked up a menu, "you got to look at our solar panel production facility." She studied his face for a second. "What did you think of it?"

"It's amazing. I don't think I've ever seen a manufacturing facility so large. As much as is going on, I'm in awe of how many solar panels that place produces in a day."

She smiled again and snapped her fingers without looking away from him. A waiter immediately appeared. "Let me order for us, Jason. I'll give you a taste of Shanghai cuisine." She spoke in rapid fire for thirty seconds as the waiter scribbled furiously on a small pad. When she stopped, he nodded, picked up their menus, and headed for the kitchen.

Seeing the worried look on Jason's face, she leaned over and patted his hand. "Don't worry, I only ordered two exotic dishes— some eel and frog legs in a white wine sauce. The rest is fairly traditional." She leaned back in her chair. "You can see that, because of the size of the plant and the amount we produce, we need to sell a large amount of product in a short time. That's why the Copper Mountain project is so vital to me. Right behind that project is the Antelope Valley project in the western Mojave Desert. That project will be twice as large and will cost around one point three billion, of which eight hundred million will be used to buy solar panels."

A mixed green salad was placed in front of him and Jason cautiously picked up a fork and tried it. This is a little on the tart side, he thought, but still pretty good.

"That's a seaweed salad with sesame seeds," Mei pointed out. "It's very good for you."

Jason raised his eyebrows. "It tastes very good. What more should I be doing to help out?" he asked between bites. "I'm confident we will win the Copper Mountain bid, and that will take all the solar panels you can make in a year and then some." He raised up his hand. "Oh, I meant to ask you something. After I was finished talking to Brian Thompson at Inter-Power about the Power Purchase Agreement for Copper Mountain, I got to thinking about the land the solar farm is supposed to go on. Inter-Power doesn't own it because it's Bureau of Land Management land, the federal government's property. How does that work?"

Mei picked at her salad with her fork. "You are correct. It is BLM land. But I'm a good friend of Congressman Eugene Waters from California, who has major influence at the Department of the Interior, who control all of the BLM land in the US. I funneled millions of dollars to his re-election campaign." She winked at Jason in a knowing way. "Congressman Waters made sure Inter-Power was given a sweetheart lease that doesn't kick in until Copper Mountain is complete. We couldn't have written a better deal for ourselves." Mei burst out laughing. "Except we did write it for ourselves!" She stopped laughing and became serious. "Of course, everything we did was legal."

Jason laughed with her. She has every base covered. No wonder she's so confident she can bury the American company, RayTech. Their own congressman is selling them out to the Chinese. I wonder what her idea of legal really is.

The main course showed up, and Jason stared at the chunks of meat and scrawny legs covered in the light-colored sauce. "It smells good," he said without looking up from the dish. "What's the saying? When in Rome?" He took a bite and smiled, savoring the flavors. "Mei, this is delicious."

"I knew you would like it. You American men are so predictable. Throw some meat in a wine sauce or a marinara sauce and you think you've found nirvana."

"You're probably right," he said, laughing. The conversation stalled for a moment while both of them sampled the various dishes around the table. Satisfied for the moment, Jason wiped his mouth with his napkin. "What about the Antelope Valley project? Is that on BLM land also? How will you get that lease?"

Mei leaned back in her chair, her head held high. "Yes, it's also BLM land, and I have a conference call with Congressman Waters next week regarding that very subject."

"Is there any chance someone else could get the lease?" Jason asked.

Mei's eyes narrowed. "Let's just say I provide many services for the congressman besides money. He likes Cuban cigars, French champagne, and Asian women. I've arranged many trips for him to the Far East, where he fulfills his fantasies. So no, no one else is going to get that lease other than who I direct, which will be Inter-Power." She raised her wine glass and looked at him over the rim. "But this information is for your ears only. I know I've told you this before, but if you're going to be taking a larger role in running Soltech, I need to know I have your complete confidence."

Jason smiled. "Of course, Mei. I completely understand." This congressman seems like a real slime ball, Jason thought. But if history repeats itself, I bet it's a matter of time before he gets caught. He paused and picked at his food for a moment, considering whether to ask about his concerns with safety at the plant. He didn't like the idea of making money off the backs of people's misery.

He cleared his throat. "Mei, when I was at the solar plant today, I couldn't help but notice that it seems a little dangerous for some of the workers. Is it possible to make the production goals you've set but at the same time keep the workers safe? It would be horrible publicity if someone were to die in the process of making our panels when a little bit of prevention could make it safer."

Mei laughed. "You Americans are amazing, always worrying about worker safety. Workers die at the factory once in a while. It's a fact of life and it's part of the cost of doing business!" She paused and put her napkin to her lips. "Look, Jason, the Chinese people are not like the American people. We are very different than you." She stopped and took a deep breath. "Have you ever heard of the Long March in regard to Chinese history?"

Jason shook his head.

"Well let me educate you for a minute. In October of 1934, three hundred thousand Chinese of the Red Army under the command of Mao Tse-Tung were being pursued by the Kuemintang, the Chinese National Party under the rule of Generalissimo Chiang Kai-Shek. To be caught meant death." She paused to let her words sink in.

"The Red Army left Jiangai province and traveled six thousand miles by foot and by donkey over some of the highest mountain peaks and hottest desert in China. They marched for a full year, fighting and trying to stay alive. Of the original three hundred thousand that started, two hundred thousand died. To the Chinese, death is part of life, as is suffering to achieve one's goals. There was a small band of women that went with the Red Army on the march, and one of those women was my great-grandmother."

"Your great-grandmother made that trip?" Jason asked incredulously.

"That's correct. That's also why my husband is so high up in the Communist Party. My grandmother was very close to Chairman Mao and stood with him through thick and thin. She and my family were rewarded for their loyalty. We Chinese understand hard work and

33

tough situations. When I was growing up, I always was pushed and I pushed myself to work hard, to be the best. We always push forward. We do not concern ourselves with niceties in our workplaces."

Jason took a sip of water. "That's an impressive story, Mei. I guess I'll have to get used to our cultural differences." He gave her a slight smile. It doesn't mean I'll agree with them, just that I'll understand who I'm dealing with better. I didn't realize how ruthless Mei can be when she wants to get something.

FIVE

Congressman Eugene Waters leaned back in his leather chair, his hands behind his head as he listened half-heartedly to his aide, John Clayton, going over a series of bills being introduced that morning on the floor of Congress. Behind him hung framed pictures of himself and a smiling President Obama shaking hands at the ribbon cutting of the RayTech plant in Fremont. There were numerous other photos of him at various events as he performed his duties as a United States congressman. His diploma from the University of California at Berkley hung in the middle of the wall surrounded by the pictures. An oak credenza held some golf trophies and other pictures of his attractive wife and two children at different family functions.

As a tall, athletic black man, he had a friendly smile and an easy disposition that disarmed even his staunchest critics. Ever since his political science days at Berkeley, he had always found politics intriguing and figured out quickly that the smart money was in pushing the renewable energy field, especially in Northern California. He was the driving force behind RayTech's successful bid to get the five-hundred-million-dollar loan guarantee, which allowed them to build the large plant in the South Bay area of northern California and to start production of solar panels, employing thousands of new people in the process.

He was not known as a zealot in the renewable field but was sure to get as much money as possible out of the federal government for green energy projects. The trillion-dollar stimulus package passed in 2009 was a godsend to many of his pet projects, particularly RayTech and the Copper Mountain solar farm. John, sitting on the chair in front of his desk, continued reading a bill out loud that was coming up for a vote. As he listened to John drone on, his thoughts drifted to his upcoming trip to Malaysia. Officially, it was a fact-finding trip about ways to harness methane gas from cows and other animals and for him to tour a newly complete biofuel plant in Singapore, but in reality he was going to do a few whirlwind stops and then head to Bali to party like a college kid on spring break.

He closed his eyes and thought about the last trip he'd taken to Jakarta. The thought of himself and the two naked women cavorting in the hot tub at his villa made him absently rub his thighs.

His thoughts abruptly came back to the present when he heard his secretary call out from the front office, "Madam Chen is on line one for you, Congressman. Would you like me to take a message for you?"

He leaned forward and shouted back, "No, I'll take it!" He nodded to the door, and John took the hint and left the room. Waters waited until he was sure the door had clicked shut and then grabbed the phone receiver. "Madam Chen, how is my favorite China doll?"

Mei laughed on the other end. "Oh, Congressman Waters, you are such a rascal. Do you flatter every woman you talk to?"

Waters laughed with her. "Of course not, just the very pretty ones. What can I do for you today?"

"I wanted to discuss the lease of the BLM land for the upcoming Antelope Valley solar farm in the Mojave Desert. As you know, the project is set to be on the two thousand one hundred acres BLM has identified and the request for proposals is out. Inter-Power is preparing their response, but I want to make sure we can cut a similar deal as we did for the Copper Mountain project."

Waters studied the back of his hands and lowered his voice. "The Copper Mountain project created a big crap storm due to the fact that some of the most influential contractors got beat out by a relative unknown in Inter-Power. There will be a lot more eyes on this auction than before. I have to be careful with what I recommend and how hard I push my sources in the Department of the Interior. I don't need a congressional investigation into improprieties of solar farms on federal land."

Mei sighed. "Okay, so what do we need to do to secure the lease for Inter-Power?"

Standing up from his desk, Waters moved over to the window looking out over the Capital Mall. "There's a couple of things I'd like to see done, and if you can accomplish those for me, I'll do everything in my power to steer the lease your way, provided Inter-Power makes some changes to their proposal. I'll get you what I need to have changed in the proposal and you can get them to Inter-Power to correct." He paused for a second and cleared his throat. "I've got a tough re-election coming up in 2010 and I'm going to need money— a lot of it. I need for you to bundle around fifteen million and put it into my campaign fund."

"No problem," Mei answered matter-of-factly. "What else?"

"There's an office building in my district that needs restoration. I want you to buy it, fix it up, lease it to me, and then give me an option to buy it once I leave Congress. At a cut rate, of course."

"Okay, get me the address and any other details I might need to know about it. What else?"

He walked back to his desk and picked up the picture of his wife and kids. "One last thing: As you know, I'm heading to Malaysia in two weeks. After all the dog and pony shows, I'm going to end up in Bali. I want our mutual friend who's helped me in the past to get me a nice villa on the beach and provide some entertainment while I unwind." He smiled as he set the picture down on the credenza. "Can you make that happen?"

"Of course," Mei answered. "Send the dates and itinerary of your trip to my personal assistant and she'll handle it. I'll make sure Inter-Power writes their proposal as you want it and gets it out by Friday. How long will it be before we find out that Inter-Power won the lease?"

"You'll know in a week, but the rest of the world won't hear until two months." He sat back at his desk and started doodling on a notepad. "If there are any hiccups, I'll let you know, but I doubt there will be any."

"Thank you, Congressman. It's always a pleasure working with you," Mei said sweetly.

"Before you go, how is Copper Mountain coming along?" he asked. "I haven't heard anything in a couple of weeks. Did you get the contract and everything else, and is everything all in order?"

Mei sighed. "No, we haven't officially got it, but I think we're getting closer. We're trying to figure out the logistics of flying all the solar panels and all the other materials to the United States."

"Where do you think you might send them? Somewhere in California?"

"No, there's too much red tape with the government in California. We're going to fly them to Steadman Airport outside Reno and store them in a warehouse there until we're ready to use them at the solar farm." She paused for a second. "You don't happen to know any companies that are in need of getting their cargo to China, do you? Once my planes offload the solar panels in Reno, they'll be flying back to China empty. I could make a good deal for someone if they need their goods shipped back there."

Waters squinted, thinking hard. "Not off the top of my head I don't, but I'll be happy to ask around for you."

"Thank you, Eugene, you're the best."

38

"And you know you're my favorite China doll, Mei." He smiled as he hung up and wrung his hands together excitedly. *I can't wait for this trip to Bali!*

His assistant, John, knocked and then stuck his head in the half-opened door. "Congressman Chambers is on line two, sir," he announced.

Waters waved his hands toward him. "Come on in and shut the door, John. I want you to hear this conversation."

John came in and took a seat, laying his hands across his lap.

Congressman Waters hit the speaker button and then bellowed in a serious tone, "Congressman Chambers, what can I do for you?" He tried to suppress a smile, but was unable.

A grunt came through the speaker as the other man cleared his throat. "Well, my appropriations bill is being heard on the floor next week and will be voted on the next day. We've talked about it before, but I wanted to confirm that I can count on your coalition of twenty congressmen and women to support me."

Waters paused for a second, letting the silence hang thick in the air. "Oh, yes, Congressman, I remember our conversation and I've read your bill. It's very thoughtfully put together. I'm leaning, as is the balance of the coalition, on giving it our support." He leaned in toward the speaker. "However, there is a favor I would like to ask of you."

The speakerphone was silent for a second. "Of course, what can I help you with?"

"You're familiar with the Antelope Valley solar farm that's being proposed. There's a lease that needs to be given to the developer across Bureau of Land Management, or BLM land. The developer is Inter-Power and I would like you to support my proposal to accept them as the lessee."

The room was silent again and Waters raised an eyebrow at John.

"Uh, Congressman Waters, didn't Inter-Power get awarded the Copper Mountain lease?"

Waters nodded. "Yes, they did. I understand they're close to letting the contract out to the PV solar panel manufacturer so that they can get started. I believe all their permits are in hand."

"Don't you think it might be prudent to see how Inter-Power performs on the first project before we give them a second project?" Congressman Chambers asked. "These are billion-dollar projects and shouldn't be taken lightly."

Waters stood up and walked behind his chair, putting his hands on its back. "Inter-Power has been thoroughly vetted, Congressman. I have complete confidence they will bring Copper Mountain to a successful completion and we will have one of the largest solar farms in the world in the western United States."

"What about the solar panel manufacturer? Do you know if the American company, RayTech, is going to get the contract? I know they were banking heavily on getting it. It would be awfully embarrassing if one of those companies subsidized by the Chinese government came in and snagged it. All the jobs and all the manufacturing, along with millions of dollars being spent overseas, would not go over well."

Waters looked over at John. "No, Congressman, I agree with you, that would not look good if a Chinese company got the job, but I think RayTech is definitely in the mix. I will make a few calls and see what I can find out."

"I think that would be a good idea." The congressman paused then switched subjects. "Well, can I count on your support for the appropriations bill?"

Waters made a funny face at John, then mouthed slowly, "I've got him by the..." as he grabbed his crotch.

John put his hand to his mouth to suppress a laugh.

"If I can count on your support of the BLM lease to Inter-Power, myself and my coalition will support you, Chambers. I wish you well with the vote."

There was a long moment of silence before Congressman Chambers answered. "I didn't expect to commit to the lease this soon, but if you're sure Inter-Power can perform, I'll support them."

Waters hopped back into his seat and made a thumbs up sign. "Thank you, sir, and I'll see you soon." He leaned forward and turned off the phone. He clasped his hands in delight. "Well, my boy, that's how things get done in this town!"

John shook his head in seeming disbelief. "Congressman Waters, you are amazing. I just hope your faith in Inter-Power is well-founded."

SIX

J ason exited Brian's Denali SUV and stood next to him, gazing at the shiny new seven-story building standing majestically if front of them, its green-hued windows reflecting everything it faced. The building stood tall against the backdrop of the foothills surrounding Fremont California. The RayTech plant could easily be seen by commuters driving north or south on the 880 freeway. Eighteen charging stations for electric cars were lined up at one side of the parking lot. Rows of carports stretched out, each carrying a bank of solar panels on top of them, all tilted at thirty-five degrees and facing to the south. Brian, the owner and Chief Executive Officer of Inter-Power, and Jason were about to be given a tour of the inside offices of the building where all the management staff worked. Brian stood straight, looking up at the sleek new building. Dressed in a pair of dark slacks and a white dress shirt, he looked the part of the successful businessman he was.

Their guide that day was a recent Stanford graduate who enthusiastically pointed out all the energy-efficient items that went into its construction. As they passed through the double glass doors of the office into the panel-manufacturing facility, he pointed at the conveyor belt that snaked around the huge warehouse. Machines and men clanged and banged away at items as they moved along, making it difficult to converse. The guide was almost yelling when he said, "Those belts carry each solar panel through the entire process from the frame to the final coating. As you can see, it moves rather quickly and some of the more delicate parts are done by the robots working along the assembly line."

Jason pushed his white hardhat up so he could see skyward better. This is an impressive assembly line, I'll give them that, he thought. They sure didn't scrimp on anything, either inside the offices or in the factory. This place makes our plant in Shanghai look like something out of the stone ages. He studied the guide as they walked toward a large crane nearby. This kid can't be more than twenty-four but he sure knows a lot about photovoltaic solar panels. He might be a good person to hire down the road.

Brian reached out, tugged on the young man's short-sleeved white shirt, and shouted into his ear to be heard. "Hey, Perry, this is impressive, but how can you compete with some of the existing solar panel makers who don't have your overhead? I mean, you told me they've spent a hundred and seventy-five million on the offices and plant. How is RayTech going to keep the price of its panels competitive?"

Jason leaned in and listened intensely.

The guide stopped and folded his arms across his chest. "Well, Mr. Thompson, our panels are so easy to install, it only takes about half the time and labor. We also have the most efficient solar panels in the world, and our twenty-five-year warranty is the best in the business."

Brian nodded. "I get that, but RayTech is a two-year-old company. How do you know your panels will hold out, and who's going to stand behind your warranty?"

Perry smiled. "We've had some of the most rigorous testing, and the failure rate is miniscule. Besides, the federal government will stand behind us."

"But what is the actual price of the solar panel itself?" Brian pressed. "It's hard to compare your cost against, say, a company like Soltech's panels."

Jason stood expressionless and listened. I'm glad Brian didn't tell Perry that I'm with Soltech. I'm not sure he would give up too much information to a competitor.

Perry made a face as he rubbed the front of his iPhone against his dark slacks. He pulled up the calculator app and started punching in numbers. "I don't like to badmouth my competitors, Mr. Thompson, but RayTech's product and Soltech's products are not in the same category as far as quality. It's like comparing a Volkswagen to a Porsche."

Jason winced as he digested that comparison. Ouch, he thought. That's not even close. We build a very reliable panel and can compete with anybody's panels. Our panels have been rated slightly higher than Raytech's by the industry's watchdogs.

"That may be true, young man," Brian said as he looked at Jason, "but the major solar farm developers like Inter-Power don't warrant a Porsche, nor would they support one." He leaned over and looked at the numbers on Perry's phone. "Humor me, Perry. Say we were talking about a five-megawatt system. What price per watt would you be able to sell these panels for?"

Perry's eyes lit up. "A five-megawatt system? We could get really competitive for a job like that. The price per kilowatt for our panels would be around five dollars and forty-five cents."

Jason nodded and watched Brian's expression. He did some quick math in his head. We're quoting four dollars and twenty cents per watt for that same panel. Even if the labor to install RayTech's system is one half of Soltech's, they aren't competitive. How are they going to stay in business? Mei Chen could be right; we might bury them.

"Is there anything else you would like to see, Mr. Thompson, or you, Mr. Ballard?" Perry asked as he led them back toward the offices.

"No, that was very educational, Perry," Brian answered. Once inside the office they handed the young man their hardhats. "You're welcome to give me a bid on the Copper Mountain project, but I think you're going to need some time to work out the bugs before you can handle an order as large as that."

"I understand, Mr. Thompson, but I appreciate the opportunity to show you what we can do. I'll get my team working on the proposal and have it to you before the deadline."

They all shook hands, and Brian and Jason headed out the front door. When they reached the black Denali parked under the one of the carports with the RayTech solar panels on top, Jason stopped and looked back at the tall building, admiring its sleek lines and sleek design. "These guys won't last three years, Brian," he stated. "The Chinese government is subsidizing this industry so much it's driving the costs down at a scary rate. With the amount of overhead these guys are generating, they won't be able to build them cheap enough. I've seen Soltech's factories with my own eyes. I'll bet RayTech pays one worker more in a day than Soltech pays the same worker in a month."

Brian shielded his eyes and looked back at the building. "I'm afraid you're probably right. It should be interesting to see what fallout there is if this company fails and all that government taxpayer money goes down the drain."

They got into Brian's SUV and slowly drove out of the parking lot. Brian looked up through his rearview mirror. "Well, even if a whole lot of taxpayer money may end up being lost, it sure is an impressive facility for what that's worth." He turned out of the parking lot and headed for the freeway off ramp. "I'll drop you off at your office, and then I've got some work to get out."

"Thanks for bringing me on this tour, Brian. I'm going to be working on our revised proposal and I'll call you when it's ready to submit."

"I'm going out of town for a few days and we can get together when I return."

♦

Two days later, Jason's cellphone rang as he was leaving the parking lot of Crystal's school after dropping her off. He answered on the second ring. "Hello?"

"Hey, Jason. It's Brian. How are you doing?"

"Hey, Brian. I'm well. What's up?"

"I'm back in town and I wanted to see if you would like to go over your Copper Mountain proposal. I'm getting close to deciding on who will get that contract and I wanted to make sure you're going to get a fair shot."

"I appreciate that, Brian, and I'm available whenever you are. I've got all my numbers put together and am ready to submit our proposal."

Jason took a deep breath as he drove. Well, it comes down to the wire, he thought. I hope I can convince Brian that Mei Chen's company can deliver these solar panels and that our quality and warranty is as good as any other manufacturer in the industry. I know she likes to cut too many corners, and I'm going to change that. But in the meantime, we need to land this job.

Brian's voice shook Jason out of his thoughts. "The deadline for the bidding isn't for two weeks, Jason, and I don't mind sitting down with you and going over everything."

Jason paused as he thought through his short-term schedule. I'm off to China a week from Monday. It will have to be next week. "I'm free next Tuesday anytime in the afternoon. What about four o'clock and then afterward we can run down to Parker's Pub and throw down a few beers?"

"Four o'clock works for me. I'll see you then."

◆

After Brian hung up the phone with Jason, he dialed the operations manager at his office. When the manager picked up the phone, Brian asked, "Hey, Phil, could you put together a summary of which bidders bid what prices for the Copper Mountain job? I'm meeting with Jason Ballard Tuesday and I want to see where the Soltech bid stands versus all the others. He's submitting a revised bid, but I still want to see where they started out at."

"Sure, Brian," Phil answered. "I can get that info for you. Are you leaning toward Soltech? The last time we talked, you were expressing concern about them."

"Well, let's just say I'm glad Jason took the job at Soltech and I like working with him. I told you I was initially worried that because we are such good friends it might be awkward if he didn't get this job, but he's a straight shooter who knows what he's talking about. He doesn't try to BS his way through projects like some of the other people in this business. I hope he understands what he's dealing with in Mei Chen. She's an amazing woman, but she's also deep into the Communist Party." He paused for a moment.

"Yeah," Phil said. "That in itself is unnerving. From the short amount of dealings we've had with that group, they're ruthless. Nothing will keep them from getting what they want if they really want it."

"You could say that again," Brian added. "That's what scares me."

◆

As Brian breezed through his office, located on the outskirts of San Jose, his secretary handed him a note asking him to call Mei Chen. Looking at the number, he thought it might be her home number in Beijing. I wonder why she would call me from there.

He shut the door to his office, tossed his car keys on the thick walnut desk, and dialed the number. Putting his shoes on the desk, he listened while the lines connected and the line on her end rang. About the third ring he heard Mei's familiar voice. "Hello?"

A feeling of friendly familiarity came through the phone and he felt his heart start to beat faster. Ending this relationship was not going to be as easy as he'd thought. He still missed the sound of her voice, the scent of her perfume, the soft feel of her flesh. He took a deep breath. "Hi, Mei, it's Brian. How are you?"

"Ah, Brian, it's so good to hear your voice," she cooed into the phone. "I miss you. It's been too long since we've been together. I'm coming back to the United States in two weeks. Can we get together when I get there?"

A knock on the door jolted him and he covered the phone with his hand. His secretary stuck her head in the door. "I'm sorry to interrupt you, sir, but James is on the phone. He says a forklift ran into one of the large inverters at the Summerhill job. He says no one was hurt, but it's created a big mess."

Brian nodded. "Okay, Bonnie, tell him I'll call him right back." He waited until she closed the door and then spoke to Mei. "I'd love to see you, Mei. Call me the night before and I'll come pick you up at the airport."

She giggled on the other line and whispered seductively, "Let's go straight to a hotel, okay? I have some things I want to do with you and I can't wait."

Brian smiled. "I'll try to envision what you might be up to, but I'm also going to be a good boy. Like we discussed earlier, I want to keep our relationship strictly professional."

"Of course, Brian," she cooed sweetly. "I can control myself."

He set the phone down and stared at it for a moment. I'm not sure I can, he thought. This is not a time to be weak. As much as it would feel great, I can't fall to her seductive ways now. I've got too much riding on these solar farms to be mixing business with pleasure, especially when the pleasure involves Mei Chen.

SEVEN

Mei set the phone on the marble counter in her kitchen and sat at a circular table centered in front of a large window overlooking the backyard. Out of the corner of her eye, she saw a small woman in a white smock silently come into the kitchen, move to the two stainless steel Samsung refrigerators, and pull out an armful of fresh vegetables. She moved over to the stove, set out a large silver pot, and set the vegetables on the white granite kitchen counter. She started rapidly cutting the vegetables on a wooden chopping block until Mei raised her head and yelled, "Ming, please do that later. I can't hear myself think!"

The shouting startled the woman and she dropped the knife. She hurriedly recovered and gathered her things before scurrying out of the room.

Mei watched her in silence and then turned and looked out through the massive windows to the three-acre garden that surrounded the back of the house. The house was built on a side of a hill above the city of Beijing, giving its occupants a breathtaking view when the smog didn't blanket everything. Today was a bad day and the visibility was only half a mile.

She stood up, moved to the large picture window, and stared down at the large pond outside the window. Large green water lilies floating on the top of the pond as colorful koi swam lazily under the lilies, comfortable with their surrounding and showing no fear of her. The sounds of laughing voices made Mei turn back, and she returned to the kitchen.

The tall double front doors burst open and her daughter came bounding in, wearing a pleated skirt with a white blouse. Following closely behind her was another young woman, probably eight years older, carrying the girl's backpack. She spotted her mother sitting in the nook area of the kitchen and immediately stood erect.

Mei raised her head, pointed her index finger at the girl, and bent it toward her. "Come in here, Chi," she said sternly. "Come tell me what you learned."

Chi stepped forward while the older girl set her backpack on the kitchen counter. Chi stopped about three feet in front of Mei and put her hands behind her back. In a high-pitched voice she said, "We studied algebra, biology, and Cantonese today, Mother. I learned about the Pythagorean theorem."

Mei's eyes widened. "Really, Chi? Recite it for me." The girl did as instructed and Mei patted her cheek softly. Satisfied the day at school had been a success, Mei spoke to the older girl. "Okay, you know what's next, Pin. Make her spend two hours on the piano and then two hours on the violin. Get going, the time's wasting."

The two girls turned and headed out of the kitchen in silence. A few moments later, the soft notes of Edvard Grieg's "Butterfly" wafted into the room.

Mei listened for a minute, then got up and hurried into the expansive family room where Chi was sitting behind the oak-stained Steinway piano. She slapped her hand on the keyboard, causing the girl to jump. "Play the piece correctly, Chi!" she shouted at her daughter, who stared straight ahead without an expression. "It's supposed to be light and feathery, not choppy!"

Mei turned and went back to the kitchen, picking up the newspaper sitting on the corner of the counter. She started thinking about David's hotels in Hong Kong and what she would do with them once she became his partner. She smiled an evil smile as she rubbed her hands together. I'm going to enjoy running those hotels the way I want to and make them even more luxurious than they already are. They'll be the talk of the world's richest people! Her thoughts where interrupted as, from the next room, violin notes from Viotti's Concerto floated across the house. Has she already practiced the piano for two hours? she thought. Mei put her fingertips to her temple in exasperation and stormed into the room. "Keep the vibrato even, Chi. Check your fingering!" She turned to the nanny, Pin, who was sitting quietly in a wicker chair across from Chi. "That sounds horrible, Pin. Make her practice an extra hour until she gets that piece correct!"

Mei heard some noise coming from the living room area, so she left the girls to their practice and went to investigate. As she entered the room, she stopped to see her husband Ho sitting on a large leather couch eating an apple.

"I didn't expect you home until later," she said, crossing her arms. Mei didn't like it when he came home early, as he was too easy on their daughter and often clashed with her regarding the amount of practice she made her put in. He was a slight man, maybe five foot seven, with a medium build. He wore thick dark glasses, and his straight black hair was combed to one side. She eyed his dark suit, an off-the-rack model that was simple but neat. Nothing about Ho was pretentious or splashy.

"Xi is heading to Chongqing, as there was a midsized earthquake there," he answered evenly. "He needs to show the people there he feels their pain and is concerned. I'll be leaving to go there in the morning to join him."

Mei didn't hide her disgust. She knew Xi was the leader of China and everybody danced to his fiddle, but she thought he was incompetent and did little for their country. She wanted more openness toward capitalism and more trade with the west, and Xi didn't. It was not the Communist way, he would always say. But he was going to step down soon—not soon enough for Mei, but soon—and Ho was in line to take over. Once that happened, Mei had big plans for China.

"I hope his train wrecks on the way and he's crushed by a herd of water buffalo as he tries to get away from it," she snarled. "The sooner he goes, the better it will be for all of China."

Ho stood up and grabbed her arm. "Do not speak such blasphemy about our leader," he hissed. He looked around the room cautiously. "Did you forget there are twelve servants running around this house? If any of them were to tell the authorities of this talk, we could be ruined!"

She wrestled her arm out of his grasp and pulled away, her face contorted in anger. "No one in this house will speak ill of me because they know what will happen to them if I find out. That is the difference between you and me. I command respect from my people because they fear me. They know I will destroy them." She almost spat out her words in contempt. "You, they walk all over. The only reason you are where you are in the Party is because of me and my family. My grandparents marched with Mao, and my parents toiled at the bottom of the Party during the Cultural Revolution. Do not forget your place!"

Ho's face grew red and his eyes narrowed. "Do not think, woman, that you are above reproach. There are a lot of people in the Party watching you. They see all the jewelry and the Mercedes Benz limousines. They see the lavish parties you throw and hear about your properties in Hong Kong. They, as am I, are aware of your scandalous affairs." He waved a finger in her face. "When you find yourself on the outside of the Party, do not look to me to help you!"

Mei stared at him for a long moment, her anger growing. She was about to let him have it when she noticed the music had stopped and the house was silent. She turned and cocked her head and yelled, "Get to practicing! Pin, why are you letting her slouch off? Add another hour to her practice time."

She turned back to Ho, who had moved across the room and was standing near the room's entrance. "Do not concern yourself with my business, husband. Those petty minds in the Party who criticize me are of no concern. There have always been people who are jealous of my success. It hasn't stopped me in the past, and it won't stop me now. I see a great future for China and I'm going to be part of it!"

Ho studied her. "You won't be a part of anything if you're languishing in jail. You won't be part of anything if you're dead."

EIGHT

The seatbelt sign went off and the lights in the cabin lit up the whole plane as it came to a full stop. Passengers jumped to their feet and reached up to the overhead bins to retrieve their carry-on baggage. Cellphones started ringing and twenty-five conversations started at once. Jason sat patiently and let the majority of passengers debark the plane before he stood up.

As the plane slowly emptied, Jason grabbed his briefcase and followed the few remaining people off the plane. The pilot stood by the cockpit and said goodbye to every passenger.

Jason headed up the ramp to the terminal, studying the emails on his phone. As he exited the ramp, he glanced around to see any familiar faces. He made his way through the terminal and ended up standing in front of the baggage claim. Although he knew Crystal was in school, he had hoped Janine might pull her out to come greet him. He stopped and set his carry-on next to the baggage carousel. When I phoned her a few days ago from Shanghai, everything seemed to be going okay. I wish I had told her when we talked how much I missed her this last weekend and how anxious I am to see her again. Oh well, he thought, I guess I'll see her outside.

As he stepped up and grabbed his baggage, his cellphone rang. He recognized the number of Debbie, his ex-wife. He immediately felt anxious and scolded himself. *Why do you do this to yourself? Get over her. She's not calling to beg you to take her back. Nor do you want her to.*

"Hello?" Jason answered in a croaky voice. His throat had gone unusually dry.

"Hi, Jason, it's Debbie. We need to talk."

He cleared his throat and kept walking. "Okay, go ahead, I'm listening."

She immediately started screaming and he had to hold the phone away from his ear. "Crystal has called me nearly in tears every day since you've been gone. She's so miserable she can barely stand it. You left her with that slut girlfriend of yours. That was your first bad idea."

Jason spoke calmly into the phone. "Whoa, whoa, wait a moment. You don't know a thing about Janine or what kind of a person she is. I had no choice but to ask Janine to watch her because I had to leave on short notice and she was kind enough to help me out. I'm sure I'll hear that this wasn't a great vacation for her either."

"I don't need to meet the woman to know her kind," Debbie said, sniffing indignantly. "Why didn't you call my mother or the Johnsons? They could have taken Crystal. She's a fifteen-year-old, for god's sake, she doesn't need a babysitter. And she doesn't need your girlfriend, whom she loathes, to be her babysitter."

"Look, Debbie, I'm doing the best I can. It doesn't help when you tell Crystal that Janine was the reason our marriage fell apart. I've spared her the real reason for the breakup. I wasn't the one who had an affair and decided to pack up and move three thousand miles away to live with the man. Don't try to use Crystal to ease your guilty conscience."

"Don't give me that BS, Jason. You were seeing that bitch the whole time we were married. You and I both know it!"

Oh no, here we go again, he thought. The fact that I hadn't even met Janine until Debbie was in North Dakota won't matter because she'd just justify her actions with fantasies. "Is there anything else, Debbie?" he sighed as if he had just lost a seven-round boxing match.

"As a matter of fact, there is," she answered. "I need you to send me more money. I think five thousand will do for now."

Jason raised his hands in frustration. "Five thousand? What is that for? I've sent you your three-thousand-a-month alimony religiously even though I'm raising Crystal and pay all her expenses. Why should I send you five thousand more? I thought Dave was killing it in the oil business there. What happened?"

"Dave's business is none of yours. If you don't send the money, I'll take you back to court. I know you're making more money than when we split up, and either way you'll have to hire an attorney and it will cost you more than five thousand dollars to fight me."

Jason pulled the retractable handle out of his suitcase and headed toward the exit. "We've already settled everything in our divorce, and at this point, going back to court would be a waste of time and money, but if that's what you're determined to do, I'm warning you, I won't roll over."

She snarled at him through the phone. "We'll just see about that!"

"Debbie, while we're on the phone, I need to know what you've decided for this summer," he said in a determined voice. "Crystal gets out of school in six weeks and wants to come stay with you. Are you going to let her?"

Her whole tone changed and she lowered her voice, speaking in a condescending manner. "I've discussed that with Dave and he doesn't feel comfortable around children, so no, she won't be coming to stay with me. I'll fly out there in a couple of months and visit with her."

Jason stopped and adjusted his grip on his suitcase, shifting it to his left hand. "Oh, that's really big of you to find the time to visit your daughter. And since when is a fifteen-year-old a child?"

"Quit trying to guilt me out, Jason. I do everything for Crystal. Good try changing the subject. You better send me the money or you'll hear from my lawyer."

Click.

Pulling his suitcase, Jason stuck the phone in his pocket and continued heading for the airport exit. Why do I let her keep pushing my buttons? If she keeps demanding this, I'm going to tell her to go stick that five grand where the sun doesn't shine. I'm tired of her trying to play the victim and extorting money from me.

As he exited the San Jose Airport into the bright sunlight, Janine pulled up to the curb in her white BMW sports coup. She popped open the trunk and pushed opened the passenger door.

Throwing the suitcase into the trunk, Jason got in the car, leaned over, and gave Janine a long kiss. "Thank you for picking me up. I appreciate it."

Putting the car in gear, Janine looked into her side mirror as she merged into the airport traffic. "You're welcome. How was your flight?"

Jason sighed as he fastened his seatbelt. "Long but uneventful," he answered. "So, how did it go with Crystal since we last talked? Did things improve any between you two?"

She turned and looked at Jason with sad eyes. "I'm sorry, Jason. I need to tell you about some things."

She steered the car down the street and headed towards a Starbucks on her left. She parked the car in front of the coffee shop and they both walked in silence through the entrance. They found a small table by a window and sat down. Janine set her purse on the chair next to hers, put her elbows on the table, and put her chin in her folded hands. She stared straight ahead for a long moment and took a deep breath.

"Jason, I honestly tried and I tried hard, but it's no use. I don't think anyone has given me the silent treatment for three days like she has. I've tried, I really have, to engage her and to interact with her, but

58

she refuses to give me the time of day. As long as Crystal is going to be in your life, which she should be, I don't see a future for us."

Jason reached across the table and placed his hands over hers. "Please, Janine, don't give up on me. I know things will get better. Crystal just needs some time to adjust to you being in my life. She'll come around. I really appreciate you staying with her and I know she can be tough, but give me a day or two and I'll have a chat with Crystal and explain to her what happened between me and her mother. I was hoping to avoid this talk to spare her feelings, but it no longer can be ignored."

She threw her hands up in exasperation. "We've been dating for almost a year. How much longer do I put up with this? As long as your ex-wife keeps poisoning that young girl's mind, I have no chance."

Jason sighed. "Just give me a chance to talk to Crystal."

Janine nodded. "Okay."

They got back in the car and headed home. Jason stared ahead at the road in silence.

♦

Papers were spread out all over the kitchen table as Jason poured over the stack of documents. Cost breakdowns, solar panel cut sheets, cash flow projections, along with the latest bid proposal to Inter-Power for the Copper Mountain job were laid out in order of priority. Jason had his laptop open and was finishing up an email when the front door opened and Crystal walked in. Her green soccer uniform had a few grass stains across her chest, and her cleats made squeaking noises as she walked over the linoleum floor. Jason got up and gave her a hug, holding her for a minute. "How're you doing, pumpkin? I missed you terribly."

Crystal leaned away from him like he had just come from a gym workout and stunk. "I missed you too, Dad," she said flatly.

He cleared some of his papers from the table and pointed to the seat next to him. "Come sit down and tell me about your week. How was school? Did you win your soccer game yesterday? What did I miss?"

She tossed her backpack at her feet and slid into the chair. She stared at him for a minute before answering in a monotone, "School was fine. We won the game yesterday and I had a goal, and Janine is a bitch and I can't stand her."

Jason sat back. "What's wrong, Crystal? Why won't you give her a chance? She's a wonderful lady with a big heart and she cares about you very much. If you would take the time to get to know her, you two would get along famously."

"Dad," she said sternly, "I don't need another mother, nor do I want one. Have you booked my flight to North Dakota? I really miss Mom and want to visit her."

Jason tapped his fingers on the table and took a deep breath. "You're not going to North Dakota. Your mom wants to fly out here and visit you in California instead."

Crystal leapt up from her chair, her arms pressed firmly on her thighs. "What do you mean I'm not going to North Dakota? Mom said you'd try this because you're too cheap to buy me a ticket. If I have to rob a 7-11 I'm going to find the money to get out of here." She grabbed her backpack and stormed out of the kitchen.

Jason sat in stunned silence. Okay, time for me to tell her the truth. Janine is right, we can't continue on like this. It's time she understands what really happened between me and her mother. Jason got up and knocked softly on Crystal's bedroom door. "Sweetie, can I come in? There's something I need to talk to you about."

NINE

The white golf ball rolled slowly toward the putting machine sitting on the carpeted floor, hit the lip, and bounced into the indentation the size of the ball. A small piston, engaged once the ball rested in the slot, punched the ball fifteen feet back, and it came to rest where it started at the face of Brian Thompson's putter. Brian was the same height as Jason, six foot two, but a few years older. His wavy dark hair had streaks of grey in it and was thinning at the top. His tanned face and arms gave him a healthy look, as if he spent a lot of time outdoors, which he did on the golf course, when he wasn't working. He was the type of person who could light up a room with his smile, but when he was serious, people listened.

Brian was still leaning over the putter when the ball returned, and with an unlit cigar in his mouth, he gave a tug to his light grey slacks and struck the ball back toward the plastic device.

Jason, sitting at an overstuffed chair in front of Brian's desk, watched the ball roll straight into the plastic cup. "You should be on tour, Brian," he teased. "Those are money putts."

Brian straightened up and rested the putter against the wall as the ball shot back. He sat down behind his expansive walnut desk. He winked at Jason and chomped down on his cigar. "In my dreams, I could be on tour. So, let's see what you've brought me."

Scooting his chair up closer to the desk, Jason reached into the briefcase and pulled out a stack of bound documents. He handed one set to Brian and kept the other for himself. Leafing through it, he stopped and looked up. "If you go to page eight, Brian, that's the amount of the bid. Behind that page are the corresponding documentation and back-up data to support the bid. If you look on page twenty-seven, I've done an analysis that shows you the price of the system and the corresponding tax credits you get from the federal government and the effective reduction in cost to the system."

He paused to let Brian catch up to where he was in the bid packet.

Jason continued. "When all the tax breaks and credits are taken into consideration, the system will pay for itself in five point three years. Your internal rate of return is close to ten percent."

Brian studied the numbers, picked up a pencil, and wrote some notes on a legal pad. He reached out and started punching numbers on the calculator sitting on the desk. After about ten minutes, he looked up and smiled. "I'm impressed, Jason. I think your numbers are very accurate and competitive. I also like the way you've shown me how the project will pencil out for my investors. I'll have to take your word that the internal rate of return is what you say it is, as this calculator doesn't do that calculation, but I'm sure you're close."

Jason smiled and closed the document. "Have you secured the lease from BLM for the land yet? I heard the Power Purchase Agreement was almost ready for a signature."

Leaning back in his chair, Brian nodded. "The lease was signed a few weeks ago. Dealing with the Department of the Interior is a pain in the ass. Even though we've got Congressman Waters pushing for us, it was like pulling teeth. I've warned Mei to make sure everything she does is legitimate and aboveboard. I don't know Congressman Waters very well, so I want to be sure we do everything according to the law."

"I've met the congressman myself," Jason said as he nodded in agreement. "He's an interesting guy."

Brian raised his eyebrows. "I'll say he's an interesting guy. He's the biggest proponent of the renewable energy movement and even runs around in one of those hybrid Priuses. But then he hops on Mei Chen's jets and flies all over the world spewing tons of carbon monoxide all over the atmosphere." He grunted. "I think his carbon footprint is as large as Bigfoot's. So much for a being an advocate for clean air."

"Yeah, I find that kind of ironic," Jason said, stifling a laugh. "There are a lot of politicians on the green bandwagon that do the exact opposite in their personal lives." He held up his document. "Back to this. Does this mean we've won the bid?"

"Not exactly," Brian answered. "I know you're aware of my relationship with Mei Chen and her involvement with Inter-Power. But I have other investors that I have a fiduciary duty to protect. I have to make sure I can get the best deal for everyone. The proposal you've put together for Soltech is impressive, but I still have to look at what the other companies bid for the job."

He got up and walked to the window overlooking the parking lot. A man was pushing a mower across a vast green lawn in the front of the building. "I need to warn you about Mei Chen. She's a very aggressive woman and will do anything to get her way." He turned and gave Jason a look full of unspoken implications. "Anything."

Jason shifted in the chair. "Why are you telling me this, Brian? Is there something she's doing that's unethical or illegal? I'm not interested in ruining my reputation or going to jail."

"Soltech's solar panels are some of the most cheaply made panels in the world, primarily because of the Chinese government subsidies. But they aren't the best solar panels out in the market, so I have to weigh that into the equation. The reason they're not the best is because Mei cuts corners in the manufacturing process."

Jason sat forward in his chair. "I thought you said that Earth-Sun was in the mix for this job. They're also a Chinese company and the government subsidizes them. There's not much difference in their manufacturing process than ours at Soltech."

Brian nodded. "That's true, they're a Chinese company and they're in the running. As a matter of fact, I've seen what they're proposing and they're going to come in more than Soltech. But the difference between your two companies is that Earth-Sun is run by a British man named Andrew Dillon, and he's been doing panel manufacturing for decades and is good at what he does. Earth-Sun puts out a great product because they pay attention to every part of the process, something Mei Chen has yet to learn."

Jason flipped through the pages of his proposal then peered up at Brian, trying to read his expression. This is bad news. I'm sure Mei Chen thought this was a done deal and was moving on to the Antelope Valley project. This is not going to be fun to explain to her. He looked down at the top sheet of his proposal. "Let me work on a couple things and finalize our price. I know I can make my proposal more competitive with Earth-Sun."

Brian shrugged. "Sure. If you want, I'll give you a few more days. But I have to be honest: Earth-Sun's proposal is going to be tough to get below, and the other issue you've got to convince me is the quality and warranty of your product."

Gathering up his papers, Jason stood up and they headed out the door. "I'll see what I can put together to show we can deliver a quality product and still get my price a little lower. I haven't told you this but Mei has been hinting to me that she wants to promote me to become more in charge of everything at Soltech."

Brian cocked his head. "Really? That would be good news. I think you'd help alleviate some of Soltech's problems. When do you think this might happen?"

Jason shrugged. "I'm not sure. She hasn't put anything down on paper for me to look at, so who knows."

Brian threw his arm around Jason's shoulder as they walked toward the exit. "Look, my friend, I'll give you the final look, and if the gap between your proposal and Earth-Sun's is large enough, I'll rethink my position. Convince me Soltech's panels will hold up in the long run. Let's wander over to Patrick's and toss down a few beers and forget about work for a little while."

Jason turned and smiled. "That sounds like a great idea."

♦

A few hours later, as Jason was driving toward his home, he dialed Mei Chen's number. After the call went to voicemail, he started to leave a message.

"Madam Chen, this is Jason. I just left Brian Thompson's and we went over our proposal for the Copper Mountain job. I need you to call me because this job is definitely not guaranteed ours."

As he was driving, he checked his watch. I better hustle if I'm going to pick up Crystal from her soccer practice.

Just when I thought things were falling into place for Soltech, I find out we have a lot of work to do if we're going to get this job. And we'd better get it. I don't think Mei will let Brian give this job away to another company without putting up a huge fight. This process is far from over.

TEN

The pool at the Sheraton Bali Kuta Resort spread out over an acre in size, and the crystal blue water shimmered in the afternoon sun. A huge water slide rose up out of one end, spiraling around a manmade foothill covered with exotic and colorful plants. A pair of peacocks patrolling the greenery stopped every so often to observe the hundreds of humans who ringed the pool as they sunbathed on white towel-covered lounge chairs. Brown-skinned servers in flowery Hawaiian shirts carried trays of margaritas, mai-tais, or coconut chi-chis to the sun worshipers. The clear water of the pool made an alluring respite from the hot afternoon sun.

With the four-story hotel in the backdrop, the pool area opened up to the pristine beach where the surf crashed noisily as wave after wave descended on the beach. Seagulls strutted around the beach as if they owned it, looking boldly for an unsuspecting sunbather to leave some food unattended.

Congressman Eugene Waters lay on a chair twenty feet from where the thatch-roofed cantina was positioned and from where all the libations being served were made. His servers didn't have to go far to take care of his needs. A young Asian woman in a bright blue bikini sat next to him and slowly applied suntan lotion to his dark back, the white cream melting into his skin as she expertly worked it with deft fingers. He had peeled back the top of his brown and tan Tommy Hilfiger bathing suit to expose his lower back and moaned contently as she rubbed the lotion in harder.

"Ah, Amy," he said to her, his eyes closed behind a pair of Ray Ban sunglasses. "You do this so well. I wish I could pack you in my suitcase and bring you home with me."

The woman leaned over and, giggling, spoke into his ear. "I would like that very much. Why don't you do that for me, Eugene? I could take care of you every day the way you like."

The congressman smiled at that thought. That would make for interesting dinner conversation if the wife ever found out. He turned to his left, where his aide, John Clayton, sat next to him in a similar chair, reading a Tom Clancy novel. He wore a floppy straw hat, and his skin was slightly pink from the sunburn he'd received after sitting out unprotected on the first day of the trip. Now, although he had applied sunscreen all over his exposed skin, he hadn't rubbed it in very well and looked half red and half white.

What a find John was, Waters thought as he watched him sitting there, absorbed in his book. I always thought UC Davis grads were just smart nerds who went on to be veterinarians. Who knew this guy would turn out to be such a tough, bare knuckles political junkie. He has no problem doing my dirty work and will go to the end of the Earth to protect me. He leaned over and slapped John playfully on the thigh.

John set his book down and looked over. With his big brown eyes, youthful face, and curly unkempt hair flowing out from the hat, he looked like he should be in a high school chemistry lab rather than a posh resort off the Indian Ocean.

"Why don't you have a mai-tai with me, young man?" Waters asked, his white teeth showing through his engaging smile. He leaned up on his elbows and waved his arm in an arc around the pool area. "Look at all this incredible talent out here and you've got your face buried in a book! I now truly believe in the saying you can lead a horse to water but you can't make him drink!"

John pulled his sunglasses down to the bridge of his nose and looked around the enormous pool. He turned back to Waters and smiled. "There's also a saying about what would the dog do if he caught the car? I'm content to live through you vicariously. You manage to squeeze enough out of life for the both of us."

Waters laughed as he reached around and patted Amy's bottom. She giggled and slapped him. "Yes, I guess I do manage to have a good time. Hey, Amy, could you give me and John a moment to talk over some business?"

She smiled demurely and stood up. "Of course. I need to get a few items from the hotel store anyway." She picked up her flowery cover-up and headed toward the hotel.

Waters watched her intently as she sashayed away. He shook his head and smiled. "I never get tired of that view." He got up on an elbow and turned to John. "Have you checked to see if the funds Mei Chen promised me have hit the campaign account? I've got to get that contract with Wo Sung taken care of by next Thursday."

John looked puzzled. "Wo Sung? I think I remember him, but refresh my memory."

"You met him with me about six months ago when we had dinner at the Golden Palace in Chinatown." Waters turned on his back and shaded his eyes with his hand. "He was the middle-aged bald guy with the thin moustache. He had two tough-looking guys with him who sat in the corner facing the door. You asked me who he was and I told you that he was the head of Fung Chi, the largest Chinese gang in San Francisco."

"Ah, yeah," John said, nodding his head. "I remember him now. I thought you said he was bad news and we should stay clear of him. What are you doing with him?"

"Well, he is bad news, but I've changed my mind about doing business with him," Waters answered as he scanned around the pool area. "He needs me to make some introductions to our Mexican contacts. He's got guns he wants to ship to Mexico, but he doesn't have a source to unload them to. I can provide that source, and he'll pay me millions for my help. I've also come up with a way to get the guns to Mexico."

A frown came over John's face. "We need to be careful how this goes down and make sure you have all your tracks covered. Remember, one of your main political platforms other than the green energy is gun control. You've pushed for, and gotten passed, the strongest anti-gun legislation in the country, and your constituents love you for that."

Waters nodded, smiling the whole time. "I'm well aware of my legislation. San Francisco and all of California should be thanking me for the strictest gun laws in the nation." He reached over and took a sip of his mai-tai through a straw, pulling out the red umbrella and setting it aside. He raised it up at the bartender, who nodded his acknowledgement.

He continued. "But here's how I justify this. These guns are going to end up in Mexico with one of the cartels. I don't know which one, as Wo has never told me and I don't want to know, but they won't end up in the US." A smiling young server showed up and handed him his drink. Waters took a long pull from the straw and then raised his glass to the young assistant. "You don't know what you're missing, John. These are scrumptious. Where was I? Oh yeah, the guns. Look, the more guns that go out of the United States the better. If the Mexicans want to kill each other in droves, I say more power to them."

"I get that," John said flatly. "But if it ever got out you were helping a gun-running operation, your career as a politician would be over. I just want you to be careful."

"Of course I am. Why do you think we're down here in Bali?" He nodded in the direction Amy had wandered off to. "Strictly for pleasure?" He lifted his head up and laughed. "Of course not. This is partial business." His face turned serious and he spoke in a hushed tone. "We have a golf outing tomorrow with one of my Mexican contacts, Juan Villa. He's flying in from Mexico City. Both parties need each other and I'll be setting up the introductions." He winked at John. "For a reasonable fee of course."

John nodded. "Of course." He put his hat down on the stamped concrete where his chair sat. "I think I'm ready to cool off. This heat is intense."

Amy wandered back over, a small package in her hand. "Are you going to go in the water John? Is it okay if I join you?" she asked, her high-pitched voice soft and innocent. "I'm burning up too."

Waters sat up in his chair, his drink not far from his mouth. "I think I'll go sit over in the cabana and get out of the sun. I've had enough for today." He put on the white terrycloth robe he'd hung over the chair and wandered over to the covered bar. He checked his phone as he walked and saw he had a missed call from Mei Chen. I wonder what she wants. Finding a seat at the bar next to a middle-aged couple who were nursing a pair of margaritas, he sat himself down. The couple next to him had their back to him, and he checked carefully around the bar before dialing Mei's number.

He heard her familiar voice answer. "Hello, Congressman Waters, how is Bali? Have you found your surroundings satisfactory?"

Waters looked over at Amy, who was sitting on the edge of the pool, her feet dangling in the water as she talked to John. Waters smiled a wicked smile. "You're good, Mei. This girl is even better than the others. I don't know how you do it, but keep it up. The room is great also. I think you picked the best suite in the hotel, and I thank you."

"You know I only want the best for you, Congressman," she cooed into the phone.

"Mei, don't be so formal. I've told you to call me Eugene. I get enough formality back in D.C. Well, I called as I was wondering if you had any good news for me. Did Soltech win that Copper Mountain job in Nevada? That will be a lot of solar panels going in up there."

"There will be approximately one million nine hundred thousand solar panels placed on that job, but as we speak, the contract has not been let out." She paused for a few seconds. "Your call to me is rather timely. I need some help with, uh," she paused, "one of the other bidders on this job."

Waters's eyes widened and he took a long sip. "What would you like me to do? I can't get involved in the bidding process. It's a private company and I have no authority to place myself in the middle of it."

"I don't want you to do anything regarding the bidding process. My main competitor is another Chinese company named Earth-Sun, run by Andrew Dillon. By all accounts, as Andrew Dillon goes, so goes the company. It's a one-man band."

"I see," Waters said, nodding. "And if Mr. Dillon isn't around to run the company, Earth-Sun doesn't compete. And if Earth-Sun doesn't compete, Soltech gets the Copper Mountain job."

Mei coughed into the phone. "Excuse me. Yes, it's something like that. Do you think you can help me out?"

Waters ordered another drink. Hmm, he thought. This might be very lucrative. That bidding process is going to end soon, so she's going to need help fast. He looked around the cabana and then spoke softly. "Of course I can't personally help you, Mei, but I might be able to put you in touch with someone who can. I assume you're going to need someone soon, correct?"

"Yes," she answered. "The next few days to be exact."

Waters hesitated and then stated matter-of-factly, "That type of quickness is going to be expensive."

"How expensive?" she asked.

Waters did some quick calculations and swallowed hard. "It will be two million for the introduction and another two million for the job."

There was no hesitation. "Done. I'll email you the details and information you'll need. I'll wire one half to your offshore account in the morning and the balance when the job's done." The line clicked dead.

The bartender came over and wiped a water spill in front of him. "Give me a shot of Patron," Waters said, smiling. "It's time to celebrate."

ELEVEN

Crystal gave an extra umph to the door when she slammed it, rattling it the in the process. She pushed aside her backpack sitting on the bed with the white comforter and two pink and mint-green pillows. Above the off-white headboard, a poster of Beyoncé was pinned to the wall while across from the bed, another poster of the group One Direction was pinned next to two shelves of soccer trophies. She lay down on the bed and stared at the ceiling, placing her hands behind her head.

Well, that was an interesting conversation. Why does Dad have to act like an ass all the time? All he seems to have time for is his job and his stupid girlfriend. And now he's making up lies about Mom. Like she would really have an affair behind his back. She reached over, picked up her cellphone from the nightstand, and dialed it. She recognized her mother's voice when she answered.

"Hello?"

"Hi, Mom, it's Crystal. I just got finished talking to Dad and he's not going to pay for my airfare to Fargo. I think he's just being cheap."

There was a pause on the other line. "I'm sorry to hear that, baby doll. I was looking forward to spending some quality time with you. I don't know why he acts like he does, because he could easily afford the ticket."

Crystal sat up and crossed her legs under her. "Can you buy the tickets, Mom? I've checked and they're only four hundred fifty dollars round trip."

"Oh, I wish I could, baby, but right now I'm struggling to make ends meet. I'm planning to come out to the Bay Area in August. We can spend some time together then."

Crystal rolled her eyes and fell back on the bed. "That's, like, in three months. How could you be struggling financially, Mom? I overheard you and Dad talking about a big check you received from the sale of the house about six months ago."

Her mother's voice grew stern. "Crystal, don't question me about money. You don't know what I'm doing here in North Dakota or what's involved in surviving in a new town. I'm doing the best that I can. Besides, I've already told you I'll be coming out in August to see you."

Crystal rolled a strand of hair in her index finger. Yeah, you'll come out here but you'll visit all your old friends going wine tasting in Napa and I'll be lucky if I see you for a few hours. Maybe Dad was telling the truth. Probably not. She sighed. "I really want to get away from here, Mom. Every weekend Dad brings Janine around and it's all I can do to keep from vomiting. I wish she would go away and stay away."

"I don't like her any more than you do, Crystal. It was my marriage she ruined, remember?"

"I remember."

"Well, there's nothing I can do about her now. Your dad made some poor choices, and eventually they will come back and bite him in the butt. In the meantime, you need to bide your time, get good grades, and in a couple of years you can be off to college. Your dad and his stupid girlfriend will be in your rearview mirror."

"Okay, thanks. I love you, Mom."

74

"Bye, Crystal, I love you."

She clutched the phone for a second. How can Mom not afford four hundred fifty dollars? Somehow she didn't seem that broken up over the fact I wasn't coming back there to stay with her. If Dad was telling the truth…

A soft knock on her door brought her out of her thoughts. "Yes?"

The door opened and her dad stuck his head in the door. "I put a pizza in the oven and it should be ready in fifteen minutes."

Crystal started to dial her phone. "I'm not hungry. Please shut the door."

He stood in the doorway for a second. He then stepped back, closing the door softly.

A young man's voice answered the phone. "Hello?"

"Hey, Steve. It's Crystal. What are you doing?"

She could hear explosions and loud noise coming through the phone. "I'm playing Call of Duty and I'm up to level five." Suddenly he yelled, "Oh crap! I can't believe I got knocked out!"

Crystal giggled. "You'll never get past level five. Hey, do you want to go over to the park and hang out? I'm bored."

"Sure, but how are you going to get out? Your dad will never let you leave your apartment."

Crystal stood up and went to her closet, pulling out a flowery blouse. "I'm going to tell him I'm going to study over at Bridget's. He'll let me go. I'll see you in fifteen minutes. Hey, did you finish your math homework? You can't afford to not turn it in or you're gonna flunk that class."

Steve stammered on the other end of the phone. "Uh, I, uh, was going to do it in a few minutes."

Crystal sighed. "Bring the assignment with you. I'll help you out." She quickly changed out of her uniform, putting on a pair of jeans and white tennis shoes. Picking up her backpack, she made her way to the kitchen. The smell of garlic, pepperoni, and cheese hung in the air, and she suddenly felt hungry. "Dad, I want to go over to

Bridget's and study with her. We have a big algebra test tomorrow and I need some help."

Her dad turned around from making a salad and studied her face. He looked out the kitchen window and saw his neighbors talking and milling around outside their building. "How long do you think you'll be gone?" he asked.

"No more than two hours. Save me some of that pizza so I can eat it when I get home."

He nodded as she made her way toward the front door. "Be home before it gets dark," he yelled at her as she left.

Fifteen minutes later, she and Steve were sitting on a wooden picnic table at the Frances Percy Park, which was one block from their apartment complex. Even though it was still daylight, the numerous streetlights surrounding them came on and lit it up like a sports arena. A couple of skateboarders were busy trying tricks at the other side of the park, but otherwise the place was deserted.

Crystal tossed her backpack on the table and folded her arms. "Okay, give me your assignment."

Steve sheepishly pulled out a piece of paper and handed it to her. She studied it for a second then pulled a pencil and small calculator out of her backpack. She scribbled numbers and punched buttons for the next fifteen minutes before handing the assignment back. "Make sure you turn it in. It doesn't do you any good if it sits in your backpack and never gets to your teacher."

Steve nodded and smiled as he folded the paper and put it in his back pocket. "Thanks, you're a lifesaver." He reached down and pulled a joint out of a front pocket of his khaki shorts and put it to his lips. He lit it and took a deep drag. He turned and held it out to Crystal. "You want some?" he croaked out.

She hesitated a second, then shook her head. "You know I'm trying to get a soccer scholarship for college. If I get caught smoking weed, I get kicked off my soccer team and there goes that dream. You enjoy it by yourself."

Steve smiled and took another drag. "Okay, I'll do that," he replied, spewing smoke out as he talked.

Crystal rested her feet on the bench beneath the table and put her hands together. "I want to get away from this town so bad. Summer can't come fast enough."

"Where would you go? Don't you have soccer practice in the summer?" he asked.

"There is some practice that I would miss, but it's not intense until the end of August so I'd be fine," she replied. "I want to go live with my mom in Fargo. It's almost been a year since I've seen her and I miss her so much."

As he blew out more smoke, he started to cough. Crystal slapped him a few times on the back and he stopped. "Thanks. Why don't you buy an airline ticket and go? What's stopping you?"

She looked at him with a scrunched-up face and threw her hands in the air. "Well, duh. How about the money for airfare? I don't have a job because of soccer and the tooth fairy didn't leave five hundred dollars under my pillow. My dad doesn't want to buy one for me and my mom says she's broke. That's why I don't just go."

He nodded knowingly. "Well, that explains it. How about if I drive you?"

She looked up at the sky and then at him. "Yeah, right. You'll just find a car out of nowhere and drive twenty-five hundred miles and drop me off at my mom's doorstep. You can't even drive."

He held up his hands defensively. "Hey, wait a minute. I meant that. I turn sixteen next month. I'm getting my license then. My uncle told me he'd let me have this older Toyota he has stored in his garage. It would be a great time."

Crystal's eyes grew wide and she grabbed his hands. "Do you mean it, Steve?" she squealed with delight. "You'd do that for me!" She threw her arms around his neck and gave him a big kiss on the mouth, knocking him off balance.

He reached out and caught himself with one hand, pulling away. "Hey, let's not go crazy here. I told you I'd drive you, and I'll stand by my word. We've got a few weeks to figure out the logistics of the trip."

Crystal stood up, jumped off the bench, and did a little dance. "Oh my god, I'm so excited." She stopped and grew serious. "We can't tell anyone. I can't let my dad find out and I want to surprise my mom. Can you keep this quiet?"

"Of course," he answered. "I won't say a word."

"Perfect," she said, clapping her hands. "I'd better get back. It's starting to get dark. Will you walk me back to the apartment complex?"

He jumped off the picnic table and dusted off his pants. "Let's get going. I've got some planning to do. Boy, will your mom be surprised when you show up at her doorstep.

TWELVE

Smoky air hung over the shabby bar room, which was dimly lit by wall sconces spaced ten feet apart with dirty yellow bulbs. A large dark-stained wooden bar stood on one side of the room, with a dozen well-worn barstools up against it. A large mirror hung on the wall behind the bar. Glass shelves with various bottles of liquor were stacked against the mirror, making it appear there were two bottles of everything. Patrons hunkered down over their drinks and conversed in low tones, their lit cigarettes hurling grey smoke toward the ceiling. The lone bartender, a slender man with wispy hair, stood with one foot resting on a sink behind the bar as he conversed with one of the patrons.

At the far corner of the bar, a short, stocky Chinese man in a dirty wife beater shirt and baggy pants conversed on a cellphone. His bald head and dark beady eyes, along with the pencil-thin moustache, gave him a sinister look, which fit in nicely with his current surroundings. A tattoo of a large dragon came from across his chest and ran up his right arm and shoulder.

He stopped his conversation short and looked down at his phone. He put the phone back to his ear. "Hey, Tom, I've got to take this call.

I'll talk to you later." He clicked the phone and put it to his ear again. "Hello?"

"Wo Sung, my brother, it's been a long time. How's my favorite Chinaman?"

Wo laughed. "I'm doing fine, Congressman Waters. It's always a pleasure to hear your voice. We haven't talked in a few weeks. To what do I owe this phone call? Is it business or pleasure? You know I specialize in both."

"Strictly business this time, Wo. I have a job that I know you'll be interested in for a couple reasons. One, the payout is very generous, and two, it needs to be done quickly."

"Well, let's start with the generous part." Wo looked over at the bartender, who was still talking to the same patron. "How much will this job pay?"

"Seven hundred fifty thousand up front and seven hundred fifty thousand upon completion." There was a pause on the line. "Is that generous enough to get the esteemed Wo Sung's attention?"

Wo checked himself out in the mirror, flexed a bicep, and nodded his head. "Yes, that's gotten my attention and I'd like to hear more. Tell me what it is you're looking for." He pulled out a small notepad and pen from his pants pockets and sat down at the bar. Listening intently, he took notes as Waters went through the job.

After going through for twenty minutes what he wanted done, Waters asked, "Do you have any questions for me?"

"Hold on a minute," Wo said as he continued writing. He slowly went back over the instructions he had written down and then answered, nodding his head, "I think I understand what you need taken care of. It shouldn't be complicated to carry out. I will text you where to wire the money and I'll get to work. If I have any questions or run into any problems, I'll get back to you."

"I'm going to be busy with some important legislation sessions this week, Wo, so I may not be easy to get in touch with," Waters said, his voice lowered. "If there are any problems, get in touch with my aide, John Clayton, and he'll relay your message to me. But I'm sure you'll be able to handle this with no sweat. You're a pro's pro."

Wo smiled and thought, And you're a dirty politician, Eugene. "I'm sure I'll be able to take care of this for you. I'll let you know when I complete it so you can pay me the balance. I'll be in touch with you soon."

"One more thing, Wo. Once you've successfully completed this mission, I'd like to meet and discuss your Mexican project. I think I've got a way to help you facilitate getting your cargo to Mexico. We'll talk when you've finished."

Wo hung up and sat in silence, his mind running through the various options for getting the job done. He called out to the bartender, "Hey, Tan, get me a tequila shot with a lime."

As he waited for his drink, he tapped his index finger on the bar and hummed to himself. I think I'll do this myself. It's just down the highway in San Jose and it'll be easier for me to do it than explain it to another person.

The shot glass of tequila was delivered, and he tossed it back with one motion. He threw a five-dollar bill on the bar and left. He muttered to himself as he pushed through the door to exit, "This job is going to be a piece of cake. Why are they paying a million and a half to get it done?" He shrugged as he walked up the steep street. "What do I care, as long as I get paid? And if Eugene can help me with the Mexican project, that's even better."

THIRTEEN

The fairway to the fourth hole at Parkland Golf Course in Walnut Creek bent to the left halfway down the hole. The manicured lawn looked impeccable except for small divots at various places on the course. Jason stuck a small tee down in the ground and set the white Titleist ball on it. In a graceful motion, he smacked it straight, watching it travel two hundred eighty yards before it ended up dead in the middle of the green. Jason glanced over at Brian and said casually, "You should save yourself a lot of grief and pay me now. If you do, I won't say a word the rest of the round."

Brian's hands rested on the top of his driver. He laughed as he stuck his tee into the ground. "You haven't beat me in two weeks, so why should I worry about you after one good shot?" He took a few practice swings and then laced his ball twenty-five yards past Jason's. He put his club on his shoulder and walked past Jason, slapping him on the back. "See, it's too early in this round for you to be cocky."

They both laughed and headed to the golf cart parked on the pathway next to the tee box.

As Jason drove, Brian adjusted the golf glove on his left hand. "When do you think you'll make a decision about Copper Mountain?"

Jason asked as he sipped an iced tea. "Will it be right after the deadline or are you going to make all of us bidders sweat?"

Brian leaned forward and checked his cellphone. "It will be right after the deadline. I'm not going to string you out. I tell you, this green movement is getting bigger by the moment. You made a great move getting into it when you did."

Jason turned to him and grinned. "Well, that was thanks to you. I didn't realize how much money was involved. With that stimulus bill that went through Congress, there's billions and billions of dollars lying around for the asking. Although I understand the construction and manufacturing side of solar farms, I don't get the economic aspects of it. Why are these projects so coveted?"

"Let me explain it in a nutshell," Brian explained. "I put together a large fund for my investors to develop these projects. The day we're done, we can take a thirty percent tax credit on the whole cost of the project or apply for a thirty percent cash grant. Then we can depreciate eighty-five percent of the whole project cost over six years. Basically, the federal government is paying eighty percent of the cost of the solar farm, and after six years my investors have their initial investment back and start clipping big coupons of money when we sell the power we generate back to the utilities. It's almost like printing money."

Jason whistled softly. "Wow, that's a pretty slick program. No wonder you people are always saying the money is green. Maybe when I save enough I could put some money into one of your projects." Jason stopped the cart at the next tee. A creek meandered down the fairway on its left side, emptying out into a small lake at the front of the hole, where several Mallard ducks swam around lazily under the weeping willow that grew out of a small island in the middle of the lake.

"Would you at least give me a hint as to where we stand on the bidding?" Jason asked.

"Do you know who you're competing against?" Brian asked nonchalantly.

"Yeah, it's Earth-Sun, another Chinese company like Soltech." Jason made a ninety-degree right turn and cut across the neatly mowed grass to where his ball rested. "They're tough to compete against. I've lost a couple of bids on solar farms to them. If we lose this bid, my boss, Mei Chen, will not be happy. She might even take it out on me and fire me."

Brian stepped out of the cart when Jason had stopped it. "Don't be so hard on yourself. You're her golden boy, the one she's grooming to run the company. Why would she fault you if you lose a bid fair and square?"

"She can do whatever she wants because she owns the company. Mei has made overtures about me running the company, to be the president of operations. It's a great opportunity, but I'm not sure I want all the pressure that comes with it. Mei is such a ruthless boss. I don't know if I told you much about my trip to Shanghai where I toured the main manufacturing facility. You talk about a sweatshop. The place has deplorable work conditions. The workers are not much better off than slaves." He shrugged. "If I were to take her offer to run Soltech, it would be under the condition that I would be able to make any changes that I see fit."

"That's one of the things that concerns me about Soltech, is their work environment. I've never seen their plant but I've heard about it, and it doesn't give me a lot of confidence in the product they'll put out. However, if she puts you in charge, that could be a game changer. I've always found that if you create a better environment for your workers, you get better products."

Jason pulled a seven iron out of the golf bag strapped to the back of the cart. "That's what I always thought. You manage a lot of workers at Inter-Power, Brian. What's your experience with how you treat your employees versus the production you get out of them?"

Brian grunted. "There's no mystery. If you treat them well, you'll get good results. I mean, there are always a few people who are jerks and no matter what you do they won't work out for your company.

But if you treat them like crap and take advantage of them at every turn, well, you're going to get crappy work out of them and, in your case, crappy solar panels. As far as bidding goes, you can only put in your best effort and try to win the bid but be profitable at the same time. Sometimes it doesn't go your way, but it doesn't necessarily mean you've made a mistake."

"That's always how I've felt, but Mei Chen has other ideas." Jason hit his ball and watched as it landed on the green, rolling fifteen feet past the pin. A single-engine airplane, its wheels lowered, flew over them on its way to the airport at the other side of the golf course. Jason shielded his eyes as he looked up at it. "She seems to think that work should be your life twenty-four hours a day. When she's around, I have to sneak out of the office to pick up Crystal, as Mei has her own way of thinking when it comes to family and it seems very radical to me."

"Really, how so?" Brian asked as he walked toward his ball a few yards ahead.

"It's a long explanation, but let's just say that in Chinese culture, children and spouses are best seen and not heard, and they too should be buried in either schoolwork or music practice at all times."

Brian reached his ball and sized up his shot. He paused and asked, "Speaking of family, how's the lovely girlfriend of yours, Janine? You and her should get together with me and have dinner. She's a lot of fun and she is sure crazy about you."

Jason waited for Brian to hit his ball before answering. "She's doing fine. We've been having some issues lately, especially after she looked after Crystal when I was in China. Unfortunately, Crystal and Janine don't get along."

Brian put his hands on the top of the golf cart and leaned in, his brown eyes curious. "Really, someone doesn't get along with Janine? She's the sweetest, most easygoing person I know. Why wouldn't Crystal like her?"

Sighing, Jason looked straight ahead. "Her mother feeds her with crazy ideas and stories about Janine. It's not fair, even though Janine goes out of her way to get along with Crystal. I've tried telling her the truth about what really happened to our marriage, but I don't think she believes me. Crystal has her own ideas on what happened to our marriage based upon her mother's version of events, which are lies."

Brian dropped his club and threw his hands in the air. "You've got to be kidding me, Jason. What is wrong with you? Your wife had an affair and left you high and dry alone to raise a kid. Why can't you explain that to Crystal so she'll understand? Of course she'll never like Janine if she thinks she stole her from her mother. Who would? Janine is a once-in-a-lifetime woman, Jason. She's got model looks, she's smart, has a good job, and really cares deeply about you."

Throwing his golf club in the bag, he jumped into the cart. "Get this through your thick skull, Jason. Debbie is not coming back, and even if by some remote possibility she did, she's not the same person you met, loved, and married. You need to let her go and move on with your life. Otherwise, you're going to be a tortured soul and your daughter will end up being a psychological mess."

Staring straight ahead, Jason drove the cart in silence. I know Brian is right and it's the right thing to do, but it's just so difficult to admit failure. I need to keep telling Crystal the truth. I'm sure she'll confront her mother and then Debbie will deny it, if that hasn't happened already. But Brian's right. Crystal needs to understand the truth, and I'll deal with the fallout from Debbie whenever it comes.

♦

Jason sat at his desk the next morning, a steaming cup of Starbucks coffee by his right hand. His attention was on an article about RayTech explaining that it had just landed a solar farm job out in Sonoma County worth around three million five hundred thousand dollars. The article went into detail about the history of RayTech in that it was a start-up American company with help from a five-hundred-million-dollar government loan and that this project was one of the largest solar farm projects on the west coast. It was a flattering article and Jason found it amusing. This distinction of building the largest solar farm on the west coast is going to be short-lived, he thought. Copper Mountain is going to be a hundred times larger.

He glanced at his watch and switched his screen to an Excel spreadsheet he had been working on for the last week. I've got half an hour before my meeting with M. I think I'll tweak this a bit and see where it takes me.

Twenty minutes later, he saved his work and gathered the paperwork stacked neatly on the corner of his desk. When he got to Mei Chen's office, he stuck his head in the doorway and rapped softly on the doorframe. Mei was standing in the corner of her office looking out the corner windows at the parking lot below the building. Her cellphone was in her ear and she spoke rapidly in Chinese. She half-turned and acknowledged Jason, indicating he sit in the chair before her desk.

As Jason sat down, he did a double take of Mei. Wow, he thought. She's really dolled herself up today. He tried not to stare at the stylish beige business outfit that fit her curvy body snuggly or the low cut white blouse that exposed her smooth white cleavage. A slit in the dress portion of the suit ran up past her thigh. I wonder who she's trying to impress today, he thought. Maybe she's going to try to close the Copper Mountain job with Brian Thompson in person. Any man would be hard pressed not to be influenced by her!

She hung up and tossed her phone onto a leather couch. "Are you ready to get going on the largest solar farm ever?"

Jason's eyes grew wide. "Did we get the Copper Mountain bid? I thought it wasn't closing until the day after tomorrow. What happened to Earth-Sun's bid? We beat them out?"

Mei grinned and held her hands out. "Hold on, Jason, you have a lot of questions. First off, technically the bid opening doesn't happen until the day after tomorrow, so we officially don't have the project, but I'm almost positive it's ours. You did an excellent job putting together the proposal."

"Thank you," Jason said, watching her as she strutted around the office. "But what about Earth-Sun and Andrew Dillon? According to Brian Thompson, their bid was going to be tough to beat."

Waving her hands dismissively, she turned her back and stared out the window. "I heard they were having some management problems over there and they're making some personnel changes. There's a rumor that their bid might be being withdrawn." She looked back at him over her shoulder slyly. "Besides, I'm meeting with Brian Thompson this evening for dinner." She grinned at him. "I'm sure it will be a long evening and very productive. I will have his assurance by today that our bid will be the winner."

Jason sat in silence, taking in what she had just said. Earth-Sun is going to pull their bid? After all the work and money they spent putting it together? This is going to be a couple hundred million dollar contract, not something you casually walk away from. Something is not adding up.

Mei stood across from him, her arms crossed, an inquisitive look on her face. "Well?"

"I'm sorry, Mei," Jason stammered. "I didn't hear your question."

"I like what you've done here. I asked you before about this, but I want to make it official. I want to put you in charge of this company in North America, to be its president. I want you to take over everything, specifically the Copper Mountain project." She walked over next to him.

He looked up at her and cleared his throat. "I'm flattered you think that highly of me, Mei. Do you need an answer from me immediately?"

A look of consternation came across her face. "No, I don't need it right at this minute, but I need it soon. Of course, this position would come with an increase in compensation for you, of which you'll find

I will be very generous. In addition, I will arrange for some profit sharing." She turned and paced behind him. "Of course, the position will require more travel for you, so that must be factored into your decision."

Jason looked her in the eyes. "That's why I would like to talk it over with my daughter and my girlfriend. It's tough on her when I'm away."

Mei turned and stared at him. "You know my position on how you Americans parent your children. Neither my daughter nor my husband would ever have anything to say about such a decision and would respect whatever I decided."

"I respect the way you raise your daughter, Mei," Jason said defensively, "but my daughter is different from yours. Our culture is different from yours. It isn't to say ours is a better way; just that we're different."

"Yes, I realize our cultures are different, but look at what a mess American youth are." She let out a big sigh. "Either way, talk to your family and let me know your decision. You are about to get really busy in a week or so." She waved her hand at him. "You can go now."

Jason gathered his file folder, stood, and returned to his desk. His mind raced. Why aren't I jumping for joy? I should have accepted that job on the spot. I'll be running one of the largest solar panel manufacturing companies in the world. It's one of the most prestigious jobs in the industry. What's wrong with me? But I've been here before. I had a hundred employees three years ago when I owned my electric company and it almost destroyed me when I had to let them all go. All of their lives were ruined because I couldn't keep my company up and running. What happens if Soltech fails under my watch? I'll have to go through the same agony of dismissing hundreds of workers again. Do I want that on my plate?

He leaned back and rested his feet up on his desk. What is Mei Chen up to? She's way too confident in Soltech getting the Copper

Mountain job. But if she can convince Brian Thompson at Inter-Power that we're the company to do the job, more power to her.

Before I talk to Crystal, I need some advice, he thought as he sat back in his chair. This is going to be an intense job, with a lot of responsibility tied to it. Is this something I'm capable of tackling? He picked up his cellphone and dialed.

Brian Thompson answered it on the second ring. "Don't tell me you want a rematch of our golf game. After the pounding I gave you, you're a real glutton for punishment."

Jason laughed. "No, I don't want a rematch with you, at least not yet anyway. But I promise I'll be coming back to you for the twenty bucks. No, I wanted to pick your brain for a second."

"Oh, so you want some serious advice. Well, fire away. I'll go ahead and start the fee meter."

"I just left Mei Chen's office and, confidentially, she offered me the position of President of Soltech. I would be in charge of the whole North American operations. If I consent to take it, I know I'll be at Mei's beck and call. It will require me to travel extensively all year, although she's going to give me a hefty raise and some sort of profit sharing deal. That part I like, but the rest scares me. What are your thoughts?"

There was a pause on the other end of the phone. "I don't see what your concerns are. You will obviously be well-compensated. You'll be able to travel the world checking out every new green energy idea that comes along. You'll be on top of your field and will have a ton of your company's money to spend to keep on top. What scares you about this? You should be dancing in the street."

"I think, deep down, Mei Chen scares me," he said, running his hand through his hair. "Sometimes I don't think she's in tune with what goes on in the real world. Because of the position she and her husband hold in China, I don't get the sense that she sees things the way normal people do."

"What makes you say that?' Brian asked. "She may do things different because we have different laws and different ways of running a business, but the bottom line is that she provides a product and the market decides if they want to buy her product. So far, it seems the market is happy to buy her products."

Jason sighed. "There's more to this, but I'm not sure I can put my finger on it. It's a feeling in my gut that she's off somehow and I'm going to be tied at the hip to her."

"Well, my suggestion is speak to Crystal and Janine and then sleep on your decision. Personally, I don't see how you can lose, but I'm not you. I'm happy for you though. Congratulations!"

"Thanks, Brian. I appreciate your advice. I'll let you know what I decide." Jason started to type a letter on his keyboard, his phone cradled in his ear. "Hey, I understand that you and Mei are meeting this evening regarding our bid. She seemed pretty confident that Soltech was going to win the bid for Copper Mountain."

"Really?" Brian exclaimed. "My understanding of our meeting was it was just an early dinner, strictly social." He paused for a second. "Oh, that Mei. She never lets any opportunity to advance her cause escape. Thanks for the heads up. It's going to be an interesting dinner."

"Yeah, I can only imagine. See you, Brian." As he hung up, a text came through from Janine.

Want to meet for a drink after work?

Pausing for a second, he texted back, *let's meet at Josh's Pub at 5:30.*

A smiley face with an *ok* came back in response. Brian is right, he thought. Janine is one of a kind, and I truly love her. I need to show her just how I feel.

He picked up a picture of Crystal, her smiling face staring at the camera as she posed in her high school uniform, a soccer ball under her arm. Oh, Crystal, what am I going to do with you? If I take this position, I'm going to be away from you for long periods of time.

Where will I put you when I'm gone? If I take this job, will you think I don't care?

Setting the picture down, he focused on another picture sitting next to it. It was photo of himself, Crystal, three years younger, and his wife Debbie, all smiling in front of Snow White's Castle in Disneyland. I wish I could turn back the clock and fix our marriage. Now that I'll be getting back on my feet and making the kind of money that kept Debbie in the lifestyle she was used to, our family life could be more stable. But not anymore with Debbie, and probably never.

FOURTEEN

The afternoon sun was slowly fading behind the tree-lined hills of San Jose, which overlooked Earth-Sun's corporate facility. A couple of cars were parked in the expansive parking lot, with most of the employees having left within the last hour. A hundred yards down the road, from a side street, Wo Sung sat in his black Escalade SUV, its windows tinted black, listening to a hip-hop station and sipping on a diet Mountain Dew, his Maui Joe sunglasses wrapped around his chubby face as he stared out at the three-story glass building. He had spent the last day and a half checking out the movement of Andrew Dillon, the CEO of Earth-Sun, and had a good idea of his daily routine. He watched the front door, where a bicycle rack stood, one lone bike still standing erect.

He glanced down at his watch. It's time to get into position, he thought. He should be coming out of there in ten minutes. Wo pulled out, drove a half mile down the road, and turned onto a side street, which was completely deserted. He put the SUV in park and reached around to a backpack sitting in the backseat. He pulled out a black hooded sweatshirt and put it on. Getting out, he glanced around the street then headed across a vacant field to a string of oak trees that lined a bicycle path. As he approached the trees, three riders came over the rise to his left and peddled toward him. He kept his head down and continued walking as they rode by. Reaching the first oak tree, he made his way to the other side and lifted up the leg of his trousers, pulling a six-inch Bowie knife out of the leather sleeve attached to his leg.

Taking a deep breath, he took another glance around the tree and looked down the bike path. A flock of starlings squawked noisily above him as they jockeyed for position for the evening's sleep. A lone car drove up the road from where he'd parked the Denali then continued down the road. Suddenly, he faintly heard the sound of bicycle gears from behind the rise in the road. His grip tightened around the handle of the knife.

A lone rider crested the knoll and headed straight toward him, the rider looking down at the path. Wo studied the rider and recognized the riding apparel and stature of the man and knew this was who he was waiting for. The rider closed the gap between them at a steady clip. As he came closer, Wo counted in his head, Thirty yards, twenty, ten, now!

Just as the rider approached the first oak tree, Wo jumped out from behind it. The rider tried to swerve to his right, but Wo had reached him first and reached out with his right hand, grabbed the bike to slow it down, and slashed the knife across the man's throat. He grabbed at his throat as the bike wobbled a few feet forward before crashing on the side of the path, throwing the man face first onto the asphalt. Wo quickly scrambled over to him, his knife at the ready. Blood was gushing out of the massive wound around his neck, and he stared at Wo with wide, frightened eyes. He tried to speak, but only gurgling sounds came out of his throat.

Seeing that the wound was fatal, Wo moved across the path the same way he had come, just as another set of riders came over the rise. One of them shouted at Wo as he headed over the small rise in the ground. "Hey, what happened? Hey, you, slow down. What's your hurry?" Wo glanced over his shoulder, his eyes peering out of the hoodie covering his face. He saw the cyclists pull up to the rider on the ground and set their bikes aside to render aid. One took off his shirt and wrapped it around the man's neck while the other furiously dialed 911.

Wo kept walking and made it to the SUV. He looked across the field, barely able to make out the commotion on the bike path. He put the SUV in gear and headed down the street. He smiled to himself. That was almost too easy. I think I'd like to bring the congressman in on the Juarez job. I owe him one and this job could be a perfect way to pay him back.

After driving a mile down the road, he stopped and picked up his phone. He texted, *Job complete, send balance.* He then added, *I'd like to meet with you to discuss what you've come up with for Mexico. Let's get together next week.* Pausing, he looked at the words and to the recipient, Congressman Waters, then hit the send button.

FIFTEEN

A tall white candle flickered at the center of the table located against the front of the window of the Stinking Rose restaurant in the North Beach area of San Francisco. The distinct smell of garlic and basil wafted around the bustling room. White-shirted servers moved quickly from the kitchen to the tables, bringing pungent dishes of shrimp, mushrooms, fresh pesto, and other items to the packed tables.

With her elbows on the table and her chin resting on her hands, Mei watched Brian Thompson as he spread creamy baked garlic over freshly baked bread. He smiled at her as he stuffed a piece into his mouth and dreamily chewed it, slowly savoring the flavors.

"Oh my, that's so good," he said as he tore off another bite. "I skipped lunch so I could stuff my face here tonight."

"I love it too. It's so delicious," Mei said as she tore off a piece of the warm bread. "But this food is so good it's worth not eating all day for it."

Setting the bread down, he turned serious. "Well, Mei, I know you didn't bring me here to discuss the garlic smells. So let me guess:

You want to discuss where Soltech's bid stands on the Copper Mountain project."

Mei looked away, trying to look as demure as possible. She lowered her eyes and dabbed her napkin daintily to her mouth. "Well, that's not the only reason I asked you to meet me, Brian. Of course I would be lying if I didn't tell you how important this job is to me and my company. I know there's a lot of competition for that job, but I thought that by you and I getting together face to face I could point out the positive things that Inter-Power could benefit from by using Soltech on this job."

Brian raised an eyebrow. "Really, other than the fact that you might not be the low bidder, there are other benefits we should consider? Go ahead, I'm listening."

Mei smiled and reached across the table to hold his hands. "Well, for one, which I don't need to remind you, is we have had a very special relationship together, which would become more solid if we were to work closely together on this project." She rubbed his hands. "But putting that aside, I'm also an investor in Inter-Power, even if it's silent, and I would like to think that I would be helping not only myself, but Inter-Power if I do this job."

Brian nodded. "That's just the point, Mei. You aren't the only investor in Inter-Power. As much as I like our relationship, I have to make my decisions based on what's best for all the investors, not just you."

Mei felt her temper flare but tried to keep calm. She pulled her hands back and set them on her lap. "I get it that you have other investors, Brian. I have other investors than myself in Soltech, primarily the Chinese government. But they don't dictate to me what to do with the company. If I wanted to do your job for my cost, or lose money on it, I could do it and none of my investors could do a thing about it. You can do the same thing. There's no rule that says you must take the lowest bid." She waved at a waiter who came by their table.

"Excuse me, sir, but could you bring me another martini?" She turned back to Brian. "Would you like another cabernet?"

He nodded and the waiter disappeared to the bar.

"Okay, where was I?" Mei asked. Before Brian could open his mouth to answer, she raised her hand. "Oh yes, the lowest bidder problem." She stopped as she collected her thoughts. "I forgot to mention to you that I have promoted Jason Ballard to be President of Soltech. He will be in charge of all of my North American operations, assuming he takes the position." She made a sly smile. "I know he'll accept the position."

"You're very sure of yourself," Brian said, "but Jason's an excellent choice. He knows his stuff and will be a great asset for you." Their waiter showed up at their table with two steaming entrees: Brian's linguini with clams, hers the baked salmon with lemon butter and dill. He leaned over and took a deep breath. "As always, it smells incredible. Let's talk business after we eat."

Between bites, they chatted about the politics in Washington, the stimulus bill, Mei's daughter, Brian's new Harley, everything but Copper Mountain. The restaurant never seemed to empty; as one group left, another was immediately seated. Laughter and voices filled the air, along with glasses tinkling and forks hitting plates.

Grabbing both hands over his belly, Brian leaned back. "I've got to stop. I don't want to but I've got to stop or I'm going to have to roll out of here."

Mei laughed as she dabbed the corners of her mouth with her napkin. "I know what you mean. My eyes are always bigger than my stomach when I come here."

Brian felt his phone vibrate in his front pocket so he leaned to his left to retrieve it. A text from his senior vice president read, *Call me, urgent.* He looked up at Mei. "Uh, would you excuse me? I need to make a call."

"Yes, go right ahead. I'll still be here when you return." She watched him go around the bar area and slip out the front door, standing on the outside of the window where she was sitting. She hummed a tune to herself and kept the beat with one of her feet crossed over the other one. She looked around at the faces of the people at the other tables. The group of six to her left looked like they were celebrating a birthday. A young couple directly in front of her seemed lost in some deep conversation. She glanced out the window at Brian standing on the sidewalk talking on the phone. His face had a pained expression on it and he put his hand to his forehead.

Hmmm, she thought. Must be some important news. I wonder if he'll share it with me.

Brian closed his phone and hung his head for a minute before turning and coming back into the restaurant. He came up to the table, an ashen look on his face, and sat down.

"Is there something wrong, Brian?" she asked in a concerned voice.

He stared at her before speaking in a soft voice. "That was Pete from my office. Andrew Dillon was attacked just outside his office a few hours ago. Someone slit his throat and he bled to death."

Mei put her hand across her mouth. "Oh my gosh! That's awful! Who would do such a thing?" Mei fluttered her hand to her face as though it had grown very hot in the room all of a sudden. "What is wrong with this country? Everywhere there is violence—guns, knives, beatings. It's terrible."

Brian looked stunned. "The police don't think it was a random act since he still had his wallet and an expensive watch on his wrist. It doesn't make sense."

"In this country it does. There's too much violence everywhere. " Mei bided her time feigning concern. "This is terrible news. Andrew was making great strides with his company." She paused a few seconds as Brian ran his hands through his hair. "Now what will happen to their bid for Copper Mountain.? They don't have the personnel to run a job like that without Andrew around. I hope they have a back-up plan. This is very unfortunate for them and sad news."

Brian blinked in astonishment. "You're kidding right? I hadn't even thought about Copper Mountain and probably won't for a few days until this sinks in. Get your coat, I need to get to the office."

Mei stood up and held her hands out defensively. "I didn't mean to be disrespectful. I was only thinking out loud. I know this is tragic, but life will go on."

"Yes, Mei, life does go on." He followed her out of the restaurant. He hailed a cab and opened the door for her. Once she was in the cab, he leaned through the window. "I'll be in touch."

Mei put her hands over his and looked up into his eyes. "I'm sorry this happened, Brian. If there's anything I or any of my staff at Soltech can do, please let me know."

He smiled faintly and backed away. "Thanks, I'll keep that in mind."

The cab pulled away as she gave the driver directions. Leaning back in the seat, she smiled. Looks like Brian will have no choice but to use Soltech. Things are starting to fall into place. Americans, they are such sentimental fools. They can't get past the fact that everyone is replaceable, especially dreamers like Andrew Dillon. If they thought like I do, they might be more formidable opponents. It's time for Soltech to become a major player in the solar panel industry, and whoever isn't with me is against me.

SIXTEEN

The long arm of the construction crane moved across the top of the twelfth floor of the newest hotel in David Wilson's portfolio, located in the high-rent district of Hong Kong. It carried a steel beam almost sixteen feet in length, dangling it high in the air as it moved along its journey to its final destination somewhere in the middle of the building.

David stood at the base of the hotel next to his construction foreman, who had a rolled set of plans under his arm. Both men wore hardhats, and even though they both wore sunglasses, they had to shield their eyes from the bright sunlight as they watched the work being done. Dust flew everywhere as concrete trucks and flatbeds drove in and out of the ten-acre site. Alarms sounded periodically as forklifts or other machinery started backing up, warning anyone nearby to be aware. Men shouted over the top of the noise created by the machines, and it seemed like the site was in a constant state of organized chaos.

David took the plans from his foreman and unrolled them across the hood of the shiny new pickup parked in front of the construction trailer. He studied the drawings for a second, then looked up at the work going on at the top of the building. He rolled them up and handed them to his foreman. Slapping him playfully on the back, he said, "Well, Rusty, you've only got forty more floors to go. I think if you keep making the same progress you've made the last three months, we might finish this thing a few months ahead of schedule."

Rusty, a forty-five-year-old former Texan, gave an approving nod and turned to look at the activity all around him. "I hope so, Mr. Wilson. If I can keep the Chinese government happy and out of our hair, we can keep up the pace." He grimaced and looked over at the crane, which was picking up a new beam off the bed of a flatbed truck. "I never know what curve ball they're going to throw at me day to day. Last week, one of the building inspectors had to be promised a remodel of his daughter's home before he would pass a crucial inspection."

David kicked the dirt with his Bostonian shoes, sending dirt flying and leaving dust on his pressed slacks. "Yeah, you told me about that. What a crock of crap. Did you figure out how much it's going to cost me?"

"It will be close to twenty-five thousand." He put his hands out defensively. "I'm sorry about that, Mr. Wilson, but this guy put us in a tough position. We were almost dead in the water without that inspection and he knew it."

"Don't fret about it, Rusty," he said. "I realize it's the cost of doing business in Hong Kong. It's happened before on other projects I've built and I'm sure it will happen again before we finish. It's part of the culture here and there's no way to fight it."

"I know it's the culture here," Rusty said. "But I don't have to like it."

David's phone vibrated in his pocket and he pulled it out. He instantly recognized the number. I wonder what Mei Chen wants, he thought as he hit a button and answered.

"What a sweet voice you have, David," Mei said in quiet voice. "It's been a long time since I've seen you. I miss you. I'll be in Hong

Kong later tonight. Could we go to lunch tomorrow and catch up with each other?"

Starting up the stairs to the construction trailer, David paused on the landing and reached out for the door handle. He sensed something in her tone but wasn't sure what it was. I have to be careful with this woman, he thought. She has way too much power, and I'm not sure what she wants from me. She's definitely a sensuous woman, and entertaining, but she always has a purpose to everything she does. "That would be great, Mei. I'll be in Hong Kong all week and I can make myself free tomorrow. Let's meet at the Royal Plantation and Polo Club around noon?"

"I love that place. I'll see you tomorrow at noon." She lowered her voice. "Maybe we can find something fun to do after lunch."

David smiled. "Maybe we can." He hung up and stared at the phone a second. Why do I have this feeling she's after something from me?

♦

A light, fresh breeze from the sea flowed through the large open windows of the Royal Plantation and Polo Club. The white linen-covered tables each had a colorful arrangement of flowers on them, with crystal glasses and Waterford plates. Every table buzzed with light conversation as servers in crisp, white tuxedos flitted from table to table. Champagne appeared to be the beverage of choice, as silver trays of it sat on the large hand-carved oak bar in the corner of the room.

David, in dark slacks and a white pressed dress shirt with three buttons opened, sat at a square table by one of the windows, nursing a Johnnie Walker and soda. He checked out the patrons in the room, noting that there was not one who didn't look like they were going to a formal dinner or a wedding ceremony. I think this is the British tradition of Hong Kong, he mused. Everyone dressed so formal for a simple lunch. Jolly good!

Looking toward the entrance, he caught sight of Mei Chen as she swept past the maître d' and headed toward his table, her long flowery dress flowing behind her.

He stood up and gave her a hug, then held her chair while she sat down. A server was at her side immediately. "A glass of champagne, please," she said to him without looking. "You look great, David. You always seem so fit. What do you do to stay in shape?"

"I try to get to the gym a couple times a week, and I have a regular weekly tennis game," he answered nonchalantly. "Thank you for the compliment. You look very pretty yourself. If I didn't know better, I would think you had an appearance at the opera later."

She threw her hand out dismissively and laughed. "Flattery will get you everywhere." Her champagne showed up and she raised her glass. "Here's to old friends."

Raising his glass, he clinked hers. "So, what brings you to Hong Kong? I thought you were busy with your solar panel company. Did you say there was a large solar project in Nevada you were about to start?"

She sipped her glass and looked at him over its rim. She smiled as she set the glass down. "Yes, you have a great memory. I'm close to getting the bid on the Copper Mountain project. It will be a huge feather in my hat and one giant step up for Soltech!"

"Congratulations." He raised his glass in a salute.

"Thank you." Her face grew serious. "The reason I'm here in Hong Kong is official business for my husband." She lowered her voice as she scanned the room. "A lot of members of the Communist Party look at Hong Kong with disgust. They think it's a capitalistic cesspool that should be nationalized, taken over, and run by the Chinese government."

David stiffened. Mei Chen reached over and grabbed his hand, patting it soothingly. "Oh, you have nothing to worry about, dear. This is just tough talk among some hotheads in the Party. They're jealous of the wealth that's created here. Unfortunately, they are too stupid to figure how to take advantage of what's available to them."

David stared at her keenly. There's more to this than what she's letting on, he thought. Is she warning me of something coming down the pike or is there something else in play here? "Why are these people concerned about the business of Hong Kong all of a sudden?" he asked. "The Chinese government knew what type of society they were getting when it was handed over from the British. They knew they weren't going to be able to change it or take over businesses without rioting in the streets."

"You are absolutely correct about that, David, and the smarter people in the government, like myself, know that." She shrugged and pulled a slice of bread out of a covered basket. "But they still want me to check out a few operations here that might be possible candidates for nationalization that wouldn't cause a fuss. So I'll spend a few days in your posh resort and pass on some suggestions to them."

David put the white napkin folded in front of him on his lap. If they can take one company, they can take any company. A company like mine with all my hotels would be a great prize for someone. Maybe I should sell out and move on to someplace that's a little different. I can build hotels anywhere in the world, so maybe it's time to move on. "Do you think there's any possibility that your government would go after landowners or business owners? What exactly are they looking for?"

Mei raised her eyebrows. "I'm not really sure what they're after. But I bet they would want something that's successful."

"Like a hotelier with a dozen luxury hotels? Would that type of business fall into their sights?"

"You mean someone like yourself?" she asked innocently.

"Precisely," he answered. "I don't like the thought of your government taking what I've built. Do you think something like that is possible?"

Mei put her elbows on the table and rested her chin in her hands. "I guess anything is possible." She paused while the server set an overflowing crab Louie covered in Thousand Island dressing in front of her.

David leaned back while the server set a plate of steaming sautéed trout with garlic-lemon butter and rice pilaf in front of him. "This looks really good, but I'm suddenly not that hungry." He picked up a fork and pushed some of the food around on the plate.

Mei picked up a fork and took a dainty bite. "If you're worried about your hotels being taken over, I might have a solution for you."

She leaned forward while glancing around the room and almost whispered, "If you were to make me a partner in your empire, the Chinese government would leave you alone and look elsewhere." She continued looking around while speaking softly. "I can also help you get control of many other sites throughout China for you to build many more hotels." Her eyes narrowed on his. "I can get you some of the best sites in Hong Kong or any other city in China you would wish to build in."

David studied her face as she ate. I was afraid of this, he thought as he set his fork down. I thought that sooner or later the government was going to step in, and now it's sooner. I didn't want a partner, particularly Mei Chen, but I may not have a choice. I need to buy some time and figure out what my next step.

He brought his napkin to his mouth and coughed nervously. "Well, I hadn't thought about a partner, Mei, so you'll have to excuse me if I'm surprised," he said, trying to keep his cool. "I will need some time to figure out if this is the best thing for me to do. I have spent a lot of energy and money on my hotels, and it won't be easy for me to bring someone else into what I have created."

"Of course, I understand," she said never taking her eyes off his. "But think of it in a positive way." Reaching across the table, she put her hand over his. "We will make such good partners and we can have a lot of fun doing it." Her eyes sparkled. "Maybe we could start having fun this afternoon. I've rented the president's suite at your Grand Palace Hotel for the next two months. Maybe we should go there and celebrate a new beginning for the two of us. But let me tell you how I think it could work."

He listened to her proposal, nodding his head periodically. This is going to take some delicate handling. I can't blow off her advances and irritate her or she could make my life miserable. On the other hand, getting intimate could open up a whole other set of problems, starting with the fact that she's married to one of the highest officials in the government. How would he react if he found out? Would he have me shot?

Taking her hand, he brought it to his lips. "Mei, your offer of an afternoon together is very enticing and generous, but I must beg for another time. As much as I'd like to spend the afternoon with you, I've got to attend a couple of meetings in regard to the ongoing construction of my hotel. I promise I'll make it up to you at another time."

He signaled to the waiter to bring him the bill and put two one-hundred-dollar bills in the leather-covered folder.

He stood and bowed to Mei, carefully setting his napkin on the table. "It was a pleasure having lunch with you. I'll think about your proposal." He smiled and added, "Both of your proposals, and we'll discuss them at a later date. I hope you have a wonderful afternoon."

His mind raced as he headed out of the restaurant. Maybe I should put all my hotels on the market and get out of Hong Kong. I could start over again somewhere else in the world where the government is more business-friendly. When he got to the outside, he handed a young valet his ticket and waited at the curb under the porte-cochere for him to retrieve his dark blue Mercedes 300 coupe.

What if I bring Mei in as a partner? Could she actually open more doors and help expand the business? She definitely knows people in high places and would make introductions I could never get.

The valet pulled round the circular drive and up to the curb where held the door as David got in. He put the car in drive around the circular drive and headed toward the exit of the club. He asked himself out loud as he drove, "Don't forget you're dealing with Mei Chen. Would the risk be worth the reward?"

SEVENTEEN

The Round Table Pizza restaurant was crowded and noisy for a weekday. Three tables of young boys, around twelve or thirteen years of age, fresh from their soccer practice, were hungrily diving into four family-sized pizzas. Six of their teammates were gathered around two pinball machines sitting in the corner of the room, watching the silver balls light up the machine amid lights, whistles, and numbers being racked up on the face of the machines.

Crystal watched all the commotion from a booth as Jason stood at the cashier and ordered their pizza. He came back with two plates and two plastic glasses and set them on the table. "Here you go, sweetie. Help yourself to some salad and a drink."

Wordlessly, she took a plate and a glass and headed to the salad bar in the center of the restaurant. Jason watched her for a second then turned his eyes to the TV hanging from the ceiling across the room to see what the score of the Giants-Dodger game was. When Crystal returned, he waited until she had situated herself then went over and helped himself to the food.

Returning, he sat down across from her. "Hey, Crystal, you're probably wondering why I picked you up from practice."

She paused, holding a forkful of salad to her lips, and looked at him for a second. "Yeah, I thought something might be up." She continued to watch him, her eyes curious.

"I've been offered a new position at Soltech," he said as he played with his salad. "The good news is that it will be more pay, which means we can move from our apartment and get something nicer."

"Really?" Crystal perked up. "Where will we move? Can I help pick the place?"

"Of course you can help pick it," he answered with a smile. "At the moment, I have no idea where we'll move, but we can take our time and decide." He glanced back up to the TV as he took a bite of salad. After a second he continued. "The bad news is I'll have to travel more. The reason that's bad is I'll need to find someone you can stay with while I'm gone."

Crystal rolled her eyes. "Please, Dad, don't tell me you're sticking me with Janine. That was the longest week in my life when you took the trip to China."

Holding his hands up defensively, Jason shook his head. "Hold on. I haven't decided who you might stay with or where. I haven't even agreed to take the position yet. I wanted to talk to you and get your input before I decided."

A number was announced over the intercom and Crystal checked their receipt. "That's us. I'll go get it." She jumped up, walked quickly to the counter, and came back with a steaming pizza. She set it in the center of the table and sat down. The smell of cheese and fresh dough was appetizing. "Well, if you want my opinion, I think if you make more money and we can move from that ugly apartment, I'm all for it. How long will you be gone at one time?"

Jason wiped his hands with a napkin. "I don't think it would be more than a week. I might have to go back to China a few times to meet with the production people once we get some of these solar farms out of the ground, so on those occasions it might be slightly longer. Other trips would probably take a few days."

"Will I still be able to go to the same school and stay on the same soccer team?" she asked him in a pleading voice. "I don't want to start over in some new school with no friends."

Shaking his head, Jason answered firmly, "No, of course I wouldn't make you change schools. You're going to be a junior next year. We can find a better place to live that's in the same school district. Besides, next year is going to be critical for you if you're going to have a chance at a soccer scholarship."

Wiping her head in mock exasperating, Crystal let out a big sigh. "Whew. That makes me feel a lot better. So, how much more money are you going to be making? Can you afford to buy me a new car when I turn sixteen?"

Jason frowned and leaned across the table. "Let's just say you're on a need-to-know basis as far as what I make. As far as buying you a new car, we can wait and see how you're doing in school when that time rolls around. I think we've got a couple of months before we need to concern ourselves about that." He reached for another slice of pizza. "Crystal, I'm leaning toward taking this position, but I need you to promise me something."

"Okay," she said. "What?"

"I will do my best to place you with one of your friends' families when I'm gone, but if I get into a pinch, I might have to let Janine watch you. Would you at least give her a chance and try to be civil with her? I'm not asking you to be her best friend, but treat her decently and try not to act like you're in a torture chamber when she's around."

"Okay, Dad," she said as she wiped her hands with a napkin. "I'll try to be nice. But don't make me stay with her often."

"Thank you, Crystal. I'll do my best to keep it to a minimum and only as a last resort."

◆

The morning sun shone brightly through the window of Jason's office as he studied his computer screen, re-reading the response he had prepared to Mei explaining the terms and compensation of his new position. Jason read the words he had typed one more time, coming to the last line, "I accept the position." He leaned back his chair and flexed his fingers. There's a lot riding on this. Brian is right. I'm one of the most qualified people to take this job, and there are a lot of people at Soltech who will be depending on me to do the job well and steer this company to the future. It's a big commitment for me, but here goes. He hit send on the computer and his reply was shot off to Mei.

Standing up, he stretched, picked up the coffee cup near the keyboard, and took a sip. I might as well refresh this, he thought, and he started off toward the kitchen. He hadn't taken two steps before his cellphone began ringing. He checked the caller ID. Why is Brian calling me so early?

He answered it. "How are you, Brian?"

"Hey, Jason. I hope I'm not calling you too early."

Jason set his cup on his desk and sat on the corner, letting his leg dangle over the side. "No, not at all. I was just thinking about you. I sent Mei Chen my acceptance of the position to run Soltech. Thanks for your guidance."

"Congratulations," Brian said, but he his heart didn't sound like it was in it. "I'm sure you'll do well."

"Is everything okay?" Jason asked. "I didn't expect to hear from you until the opening bid date."

Brian heaved a heavy sigh and spoke in a somber tone. "Have you heard the news about Andrew Dillon?"

Jason scanned a new email from Mei, saying how delighted she was at his decision. He looked up from the screen. "No, I haven't heard anything about Andrew." Concern showed in his voice. "What's up with him?"

"He was attacked and murdered yesterday afternoon while riding his bike home. The police don't have any suspects and the few witnesses that arrived on the scene didn't see anything. It's a sad day around here. Andrew was a great guy."

Jason stood up, his mouth open. "Oh wow. I missed that on the news. Who would want him dead? He was one of the nicest guys in the industry." He slumped down in his chair. "I can't believe what I'm hearing. I just saw him at the renewable energy convention at Moscone Center last week. He was happy and excited about some of the new projects Earth-Sun was getting ready to start."

"I know it's pretty unbelievable. I guess you can't be too careful nowadays. The area where he was riding his bike has nothing but million-dollar homes. It wasn't exactly a high crime area." Brian paused for a second. "Because of the suddenness of his death, Earth-Sun pulled their bid for the Copper Mountain job and Soltech looks like they're in the first position."

"I sure didn't want to win the bid this way, Brian," Jason said somberly. He sent a quick email to Mei about Andrew's death.

"I'm sure you didn't, Jason, there's no question in my mind. Out of respect for Andrew and his family, I'm going to push back the bid opening for three more days. I'm sure there will be a church service right in the middle of the bid opening, and that wouldn't be good for anybody."

"I completely understand," Jason said. "I don't know if there's anything I can do, but if you think of something, please let me know."

"Thanks. If I hear anything further about the service and such, I'll pass it on to you. Let me ask you something. If Andrew was murdered as reported, who would have benefited most from Andrew's death?"

Jason drew a deep breath and put his hand to his forehead. "Uh, I don't know what to say. The thought hadn't occurred to me until you mentioned it. I didn't know Andrew that well personally, so I don't know what he had going on in his personal life. I'll have to give it some thought."

"I'll do the same."

Jason hung up and walked to the window, staring out over the vast manicured lawn area below his office. This is unbelievable, he thought. Andrew leaves a wife and two little kids. What a tragedy.

His computer dinged, telling him he had an email.

Turning from the window, he leaned down and checked the screen. The email was from Mei, so he quickly opened it.

It's really terrible what happened to Mr. Dillon. I know this death is still fresh in everybody's minds, but you need to get in front of Brian Thompson and secure that Copper Mountain deal. Because of this unfortunate circumstance, we're in the first position and I don't want anything to get in the way of us getting that project. We can grieve for Mr. Dillon, but the world will not stop and we must keep moving.

Jason read it again in disbelief. He thought about what Brian had just said to him and then he remembered his last conversation with Mei. She predicted Earth-Sun was going to pull their bid. Was there really management turmoil there or did she know about something else? A chill rose up his spine. I've just committed to work for her. Another thought, more horrible than the first, hit him. If I don't meet her expectations, will the same happen to me?

He started to pace the floor in front of his office, wringing his hands in front of him. I know Mei is callous and a ruthless businesswoman, but is she capable of murder? I hope I haven't made a colossal mistake.

He re-read the email one more time, then picked up his phone. Janine picked it up on the third ring. "Hi, baby, are you calling me with good news? Did you land that Copper Mountain job?"

He sighed, running his left hand through his hair. "I think so, but not the way I wanted to. I think we got it by default."

"What's wrong?" she asked. "You sound like you've had a death in the family."

Jason let out a breath of air. "It isn't exactly a death in the family, but one of my colleagues is dead. The guy who was running the solar company that was competing with Soltech for the Copper Mountain job was murdered yesterday afternoon. Now his company, Earth-Sun, has pulled their bid."

Janine was silent for a moment. "I see how you got it by default." She paused then asked, "Do you think there's any connection to the Copper Mountain job and his murder?"

"Uh, Brian more or less suggested that, but I don't know. This has all happened so fast, I don't know what to think. The person who benefits from this tragedy is Mei Chen if we get the job. But that would mean she'd be involved with a murder."

"How well do you know Mei?" Janine asked. "You mentioned she's well connected in the Communist Party. It's not like they play paddy-cakes all the time. You might want to do some research on her, but be careful. Maybe she's completely innocent in this but, if she had a hand in it, she's a dangerous lady."

"Yeah, I'll do some checking around," Jason answered. "Should I resign from the company?"

"Don't be silly, Jason. You have no proof she's done anything other than having a big bid fall in her lap. Keep doing what you're doing, but keep your eyes open."

"Yeah, you're probably right. Like you said, she's probably got nothing to do with the murder, but all the same, I'll keep alert. Thanks for being my sounding board. I'm so stunned I didn't know who to call."

"I'm glad you called me, sweetie. Anytime you need to talk, I'll be available for you."

"Thanks. I'll talk to you later." Jason set his phone down and folded his arms around his chest. He shook his head. There's no way she's involved. She's got too much to lose if things go bad.

EIGHTEEN

Jason sauntered casually up the narrow walkway that led to Janine's front door. He glanced at the manicured flowerbeds on both sides brimming with colorful pansies illuminated by the soft Malibu landscape lights. He barely made out the well-maintained lawn that smelled as if it had been freshly mowed. Even though it was Saturday, he had worked most of the day before picking up Crystal to run her to a friend's home where she was staying the evening.

This will be great, Jason thought. I'll finally have an evening alone with Janine. It's been too long since we had one of those.

A cool breeze blew in from the west as the quarter-moon started to rise just above the horizon. It won't be long before summer is here, he thought.

He reached the porch where the front door was set back a couple of feet from the house. He reached up to rap on the door, but before he could, it flung open and there stood Janine, one hand on the door and another on her hip. Jason recognized his white polo dress shirt she was wearing, with the sleeves rolled up and the front unbuttoned. He also noticed she was wearing nothing else.

She grabbed his arm and pulled him into the house, shutting and locking the door behind him. She brought him close and kissed him firmly on the lips. Jason reached his hands around her and held her tight. He felt himself becoming aroused as she slipped her tongue over his. Over her shoulder he caught a glimpse of a vase of red roses sitting on the coffee table in the front room, a small white card protruding out of the top with the words "I love you, Janine" written on it.

He pulled back, smiling. "I wanted to show you how much...."

She placed her index finger to his lips as she reached for his hands. "Can't we talk it over in bed?" she asked as she led him, walking backwards, to the master bedroom. Taking off the shirt, she pulled back the bed sheets and flung herself onto the bed. Patting the mattress next to her, she smiled sweetly. "Get those clothes off and join me."

Jason didn't hesitate, undoing his shirt and jeans and flinging the rest of his clothes onto the floor. He fell into her arms and kissed her passionately on the lips as his fingers gently caressed her breasts and moved down to her flat stomach. He felt her hands going up and down his back, causing a tingling sensation all over his body. I wish I could feel like this every day, he thought. I want to be with her every day.

♦

Lying on his back, Jason stared at the ceiling as his breathing slowed back to a normal pace. Janine was lying on her side next to him, her finger drawing circles on his chest. He turned his head and stared into her light blue eyes. "I love you so much, Janine. I sent you those flowers because I wanted to let you know how much I appreciate everything you do for me and how lucky I am to have you in my life."

Janine rolled to her side, her curvy silhouette accentuated by the soft moonlight flowing in through the open window. A light breeze made the curtains flap quietly. A tree frog outside in the yard croaked, making the only sound in the night.

She smiled at him as she continued running her finger over his chest. "I know you love me, and I love you as much. That was a wonderful gesture, and you know I'm a sap for flowers. We don't get enough quality time together, and I wanted to make sure we took advantage of our being alone for the evening."

Jason smiled back at her. "Well, you sure started the evening off with a bang. I'm going to make it a point to make more time for us."

Janine rolled onto her back. "Well, there is one reason we don't spend time together and we both know who that reason is. I know you love your daughter, Jason, and believe me, I would never ask you to put my interests between you two." She turned her head to look at him. "But we can't continue this way." She paused for a second. "Or I should say, I can't continue this way. I'm trying to compromise with Crystal, but she doesn't want to give an inch. I don't know what else to do."

"You've been more than fair with Crystal, and I don't blame you at all," he said, his eyes back staring at the ceiling. "I know it's easy for me to say, but since I've told her the truth, she's slowly starting to question her mom's version of events. You probably can't see it, but I can. She needs a little more time, and I think her attitude will begin to change."

"You're right. I can't see it, nor did I see anything like that while you were gone and I was watching her." She sighed and sat upright in the bed, the covers bunched up along her waist. "I'm willing to give her some time, Jason, but I'm not going to wait forever. If she doesn't change her demeanor toward me and accept that you and I are a couple, I can't stay in this relationship."

Jason put his arms around her waist and kissed the lower part of her back. "Things are going to change, I promise you."

NINETEEN

Congressman Eugene Waters sat back in the chair behind the desk in his San Francisco office and listened to the pitch of the two men sitting in front of him. They were both in crisp dark suits with white shirts and could easily have been coming out of a high profile court case or a major financial deal. He pretended to be listening intently but his mind was still back in Bali, with the beautiful Amy rubbing oils all over his body. John Clayton sat in a chair next to the congressman, busily taking notes.

Finally, after the twenty-minute presentation, the man on the left asked, "What do you think of our proposal, Congressman? Is it something we could count on your support for?"

Waters leaned forward, putting his elbows on the cluttered desk. He looked at one man and then the other. "First off, the reason we're having this meeting is that my good friend Mei Chen vouched for your credentials. If she says you guys are players, I believe her. Now, here's what I think. I'm all for any project that helps out the environment, and the one you're proposing is a very ambitious one, which I like. Solar farms are a great thing, and fortunately, because of my strong pushing, we have a way to finance these things through the stimulus bill." He rubbed his hands together as his eyes went from one man to the next. "But I get asked to get behind fifteen projects a week, and as much as I'd like to help them all, some are better than others." He paused and stared at the men.

The only sound in the room came from John's pen scratching notes on his legal pad, but then he stopped and looked up. He looked at Waters, then at the two men, but no one moved.

Finally the first man spoke. "We, uh, are completely on board with your work in the renewable energy field and would like to help ensure you stay in office to complete this important work. Our company would like to contribute to your campaign fund so you can focus on your work and not worry so much about fundraising."

A big smile came over Waters's face. "Well, that is very generous of you, gentlemen. I could use all the help I can get."

The man shifted in his chair. "What amount would be most helpful to your campaign, and uh," he cleared his throat, "help our project get toward the front of the pack?"

Waters leaned back and gave them a thoughtful look. He turned to his aid. "John, how much did Inter-Power help us raise for the Antelope Valley project? Wasn't it close to two million dollars?"

John nodded as he wrote some notes on a legal pad he had on his lap and added, "The amount raised for that project was two point two million to be exact. That was a one-point-three-six-billion-dollar project and there were many extenuating circumstances to it that made it unique and challenging to get done."

"Do you mind us asking what those circumstances for the project were?" the second man asked.

John looked at Waters, who gestured with his hand at the men. "Go ahead. Mei Chen vouched for these gentlemen. Tell them what happened."

John took a quick swig from his water bottle and set it down. "That project is a two-hundred-thirty-megawatt solar farm and was pinpointed to be on twenty-one hundred acres in the western Mojave

Desert on Bureau of Land Management, or BLM, land. It was a perfect spot for solar except there were some ranchers who had grazing rights across a large swath of the land, which made it unfeasible for the use we wanted. We needed a way to break the leases for the grazing rights of those ranchers. We did it by getting the Fish and Wildlife people to put the California Great Tortoise, whose habitat was near the BLM land we had picked, on the endangered species list." He looked across at the congressman. "This was the beautiful part, and Congressman Waters thought that one up."

Both of the men listened intently as John continued. "The Fish and Wildlife determined that this particular area was the tortoises' habitat, and since they were endangered, it couldn't be used for cattle grazing. The BLM either cancelled or didn't renew the cattlemen's leases." A smile came over his face. "You talk about a crap storm, these ranchers created a huge fuss about it and threatened all sorts of legal action, but in the end, all but one of them went away. It took a number of years for that to happen, but it's completely done."

The first man asked, "What happened to the last rancher? Is he still around?"

John nodded. "He's still around and is still fighting. He sued the federal government twice and lost. Of course it helped that the judge who heard the lawsuit was active in the environmental movement. That poor rancher didn't stand a chance."

He burst out laughing and was joined by Waters, who added, "Yeah, that judge was in the bag."

"So, anyway," John continued, "while the government was cancelling the leases for grazing, Mei Chen introduced us to Inter-Power, which was an impeccably run solar farm developer, with unimpeachable credentials. They started working on getting the permits, the lease for the land from BLM, and the Power Purchase Agreement from Nevada Power, the biggest utility company in Nevada."

"What happened to the tortoises?" the second man answered. "How could the BLM lease land that is habitat for an endangered species?"

"That was easy," Waters said, smiling, his perfect white teeth shining. "We moved the tortoises to another spot about fifty miles away."

The first man looked in astonishment at the second man and then back at Waters. "You moved them? Just like that?"

"Yep, just like that," Waters answered. "And they are happier than hogs in crap in their new home. From what I hear, they're breeding so fast they might get taken off the endangered species list. But to be honest, the only reason they were listed in the first place was to get the ranchers to lose their grazing rights and now, ten years later, they did."

John jumped in and said, "But back to your point about what amount of money might be necessary to move your project along. Your project doesn't have as many problems nor is as large as Antelope Valley."

"Uh, not many solar farms are as large as Antelope Valley," the first man said.

"That's a good point. But I would say a million and a quarter would be sufficient?" John looked at Waters. "What do you think, Congressman? It's your call."

Waters was leaning back in his chair, one foot resting on the edge of his desk. He twirled a pen back in forth between his fingers. "Yeah, one million two hundred fifty will get your project where you want it to be. Coordinate the money transfer with John and we'll get the ball rolling on our end." He stood up, straightened his starched shirt, and reached out with his right hand. "Gentlemen, it's been a pleasure meeting you. I look forward to working with you on this exciting project. If we keep doing this, future generations of people will thank us for being good stewards of the planet."

The two men exchanged handshakes and made their way out the door, closing it as they left.

Waters came around the desk and slapped John on the back. "Well done, young man. I think they'll be a great resource for us going forward. Make sure you have them wire the money to my account in the Dominican Republic. I don't want to have to disclose this."

"Thank you, Congressman Waters," John said. "I'm glad you approve and I'll make sure the money goes to the right account." He wrote some notes on his legal pad then glanced at his watch. "You had better hurry, sir. You've got a two o'clock meeting with Wo Sung at the Golden Palace in Chinatown. Traffic might start to back up soon."

"Okay," he said as he grabbed his suit coat from the chair behind his desk. "He's going to like what I'm going to tell him."

◆

The two men made it out of Congressman Waters's office and stood at the curb. Within a minute, a white limousine stopped in front of them and they scrambled in. A middle-aged black man wearing a black driver's hat sat behind the wheel, staring straight ahead the whole time. They sat in silence through the streets of San Francisco until the limo entered the onramp to Highway 101. The limo continued down the highway for twenty more minutes and exited at the first park-and-ride lot a couple miles from the San Francisco Airport. The driver pulled up behind a black Lincoln town car parked in the back of the lot and stopped.

As the men exited, the first one said, "Thanks for the lift, Charlie. We'll see you back at the Bureau." As they put on dark glasses to shield the bright sunlight, they watched the limo drive away, then one said to the other, "Did you get all that inside the congressman's office?"

The second smiled and patted the breast pocket of his coat. "Oh yeah, I got it all. That was mighty nice of them to explain all the ins and outs of the Antelope Valley project. There have been so many rumors swirling around, I never thought half were true. I guess I was wrong."

"Well, this is another piece to a fascinating puzzle. The chief is going to like this."

"Do you think Brian Thompson knew anything about all the backdoor shenanigans? That was pretty slick how they got those ranchers off the land."

The first man shook his head. "Nothing's come up about him in our investigation. He'll probably be as surprised as anyone once he finds out how this all went down. But Brian was the person who got us the introduction to Mei Chen last month. Apparently what we presented impressed her enough to vouch for us to the congressman." He reached into his pocket and pulled out a set of keys. "Let's head back there and give the chief a full report. Do you mind if we stop at In-N-Out on our way? I'm starving."

The first man hit the fob on the keyring and the horn honked briefly. He opened the door and slid into the driver's seat. "I don't mind at all. All that talk about ranchers and cattle has got me hankering for a hamburger myself."

TWENTY

Crystal was lying on her back in bed, holding John Steinbeck's *Of Mice and Men* a few inches in front of her face in one hand while taking a bite of an apple in her other, when her cellphone rang. She recognized Steve's number and excitedly answered it. "Did you pass the driver's test?" she asked breathlessly.

A pause on the other line made her anxious. "What, no 'hello' or nothing?" Steve answered with an indignant tone in his voice. "Geeze. Of course I passed. Who do you think you're dealing with? Some dumbass?"

Crystal squealed in delight, clapping her hands together. "That is so awesome. I'm so proud of you. When do you think your uncle will give you his car?"

"I talked to him a few days ago. He says he wants to get it tuned up for me, so I think it will be next week before I get it."

"I can't wait." Crystal moved off the bed and paced her room. "I want to be the first person to ride with you. Promise me you'll let me be the first."

"No problem, I promise you'll be first."

Crystal heard a beep in her ear and pulled down to see she had another call. "Hey, Steve, let me call you later. My mom's on the other line." Hanging up with Steve, she switched lines. "Hey, Mom, how are you doing? I haven't talked to you in over a week."

Her mom answered in a dull tone, "Okay, I'm doing okay. It's been a long week. A couple of David's jobs fell through and it's been a struggle tracking down new leads."

"I thought David had a lot of work lined up," Crystal said as she walked around the room. She stopped at the vanity mirror above a chest of drawers, reaching up and playing with her hair. She turned away and continued pacing. "Wasn't that the reason you left here? Because he had so many opportunities in North Dakota."

"It's complicated, Crystal. I don't have time to explain everything."

Doubts cropped up in Crystal's mind, but she pushed them away. "Hey, guess what. Dad got promoted to a new position at Soltech. They made him president of the company. We're even going to move out of this apartment and get a new place."

There was a long pause on the other line. "You don't say. I bet they probably doubled his salary. That's really good news for all of us, Crystal. I can't wait to call him and congratulate him on his new position."

Crystal flopped back on the bed. "Why would it be good for you, Mom? Dad got the raise, not you. I thought everything was settled after the divorce."

"Don't worry your pretty little head about grownup things, Crystal," she said in a condescending tone. "This has nothing to do with you. Do you know where you'll to be moving?"

"Dad said he's tired of apartment living, so we'll be looking at a house. He promised me he'd let me help. We're going to stay in the same school district so I won't have to change schools. Isn't that great?"

"Yeah, that's just grand," her mother answered. "You guys are moving on up while I'm stuck busting my ass in the badlands of nowhere trying to stay afloat. By the way, how's that skanky girlfriend of your dad's? Is she moving in with you also? I hope you remember what she put me through."

"No, Mom," Crystal said as she lay across her bed. "There are no plans to have Janine move in with us. I wouldn't put up with that and Dad knows it." She paused and sat on the edge of the bed. "You don't seem too excited that Dad's doing better. Wasn't that one of the issues you had with him before? That he lost his business and didn't make enough to support us?"

"Look, Crystal, your dad's inability to survive the recession was one of our problems, but you and I both know what was the real cause of our divorce was. I don't think I need to be jumping up and down like a cheerleader just because your dad got a big raise. How about me? He's not doing anything for me."

Crystal was silent for a minute. "I just thought you might be happy that things are getting better," she said in a sad voice. "That's all I meant."

"Let's change the subject. I don't want to discuss your father anymore."

"I sure would like to come and stay with you, Mom. I'm going to have a few months off soon, and if you could get me there, I'd be a big help to you and Dave."

"Crystal, we've already been over this," she said in an irritated tone. "I don't have the money to buy your ticket and there really isn't a lot of room at the place we're staying. I'll be out there to see you in a few months and we can catch up then. Hey, I hear David coming up the walkway and I've got to run. I'll talk to you later."

Hanging up, Crystal held the phone to her chest. Yeah right, she thought, when you find a few minutes to squeeze me into your schedule, like in a month or so. Why did you run all the way to North

Dakota if it wasn't to make a lot more money than you could have made here? Maybe Dad was telling the truth. Probably not.

TWENTY-ONE

As he drove to the meeting with Brian Thompson, Jason went over the points of discussing what he wanted to focus on. Had the Power Purchase Agreement been signed? Was everything in place with the lease for the BLM land? What would be the logistics of staging the project and what were the access points? His cellphone went off and he quickly put on his Bluetooth. Glancing down at the phone, he saw it was a 717 area code. His breathing quickened as realized it was Debbie and he hit the answer button. "Hello?"

"Hi, Jason," she said sweetly. "It's Debbie. How are things with you?"

"Uh," he stammered, "things are doing well. How about you? How are you and Dave doing out there in North Dakota?"

"We're doing just fine, thank you," she answered, her voice sharpening. "I was just talking to Crystal and she mentioned you've got a new position with Soltech and a hefty new raise. Were you not going to tell me about that?"

Jason started to turn off at an off ramp near Inter-Power's headquarters. He cleared his throat and answered defensively. "It just happened, but to be honest, I hadn't thought about telling you. I wasn't hiding anything, it just that it really didn't concern you."

"Didn't concern me!" she exclaimed. "What are you talking about? I'm barely getting by and now all of sudden you get a big windfall and it doesn't concern me? You are dreaming if you think I'm going to stand still and watch you bull me over. I want to know how much more money you're making because I'm entitled to half of it!"

"Debbie, our divorce was final over a year ago, and everything was settled," he said in an even tone, trying to calm her. "You signed off on the settlement and you signed off on the alimony I've been giving you. I've never missed a payment and even give additional money when you've requested it. You can't demand that I start paying you more because I've been rewarded for my hard work."

"Oh, do you want to make a bet? Listen to me, Jason. We can do this either the easy way or the hard way. Either you tell me what you're making and start coughing up half or you'll hear from my attorney, and not only will you have to pay me but you get to pay his fees, which, if you recall, aren't cheap."

"Debbie, be reasonable," he pleaded. He parked his car in Inter-Power's lot and shut off the engine. "I almost got on my hands and knees and begged you to stay, but you chose to move on. I'm finally getting on with my life and I think you should accept the decision you made and do the same with your life. You can threaten me all you want, but you can't bully me into paying you more money."

"Oh yes I can!" she screamed. Jason had to hold the phone away from his ear. "Don't try to throw a guilt trip on me, because it's not going to work. It was because of you that your business failed and it was because of you that we lost the house! I deserve to be treated better! None of this was my fault!"

Jason covered his eyes with his hand and sighed. "Debbie, I've got to go into a meeting. We'll have to discuss this another time when you calm down."

"Let me tell you something. This is not the end of this. If you think I'm going to let this go, you better think again. I deserve more money and you're going to pay me!"

"Don't bet money on it." He hung up and stared at the phone for a second. This isn't the same woman I loved years ago. Or did I never really see her as she really was? The more she acts like a spoiled brat, the more I'm feeling better without her. I realize because of Crystal I have to deal with her, but I don't need her to ruin my life. He grabbed his briefcase and headed toward Inter-Power's offices.

Brian Thompson was on the phone when his secretary brought Jason to his office. Sitting behind a massive oak desk topped with stacks of documents, Brian signaled for Jason to come in and sit in one of the hand-carved wood chairs.

After a minute he hung up and shook Jason's hand. "How are you doing there, buddy?" he asked in a jovial tone. "I'm sorry for holding you up, but my attorney was going over some final changes to the BLM lease for Antelope Valley."

"No problem," Jason said as he opened his briefcase. "Do you know anything more about Andrew's death?" he asked in a somber tone. "I mean, it seems so senseless and random."

Brian shook his head. "I haven't heard anything other than his funeral is on Thursday. The police have no suspects or motives. I don't know why anyone would want him dead."

"I don't either. What a shame."

Brian nodded. "Sure is."

Jason pulled out a document and handed it to Brian. "I'm sorry we have to talk business at a time like this, but I know you're running short on days before you have to make your decision. Here's my revised bid for Copper Mountain. It has all the changes you requested and includes everything we discussed. Do you want me to walk you through it?"

Taking the document, Brian set it on the corner of the desk without looking at it. "I don't think that will be necessary." He put his elbows on the desk and rested his chin in his hands. "I wanted you to come here and see me so I can tell you personally where I'm coming from on this project. Soltech is the low bidder and I should give you the job. But I'm still having reservations about how the products are made and the warranty behind it. Mei Chen is a good businessperson, but I'm responsible to my investors and if the product I chose for this solar farm isn't up to the industry standards, I'm the one who's going to have to answer for that."

Jason leaned forward in his chair. "I completely get that, but one of the reasons I took this position at Soltech was to change the way we did things. I can assure you that the product we sell to you and the product that ultimately generates electricity for your solar farm will be as good as or better than any other solar panel on the market."

"That's what Mei Chen has promised," Brian said. "I'm leaving right after the funeral to meet her in Hong Kong to discuss that very issue."

"You're not considering using someone like RayTech are you? This isn't a made-in-the-USA thing, is it?"

Brian waved his hand dismissively. "Oh hell no, I'm not using them, although the public relations angle of that might be good. Their solar panels are way too expensive. I've also heard they're having major cash flow problems and might be out of business in less than a year." He laughed. "After a five-hundred-million-dollar loan from the federal government, they still can't be competitive. Great use of our taxpayer money, isn't it?"

Jason shrugged. "I'd heard those rumors also. But I wasn't sure who else's panels you would be using instead of Soltech's. With Earth-Sun out of the picture, we're the best option for you."

"And you still might be. Mei Chen has a way of getting her way with me." He winked. "She can be very persuasive, but I'll be careful with her. I just want to hold off my decision until after we meet. I want to hear it from her how she's planning to stand behind her product."

"So you'll let me know after you meet with her this Friday?" Jason asked. "Because if we get the job, I've got to gear up the production facility. Spitting out nine hundred thousand solar panels in six months is going to require some preparation." He pulled out a flow chart and scanned it for a second. "We had talked previously that you were going to start grading the site to make it flat and even next month. Is that still the target?"

"Yes, that's still the plan, and I'll let you know Friday if it's yours." Brian stood up and stretched. "Everything is on schedule to start in three weeks. I've got all the permits pulled, the land lease with BLM is executed, and the Power Purchase Agreement is finalized. All we need to do is build this thing and start collecting revenue from the sun. How exciting is that?"

"It's very exciting, and I want to participate in it. I want Soltech to be the supplier of your solar panels. Is there anything I can do to convince you you're in good hands and that our warranties are solid?"

"No, Jason, you've done everything I've asked and then some. I just need some reassurance from Mei Chen." He sat back down at his desk. "Just out of curiosity, when are you going back to Shanghai to check out your facility? If Mei Chen is convincing enough and I give Soltech the job, I might want to meet up with you and take a look at what you're doing there."

"If you want, I'll meet you there right after you meet with Mei Chen," Jason said enthusiastically as he moved to the edge of his seat. "You let me know when you want me there and I'll make arrangements to join you. I would be happy to give you a tour of our Shanghai facility." He closed his briefcase and stood to leave.

"Uh, one more thing before you head out of here. One of the other reasons I want to meet with Mei is to discuss the way she does business. I'm sure you're going to make a difference in how Soltech will manufacture its solar panels, but I want to make it clear to Mei that I won't tolerate any slimy deals or underhanded transactions. I want to know that her hands are clean and she had nothing to do with

Andrew Dillon's death." He paused to let his words sink in. "I have no knowledge she was involved, but we both need to be aware there is that possibility she was involved and, as such, both you and I could be in danger if we do something she's not happy with. We can't forget which country she owes her allegiance to and how they solve problems—usually by eliminating them. I'm also somewhat concerned that by not picking Soltech, I might be putting myself and my family at risk of Mei's retaliation. Who knows what she or her government might do."

Jason somberly shook his hand. "I get what you're saying. I'll be vigilant." He turned and headed out of the building, rubbing his sweaty palms together. Oh boy, he thought. I hope Brian is wrong about Mei, but I'm getting uneasy about her too. She has a callousness about her that's unnerving.

As he drove away from Inter-Power's facility, he tapped his index finger on the steering wheel. I need to figure out what to do with Crystal. This is very short notice if I'm going to be on a plane to Shanghai in two days. Should I try to let Janine keep her one more time? It would only be for a couple of days.

He turned the stereo down and dialed his phone. Janine answered on the second ring. "Hi there."

"Hey, good looking. What are you doing?" Jason asked, trying to make his voice upbeat. "Do you have time to meet for lunch?"

"Of course," she answered. "Where and what time?"

Jason thought for a moment. "How about Angela's over in Fremont? I can be there at 12:15."

"You've got a date. I'll see you at 12:15."

He turned the stereo up. John Mellencamp's "Pink Houses" was on and he hummed along. What a breath of fresh air she is. She's never demanding, is always in a good mood, and seems to appreciate our time together.

His thoughts turned back to his conversation with Brian. He furrowed his brow, took a deep breath, and sat up in his seat. He reached up to adjust his rearview mirror, but abruptly stopped. That white van looks like the one that was following me earlier this morning, he thought as he nervously pulled on his collar. He half turned in his seat to get a better look. I can't make out who's driving.

The hairs on the back of his neck started to stand and his palms felt sweaty holding the wheel. He tried speeding up, only to see the van had sped up as well. He put on his blinker and slowly merged into the right lane, his eyes nervously checking the van. Who are those guys? He slowed down, and the van crept up and slowly went by him. He turned and looked at the passenger and the driver, but neither of them paid any attention to him as they made their way down the freeway. Jason's breathing slowed down as he wiped his forehead with the back of his arm. "Jason," he admonished himself out loud, "you're being a paranoid moron! Nobody is interested in you!" He checked the mirror again and let out a sigh. "At least not yet. Maybe when I return from Shanghai, but not yet."

TWENTY-TWO

The enormous black Steinway piano's notes carried softly around the room, resonating off the light-stained hardwood floor and the thickly paneled walls. A violin joined in, its notes intertwined with the piano's, creating a full, rich sound that resonated around the house. An older Chinese woman, dressed in a starched white smock, sat stiffly at the piano, her legs crossed and at least a foot above the ground. Chi, her hair in pigtails and still in her school uniform, stood next to the piano bench, reading the music score over her instructor's shoulder. Pin, the nanny, sat across the room in an overstuffed chair, silently listening, her hands folded across her lap.

The woman stopped playing suddenly and pointed at the music score. "That's an A flat, Chi!" she said angrily. "Why can't you get this part correct?"

Chi brought the bow and the violin to her side and started sobbing. "I can't concentrate anymore, Miss Kim," she said through sobs. "I've been practicing for four hours and I'm tired."

Her instructor slammed her hands on the piano. "You don't have time to be tired, Chi. *We* don't have time to be tired. If you don't do this duet perfectly, you will embarrass your parents in front of the whole Party."

Pin, her nanny, stood and walked over to where Chi stood, her shoulders heaving. Pin put her arm around her and spoke to her softly, "How about if you take a fifteen-minute break? Go into the kitchen and see if you can find yourself a treat. Nothing too sweet though."

After Chi left for the kitchen, Pin came and sat next to Kim at the piano. "You know how anxious she gets when her mom is about to come home. She'll be here tonight and I think it affects her a lot." She patted Kim's hand. "Try to be patient with her. This concert will come and be gone before you know what happened and she'll perform it perfectly."

Kim looked at her with a resolved expression. "That's probably true, but then her mom will sign us up for another intense concert with a more intense music piece, and she'll demand that we practice twice as long. Besides, it's easy for you to find time to take a break, but you won't be the one who's fired and sent to a Chinese prison if Chi isn't perfect at the concert. I know about a lot of things that go on in this household, and if I wanted to make trouble for Mei, I could easily do it."

Pin sighed and stood from her chair. "I don't think that is wise to speak like that in this house. Why don't we go join Chi?"

♦

The limousine pulled up through the circular drive and stopped in front of the massive hand-carved oak doors. A short young man leapt out of the front passenger's seat and hustled to the back door, opening in a swooping motion.

Mei Chen stepped out, pulling her blue skirt down and brushing it off. Without hesitating, she strode by the man, walked up to the doors, and stopped. She could hear the piano and violin coming through the doors. She turned her head to one side and listened for a minute. Finally she yelled out, "Chi, make the vibrato even! It sounds like you've got blisters on your fingers!"

She opened the door and stepped inside. She walked past the startled Chi and Pin and went to the master bedroom. As she walked by them, she yelled over her shoulder, "Don't stop. You need to keep practicing. Right now you sound like two cats in a gunny sack."

Upon reaching the walk-in closet, she flung racks of clothes aside as she searched for a particular dress. She pushed wave after wave of clothes to the side until she finally found what she was looking for. All right, she thought. This is what I need for tonight. She pulled the outfit out—a long velvet evening gown with sequins up and down the sides. She laid it across the bed and returned to the closet to look for a matching set of shoes.

A soft rustling noise caused her to look up to see Pin standing contritely in the doorway, her head looking down at the ground. "What is it, Pin?" she demanded.

Pin shuffled her feet nervously. "Excuse me, Madam Chen, but your husband, Ho, has arrived and requested to speak with you. What should I tell him?"

Mei gave her a look of disgust and waved her hand in the air. "Tell him I'll be with him in five minutes." She turned and focused back on matching her shoes. What could Ho possibly want now? I'm sure it has something to do with the Party and all the drivel that goes with them. I can't help that those people are a bunch of sheep willing to follow whatever order that comes down from the top. That's not how I operate.

A shadow was cast over the room and she could feel Ho's presence. Without looking she asked, "What is it, husband? I told you I would see you in five minutes. What have you asked to see me about?"

Ho moved a few feet from her. "It has come to this," he said in a firm but low voice. "I must ask permission to see you. Do you not see how this looks to the outside world? Do you not know what a mockery you are making of our marriage?"

Mei turned to him, her hands on her hips, frowning. "You asked to see me. I'm a busy woman and I don't have time for one of your foolish lectures. If you have something to say, say it. Otherwise leave me alone."

He cleared his throat and put his hands behind his back. "I have received word that you have told David Wilson, the hotel magnate, that the government of China is getting ready to nationalize his hotel chain." He started to pace in front of the bed. "And you have informed him that, of course, there is one way to save Mr. Wilson's properties and that is for him to cede one half of his interests to a citizen of China. A citizen such as yourself." He stopped and stared at her. "Is this true what I've heard?"

Mei laughed at him. "This is the reason you interrupt me while I'm getting ready to go out? I'm meeting with Mr. Wilson tonight, and what I tell him is my business and nobody else's. Whatever myself and Mr. Wilson work out is between us."

Ho pointed a finger in her face. "Oh no, Mei, you are so wrong. A lot of people are interested in what you do. You are married to a high member of the Party and as such are very visible to the common man. You cannot go around and use the threat of the government to make private citizens give up their possessions to you."

She picked up a shoe and threw it at him, missing his head by a few inches. "Who says I can't?" she screamed. "I am the government! It was my family who marched with Chairman Mao in the early days of the Revolution, not yours. We were the ones who sacrificed and suffered. Don't tell me I can't use the government to get what I want!"

Turning away from him, she stormed past him. Ho followed close behind.

"Everyone knows the role your family played in the Revolution," he said, his voice rising. "Your indifference to me makes it clear to the Party members that you feel you are the reason I have my position and that, because of that position, it allows you to do whatever you want." He stopped a foot away from where she was leaning over the bathroom vanity mirror and applying mascara. "I am warning you, Mei, for your own good. You cannot flaunt your wealth like you do or seize private property. The Party has many eyes, and many eyes are watching what you are doing. They don't like what they are seeing."

She sneered at him in the mirror. "Those people in the Party whom you refer to are jealous jackals. They can't hide their loathing because they don't have what I have. But they don't have what I have because they're lazy. They want to hide behind the shield of the Party and have the Party take care of them." She set her mascara case down on the counter. "Nobody is going to do a thing to me. If I want to nationalize a business or seize a property, I will do it. Now leave me alone and let me finish getting ready." She pushed him out of the bathroom and slammed the door shut. Taking a deep breath, she picked up her mascara and started applying where she'd left off.

His voice thundered through the door, startling her. "I've warned you, Mei. Do not come crawling to me looking for an ally after the Party turns on you! You will be on your own!"

She stared at herself in the mirror in silence. Humph, she thought. Why did I choose such a gutless man to marry? I could have had any man in the country yet I chose Ho. I was too young to understand that his standing in the Party would be eclipsed by my own and I wouldn't need his influence. What does he know anyway? He's always kissing up to the President and Vice Chairman. He can never have his own mind.

Pulling out a small tube from a drawer in the cabinet, Mei started to apply a bright red-colored lipstick. After a minute she smacked her lips and checked to see if it was on evenly. She held her head high. Nobody is going to tell Mei Chen what she can or can't do. Nobody! Tonight I will talk some sense into Mr. David Wilson, then tomorrow it's off to Hong Kong to close the Inter-Power deal with Brian Thompson. It's good to be the queen!

◆

David Wilson sat alone in a corner table in front of a floor-to-ceiling window that looked out to the west side of the city. Two pigeons, one with a colorful ring around its neck, strutted on the cornice below. The view from the Longang restaurant at the top of the Ritz-Carlton gave a breathtaking sight of Beijing, twenty-five floors above the city, except that most days the pollution was so intense, only vague outlines of buildings could be seen. Crystal glasses clanged and voices speaking various dialects of Chinese filled the vast room as male servers in white coats and black ties made their way around the white linen tables, balancing silver platters filled with succulent dishes of veal, prime rib, and the like.

"Flying rats."

David jumped. He looked up to see Mei Chen standing over him. She was smiling and looking in the direction of the pigeons.

"I wish the city would declare open season on them and have anyone who wanted shoot as many of them as they could. Get rid of all of them."

David stood up and picked up Mei's hand, giving it a gentle kiss. "Ah, Mei, you always show a soft side to your tough exterior." He let her hand drop and looked her up and down. "You look splendid as always." He held her chair as she sat down, and he returned to his seat.

Mei took a sip of water and looked out of the window. "You have chosen an excellent table, David. If it wasn't for the horrible smog, we would have a wonderful view of the city."

"Well, this is one of the benefits of owning the hotel. I get to choose the best seat in the house." He waved his hand at the window. "The smog, there's nothing I can do about that." He leaned his head forward. "Now, you, on the other hand, as high up as you and your husband Ho are in the government, you could do something about the smog."

141

A young man in a crisp military uniform appeared at their table and bowed before Mei. "Excuse me for interrupting you, Madam Chen," he said in a low voice as he reached out to hand her an envelope. "A message from the Interior Department." Mei snapped the envelope from his hand as the man backed away and left. She looked up at David as she ripped open the envelope and quickly scanned its contents. She folded it and stuck it in the small purse by her side.

A server appeared with two glasses of champagne and set them down. Mei raised her glass in a toast and took a sip. "Where were we? Ah yes, fixing the smog. Don't confuse me with my husband. If I want something done to fix the smog, I promise you it will get done." She looked out the window. "But remember that smog is because of progress. China has grown from a poverty-stricken, backward country to a world power in a matter of decades. That is progress, and sometimes there are side effects of progress. Smog is one of them."

"Well, I hope progress doesn't choke everyone to death. Enough about the smog." He nodded toward her purse. "I hope the message you received wasn't bad news. Things appear to be changing in China, especially in Hong Kong. The Interior Department seems to have their hand in everything."

Mei waved her hand dismissively. "They want me to attend a Party function tomorrow night. There's a lot of angst lately about what to do with Hong Kong, as it appears its citizens have grown accustomed to British rule and law and don't understand the Communist way." She sipped her champagne and kept her gaze on his. "This will change with time."

David took a sip from his drink and set his glass down, cocking his head slightly. "I hope you'll keep me informed if anything transpires that affects my business."

She smiled sweetly. "Of course, that's why I wanted to meet."

David snapped his napkin and placed it on his lap. "I'm sorry, Mei, I've almost lost all my manners talking all this business and ignoring you. How have you been? I assume you've been busy with the solar factory pumping out panels and saving the planet."

Mei shifted in her seat and crossed her hands on the table. "The solar factory is doing well. I'm on my way to Hong Kong to close a deal on one of the largest solar farms in the world. It's all very exciting." She looked into his eyes. "Have you thought about my proposal we discussed the last time we were together?"

"You mean the one where if I don't give you one half of my Hong Kong hotel holdings, the Chinese government steps in, nationalizes them and takes one hundred percent of them?" He raised an eyebrow as he sipped his champagne. "That proposal?"

Mei leaned back in her chair and held her chin up. "It isn't quite that cut and dry. I'm offering you a way to keep your hotels from the government. It's only a matter of time before they get them from you. I've got inside information and I'm sharing it with you. I'm trying to help you out."

"Let's order while I figure out how to repay your kindness," he said in a sarcastic tone. He picked up the menu and studied it for a second. "Ah, they have braised lamb shank tonight. The chef here makes the best lamb I've ever eaten."

She crinkled her nose. "I've never been a lamb fan. I'll try the salmon." She set her menu aside. "Listen, David, I'm serious when I tell you the government is looking for different sources of revenue. Your portfolio is a perfect fit for them. They could retain you as a manager and even pay you for your services. They, in turn, get some great assets and steady income."

"I get why they would want my hotels, Mei," he said, the frustration in his voice rising. "But I feel I'm being blackmailed. I don't seem to be given a voice in this conversation."

"Is that why you made inquiries at the government?" she asked sweetly. "Somebody told someone that I had threatened you, and that, in turn, got back to my husband." She waved a finger in front of his face. "That's a no-no. There is no one else involved in this negotiation at this time but you and me. If you try to go around my back again, it would not work well in your favor."

David studied her face. This gal is not bluffing, he thought. She is dead serious about taking my hotels. When she first brought this up, I thought it was just some fantasy of hers. I need to buy some time and figure how to keep her at bay. But how? I can't go to the government; she'd find out. My government, Great Britain, has no control anymore in the matters of Hong Kong. Besides the fact that I would be giving up fifty percent for nothing, I'd also have Mei Chen for a partner.

Their orders came and they both ate in silence. The string quartet continued to play softly as the notes resonated around the room. David finished his meal and set his knife and fork on the plate. "Look, Mei, I understand you're giving me a heads up and a warning and possibly a way to keep my holdings, and for that I am very much indebted. But this is all such a shock, I really need more time to figure it out. I would like to see if I have any other options than what you're proposing."

Mei tapped her napkin around the corners of her mouth delicately. "That's fine, David. See what, if anything, else there is for you to do." She set the napkin on the table and stood up. "I'll give you two weeks to give me an answer." She turned and glided out of the restaurant.

TWENTY-THREE

The bar at the front of the Golden Dragon was deserted except for the middle-aged, balding bartender who had a cigarette dangling precariously from his mouth. A large aquarium stood behind the bar and a dozen orange and white koi the size of small mice floated lazily back and forth. Wo Sung, in his usual wife beater shirt and dark slacks, sat at the corner of the bar reading the sports section of *The San Francisco Chronicle*.

"Stupid Giants," he muttered as he read the lead article about the day's previous game at 3-Com Park, where they had blown a three-run lead in the eighth inning to lose to their hated rival, the Dodgers. "They need to fire the manager."

He raised his shot glass up, and the bartender ambled over with a bottle of Patron tequila and poured Wo another round. "I should just leave the bottle here in front of you, Wo," he said, laughing.

Taking the glass, Wo looked at him in silence, tossed the drink down, and went back to the paper. The bartender moved quickly away.

The front door opened and an impeccably dressed black man with a younger white man at his side entered the bar. They waited for their eyes to adjust before spotting Wo and then heading to where he sat.

"It's good to see you, old friend," the black man said to Wo as he extended his hand. "You remember my aid, John Clayton?"

"I do indeed remember him, Eugene," he said as he shook their hands. "It's nice to see you again, John." He got off the barstool and nodded across the room. "Why don't we move to that booth over there where we can be more comfortable and talk in private?"

"Sorry we're late, but I wanted to be sure that I wasn't followed. It might not look very good if I was spotted in your company."

Wo bowed and smiled. "I completely understand."

Once they were situated in a dark corner, Wo asked, "Would either of you like a drink?" He turned and signaled the bartender, who came around the bar and headed to where they were sitting.

Looking at his watch, Waters shook his head. "No, it's only ten o'clock. That's a bit early for me."

John shook his head.

"It's never too early for me," Wo said, laughing. He nodded to the bartender, who nodded back and returned to the bar to get another shot.

"I don't want to be rude, but I've got a busy schedule today and I leave for Washington D.C. in the morning. So if you don't mind, I'd like to get down to business." Waters looked Wo in the eyes. "I've got to get back to work to do my constituents business. Tell me more about your proposed business deal that involves getting guns into Mexico."

Wo smiled thinly and spoke. "I think I have an opportunity again to make some serious cash for the both of us. We did this type of job a year ago and it turned out well. You remember the operation for the Marcos Cartel, Eugene?"

He nodded, smiling. "I do indeed. That was a great haul. We both made two million, if I recall."

"Your memory is good, Eugene." The bartender placed his shot in front of him and Wo tossed it back. He waited until the bartender was well out of earshot and continued, "This is also a Marcos job, but it's going to be a little bigger and I think I've got an idea that would

146

make it easier to pull off than the last one. I've got a source that will supply us with eight thousand assault type rifles of various makes—AK-47s, Capitols, and Springfields. In addition, they'll supply five thousand hand guns—Rugers and Colt 45s." He paused to let the numbers set in.

Both Waters and John leaned back in their seats. "Eight thousand assault rifles." He whistled softly. "That's a lot of weaponry."

"Hold on," Wo said, putting up his hands. "Let me explain. My source can get the guns to us; our job will be to get them down to Juarez, where the Cartel will pay us six point five million over cost for our efforts."

Waters started laughing. "Oh, is that all?" he said sarcastically. "We just need to cart a few railroad-sized cars full of guns across the Mexican border and we make a ton of money? I'm sure that's never been thought of before." His eyes narrowed. "Come on, Wo, that's a fools errand. There's no way we could get that amount of guns across the border that way."

He stopped suddenly and stared at Wo. "But, I've got a better idea. My good friend, Madam Chen, is going to be supplying a huge amount of solar panels to a new solar farm project not far from Reno Nevada. Most of the panels will be coming by container ship, but she wants to get the first batches of panels here quickly. She'll be transporting those panels directly from her factory in Shanghai and will need a number of transport planes to get them here."

He watched as Wo leaned forward, listening intently.

He continued. "Madam Chen uses government transport planes to move her products all the time."

"Why would she use government planes?" Wo asked.

"Because," Waters answered, looking at him directly in the eye, "she can't own regular jets, as it would look too ostentatious to the regular Chinese people. The higher ups in the government have to be careful not to flaunt their wealth, so they use government equipment. She helps herself to government jets. So, here's the plan. We get Mei involved. Once her planes unload the solar panels, they fly back to China empty. She ships her panels in large covered wooden boxes. When they unload the panels in Nevada, we fill the empty boxes up with the guns. She arranges for the jets to fly to an airport outside Juarez and we offload the guns to the Cartel. It can be done in a matter of hours."

Waters started rubbing his chin, a grin on his face. "Since the plane's a Chinese government plane, it won't get the scrutiny of a private jet and it can get in and out of Mexico quickly. Plus, the airport and the warehouse in Nevada are off the beaten path. There aren't a lot of people sniffing around out there. "

"That's genius, Eugene," Wo said as he signaled to the bartender for another drink.

"Thank you. After we remove the guns, the plane gasses up and flies back to Shanghai to load up another batch of panels. All we need to do is come to an agreement amongst ourselves and get Mei onboard. This could be a huge moneymaker for all of us."

The bartender set Wo's drink in front of him, and Wo raised in it a toast. "I'm all in. Let's get Mei in."

"I'll contact her right after I leave you and run this by her." He turned to John. "Is there anything you want to add?"

"I would be concerned how to get the cash into Congressman Waters's re-election account. We can't just walk into a bank with a wheelbarrow full of money and deposit it." He waved at the bartender. "Could you bring me a water?" He continued, "Are you going to try a couple of dry runs before you actually put real guns on the plane? This sounds like it could work, but there are a few bugs that need to be worked out."

Waters nodded his head. "Absolutely we'd do dry runs. My thought is if we get Mei on board, she makes the stop in Mexico a regular part of her shipping. They put the panels on the plane in Shanghai, fly to Nevada, then fly to Mexico and then back. Four out of five times, there would be nothing on the plane going from Nevada to Mexico, but once every fifth time…" He held his hands up.

"I'm liking it, Eugene," Wo said. "But one question: Who fronts the money for the guns? That's a lot of money to be put at risk."

"Don't worry, I've got that covered," he answered. "If we can use Madam Chen's government planes, the money will be there." Eugene looked at Wo, then at John. "Okay then. I'll make a call to Mei and see if we can make this happen. It should be a profitable experience!"

♦

The next morning, Congressman Waters and John were seated in the back seat of a white limousine, going over upcoming legislation as they drove to the San Francisco International Airport. The traffic was heavy, as it was still rush hour, and the limo only moved about fifteen miles an hour. John had highlighted certain parts of a proposed bill that Waters held in his hand as John explained it to him. Waters pushed his eyeglasses to the bridge of his nose. "This was supported by the Friends of the Earth, right? I can't vote for anything they're opposed to or we'll never hear the end of it."

John nodded. "Yes, they are definitely behind this. There is a provision in the bill that gives preference to energy-efficient use of cars like hybrids or electric cars, so they're very happy about it."

"Okay, that's good. What's the next bill?" he asked. Before John could answer, Waters's phone rang. He checked the number and answered it in a deep-sounding voice, "Madam Chen, what a pleasure to speak to you. How are you doing?"

He heard Mei's high-pitched voice answer sweetly, "I am doing well, Congressman Waters. I apologize for not returning your call yesterday. It was a crazy day at my Shanghai plant and I barely got to speak to anyone not associated with the operation."

"I hope it was all good crazy for you, Mei," he said, trying to sound sincere.

149

"Not exactly. A couple of my workers managed to get themselves killed in one of the aluminum vats and it created a lot of havoc." She paused for a second. "But everything is back to normal, thank you for asking. What can I do for you?"

Waters cleared his throat. "I've come up with a way to fill your planes with cargo on their way back to China. Let me explain what I have in mind." He went through it in as much detail as he could remember, explaining Mei's role and her cut of the profits. When he finished, he added, "There's so much buzz and excitement regarding getting the Copper Mountain solar farm off the ground, we thought it would be a perfect cover for this operation. You're going to have to get the panels to Nevada, and Reno has a nice airport away from a lot of prying eyes. Your planes are going to be coming and going at such a rapid pace, there wouldn't be much scrutiny paid to what's leaving on them once your solar panels are unloaded there." He paused for a second and then asked, "Well, that's what we have in mind and we want to know if you want to participate."

The phone was silent for a minute and Waters asked, "Hello? Are you still there, Mei?"

"Yes, I'm sorry, Congressman, I was just thinking about your proposal," she answered. "I like your idea, but it seems to me that my government plane is the key to the success of this operation since they would be carrying all the solar panels to Nevada, don't you think?"

"Yes," he answered. I think I know where this is going, he thought. "The planes are a crucial part, without a doubt."

"Then my planes will be carrying your cargo to Mexico, right?"

"That's correct."

"Well then, shouldn't my cut be bigger than everyone else's? The only reason my planes are going to be in Nevada is to get the panels to the solar farm. I'm taking a big risk, and the success or failure will depend on me. If you want me in, I want fifty percent of the profits."

Waters did some mental calculations. Fifty percent of six million is still three million for Wo and myself to split. And that's for the first attempt. If we're successful and make more than a few runs, the profits would be enormous. "Mei, I think what you're asking is not unreasonable. Let me check with my other partner and get back to you. Assuming he agrees, we would like to get this operation going fairly soon." He gave John a thumbs up and smiled. "Do you think you could make your planes available for us to do a dry run in the next few weeks so we can test out this idea?"

"Of course, I can make it happen," she answered. "I believe we're already scheduling panel shipments to Reno as we speak. Get back to me after you've cleared my percentage with your partner and I'll make arrangements for you on my end." She paused and then added, "Oh, Congressman. The girl you met in Bali, Amy. She asked me to ask you when you might meet up again. I guess you made a real impression on her."

Waters smile and rubbed his thighs subconsciously. "Well, you pass on to Miss Amy that I would love to see her again really soon. As soon as I get a break from this session in congress, I'll figure out where to hook up with her. I'll talk to you soon, Madam Chen."

He hung up. Oh my, that Amy was just too luscious. For such a young woman, she sure knows a lot about pleasing a man. He closed his eyes and envisioned her naked body and his hands running over it.

"Is everything okay, Congressman?" John asked.

Waters opened his eyes and saw John staring at him with a puzzled look. Waters rubbed his hands together. "Everything is just fine, John, just fine. I think we're on our way to some big, exciting deals!"

TWENTY-FOUR

Classical music played softly from the Bose stereo system sitting on the large bookcase on the far wall of the living room in the president's suite of the International Hyatt Hotel. Mei used the suite as her base of operation whenever she stayed in Hong Kong. There were two additional rooms other than the master suite, and she had converted one of those into an office. She lounged on a flower-printed couch, dressed in a silk bathrobe, her hair put in a bun behind her head. She sipped champagne slowly from a crystal goblet, watching Brian Thompson, who was sitting in a matching chair across from her.

Dressed casually in a pair of light brown slacks, Polo golf shirt, and a pair of brown loafers, he stirred the ice in his glass of Kentucky bourbon with a glass stirrer. "These deaths that occurred yesterday at your factory are what bother me about Soltech's operation, Mei," he began in a serious tone. "I don't need this kind of negative publicity in the United States when I'm attempting to get the US government to lease me huge swaths of their land." He stopped swirling and took a sip. He held two fingers with a very little space between them. "I'm this close to getting the BLM to sign the lease for the Antelope Valley project in the western Mojave Desert. Do you realize that it's twenty-one hundred acres they're going to let me lease?"

Setting her glass on the coffee table between them, Mei rolled her eyes. "I also know that that's a one-point-four-billion dollar project," she said, her frustration showing, "and if you don't give Soltech Copper Mountain, we will have no chance for Antelope. I want both! Don't forget I'm an investor in Inter-Power and I have a say in how its business is run."

Brian put up his hands defensively. "Calm down, Mei. I know what your investment in Inter-Power is; you tell me of it often enough. Let me remind you that that ownership is silent and that's because you wanted it that way. You don't want that fact to become public knowledge, as it would put you and your husband in an awkward spot. Here you are getting subsidies to build your solar panels only to turn around and make a huge profit as an owner of a solar farm using those subsidized panels." He shook a finger in her face and shook his head. "That would not look good, Mei."

She held her chin up and replied petulantly, "The Communist government is for me to worry about, not you, and my husband has no say in my dealings. I would prefer if you keep him out of our conversations!"

Bowing his head, he replied, "As you wish. It still does not change the fact that Soltech has had issues with its production and quality control, and even though Earth-Sun has to drop out of the bidding, I still can't award the bid to you as low bidder. To be honest, you have always worked on the fringes of ethics and I can't afford a public relations mistake if something ever comes out about your business dealings."

"What are you talking about?" Mei screamed as she stood up, her fists balled at her side. "I have had nothing to do with Andrew's death and everything Soltech has done has been aboveboard. I promoted Jason Ballard to make sure everything we do would withstand any kind of scrutiny. On this project we have the best at the best price and the best product. Copper Mountain should be Soltech's project!"

Brian looked at her in silence, slowly sipping his drink. He shook the almost empty glass, rattling the ice cubes around. "Look, I'm sorry," he said softly. "Once you get some of the bugs worked out of your company and Jason has a chance to change some of your business practices for the better, I swear I'll give you a shot at one of our projects. I think Copper Mountain is just too big for you at this stage of your growth."

Seething, Mei looked at him for a second. "Does anybody else know of your decision?" she asked.

He shook his head as he shifted to the edge of his chair. "No, I haven't shared this with anyone else. I wanted you to hear it first. I thought it would only be fair."

You wanted to tell me yourself, right, Mei thought. Too big a project for Soltech. What a crock! My solar panels could hold up as well as any made. They've made it through some of the most rigorous testing done on panels. Is he just being stubborn or is he trying to punish me? What does he know about Andrew Dillon's death? Did Congressman Waters's hitman screw up and leave a trail? I doubt it. Brian's probably guessing, but still, I don't like where this is going.

Reaching out, she grabbed the glass from his hand. "I'm sorry, I almost forgot my manners. Let me refresh this for you." She turned and walked out of the room into the spacious kitchen. She barely heard him say, "Thank you," as she turned the corner.

A bottle of Maker's Mark Kentucky Bourbon sat on the off-white Corian countertop. Pushing his glass against the indented ice dispenser on the stainless steel refrigerator, she watched as the ice cubes tumbled into the clear glass. It's time for a new approach, she thought. I don't seem to be getting through to him, and I think he's made up his mind to give Copper Mountain away to someone else. She pulled open the refrigerator and grabbed the tall bottle of clear liquid from the door's shelf she had placed there the day before. It had a white label across the front with the word "tea" written across it. Spinning the lid off quickly, she poured an ounce and a half of the liquid over the whiskey drink and set the bottle back on the shelf. As she closed the refrigerator door, she swirled the drink around, holding it up to the light. Filling the glass with the Maker's Mark, she took a sniff and smiled to herself. It smells like bourbon. This will be a game changer.

Returning to the living area, she handed Brian his drink, poured herself some more champagne, and curled up on the couch, adjusting her robe to cover her legs. She raised her glass in a salute. "Well, Brian, here's to Copper Mountain success. I know you'll do well with it, whoever you chose to buy the solar panels from."

He smiled and lifted his glass. "Thank you, Mei. You've always been a good sport. I know there will be many more projects for us." He took a long drink and set his glass on the coffee table. Pointing at his glass he commented, "That is such great bourbon, I could drink the whole bottle."

Mei returned the smile as he looked over the top of her glass at him. "I think you should do that.

TWENTY-FIVE

Jason set the phone down on his desk and ran a hand through his hair. He knew this time was going to come; now he had to get ready. That sure was odd about Brian. That was the fourth time he'd left him a message in three days and he hadn't heard back from him. He knew Brian and Mei were meeting in Hong Kong, but he hadn't heard from her either. That was unusual for both of them. The pieces weren't fitting together. He picked up his phone and dialed. Janine answered on the first ring.

"Hi, Jason, thank you for last night. That was nice."

The thought of her naked body in bed and the sensual lovemaking they'd made came flashing to his mind. Crystal had had a school function to go to, which freed him up to be with Janine for part of the night. I wish every night could be like that, he thought. "No, thank *you*, Janine. I had a wonderful time. It was a special evening for me." He paused, trying to figure out how to continue. "I just got a call from my boss," he said. "We landed that big project I told you about and she wants me to be in Shanghai on Saturday to get the facility geared up to meet the production goals required by the developer."

"Wow, congratulations! I know you've spent a lot of time on that project and I know how much it means to you. I'm excited for you."

"Thank you, but now I need to ask a favor." He took a deep breath. "I'm going to be gone for about six days and would be hugely in debt to you if you could stay at my place with Crystal while I'm gone. I know we talked about this before, but it came up faster than I thought it would."

Janine paused for a second and cleared her throat before speaking. "Of course I'll stay with her, Jason. Don't worry about a thing. You go over to China and do your thing and we'll both be fine. Both of us can survive six days with each other."

I sure hope so, he thought. It's not you I worry about, Janine. He breathed a sigh of relief. "Thank you so much, Janine. I'll go over the details with you later. I've got a few errands to run before I pick up Crystal. I'll call you later."

Hanging up, he stared at the phone for a second. I've been a fool for a long time. Janine is a beautiful, sincere, and good person, and yet I've not given her the love that she deserves. That's going to change. He set the phone down and called out to his administrative assistant who sat outside his office. "Susan, I need for you to arrange some flights and hotels for me for Saturday. I'll write down the details for you."

His cellphone vibrated in his pocket. He pulled it out and stared at the number. Who's this? He answered, "Hello?"

A male voice on the other line said, "Andrew Dillon's death was no random murder."

Jason bolted upright in his chair. "Who's this? What do you know about the murder?"

"Who I am is unimportant. Do some homework. You're playing in dangerous waters."

The line went dead.

♦

157

Crystal spotted her father's white BMW as she and her teammates were doing their final wind sprints to end soccer practice. She knew his presence meant something was up, as she normally caught a ride with one of her teammates' mothers. *Maybe I can talk him into going for pizza after we're done.* She finished her sprints and listened to her coach's final thoughts for the day, then grabbed her backpack on the sidelines and headed to the car.

She opened the back door and flung her backpack in before sliding into the passenger seat. "Hi, Dad," she said cheerfully. "I'm surprised to see you here. What's the occasion?"

He smiled at her and then made a disappointed face. "What, I can't come and watch my wonderful daughter practice soccer?"

She turned and narrowed her eyes. "Of course you can. It's just not that usual for you to do it. Games, yes, you're always there. Practice, no."

Putting the car in gear, he pulled away from the curb, slowly checking his side mirror for traffic. "Okay, I have to confess. I've been called to go to China for a few days starting Saturday. I'm going to try to get a flight late enough that I can catch your game but I'm not sure that will be possible."

Crystal leaned back in her seat and turned to look out the window. "Okay, I see. So who will you pawn me off on while you're gone? Please don't tell me I'm staying with Janine."

He gripped the steering wheel and sighed. "Look, Crystal. I'm in a bind and Janine volunteered to help out. It will only be for a couple of days and then I'll be back. I thought maybe she could take you to look at those houses we checked on last Sunday. If you like one or more of them, when I get back we can see if we could put in an offer to buy it and then arrange to move."

Folding her arms across her chest, she continued to stare out the window. "So, is Janine going to move in with us now at our new place?" she asked in a defiant tone. "Why should she be involved in choosing where we live?"

A car zipped by on their right side, startling him. "I didn't say she was going to help you choose a place, only that she could drive you to the places to check them out. What would you like to do for dinner? I'm hungry."

"How about a pizza? We haven't done that in a couple of weeks."

"Okay, a pizza it is," her dad said as he started to merge into the right lane.

After eating, they got home and Crystal headed to her room, closing the door behind her. She dialed Steve and waited for him to pick up.

"Hello?"

"Hey, meet me in the park in twenty minutes," she whispered into the phone.

"No, let's meet at the burger joint across the street from the park. I'm hungry for some French fries."

"Okay, I'll see you there."

Crystal came out of her room and stood by her dad, who was sitting at the kitchen table reading the paper. "Hey, Dad, can I run over to Claire's and go over my history homework with her?"

Setting it down, he looked up. "Sure, go ahead. Make sure you get home before dark, okay?"

She nodded and headed for the front door. "Okay."

Ten minutes later she was sitting next to Steve outside the restaurant under an umbrella covering a white metal table. Steve took the last French fry and popped it in his mouth, wiping his fingers with a small paper napkin as he slowly chewed it. After a couple of minutes, he reached into his shirt pocket and produced a joint and promptly lit it. He took a drag and then held it out to her.

Shaking her head, she said to him, "Steve put that away. You're in a public place and that stuff is illegal. You know there are studies that say smoking weed gives you brain damage."

He started laughing, coughing, and spitting smoke out. "I'm already brain-damaged," he croaked. "What's a little more gonna do?"

She pushed him playfully. "Yeah, you've got a point. I guess the only thing that could get worse for you is if you become braindead. I'm not even sure that hasn't occurred already." She looked around the deserted courtyard nervously.

"Oh, look at you, Miss Four-Point-Oh. Just because I don't get straight A's like you do doesn't mean I'm dumb."

"I didn't say you were dumb, just that if you continue smoking weed every day you're not going to grow smarter. When do you get your permanent driver's license? Aren't they going to send it to you?"

"Yeah, I get it a week from tomorrow." He took a deep drag and held his breath for a few seconds before exhaling. "Then it's going to be a new world for me."

Tugging on his shirt she said to him, "And for me too. Don't forget."

He smiled and leaned into her. "Of course I won't forget you. We've got a big road trip coming up."

She clasped her hands together. "I can't wait. My dad is leaving for China on Saturday and I'm going to be stuck with his bitch girlfriend for a week. I can't wait to surprise my mother and get away from all this crap."

"But your dad is cool. I thought you get along well with him."

"I do get along with my dad, as long as he's not around that dopey girlfriend." She rubbed her hands on her thighs. "My mom hates her worse than I do, and just being around her bugs me. She's always trying to be nice and trying to be my friend." She closed her eyes and wrapped her arms around her chest. "Ugh, it drives me nuts."

"Your dad isn't an idiot. She must have some good qualities for him to date her. She can't be that bad."

Crystal felt her cheeks flush in anger. "You don't know what you're talking about, Steve. This woman is an evil homewrecker and

I don't want anything to do with her. If I can ruin my dad's relationship with her, I will. Gladly."

"Hey, Crystal," he said defensively, "I didn't mean to get you all fired up. I was just saying this lady seems to be a nice woman and is only trying to help out you and your dad. I don't know the history she has, but it seems she's trying to make an effort to be friendly, and maybe you should too."

Crystal put her chin in her hands and let out a big sigh. "I don't know, Steve. I don't know what to believe anymore. My mom tells me one story and my dad tells me another. I don't know who to believe. All I know is I can't wait to get out of this town."

Twenty-Six

The floor of the House of Representatives of the United States was alive and buzzing on Wednesday morning as congressmen and women, all dressed in business suits and looking professional, gathered in groups of threes and fours to discuss upcoming legislation. The Speaker of the House stood at the podium, a serious expression on her face as she listened to a congressman from New York introduce a bill requiring car companies to cut back the emissions of all new cars thirty percent after the year 2025. Hardly anyone listened to the congressman, as they all had previously received a condensed version of the bill. Most house members gave it to one of their staff members to read and dissect and to advise on whether to vote yea or nay on the legislation.

Congressman Waters stood off to the side of the Speaker's podium, flirting with a young female aide to another California congressman who was in the chamber to listen to the bill.

She looked to be about twenty-five, with long blonde hair, blue eyes, and a tall slender physique. She held a file against her chest and tried to listen to the congressman at the podium introducing the bill and still not be rude to Congressman Waters.

"So, Julie," Congressman Waters said to her as he sipped coffee from a white porcelain cup with the Seal of the Congress on its side. "When are you going to join me for a drink at the Downtown Club? Every Thursday they have an acoustic guitar guy playing music, and the guy's phenomenal. You have to hear him."

The young woman turned. "I can't get into the Downtown Club, Congressman. You know that. It's for members only, and I'm not a member."

"Of course you're not a member," he laughed. "I know that. But if you say you'll come this Thursday, I'll arrange for a pass to be waiting for you at the front door."

She smiled at him. "I'll let you know tomorrow. I don't know what Congressman Daugherty has in store for me, but if I can get off early, I'd like to go." She focused her attention back to the podium.

John Clayton came up and softly tugged Congressman Waters's arm, causing him to turn around. "What's up?" he asked.

Looking around slowly, John leaned in and whispered in his ear, "Wo Sung called. He wants you to return his call as soon as you can."

"Is it urgent?" Congressman Waters asked, concern tingeing his voice.

"No, Wo didn't indicate there was anything amiss, just that he would like to speak to you soon."

"Okay, good." He pulled a handkerchief out of his breast pocket and wiped his forehead. He then took off his wire-rimmed glasses and wiped them also. "I'll wait for the vote on this bill to be finished and then go outside and call him." He glanced up at the podium and saw that the other congressman had stopped speaking and the Speaker of the House was calling for the vote. He patted John's arm. "I'll be done in about fifteen minutes with this vote. Meet me back at my office in an hour."

John nodded and headed toward the huge hand-carved oak doors that served as the entrance to the chamber.

Twenty minutes later, Congressman Waters was outside the Capitol, leaning on one of its massive white pillars, his cellphone at his ear. Every so often he would glance around the premise, checking the surroundings. A voice came on the phone after a couple of rings.

"Eugene, how are you doing this fine day?" Wo Sung asked, his voice bright and chipper.

"Wo, I'm good. John told me you called earlier. What can I do for you?"

"I just wanted to let you know that we've made two practice runs with Mei's plane to Mexico and back and everything went along without a hitch," Wo told him in an excited voice. "We're going to try the real thing on Tuesday. If everything goes according to plan, we all are going to be a whole lot richer come next Thursday."

"This is great news, Wo. Excellent work." Waters smiled and nodded as another congressman walked by him heading toward the chamber hall. "You had no problems. That's great. I'll pass this information on to Madam Chen. She'll be very pleased to hear this."

"That would be good. It would be very helpful to keep her in the loop in case any problems arise with the Mexican government." Wo paused a moment. "Assuming this is a successful mission, we plan on another operation in two weeks. Same cargo, same routine. Hopefully the results will be the same."

"If this is successful, which I believe it will be, we could do this for years," Waters said, lowering his voice, trying to hold his excitement. "The Cartel has an insatiable appetite for guns. We could be set for life!"

"Set for life is a good thing. Alright, I won't keep you any longer. I'll call you on Tuesday and let you know how everything turns out."

"I'll be waiting anxiously for your call, Wo."

He looked around the Capitol for a second and then headed down the massive steps toward the sidewalk. A brisk fifteen-minute walk brought him to his office, where John was waiting. Congressman Waters motioned for John to follow him inside. Taking a last look out at the area outside his office, Congressman Waters shut the office door.

Stepping around the desk, he plopped into his chair and put both hands on it. "Well, John, we're going for the real deal on Tuesday." He rubbed his hands together, smiling. "They've done two dry runs and everything went according to plan. This could be a very profitable two weeks!"

John nodded. "That's great, Congressman. That will make our lives easier if we don't have to go begging for money every couple of years to finance your re-election."

"Amen to that," he said, clapping his hands together. "I won't miss those laughable fundraisers at those senseless churches. I could really cut back on them."

Pulling a file he had sitting on his lap, John asked, "Do you want to go over these now? There are a couple bills in here that you volunteered me to co-sponsor."

"Yeah, let's get it over with." Waters looked down at his watch. "I've got a drink appointment with a friend at five o'clock." He leaned across his desk and winked at John. "A fine-looking lady friend, I might add. You've met Gloria, I believe."

John smiled and shook his head. "Indeed I have. I don't know where you find all the stamina to keep these ladies happy. You are the man!"

Straightening his tie, the congressman nodded his head. "Somebody's got to do it. Okay, what's the first bill I'm co-sponsoring?"

John flipped open the file and started reading. "This one is the semi-automatic and automatic weapons restrictions bill." John looked up, a puzzled expression on his face.

Congressman Waters started laughing out loud and then John joined in, their voices filling up the room. Finally, Waters pulled his handkerchief from his coat pocket and wiped his eyes. "Oh my god, that's precious. If anyone ever found out what we're doing in our spare

165

time while we work to keep these other rifles off the streets of America, they would have a field day with me."

Putting his hand to his mouth, John started to cough. "Yeah, they would have a field day with you," he said between coughs. "Let's just hope they don't find out."

"Let's move on," Waters said as he set the bill aside. "I know that bill backwards and forward and it's got wide support, especially after that massacre at that high school in San Diego. The timing of this bill is perfect. My record on gun control has to be the strongest in Congress. What's the next one?"

John set the first file on the floor by his foot and started to read the second one. "This bill you're co-sponsoring with Congressman Milken of Delaware. The bill states there should be a cap on all emissions from factories in the United States. If a company can't meet the standards we set, they either have to pay a fine or they can trade with another company who doesn't put out as many emissions. Either way, we'll tax the exchange. It's another form of cap and trade. The revenue which is generated is intended to be put into more social services."

"That's the one the Friends of the Earth are strongly behind, correct?"

John nodded. "Yes, they're one hundred percent behind this one. This will make you a lot of friends in the environmental movement and will open some major doors to their large donors for your campaign. This one is a no-brainer."

"I like no-brainers," Waters said as he looked over John's shoulder at the clock on the wall. I wish he would hurry up, he thought. Gloria's gonna be at the Haight Street Grill in about a half an hour and I can't wait to run my hands over her silky thighs. He leaned back, closing his eyes and barely hearing John as he droned on. Oh, what I'm gonna do to that woman when we get back to her place tonight. Hmmm, I'm getting a tingling sensation just thinking about her. His thoughts were interrupted when John called his name a second time.

"Excuse me, Congressman, did you hear what I said?" John asked inquisitively. "I asked if you want me to go ahead and sign your name to these bills and send them back to the other sponsors so they can introduce them at the next session."

Waters leaned forward and slapped both hands on the desk. "Yes, that would be splendid, John. Sign my name and send them on. Well, I guess we're finished here for the day, correct?"

John bent down, picked up the files by his feet, and stood up. "I believe we are, Congressman. I hope you enjoy your drink with Miss Gloria tonight, and tell her I said hello. I'll see you first thing tomorrow morning." He turned and left the office.

Waters watched him leave. I'm lucky to have John as an aide. He does the work of four others and keeps his mouth shut. I'm going to help him get into Congress some day and he can take over where I leave off. Well, I shouldn't keep Gloria waiting. It's time to clock out for the day. He stood up, grabbed his coat, and strode out of the office.

TWENTY-SEVEN

Mei stood over the kitchen sink, a tall slender plastic container with a plastic straw coming out of the top in her right hand. Unscrewing the top, she added a small amount of the clear liquid to the juice already in the container. She swirled it around and headed toward the second bedroom. When she approached, she could hear Brian's soft moaning. He lay in the bed in only a pair of white boxer shorts, the sheets pulled up over his waist. His hair was soaking wet and he was sweating profusely. Mei sat on the bed next to him and picked up a washcloth soaking in a bowl of water. She washed his forehead and chest.

"Here, Brian, I've brought you some more juice," she said to him as she helped him sit upright. "You're terribly dehydrated and you need more liquids."

He feebly sucked on the straw for a few minutes, and then fell back on the bed, his eyes rolling. He squeezed her hand and mumbled almost incoherently, "Mei, please, take me to the hospital. I need a hospital."

Patting his hand, she scolded him, "Now, now, Brian. I've treated fevers and colds before. You'll be good as new in a few days. I promise you, though, if you're not better by tomorrow, I'll get you to a hospital." She stood up and grabbed the drink from his hand and replaced it with a pen. She placed a document on a clipboard on his lap and helped put his hand at the bottom. "Sign your name on this line. It's a letter to your staff that you'll be out for a few days but that everything is fine."

Brian mumbled something incoherently and she helped him scribble a semblance of his signature at the bottom of the document. She pulled the document from him, took the pen out of his hand, and patted his forehead. "Now get some rest. I've got some things that I need to take care of. Don't worry. I'll take care of Copper Mountain while you gain your strength."

Brian said something slurred, then rolled over on his side. Mei put the top sheet over him and left the room, shutting the door behind her. She went into her office and held the document up to the light. "Perfect," she said out loud. "The signed contract for Copper Mountain." She dialed her cellphone.

Jason picked up on the third ring. "Hello?"

"It's Mei. I need you to do a couple of things for me."

Jason answered in a worried voice. "Mei, where have you been? I've been trying to track you down for almost four days! I wanted to discuss the two deaths we had at the factory a few days ago."

Looking back at the bedroom where Brian was lying, she said, "I've been very indisposed the last few days, so I haven't answered my calls. I don't have time to talk about the factory deaths right now. Those two workers were fools. If they were doing their jobs properly, they wouldn't have gotten hurt. Listen to me, Jason, Brian signed the contract for Copper Mountain and we're good to start. I want you to gear up the Shanghai plant and get ready to start shipping the panels in less than two weeks."

"That's great news about the contract, Mei, but you can't just brush those deaths under the rug. I want to make the factory safer for our workers. Where's Brian? I haven't been able to reach him for a few days. I want to tell him thanks for the opportunity."

Mei took a deep breath. "Uh, Brian has become very ill and he asked me to make sure Copper Mountain gets off to a good start. I promised him I'd help keep everything going until he gets better."

"What's wrong with Brian?" he asked. "He's always been healthy as a horse. Is he going to be down for very long?"

"That's one of the problems," she said. "No one knows what's wrong with him. He's got symptoms of the flu, but usually that goes away after a day or two. He's been sick for four days. If he doesn't improve, I'll have to take him back to the hospital."

"What are his doctors saying?"

Mei held the fingernails on her left hand up to her eyes. "They aren't sure. They sent him home with me yesterday and told me to keep him comfortable and give him lots of liquids. That's what I'm doing." She looked over at the room as if she suspected Brian would miraculously leap out of bed and hear her conversation. "Anyway, Brian gave Soltech the Copper Mountain contract to supply all the solar panels and I'll send it to you in the next half hour or so."

"I can't believe it. Copper Mountain is ours for sure?" he asked. "That's incredible news. Congratulations."

Before she could answer, she heard Jason let about a big whoopee and then shout out to the people in the office that Soltech had gotten the Copper Mountain job. She could hear the pandemonium break out on the other side of the phone. "Jason!" she shouted. "Jason!"

"I'm sorry, Mei," he said as he came back on. "I had to share the news with the staff here. We're all pumped up about it."

"Well, I'm glad to hear that," she said with a hint of irritation in her voice. "I want you to start accumulating the panels we're going to need at our hangar at the Shanghai Airport. I want to be in a position to ship the first batch of solar panels to Nevada in a couple of weeks."

There was a pause on the line. "Will Inter-Power be ready for the panels that early?" he asked. "I thought they had barely begun grading the area where the panels were going to be installed. There still needs to be months of underground work done before the panels will be installed."

"I know the process, Jason," she said. "But I want as many panels to be in Nevada as soon as possible so that when they're needed we'll have them ready. We've got a place to store them in Nevada so they're not going to be damaged, and," she paused to emphasize her point, "once they're shipped from China, I can bill Inter-Power for them. Also, contact Bill Howard, Brian's point man for the Copper Mountain job, and co-ordinate his scheduling needs with ours. Brian contacted his staff at Inter-Power that Soltech was the winning bidder, so everyone there knows we'll be the working on Copper Mountain together."

"Okay, I'll do that," he said. "I'll send notice to Shanghai to start gearing up. But you need to let me implement some safety measures there, Mei. We don't need any more industrial accidents at our factory."

"You can make changes, Jason, but don't do anything radical that's going to cost a lot of money. Right now I'm selling the panels at a profitable price. I don't want that to change because our costs are going through the roof."

Mei walked back to the bedroom and poked her head through the door. Brian was still writhing in pain, sweating and mumbling incoherently. She pulled back and sat down on the couch in the living room.

"I want you to go to Shanghai, Jason, and personally oversee the gearing up of the production line," she said. "How soon can you make arrangements to be there?"

There was a pause on the other line. "Uh, today's Thursday. I think I could get there by Saturday. The plant will still be open and operational."

"Good, Saturday will work," she said. "And by the way, the plant will be operational seven days a week, twenty-four hours a day from

171

now until the last panel is shipped. There will be no exceptions. When you get to Shanghai, call me and we'll compare notes on what needs to be done next."

"Okay, Mei, I'll do that. Tell Brian I hope he gets well soon. I'm looking forward to working with him on Copper Mountain."

Mei leaned forward and looked toward the bedroom. "I'll be sure to tell him for you, Jason, and I'm looking forward to working closely with you." She smiled and ran her tongue across her lips as she set the phone on the desk. *You don't know how close we're going to get, Jason, and it will be more than just work.*

TWENTY-EIGHT

The white iPad sitting in its docket on the Formica kitchen counter top softly played a song from the 80s band The Outfield. Janine hummed along as she carefully stirred a simmering pot of pasta sauce that she had made from scratch. She wiped her hands on a white apron that covered her light-colored jeans and set a pot of water onto a burner next to the sauce. A glass of chardonnay sat on the other side of the stove, beads of condensation covering it.

The front door opened and she heard some rustling in the entry. "I'm in the kitchen, Crystal!" she called out. She listened for a minute and waited for a response. Finally, Crystal appeared carrying her backpack at her side.

"I'm going to go study in my room," she said flatly and turned away.

"Okay, but if you're hungry, dinner will be ready in about twenty minutes." Janine listened for a response but none came. She looked up at the ceiling and sighed. What am I going to do with this child? Jason's not going to be home for another day, but it's like living with a mime. How do I break through to her?

She shrugged, picked up her glass of wine, and leaned against the counter, away from the stove. Crossing her arm across her chest, she sipped her wine.

A noise from the living room brought her out of her thoughts. She turned back to the stove and continued stirring the sauce.

Crystal poked her head around the corner and then came into the kitchen, taking a seat at the breakfast table. She had changed from her soccer uniform into a pair of shorts and a tee-shirt with a San Francisco 49ers logo on it. "What are you cooking?" she asked in a soft voice.

"Oh, it's a Bolognese sauce my grandmother used to make for me when I was a child," she answered without turning from the stove. "She was an Italian woman whose parents immigrated to the United States from Naples at the turn of the century." She turned and looked at Crystal. "My, that woman could cook. She made some of the most fantastic dishes I've ever eaten. She taught me to make some of her dishes and this is one of my favorites. I'm boiling some water for pasta shells and when they're done I just pour some sauce over the top and serve. Are you hungry?"

"Yeah, I am," she answered.

Janine smiled at her. "Good, it should be ready soon." She came over to the table and pulled out a chair, setting her wine glass in front of her. "How was school today? Did you learn anything interesting?"

Crystal shrugged. "It was the same as always. We're studying United States history during the Civil War. A lot of stuff about battlefields I have no intention of ever visiting. Other than that, the rest was boring."

"Your dad says you're going to try and get a scholarship to go to college. Do you have any particular one that you would like to attend?"

Crystal answered, "I'd love to go to Pepperdine University, over in Malibu. To be right on the beach and attend college would be awesome. Or UC Santa Barbara would be cool too. Both of them have great soccer programs for women."

"Yeah, those are good choices. They're tough academically to get into also, but I understand you've gotten good grades, so that shouldn't be a problem. Have you ever thought about an out-of-state school?" Janine asked.

"No, why?"

"No reason. I graduated from Arizona State and it was a wonderful experience at a wonderful school. If you get a chance, you ought to visit it."

Crystal studied her in silence for a minute. "How long have you dated my dad?"

Janine rose up and stirred the sauce. She pulled a wine bottle from the refrigerator and refilled her glass. I wonder where this is going, she thought. At least she's talking. "I think it's been about thirteen months, maybe a little less. We met at a Christmas function at the Galleria. We've been seeing each other ever since."

"Are you sure it's only been thirteen months?" Crystal asked, her eyes boring into Janine's. "It seems a lot longer to me."

"No, it's been twelve or thirteen months. I remember very distinctly the first time I met your dad. Is the date important to you for some reason?"

"No," she answered. "I was just wondering. Is the pasta ready yet? I'm starving."

Janine turned back to the stove. She poured the pasta into a colander and set it in the sink to drain. "Let me get all the water out of the pasta and I'll serve you right up. There's some parmesan cheese in the fridge if you want to get it. I love it on my pasta."

Crystal pulled out the green canister of grated cheese and set it on the table. Soon she was stuffing a forkful of sauce-laden pasta in her mouth. They both ate in silence for a few minutes.

Finally Janine asked, "Well, what do you think? Should I keep the recipe?"

175

Crystal, her mouth full, nodded.

"Good, I'm enjoying it myself." She put another mouthful on her fork and then paused. "We haven't checked out those houses you and your dad had picked out to buy. Do you want to go see some of them tomorrow? Your dad will be home in a couple of days and maybe you could narrow down the choice of houses for him to look at."

Crystal set her fork down and her eyes narrowed. "Are you going to move in with us?" Her voice was hostile. "My mom says you're just waiting to make your move so you can get your hands on my dad's money."

The tone of her voice startled Janine and she was caught off guard. "I have no intention of moving in with your dad, Crystal. I've got my own place," she said. "I've got a good job and have my own money. I don't need or want your dad's money."

"Oh yes you do. My mom says you just won't admit it."

Janine felt her anger mounting. "Let me set something straight for you, Crystal. Contrary to what garbage your mother is feeding into your head, I met your dad long after they were split up and divorced. I have no interest in his money or any other material thing he has. I'm interested in Jason the person. You're a smart young lady. Why don't you do a little research and figure out when exactly your father and I met? I can give you the date and the function we attended. I know it might not fit the fantasy your mother is spinning, but it will be the truth!"

Tears gathered in Crystal eyes, and she got up and headed for her room. "I'm sorry," she said over her shoulder. "I've got homework to finish. Thanks for dinner." She shut her door and the apartment went silent.

Janine sat for a moment. Well, she thought, at least that's out in the open. I've tried to be reasonable, but if Crystal is going to continue treating me like this, it may be time for me to move on.

◆

The soft knock on the door brought Janine to her feet, and before she could get to it, Jason had opened it and stepped into the apartment. He slid his rolling suitcase to the corner and came up to Janine, kissing her on the lips.

She wrapped her arms around his neck and kissed him back. "Welcome home. How was your trip?"

"It was good, except I didn't have as much time as I needed to get the changes I wanted implemented done. The plant we run in Shanghai has so many things that need to be fixed, I'm going to have to go back there in a week."

"Really?" she said as she let her arms fall from his neck. "That soon? I hope you're not going to ask me to take care of Crystal again."

He turned and looked at her, an expression of concern on his face. "I assume things didn't go well with Crystal? You didn't say anything to me on the phone."

Janine blinked back tears and moved to the couch in the living room, where she took a seat, her legs curled up under her. "It's not going to work, Jason," she said. "I can't fight them both. It's not fair and I don't have a chance."

"Fight both who?" he asked. He moved across the room, taking a seat next to her, reaching out to hold her hand. "Tell me what happened."

"I can't fight Crystal and her mother. They're not going to let me have a relationship with you. They'll sabotage everything I try to do. Nothing I can say or do will ever convince Crystal that I had nothing to do with your breakup or that I am anything other than some cheap tramp who only wants your money. It just isn't fair." She started crying and tried to wipe away her tears with the back of her hand. She reached down to the coffee table in front of her and pulled out a Kleenex from the box sitting there.

"I'm so sorry, Janine," he said, his voice strained. "You're right, it isn't fair. I don't know everything Debbie's told her, but I can

177

imagine none of it is going to put you in a positive light. I was hoping that Crystal would come around, but I see that it's going to be impossible with her mother in her ear." He squeezed her hand. "I'm so sorry I placed you in this mess. I hoped that it would work out, but I don't want you hurting. I care about you too much."

She dabbed her eyes softly. "I think I need to stay away from you for a while, Jason." She sniffled back a tear. "I love you so much, but as long as your daughter feels this way, there will no chance for us. As much as I want to will this relationship to work, I don't see it happening."

Jason pleaded with her, "Please don't give up on us, Janine. I can do more to help diffuse the situation. I've felt so guilty about our divorce, I've let Crystal run amok with her feelings. I've told her what really happened and all it's done is make matters worse. She thinks I'm lying to her."

"I'm not asking you to alter your relationship with Crystal because of me, Jason," she said, her eyes red from crying. "That would make me sadder than anything if I caused a rift between you two. She's your daughter and she needs your love. I don't want to have any part in changing that."

Jason took a deep breath and let out a sigh. "I promise you that won't happen. I'll be home for the week and I'll have a chat with Crystal. I've already told her the circumstances of our divorce, but I guess I'm going to have to be more forceful and actually show her how you weren't involved. I won't jump her case or raise hell with her if that's what you're thinking, but this incivility has to stop."

"Please don't drag me into this, Jason," she said. "Crystal already can't stand me and I don't want you to try to stuff me down her throat. It won't work and she'll resent me even more."

"I will not stuff you down her throat. I know her better than that and I know that won't work." He turned and stared out the window. "I know what to say and how to handle her. Things are going to change, just wait and see."

◆

Crystal sprinted left, her cleats digging into the turf as she cut off the wayward ball her teammate had passed. Deftly, she stopped the ball with the side of her foot and stopped next to it. Laughing, she shouted at her teammate, who was twenty yards across from her, "Nice pass! I hope you don't do that in the game."

The teammate, looking sheepish, laughed back, "I put it there on purpose. You need to run a little harder."

Crystal was about to retort when she spotted her dad leaning against his car, his hand shielding his eyes from the sun. Even though he wore dark glasses, the glare was intense. Crystal yelled at her coach, who was across the field showing a couple of girls a new move, "I'm gonna take five!" She sprinted across the field and came up to her dad, giving him a big hug. "Daddy! I'm so glad you're home. I've missed you!"

Jason leaned down and kissed her on her forehead, holding her tightly. "I missed you too, pumpkin. Go ahead and finish your practice. I'll wait for you."

The next twenty-five minutes flew by as Crystal went through the motions. The coach blew a whistle and brought all the girls to a circle around him in the center of the field. After a brief pep talk, he dismissed the team. Crystal grabbed her backpack from the sideline and walked to where her dad was parked.

After she threw her backpack in the back, she settled in her seat next to her dad.

"Hey, do you want to get a yogurt? That Honey Bear shop you like is right up the street," he asked.

Crystal gave him a smile. "Yeah, that would be great. I haven't had one of those in weeks." She leaned down and untied the laces to her cleats. "So, how was the China trip? It seems like you were gone a long time."

179

"Everything went well in China. There are lots of things going on there. We're buried trying to ramp our production up to service the Copper Mountain job."

"That's a good thing right?" she asked as she switched from her cleats to tennis shoes.

"Oh yes, it's a very good thing," her dad answered. "It's just a challenge for me to herd all these cats at once." He pulled the car into a strip mall down from the soccer field and parked in front of a shop with colorful rabbits eating yogurt cones painted on the windows.

After ordering, they took a table with an umbrella outside the shop and sat down. Crystal eagerly spooned out the contents of her chocolate peanut butter special. "I forgot how good this stuff is," she remarked between spoons of yogurt. "We should do this more often."

"We should," he said, nodding. He wiped his hands with a paper napkin and pushed his cup away. "I'm glad to be home and it's great to see you again, Crystal. But there's something I want to talk to you about."

Crystal finished scooping out the last remnants of the yogurt. *Uh oh. Here comes the lecture. I wonder what Janine told him. Every time he leaves me with her I get into trouble.*

Jason cleared his throat. "I kept a lot of things from you regarding what happened between me and your mother because I thought it best to keep you out of the sordid details." He locked his eyes on hers. "But I think it's time you know the whole truth. Back in 2007, we all were living well. My business was booming; we had lots of money and took lots of trips."

"I remember," she said, looking confused.

"Well, our world got turned upside-down in 2008. The recession hit, money dried up, my business almost stopped cold, and the income drastically declined. I had to lay off my entire staff and tried my best to keep the doors open, but it was in vain. We ran out of money, and the bank took our boat and eventually the house."

He tapped a finger on the table nervously. "I would have felt worse if I were the only one going through this, but anyone who was in the construction industry like I was went through the same thing."

"I was with you, Dad, remember? What are you trying to tell me?"

"What I'm trying to tell you is not having money and moving into an apartment was hard for your mother. She was used to our other lifestyle and blamed everything on me. When she met her current boyfriend, she was in a vulnerable, emotional state, and it seemed he could give her what I couldn't, so she moved out and left with him."

He paused for a moment as a woman with two infants in a double stroller passed them by. "I'm not the one who had an affair, Crystal. I'm not the one who wanted the divorce. I did everything I could to keep our marriage intact, but she wanted out and filed for divorce." He paused for a second. "I want you to get that. You mother moved out and filed for divorce."

Crystal stuck out her chin defiantly. "You're lying!" she yelled. "You kicked mom out so you could have sex with Janine. Don't try to rewrite history, Dad!"

"Stop yelling," her dad hissed. "I am not lying and Janine had nothing to do with our divorce. Here's a question I want you to ponder: When did we move into the apartment? I'll answer that for you. It was when you were finishing the sixth grade almost four years ago." He stopped and took a sip of water. "Do you remember that?"

"Yes, I remember," she answered firmly. "I had to transfer schools in the middle of the year. That sucked."

"I'm sure it did," he said. "But do you also remember that summer when you were getting ready to go into the eighth grade? Your mom told you that she was going to take a trip back east to get her head right."

"Yeah, I remember."

"Well, your mother's head-clearing trip was to go live in North Dakota with another man. That man was Dave, her current boyfriend.

Three months after she left, she served me with divorce papers, and our divorce was finalized by the time you were out of school for the summer."

Crystal stared at him, clenching her teeth.

He continued. "I met Janine at a charity party the following May. It's not even close. You have to quit letting you mother convince you she's a victim. She's made her own bed and she needs to sleep in it."

Crystal's cheeks grew flushed. "Okay, if Mom really is the cause of all this, then why won't you buy me an airline ticket and let me go stay with her? It's because you're too cheap, that's why. You're probably saving money for your honeymoon in Hawaii."

Her dad threw his hands in the air in exasperation. "Crystal, what the hell are you talking about? The reason I didn't send you to North Dakota is because Dave doesn't want to deal with children, and in his mind, you're a child. Your mother told me not to send you there because he didn't want you to come and stay with them."

"I am not a child!" she said, her voice rising in anger. "Mom told me she wanted me to come, that she misses being with me. You keep telling me that Mom doesn't want me flying to North Dakota. Why would she not want me to visit her?"

Her dad shook his head. "Why would I lie to you, Crystal? I have no plans on getting married or going on a honeymoon. I don't have time for a vacation in Hawaii. I have more than enough money to send you to North Dakota if your mom wanted you to come."

Crystal sat at the table and seethed. "I still don't believe you, Dad," she said, not taking her eyes off him. "Mom has told me what happened, and she has told me I'm free to visit her anytime. She wouldn't lie to me." She stood up abruptly. "I need to get home. I've got an English paper I need to finish. It's due in the morning."

As they drove home in silence, Crystal pulled out her phone and texted Steve. *How is it going with your new license?*

A few seconds later he replied. *Sweet!*

She typed back, *Next Fri is last day of school. You ready for our trip?*

I'm more than ready, came the reply. *Tell me what time and we'll meet and blow this town.*

Crystal sat back in her seat and smiled. She looked over at her dad, who was squeezing the steering wheel with an intense look on his face. I'll show you, Dad. When I surprise Mom next week by showing up on her doorstep, I'll prove you're wrong. I know she wants to see me, but if you're telling the truth, I'll soon find out. She turned and stared out the window, watching the traffic pass by their car. This is going to be a trip that I will never forget!

TWENTY-NINE

The inside of the van was covered wall to wall with television monitors, each one focused on different sections of the airport hangar a hundred yards away. Three men in dark clothing sat silently watching the monitors, once in a while pointing something out to each other. Their main focus was a Boeing 747 cargo aircraft parked in front of the hangar, its large nose tilted up to expose the main body of the aircraft. The airplane was so huge it almost dwarfed the hangar, and troop trucks could easily drive in or out of it.

A Chinese flag was painted on its tail, and two soldiers with Chinese military insignia on their uniforms stood guard on each side of the entrance to the aircraft. Three forklifts drove from the plane to the hangar and back again, each time carrying a pallet of solar panels packed in open wooden boxes to be stored in the hangar.

The tallest of the three men pointed to the monitor in the center of the van. "That should be the last of the solar panels," he said in a monotone voice. "They should start packing the guns in the panel crates and reload fairly soon."

"How long do you think it will take to load the cargo up?" the man to his left asked.

"About the same as the last load, about six or seven hours," the first man answered. "It's almost ten o'clock. They'll want to be finished before daylight. Keep an eye on things. I'm going to get some rest for a few hours. Wake me up if anything changes."

"You got it."

♦

The cellphone sitting on the kitchen counter rang incessantly. The first time, Jason let it go to voicemail. The second time, he rose up from the chair in the living room, lowering the volume on the TV. *Who's calling me at 10:30 on a Tuesday night?* He hit the green button. "Hello?"

"Mr. Ballard?" the male voice asked.

"Yes, this is Jason Ballard. Who's this?"

"Mr. Ballard, this is Benny Teller. I apologize for calling you so late but I wasn't sure what to do or who to call. I'm the foreman at the Reno hangar where we're storing the Soltech solar panels for the Copper Mountain job. I got to my shift and there are some people here emptying the panels out of their shipping crates and then storing some other stuff in it." He waited for a second.

"I'm listening, Benny, keep going," Jason said, his eyebrows furrowed. *What is going on over there? They shouldn't be uncrating those solar panels.*

"Well, anyway, I went over to ask the guys what they were doing and they told me to get lost. One of them showed me some kind of military ID. I think you should come over here and take a look at this. Something doesn't seem right."

Jason looked down at his watch. *I could use one of the corporate jets and be there in an hour and a half.* "Hold on a second, Benny." He walked to Crystal's bedroom and quietly stuck his head in to check on her. *She's sound asleep,* he thought. *I'll leave her a note and alert Janine in case there's an emergency. I can be back here in about five*

185

and a half hours and she'll never know I was gone. Seeing Crystal's cellphone on her nightstand, he picked it up and programed Janine's cell number in it, adding the numbers 911 to the end of Janine's name that he added to the contact list. I'll let her know in the note that if something happens to contact Janine first.

He shut the bedroom door and stepped back into the living room. Talking softly he said, "Okay, Benny. I'll be there in a couple of hours. Keep an eye on things."

Thirty minutes later he was resting in the beige leather tuck-and-roll seat of Soltech's Cessna Citation jet as it lifted off the San Jose International Airport's runway on its way to Nevada. He thumbed through a *Sports Illustrated* he had brought with him, but his mind wasn't on pampered athletes. Somebody's about to get an ass chewing, he thought. I never authorized the uncrating of the solar panels. We've got a month or so before they'll be needed at Copper Mountain. That project's just getting underway. It's going to be months before all the wiring, underground inverters, and odd work will be done, before we can even place one solar panel. He stared out the window into the darkness. Would Mei have authorized this work? If so, why? Uncrated, those panels can easily be damaged. This makes no sense.

After the plane landed at Stead Air Force Base, Jason came up to the cockpit and directed the pilots to where the Soltech hangar was located. It was lit up from huge floodlights in front of the hangar and from the lights hanging from the ceiling on the inside. He instructed to have the pilots taxi the jet a hundred yards away from the C-47, which was still parked in front of the hangar, its nose still in the open position. Once the jet stopped, Jason scurried down the stairs and walked up to the massive hangar, keeping to the shadows. He could hear the sound of a vehicle inside the hangar, so he opened the main door on the side of the building and cautiously peeked inside.

Stacks of Soltech solar panels, with small fillers between each panel, rose from the floor of the hangar to the ceiling on the far wall.

Opposite the panels were the wooden crates the panels, ten to a crate, had been shipped in. A young Chinese man with a dirty baseball cap over his head and earphones in his ears operated a forklift, which lifted up two wooden boxes from the stack. The man then backed up the forklift and headed toward the C-47 on the tarmac. He passed two sentries guarding the entry of the plane. Two other young men, also Chinese, were smoking cigarettes and laughing at the far end of the hangar, their backs to Jason.

The noise from the forklift echoed around the hangar, and the exhaust covered Jason in a gray smoke. None of them—the forklift driver, the men smoking, or the sentries—had seen Jason, so he slowly walked over to the stack of wooden crates.

He checked over his shoulder and, seeing no one was paying attention to him, reached down and slid open the lid of the crate sitting on the top.

His eyes widened and his heart started racing. Holy crap! he thought. There has to be a hundred assault rifles in here. He reached down to touch one just to make sure he wasn't dreaming. He wasn't. Stepping back, he looked up at the stack that towered eighteen feet above him and whistled softly. This is not some small potato operation.

Men's voices shouting and cursing made him turn to his left. He saw the two men smoking the cigarettes running toward him, screaming at him in what he assumed was Chinese. They skidded to a stop in front of him and pushed him backward, all the time screaming and yelling. One of the sentries, hearing the commotion, came racing over, his rifle up at his shoulder ready to shoot.

Jason held his hands up and shouted, "Hold on! Hold on! I'm with Soltech! I'm the president of the company!"

The men were still yelling excitedly and gesturing wildly with their hands. Jason's heart was doing double time as he stared down the sentry's rifle aimed at his forehead. He was sweating profusely. A thought came to his head and he yelled out to the sentry, "Madam

Chen! Madam Chen!" The guard looked at him with a puzzled expression. The other men stopped their yelling and looked at him.

Jason slowly reached back to his back pocket with his left hand, keeping the right in the air. The men started chattering excitedly and gestured for him to raise his arms. Jason pulled out his cellphone and yelled again, "Madam Chen!" The sentry slowly lowered his gun as Jason opened the phone. He tapped his contact list and pulled up a name on the screen. He showed them Madam Chen's name and pointed to himself. "I'm with Madam Chen!"

The forklift came roaring around the corner and pulled to a stop in front of the group, and the driver shut the engine off and jumped out. "Who are you?" he demanded. "What are you doing here? This area is off limits to anyone who doesn't have the correct credentials."

"I'm—I'm Jason Ballard," he stammered as he lowered his arms. "I'm the President of Soltech, which is owned by Madam Mei Chen." He pointed to the stack of solar panels in the corner of the building. "Those are my panels."

The driver turned to look at the panels then said something in Chinese to the other three men. They nodded as if they understood. He turned to Jason and pointed at the entrance of the hangar. "I'm sorry about the confusion, Mr. Ballard, but this is a restricted area. You're going to have to leave."

"Where's Benny Teller, the warehouse superintendent?" Jason asked as he lowered his hands and his breathing returned to normal. "I was supposed to meet him here." He turned and scanned the hangar to see if there was anyone else around. Does Mei know about this? he thought. Someone high up has to have authorized this. What the hell is going on?

"I don't know who Benny Teller is," the driver answered, his jaw set and his tone firm. "There was some skinny guy snooping around here earlier but we ran him off. You need to leave, sir. Now! These are orders form Madam Chen."

Jason saw the intensity on his face and decided he'd better do as he was told. "Okay, I'll leave. But I want to know what's going on here and who authorized this."

"Take it up with Madam Chen," the driver said, sneering. "Now, get out of here!"

Jason headed out of the hangar, walking a wide arc towards the C-47. Checking behind him, he heard the forklift fire up and watched the other men head back into the hangar. After he made it past the entrance, he turned left, away from the spotlights. He ducked under a wing and walked around to the tail section of the plane, examining its exterior. Even though it was dark, he recognized the logo of the government of China on the tail.

As he rounded the back of the plane, he felt a hand grab his arm and push him forward. A man's voice spoke softly in his ear. "Don't make any noise and do as I say." For the second time Jason's heart raced. Oh no, what have I gotten myself into?

The man steered him away from the plane and the hangar, and they walked in the dark until they reached a dark van a hundred yards away. Jason's mind raced as he wondered what the guy was going to do with him. The door to the van opened and Jason was pushed inside.

Two other men, both dressed in dark shirts with the sleeves rolled up, were seated on a bench on one wall. One of the men indicated to Jason to sit down next to him. "Mr. Ballard," he said as he pulled a silver badge out of his coat pocket and held it up for Jason to see. "I'm Special Agent Mark Namath. This is Agent Pete Clark." He then pointed to the bald black man in his mid-forties who had escorted Jason to the van, "And that is Special Agent Willie Wilson. We're all with the department of Alcohol, Tobacco, and Firearms, or ATF for short. You've walked into one of our operations. Agent Clark did the Benny Teller imitation to you over the phone. We wanted you to come here to this warehouse so we could explain how you're going to help us. We tried to intercept you when you got off your plane, but you moved too fast. Sorry to scare you."

Jason took a deep breath. "I wasn't sure what I had come across. I have no knowledge of what's going on inside that hangar other than my company has shipped thousands of solar panels here to be placed on a job nearby."

Agent Namath watched him talk, his hands folded in his lap. The other two agents had slipped on headphones and were back watching the monitors on the walls. "We know that. We're monitoring everything that goes on inside the hangar and we heard your conversation with those people in there." He leaned forward, his face growing serious. "You were lucky. Those military personnel don't mess around. They have no problem putting a bullet into trespassers." He smiled. "Of course, we wouldn't have let that happen."

Jason pointed at the TVs around the van. "So you guys have been monitoring the activity around here? What have you found and what do you need me to do?"

"This is part of an ongoing gun-running operation that we've been tracking for some time," the agent answered. "We're trying to find out who's behind it. We know where they get the guns, but we're not sure what the ultimate destination is for them. You said you were the President of Soltech, right?"

Jason nodded.

"Why would your company be using a Chinese military plane to move your products?" he asked. "Who authorizes that?"

Reaching for a legal pad sitting on a countertop under the monitors, Jason started sketching out a company schematic. After he was finished drawing, he walked the agents through the hierarchy of Soltech, the Communist government, and Mei Chen's position in both. He explained Inter-Power and the Copper Mountain project and their presence at the airfield in Nevada. When he was done, he set the pad back on the counter.

Agent Namath looked at the others and then spoke. "What you've showed us has been very educational, but we need your help in pinning down and catching the players who are behind this. We would like your cooperation."

"Do I have a choice?" Jason asked, looking from face to face.

Agent Namath smiled. "Of course you do. We're not going to force you to help us. But your company and your solar farm could be in jeopardy if we find either of them are willing participants in a gun-running scheme. We think that your company is legitimate, but someone is using it to front the gun operation. We also know from past experience something this big has more than one big player involved."

Jason swallowed hard. "So, what do you want me to do? I'm not privy to the operations of the Chinese plane. That's my boss, Mei Chen's, department. I don't know where it goes from here."

"Here's what you can do for us," Agent Namath said, moving to the edge of his seat. "We know your boss, Mei Chen, has some involvement here. You're close to her. Get us as much information as you can about her dealings and who she does business with. Anything and everything you can get your hands on. We'll determine if it's worthwhile information. There's also evidence she's getting help from people in the United States government. There have been some suspect dealings with the Copper Mountain lease with the BLM. There has to be a connection between who she's dealing with and how the guns get to this spot. Who is that person? Start with her closest aides and work outward from there. We think there might be someone back in China or Hong Kong that might be pulling the strings. Or there might be someone closer to home, possibly in the government."

"Okay," Jason said nervously. "How do I contact you with anything I discover?"

Agent Namath handed Jason a card. "You can get me day or night at this number. We'll also be watching out for you to keep you out of trouble. We're not dealing with Boy Scouts here."

Jason studied the card. "Great. It's comforting to know you'll be watching me." He looked back at agent Namath. "Does this operation have anything to do with Andrew Dillon's murder?"

Agent Namath stared back at him. "We're not sure yet, but there's some belief that these events are related. Stay alert and stay in touch."

THIRTY

The stuffed heads of antelope, wildebeest, and water buffalo—all shot on various African safaris—protruded from the walls of the massive living room. A zebra skin lay stretched out on the plush white carpet, a hand-carved cherry wood coffee table sitting over it. David Wilson sat on his black leather couch looking up at the flat screen TV on the wall, the remote control in his hands. The Monaco Grand Prix, one of the premier formula one car races in the world, was down to the last ten laps, and Damon Belch, the dashing young British race car driver who had captured the hearts of his countrymen, was in the lead. As the race wound down to its final laps and Belch was comfortably ahead, David tossed the remote to the leather chair and stood up. Looking down at his watch, he said to himself, "It's past noon. I think it is time for a celebratory drink."

Meandering to the long mahogany bar on the other side of the room, he poured himself a double shot of Glenlivet over a few ice cubes. This was his favorite suite, which he used exclusively. It was thirty-five hundred feet of pure luxury at the top of the Grand Hyatt. As he sipped his drink, he moved to the two French doors leading to the exterior deck and stepped outside, putting on a pair of sunglasses he had in his breast pocket as he went. The sun beat down on him as he moved over to the railing and looked down to the street twenty-seven floors below him.

The building sat just outside of downtown Hong Kong, and even though this was a Sunday, the area was bustling with activity. Car horns honked every two seconds, along with shouting and yelling from a nearby construction site where work went on twenty-four hours a day, seven days a week. Standing in a short-sleeved shirt and khaki shorts, he felt a soft breeze blow over his face, a relief from the dry heat.

I can never get enough of this view, he thought. Hong Kong is such a vibrant city and I'm sitting right in the heartbeat of it. There is no amount of money in the world that would make me give this up. He turned his head and watched a group of cyclists biking through the nearby park. What a beautiful day. I should be sharing it with a beautiful woman.

The image of Mei Chen's face came to his mind and he smiled. Oh no, not you, Mei. You are beautiful, but way too dangerous for me. Ever since I turned you down to be my business partner, you've gone from steamy vixen to tiger shark. People like you need to be kept at a safe distance.

His thoughts were interrupted by a set of sirens, and he looked to his left to see where the source was coming from. Three white and red police cars, lights flashing, came screaming around a corner and skidded to a stop at the entrance to the hotel. Two camouflage-colored jeeps with two soldiers inside each, followed right behind them. Six uniformed policemen stepped out of the cars, along with the four military personnel, and raced into the hotel.

This can't be good, David thought as he took a long sip from his scotch. He spun around and headed back into the suite. I guess I should find out what this is all about. He picked up a couple of glasses sitting on the counter and set them in the dishwasher. He looked about the room and, satisfied everything was in order, headed to the master bedroom to change.

He rifled through his closet and settled on a dark pair of slacks with a light blue shirt. Before he could finish changing his clothes, he heard a loud rapping on the front doors. Opening the doors, he saw the two soldiers standing in the doorway, the four policemen behind them, and all of them with their hands on their weapons. David looked them over, then turned to the one soldier who had more stripes on his shoulder.

"To what do I owe the honor of hosting Hong Kong's and the government of China's finest?" he asked in a pleasant tone, trying not to show any nervousness in his voice.

"Mr. Wilson," the soldier said to him curtly as he stepped forward onto the marble floor of the entry, "we have a warrant for your arrest." He held up a signed piece of paper and waved it in front of David's face. "We would appreciate it if you would come quietly so no one gets hurt. Especially you."

David felt the hair on the back of his neck rise. This has to be payback from Mei Chen, he thought. She's going to try to steal my hotels from me one way or another. He held his hands up in protest. "What is the purpose of my arrest?" he asked. "I haven't broken any laws. You can't just come into my house and drag me away without telling me what I did."

The soldier put the arrest warrant in his pocket and declared, "You are under arrest for crimes against the government. You will be given a fair trial and will have a chance to express you innocence in a court of law. Now please, come with us."

"That's a bunch of rubbish," David spat. He turned and moved back toward the living room. "I'm going to call my lawyer. This isn't legal. I haven't broken any law."

He had almost made it into the living room when he felt a crushing blow to the back of his head, knocking him to the ground. His head immediately started pounding and his vision blurred. He could feel warm blood running down the back of his neck as he tried to stagger to his knees. Another blow to his head sent him slamming face first into the marble floor.

The soldier stood over him as David stared at his spit-shined black boots. "Mr. Wilson, I don't think I made myself clear. You are to come with me now. There is no need to call a lawyer. Now get up and get moving before I am forced to have my men carry you out."

David struggled to stand up, putting his hand to the back of his head in a vain attempt to stop the bleeding. His eyes grew wide as he tried to clear his head. Is this Mei's idea of a payback for turning her offer down? This can't be happening. Things like this don't happen in Hong Kong.

He was pushed roughly out the front door and half-dragged, half-walked to the elevator. When they got to the ground floor and made their way through the lobby, a crowd of people gathered to watch the spectacle. When one of the military men dropped his rifle to his waist and gave a menacing glare to the crowd, they quickly dispersed.

After a bumpy drive through the city, where he was squeezed between two policemen, they arrived at a military facility on the outskirts of town. David's head pounded, and a gash over his eye started to bleed, making it difficult to see where they were taking him. They drove through a fenced-in area with razor wire at the top and ended up at a drab two-story complex in the middle of the compound.

They dragged David out of the car and into the building, which was guarded by young, fresh-faced sentries, all of whom carried AK-47 assault rifles. The steel entry door clanged heavily shut after they passed through it.

David tried to make out where he was, but his pounding head and limited vision made it impossible. The smell of the place—human sweat, vomit, urine, and feces—almost made him gag, and he could hear men moaning and groaning from all around him. After going halfway through the dark hallway, they stopped at a metal door, where one of his captors produced a key and opened it.

One of the guards pushed David hard with his boot, causing him to fall forward onto the dirt floor of a cell. As he lay on the dusty floor, he tried to make out the cell's surroundings. There was no light, only a small mat in one corner and another small bucket in the other.

"Please," he pleaded. "There's been a mistake. You must have the wrong man. I haven't done anything to warrant this."

The soldier who had beaten him earlier took a step into the cell. "We have the right person, Mr. Wilson. We don't make mistakes when it comes to crimes against the government. You will remain here until your trial."

David propped himself up on an elbow, struggling to see the man who was talking. "Wait, please. Can I speak to Madam Chen? I know she'll help clear this up. Please let me speak to her."

The soldier laughed at him then spoke in a condescending tone. "Madam Chen? You want to speak to Madam Chen? Do you think an important woman like that has time to speak to a prisoner like yourself? There is no chance. When your trial comes, you can have your say. Until then, enjoy your stay with us."

The soldier turned and said something in Chinese to the other men, and they all laughed. The door slammed shut and David heard the rusted key turn in the lock. He lay on his back and stared at the ceiling. How am I going to get out of this mess? How long will Mei keep me here? Will she just take my hotels and leave me here to rot? He felt something brush up against his leg. He tried to kick it but he immediately felt a piecing jab in his calf. He screamed in pain and then realized he had just been bitten by a rat. He recoiled away and sat against the cold brick wall. "Please, Mei, don't do this to me," he yelled out. "You're not going to get my properties by torture!"

THIRTY-ONE

The windshield wipers went back and forth in a steady beat as the rain poured down upon the dark Mercedes limousine. The driver, a young man in his twenties wearing dark gloves and a black cap, drove slowly but steadily through the heavy traffic alongside the National Convention Center just outside downtown Beijing.

Mei, a glass of champagne in her right hand, stared vacantly out the window as they made their way from the venue. The annual Communist Party Convention was over, and it pleased her that she wouldn't have to think about it for another year. She smoothed out her full-length chiffon evening gown and, putting her glass down, started to pull off the white gloves from her arms. She pulled out the clip holding her hair in a bun and let her hair fall down to her shoulders. The diamond necklace she wore shimmered from the headlights of the oncoming traffic.

Her husband Ho, in a black tuxedo with a starched white shirt, sat across the limo from her and watched, a stoic expression on his face. Finally he spoke. "You were well received, Mei. I was worried you might use your tongue to lash out of some of the members who are not up to your standards, but thankfully you refrained."

Glaring at him, she retorted, "It would be easy to slice them into little pieces with my words, but there is nothing to be gained by that. I know what they're saying behind my back and I refuse to give them any more ammunition. I don't care what they say, they are not in my same class."

"You give yourself too much credit, Mei," he said, squirming forward to sit on the edge of his seat. He pointed his finger at her. "Those so called people who are beneath you are the same ones who can take you down. Do not forget that Chairman Xi is going to step down in the next two years. I'm in line to take his position if everything works out and if I remain in good favor with the Party. I don't need you to sabotage that."

Waving her hand in a dismissive way, she took a drink from her champagne. "Don't be ridiculous, husband. They'll put you in the President's position because of me and my family ties. You worry too much. Once you gain the presidency, there will be great changes in China, especially Hong Kong."

"Oh, really?" he said, raising his eyebrows. "And I bet a lot of the changes involve Mei Chen taking over a lot of privately owned businesses just like you did with David Wilson's hotels."

Putting her glass down, Mei bristled. "Who told you that? That's a bunch of lies. I will have whoever spread that lie shot! I don't intend to take over anything, but whoever does business in Hong Kong should share the wealth we're letting be created with certain members of the Party. That's not taking over anything!" She folded her arms across her chest and leaned back in her seat. "Now that I'm done here, I need to get back to the US to get prepared for the next big solar farm project. I'm tired of all this political nonsense."

"Mei," he said to her in a stern voice, "why must you continue to pursue these high-profile projects? I'm assuming you're referring to the Antelope Valley project in the Mojave Desert. The project is subsidized by a huge amount of money from the United States Government. Do you know how much scrutiny the project will get once it gets started?" He paused, letting his words sink in. "Soltech is a Chinese company that's furnishing the solar panels and a high ranking person in the Chinese government is a part-owner of the solar farm. Do you not think that will play poorly in the United States, not to mention in China, when the people find out your involvement? This could all end up badly."

"Shut up, Ho," she snapped. "I'm not going to stop what I'm doing because some small-minded people might not approve. I've got bigger things to worry about. You focus on the Party and becoming the next President and I'll worry about me."

"Okay, Mei, you win. Go ahead and be the big capitalist, but don't tell me I didn't warn you." He softened his tone. "What about our daughter? You never see her except when she's playing at a major concert hall or in some school project. She deserves more from her mother."

Lifting her chin up, Mei narrowed her eyes at him. "You are a wimp like her, Ho. She needs to be pushed. She is Chinese, not a coddled American! Quit pampering her! Make her work harder and she will thank us later when she grows up."

"She doesn't need to be treated like a slave for her to be successful in life. We have a wonderful, smart, and ambitious daughter in Chi. She will grow up and be a wonderful and successful person."

Mei laughed at him. "Don't be such a fool, Ho. She will be successful because I will push her to be successful. The only reason she might fail is if you step in and undo all my hard work."

◆

Two days later, Mei was at Soltech's office in San Jose before 7:00 a.m. She was pleased to see Jason's BMW parked in his usual spot in the company parking lot. I made a good choice in Jason, she thought. The more I throw on his plate, the better he responds. But he might be too smart for his own good. I'll keep him on a short leash.

She spent the next hour going through her mail and phone messages. After the last message was dealt with, she buzzed Jason at his office. "Jason, can you come in and see me?" she asked through the intercom.

A minute later he was standing in her doorway, a legal pad in his hand. She indicated for him to sit at the chair in front of her desk. "I understand you paid a visit to our hangar in Reno recently." She looked at him coolly. "After our panels are unloaded, what goes on there is official business of the Government of China and no one else's, including yourself. It is restricted space and no one is to go near those planes." She paused for a second. "Do I make myself clear?"

Jason nodded slowly. "Yes, I get your point."

Mei smiled and changed the tone of her voice. "Now, bring me up to speed on the Copper Mountain project," she said as she leaned forward on her desk. "I'm anxious to hear what's been happening in my absence."

Jason cleared his throat, looking down at some notes on his legal pad. "As you were probably aware, they have started grading the site." He looked up for a second. "It's over nine hundred acres, so it's going to take at least three months to finish that portion of the project."

He looked down again. "The infrastructure of the project, the underground wiring, the PVC piping—all of that can be started in the first phase in about two months." He crossed something out on his pad and continued. "Even though our solar panels won't be needed for about five months, per your request we've started shipping them to our warehouse in Nevada."

Flipping over a new sheet, he stopped and looked up at Mei. "Everything at the plant in Shanghai is running more smoothly. I implemented the safety measures I ran by you, and so far the accidents have ceased."

Mei frowned. "I'm sorry, Jason, but you can't cure stupid. Those workers who died weren't doing their jobs correctly. That's why they lost their lives. It had nothing to do with the way the plant had been operating."

Jason stared at her for a second. "I'm sorry, Mei, but I strongly disagree with you. Those deaths were preventable. I want to ensure that it doesn't happen again."

Throwing her hands in the air in exasperation, she said, "Okay, I give in to you. You made the changes, so let's move on. What else?"

"Well," he said, "I need to ask you something."

"What?"

"How is Brian Thompson doing? Who's going to be in charge of Inter-Power?"

She lowered her head and sighed. "Brian's not doing well. When I left Hong Kong last week he was still at the hospital. The doctors can't figure out what's wrong with him." She looked up at him. "Greg Arnold will be the interim project manager while Brian is gone, and Brian asked that I help Greg with running the company until he returns."

Rolling a pencil between his fingers, Jason stared at her in silence. "Isn't it going to be a conflict of interest for you to award Antelope Valley to Soltech? This is a one-point-three-billion-dollar project, which is not small potatoes. Aren't you worried about negative press?"

"No, I'm not," she said emphatically. "I'll be helping Greg make decisions based on what's best for Inter-Power. If Soltech's bid is the best bid for Antelope Valley, that's who will be awarded it."

"Do the doctors have any idea when Brian might be released from the hospital?" Jason asked. "There are still a few months to go before that bid is let out. He should be back running things by then, shouldn't he?"

"I don't know," she said with a shrug. "He didn't look very good when I last saw him." She leaned forward on the desk and said with a soft voice, "I'm not sure he's going to live much longer, Jason. I hope he can recover, but it doesn't look good."

Jason's jaw dropped and his eyes widened. "Oh my god, Mei. I didn't realize it was so serious. Do they have the proper health care in Hong Kong to care for him? Should he be moved back to the United States? I can't believe this. Brian was as healthy as a horse."

"He's in great hands in Hong Kong," she said to him. "I made sure he was put into the best hospital and had the best doctors attending him. If anyone can help him get better, they can, but I'm not sure they'll be able to save him."

A young woman showed up at the doorway and tapped softly on the door. "You're eight o'clock appoint is here, Madam Chen," she said in a soft voice.

"Alright, I'll be right out." She turned back to Jason. "Is there anything else?"

"Uh, yes," Jason said as he flipped the papers on his legal pad over. "We've shipped about three hundred thousand solar panels to Nevada and we're almost out of storage space. Should I wait until the project is further along before I have Shanghai ship out more?"

Mei shook her head. "Keep shipping the solar panels. You'll find a place to store them. The more we ship, the more we can bill. It's a simple formula."

"Okay, there's another warehouse about a mile from the airport that's available to lease. We'll store them there." He got up and left her office.

◆

By the time Jason had reached his office, his head was spinning. He picked up the phone and dialed Janine's number. As soon as she answered it, he started to speak quickly. "Hey, babe, I just needed someone to talk to." He took a deep breath. "I've been telling you about Brian's sudden sickness and I feel something is wrong here.

That guy was so healthy, he'd be the last guy I'd pick to get sick. He's been to Hong Kong many times and never been sick. Why now?" He walked over to the window of his office and looked down at the parking lot.

"You told me you were worried about him since he hadn't returned your calls. Have you had a chance to talk to him?" she asked.

"No," he answered. "He's staying at a prestigious hospital in Hong Kong, but she tells me he's too weak to come to the phone."

"That does seem strange to me also. Is there anything you can do?"

Jason came back to his desk and sat down. "I don't know. Listen, thanks for letting me vent. I need to get going. I'll see you later on tonight."

"Any time. I love you. Bye."

Jason sat at his desk, his chin resting on his hands, and stared at the computer monitor. There must be a better reason why Mei's been shipping all these panels early to Reno. How deep is she in the gun-running deal? Maybe I should get over to Hong Kong and see for myself what's up with Brian. I would sure hate to have Mei's relationship with Inter-Power screw up the Copper Mountain project or ruin our chances at the Antelope Valley project because of a conflict of interest. Maybe I can find out more about Mei's dealings while I'm there. Andrew's murder, the gun running, now Brian's sickness. There're too many bad coincidences going on here.

He sat down at his desk and typed out an email explaining to Mei that he was going to the Shanghai factory next week to check on its progress. After he sent it, he stared at his computer for a moment. I'll travel to Hong Kong first, he thought. I'm going to get to the bottom of this and figure out what's really going on. If Brian needs medical attention, I'm going to help him get it. He's not going to die on my watch!

Putting his hands behind his head, he leaned back in his chair. Am I going to be putting Janine and Crystal in danger? There's no telling what Mei will do to me if she finds out I'm interfering with her operation. She's already proven she'll stop at nothing to get her way. He closed his eyes and shook his head. I need to get them to a safer place while I'm gone. I'm going to alert Agent Namath about these suspicious things and have him keep an eye on Janine and Crystal. They don't need any of Mei Chen's goons paying them a surprise visit.

♦

Three days later, after placing Crystal with one of her teammates' families and making sure Agent Namath had both that family's and Janine's addresses, Jason arrived at the Hong Kong hospital Brian had been taken to and found Brian's room. He set his carry-on luggage outside the door and knocked softly. Hearing no response, he opened the door slowly and stepped in. What he saw stunned him. The person lying in the bed with four IVs coming from his arms and a monitor with three tubes stuck to his chest did not look like the person he had sat in front of one month ago. His breathing was slow and labored, and he seemed to be in a constant sweat. Crusts of spit accumulated in the corner of his mouth and his lips were dry and cracked.

Jason moved over to the bed and sat in the chair next to it. He reached out and grabbed Brian's hand, rubbing it softly. "Brian, it's Jason," he whispered. "I came by to see how you're doing. I'm so sorry to see you this way. I want you to know I'm thinking about you and hope you can beat this thing."

Brian lay there without moving for a minute and then slowly turned his head an inch or so. His eyes flickered a bit and he nodded to Jason. He reached across his body with his right hand and squeezed Jason's hand weakly. "Out," he croaked.

Leaning in to hear better, Jason asked him, "Say that again. I didn't understand you. What did you want?"

Brian opened his eyes wider, a pleading look in them. He squeezed Jason's hand harder. "Out. Get me out!"

What? Jason thought. Does he want me to take him out of this hospital? That won't be an easy task. Jason leaned in closer. "You want to leave this place, Brian?"

Brian blinked and nodded slowly.

"Aren't the doctors here taking care of you? Mei Chen told me these were the best doctors in all of Hong Kong."

When the name Mei Chen was said, Brian squeezed Jason's arm harder. "Mei, she's giving me poison," he mumbled in a barely audible voice. "Get me out."

Jason straightened up. Poisoned? He looked around the room and saw a chart attached to the end of the bed. He reached out and grabbed it. The writing was in cryptic Chinese doctor speak and he couldn't make any sense of it.

He leaned back down to Brian's ear. "Why do you think you're being poisoned? Do the doctors know about that?"

Brian nodded as a tear built up in the corner of his left eye. "Every time Mei shows up, she does something and I get worse," he said haltingly. "When she leaves, after a few days I feel stronger. She's coming back soon. You need to help me get out."

Jason was stunned. Is it possible Mei Chen is poisoning Brian? But what if he's right? There are too many strange things swirling around Mei. He paused for a second. What about Andrew? Was she somehow involved? A better question is, how am I going to get Brian out of here and where would I take him? I have to be careful and keep a low profile, as Mei doesn't know I'm in Hong Kong and she won't be happy if she finds out, because she'll know I'm checking on Brian.

Jason stood up and patted Brian's arm. "I'm going to leave you for a little bit while I figure out what to do here. I don't know how I'm going to get you out, but I will." Letting go of Brian's hand, he headed out the door. He turned and said, "Keep trying to get your strength up. I'll be back." He shut the door and moved down the corridor to the nurses' station situated in the center of the floor. Two young women in white hospital smocks were sitting at their desks typing on computers.

He stopped in front of the first woman and leaned forward on the counter. She stopped her typing and asked him, "Can I help you, sir?"

With his thumb, Jason gestured to the room behind him. "The patient in room 1431, does his doctor have any idea what's ailing him? He seems to be in a lot of pain."

The nurse half stood up and looked down the corridor. Then she answered, smiling, "Oh, you mean Mr. Thompson? His doctor doesn't know what's wrong. He's run a lot of tests but found nothing. He guesses it's a bad flu bug."

"Has anyone run any test for poisoning?" Jason asked, looking back at Brian's room. "I know the doctors have tested him for a lot of things, but has poison been one of them?"

The nurse shook her head, a surprised look on her face. "No, there have been no tests for poison. Madam Chen brought him in and consulted with the doctor. She gave strict instructions as to what to do for him. She thinks he has the flu, and that's what the doctor thinks too. You watch, he'll get better soon. It'll go away."

Jason thanked her and stepped away, heading down the corridor for the elevator. Nurses and orderlies brushed past him as they made their rounds around the hospital, but he barely noticed them. Mei Chen owns this doctor, he thought. If Brian is right, she's going to keep this up until he dies, and no one will interfere. I need to get him out of here, but how? He pulled out his wallet and removed the card that the agent had given him in Nevada.

Once he made it to the ground floor, Jason hurried out of the lobby and walked down the sidewalk away from the entrance to the hospital. He pulled out his phone and dialed the number on the card. As he waited for the recipient to pick up, he glanced around the hospital grounds, which were lush with well-kept flowerbeds and manicured lawns. He spotted a young man in dark sunglasses leaning on a white Mercedes across the parking lot, about fifty yards away.

He was staring intently at Jason. Jason could see the silhouette of another man inside the car, also looking his way. Oh crap, have I already been spotted?

A voice came on the phone, which startled him. "Hello?"

"Agent Namath, this is Jason Ballard. I'm going to need your help." Jason then explained the situation regarding Brian, the possible poisoning, and his treatment at the hospital.

After he finished, Agent Namath paused for a second. "Madam Chen has a lot of tentacles that reach into many parts of that society. It doesn't surprise me that she has a doctor in her back pocket. From what you've described as his symptoms, my guess is she used glycol to poison him."

"Glycol? What's that?" Jason asked.

"Anti-freeze, the stuff you put in your car. It's clear and odorless and if you slip it into a drink it will become lethal. It attacks the kidneys and causes them to fail. If the medical team isn't looking for poison when they're treating a patient, it's overlooked and the patient will eventually die."

"If we get him out of that hospital and to another doctor to treat the poisoning, can he be saved?"

"It depends, Jason. It depends on how much he's ingested and for how long. But for sure leaving him where he is will be a death sentence. This will not be an easy task removing someone from a hospital who was placed there by a high-ranking Party member." The agent paused for a second and then continued. "Give me a couple of minutes and I'll make some calls and see what we can do. Have you found anything out on your end about a connection between Mei Chen and the gun running?"

Jason couldn't help noticing the guy on the Mercedes was still staring at him. "I haven't had a chance to check out much, since I came here once I heard that Brian was in bad shape. I was going to check out Mei's suite here in Hong Kong since she always allows me to use it when I come here. I'll let you know if I find anything."

"Okay, Jason. I'll get back to you soon."

He hung up and moved to the curb to hail down a passing cab. He directed the driver to the Grand Hyatt where Mei's suite was located. As they drove, he kept turning and looking out the back window, trying to determine if they were being followed. The traffic was semi-heavy and he could only see a few cars back behind them.

The driver pulled into the circular driveway of the Hyatt and parked beside the main entrance. A young valet dressed in a neat, sharp uniform with a captain's hat rushed to open his door. Jason threw some Chinese money at the driver and headed toward the entrance, the valet following behind with his one suitcase. He stopped at the entrance and scanned the driveway entrance and the road behind it. If I was followed, they're good at not being noticed.

The elevator ride took twenty seconds, and he ended up on the twenty-first. He opened Mei's suite with his key and allowed the valet to go in and set his suitcase on the floor. As he left, Jason handed him a twenty-dollar bill. The young man tipped his hat with his white-gloved hand and bowed. "Thank you very much, sir. If there is anything you need, please give us a call."

"I'll do that," Jason said as he shut the door. He turned and scanned the living room where he was standing. It's just as I remember from the last time. Nothing's changed. He wandered from room to room, checking for anything that might be out of place, but everything was as he remembered it. I shouldn't be surprised. This place has daily maid service and Mei would demand perfection.

He shut the bedroom and wandered to the kitchen. Opening the refrigerator, he checked the contents inside. Let's see, he thought as he moved items around—orange juice, lettuce, various vegetables, a few apples, and a couple cartons of Chinese takeout. He picked up one of the cartons, opened it, and took a sniff of its contents. Hmm, that actually smells good.

Setting the carton back, he scanned the shelf of the door. It was crammed with jars of relish and condiments. Jason picked them up one by one, looking at them closely, then set them down in the exact same position he had found them. He bent over to look on the second shelf and picked up a small clear jar hidden behind some mayonnaise that looked like it had been previously used as salad dressing container. He held it up and saw it was half full and contained some type of clear liquid. Unscrewing the lid, he put his nose up to it cautiously and took a sniff. There's no smell, he thought. I need to save some of this.

Moving to the other side of the kitchen, he opened the cabinet door next to the sink. He studied the small empty glass jars that lined a middle shelf and grabbed one. Pouring a small portion of the clear liquid into the jar, he placed the original container back on the shelf on the refrigerator door. Whatever doctor ends up treating Brian, he's going to need this, he thought. Returning to the living room, he bent down and set the bottle inside the side pocket of his suitcase.

Standing up, he turned and looked down the hallway, noticing the third bedroom had the door closed. He went down, opened it, and stepped inside. Mei's large-screen computer sat on an ornate desk in the center of the room. Two upright file cabinets stood against the opposite wall. A large white couch sat across from the desk with a huge watercolor of a cherry blossom limb hanging behind it.

I've only been in this room a few times, he thought. I wonder what she's got in here. He sat down at the desk and turned on the computer. While it booted up, he perused the papers stacked neatly in one corner. The drawer in front of him was partially opened, so he leaned back and pulled it out all the way. He became aware of the loud ticking of the antique clock hanging on the wall behind the desk. He turned and looked at it for a second. Wow, it's already four o'clock, he thought before returning his attention back to the contents of the drawer.

Paperclips, highlight pens, and business cards were set neatly in a plastic organizer, which filled most of the drawer. He slid the organizer forward and reached to feel around the back of the drawer.

His fingers felt a small metal object hanging by a nail on the back left. Pulling it out, he saw it was a small key. He looked over at the file cabinets on the opposite wall.

In a second he was across the room and had the key inserted into the first cabinet, but it wouldn't budge. He tried the lock on the second and it popped open. Standing to the side of the cabinet, he pulled it all the way open.

Manila files were neatly stacked in folders hanging from metal rods on either side of the drawer. With his fingers he thumbed through them, glancing at the labels. He came to one and pulled it halfway out of the drawer. The label, in Mei's handwriting, read: "Congressman Waters."

He frowned as he pulled the file out and opened it. Is this the same Congressman Waters from San Francisco? He saw that the file contained a series of faxes between Congressman Waters and Mei Chen. None of the faxes seemed to contain anything important, except one caught his attention. A chill ran down his spine. There was a copy of a news article from *The San Jose Mercury News* on Andrew Dillon's murder. He re-read the handwritten note at the bottom of the fax again to make sure he understood it. *Thought you might be interested.*

Jason studied the fax and checked its date. April twenty-third. He sat down and leaned back in the chair, holding the letter, trying to gather his thoughts. That's the day after Andrew Dillon was murdered. What is Congressman Waters referring to? Would he know that if Andrew were dead Earth-Sun would pull their bid for Copper Mountain?

He continued looking through the letters, stopping at one more. The middle paragraph caught his eye and he read it out loud. "'The desert tortoises are no longer an issue. An environmental assessment on endangered species is being prepared by a firm friendly to my office, and we should receive a negative declaration giving the project the green light to go forward. Now that you are helping run Inter-

Power's day-to-day operations, both it and Soltech will be in a position to greatly profit from the funds set aside for such projects in the stimulus bill. Please don't forget your good friends who helped you get this project funded.'

"So that's how Antelope Valley got approved," he said to himself. "They moved the tortoises away. That project should have taken two more years to get its permits done. Now I know why and who was behind it. Was Brian involved in this too? I hope he wasn't involved in something so illegal."

A loud banging on the front door made Jason jump. He swallowed hard. This can't be good, he thought.

THIRTY-TWO

Crystal held the bed sheet tight up to her chin and stared at the ceiling. The room was dark except for the small nightlight in the far corner of the room giving off a soft glow. Her heart raced in her chest as she lay there, silently listening to the shallow breathing of her friend Amber, who was sound asleep in the bed next to her. Since her dad had left for China two days ago, she had been staying with Amber's family.

Picking up her cellphone, she activated it and it glowed, showing her the time: 11:30. Ambers' mother, father, and brother had gone to bed an hour ago, and the whole house was deathly quiet. The sound of a car slowly approaching made her excitement grow. She threw back her covers and reached down to find her tennis shoes under the bed. Silently, she laced them up, picked up her small suitcase, and tiptoed out of the room. She made her way to the front door, where her backpack sat. Carefully, she unlocked the door and slid outside.

She spotted Steve's car across the street, its engine idling. Without hesitation, she made her way to him, flung her belongings into the back seat, and jumped inside. She barely noticed an older boy sitting quietly in the back. Clapping her hands together excitedly, she squealed, "Let's go! Let's get this thing on the road."

Trying to act as cool as possible, Steve threw the car into gear and headed away from the house. "Well, are you ready for this adventure? We should be in North Dakota in a day or two."

"This is all I've been thinking about for a week."

"Oh," Steve said casually as he looked in the rearview mirror. "That's my cousin, Jimmy, sitting behind you. He wanted to tag along because he's never been outside California. Besides, he's twenty-one. When we get outside of Utah, he can buy beer for us."

Crystal turned and looked at the youth sitting behind her. He wore a dirty tee-shirt, and his hair was greasy and unkempt. A cigarette dangled from his lips and he gave her a wry smile. This guy looks like he just got finished dumpster diving, she thought. I hope he doesn't turn out to be a jerk. She smiled a nervous smile at him. "Hi."

"Nice to meet you, Crystal," he said as he stuck his hand across the seat. "Steve has told me a lot about you."

She shook his hand quickly, discreetly wiping it on her jeans when she was done. She looked at Steve, who seemed oblivious to anything but the road. Without turning back she asked, "You're not going to smoke that thing in here, are you?"

"Maybe," he answered in a defiant tone. "And then again, maybe not. I haven't decided."

"Smoke it when we stop," Steve said, looking back at him. "Crystal here is an athlete and she doesn't need that crap clogging up her lungs. I'll join you in a smoke the next time we stop."

Crystal narrowed her eyes in distaste. "When did you start smoking, Steve? I know you like weed, but I didn't know you picked up cigarettes. You know those things will eventually kill you."

Smiling, he turned to her. "I only smoke once in a while. I don't intend to make it a habit."

"That's what everybody says," she retorted, folding her arms across her chest. A bottle of Jim Beam appeared in front of her face.

"How about a swig of some bourbon there, sweetie?" she heard Jimmy ask. "It'll put hair on your chest."

214

Pushing the bottle away with her hand, she answered, "I don't think I need hair on my chest, thank you. You enjoy yourself."

Taking a big swig, Jimmy swallowed it and grimaced. He pounded himself on the chest a couple of times and let out a big yelp. "Damn," he said as he wiped off his mouth with the back of his arm. "That's some nasty stuff. Steve, do you want a hit?"

"Yeah, give me a pull of that bottle," he answered as he reached behind to the back seat.

Crystal was shocked. "Steve, what the hell are you doing? You're driving. You can't be drinking and driving. It's dangerous, not to mention since we're all underage." She looked up at the sign along the interstate that said they were thirty miles from Auburn. Wow, we're still a long way from Reno.

Grabbing the bottle, Steve turned and gave her a wink. He tossed his head back and tilted the bottle, taking in a few gulps. When he finished, he had bourbon running down his chin. He handed it back to Jimmy. "Ah, that's good," he said. He slapped Crystal on the thigh and laughed. "Relax, Crystal. I'm not gonna get drunk. A few nips from that bottle won't bother me. I've had a few drinks before."

She stared at him as if he were an alien who'd dropped into the driver's seat.

"Come on, Crystal," he said as he saw the concerned look on her face. "Don't be so uptight. This trip is supposed to be fun and an adventure. You can't have an adventure without a little excitement, and you can't have excitement without some booze."

Turning and facing the windshield, she crossed her arms in irritation. "Yes, Steve, it's supposed to be an adventure. But we never discussed bringing your cousin along or drinking on the way." She turned to the side window and watched the landscape fly by, illuminated by streetlights located every hundred yards along the interstate. She could hear Jimmy talking to himself and laughing, interrupted every minute or so by the sound of noisy slurping, which she figured was the bottle of bourbon.

They had driven two and a half hours and were just passing through Sacramento when Jimmy came up and leaned over the front seat. Crystal backed away against the window and waved her hands back and forth in front of her face. "God, Jimmy, you reek!" she exclaimed. "Stay in the back. You're going to make me puke!"

"I gotta pee," he said, his speech slurred. "Find me a place to pee, cousin."

"Okay, hang on," Steve said. "There was a sign we just passed that said there's a rest stop up here in about five miles." A short time later, he had pulled off the freeway and parked, and they all went to use the facilities.

When Crystal came out and got into the car, Jimmy was already sitting in the back seat. She had just buckled her seatbelt when she felt a hand going through her hair.

"You know, you're a pretty girl," he said to her. "I bet we're going to get to know each other very well by the time this trip is over."

Crystal froze in her seat, a chill going up her back. She scanned the restroom area for any sign of Steve, but he was nowhere to be seen. I hope this jackass doesn't try to do anything stupid, she thought. I'd hate to have to rip him a new one. Maybe I could convince Steve to ditch him. She felt his hand start to rub her shoulder, and she immediately tore it away and turned to face him. "If you want me to lay a nice patch of fingernails across your face to make it uglier than it already is, keep doing what you're doing!" she snarled at him. "I have no interest in you. Don't touch me again!" She could smell the alcohol from his breath and see he had a goofy look on his face.

Holding his hands up in mock innocence he backed away. "Hold on there, sugar. I was only playin'. There's no need for you to get hostile." He flashed an evil grin, showing a missing tooth. "Remember, this is going to be a long trip, and you and I are going to be real close friends when it's done." He put his hand to his mouth and blew her a kiss.

216

Crystal spun around, seething. How could Steve let this jerk come along? This isn't going to turn out like I thought. She spotted Steve coming out of the restroom, buckling his belt as he walked to the car. He jumped in, but before he turned on the ignition, he looked into the rearview mirror. "Hey, cuz, how about another swig?"

A hand with the bottle appeared from the back seat. "Absolutely, cuz. Here you go." Jimmy came forward and rested his arms on the seat back. He looked at Steve and said, "You didn't tell me your friend here was such a firebrand." He grabbed the bottle from Steve and took another swig as Steve started the car. "Heck, I thought we'd just take some time to get to know each other and she about bit my head off. But I like a woman with some fight in her."

Crystal could feel Steve's gaze on her, but she continued staring out the window into the darkness. He stepped on the accelerator and moved the car onto the freeway. "Don't listen to Jimmy. He talks a big game but he's harmless. He'll run out of steam in a little while and will be sleeping like a baby."

A hand came up and whacked him on the head, causing his head to lunge forward. "What the hell are you talking about?" Jimmy yelled, his eyes wide with anger. "What do you mean I talk a big game? I'll climb over this seat and beat the crap out of you, even if you are my cousin. Don't you go talking crap about me in front of this girl."

Steve rubbed his head and scrunched down in his seat. "Calm down, Jimmy. What's gotten into you? Can't you relax and enjoy the scenery or something?"

"I'll tell you what's gotten into him," Crystal said in an irritated voice. "He's drunk. He can't hold his liquor. He tried to make a pass at me and I told him to shove off. Now he's pissed." She turned and put her arm on the back of her seat. "Why don't you try to make this trip as pleasant as possible by not saying anything for two hours? Think you can do that?"

Jimmy glared at her and took another drink from the bottle. "Why don't you lighten up, Miss Goody-Two-Shoes? I wasn't talking to you anyway. This discussion is between me and my cousin, so just butt out!"

Crystal turned back around and raised her eyebrows at Steve. "This was a great idea of yours, bringing him along. We're going to be stuck with him how long?"

Suddenly she felt hands around her neck, choking her. She reached up to pull them off, fighting for breath and feeling lightheaded. She kicked and squirmed, but the grip only tightened.

"What were you saying, you stupid bitch?" Jimmy yelled as he leaned across the back of the front seat, his hands firmly around her throat. Crystal fought, her arms and legs flailing around the front seat.

Half turning his body and keeping one hand on the steering wheel, Steve pounded Jimmy with his fist. "What are you doing?" he screamed. "Let go of her, Jimmy, you dumbass." He continued pounding on his cousin's chest, but it seemed to have no effect. "Let go Jimmy, you're going to kill her! Let go!"

"Nobody talks to me like that," Jimmy snarled as he shifted his weight. Crystal struggled to get her hands under his. Jimmy looked into her eyes, his face contorted into an ugly rage. "I'm going to teach you how not to talk."

When Jimmy wouldn't let go, Steve released the wheel and lunged at him. He grabbed him by the shoulders and attempted to pull him away. Steve's knee hit the steering wheel, and the car turned sharply to the left into the oncoming traffic. Headlights lit up the car as Steve reached back and grabbed the wheel, over-correcting and sending it cutting across the interstate slow lane, just missing a car on his right.

Crystal looked up to see their headlights shining on the upcoming embankment as the car hurled quickly toward it. Jimmy let go of Crystal, screamed, and covered his face as the car plowed into the hillside, flipped, and smashed against a huge Douglas fir. Crystal heard the sound of rubber screeching, metal crunching, and glass breaking. Dust and smoke swirled all around the car, and then there was silence.

THIRTY-THREE

The Barrister's Club in Washington D.C. prided itself in catering to the members of Congress and had been a regular stop for legislators of both parties for over fifty years. The restaurant was located just a few blocks from Georgetown University, which helped fill it with a steady supply of beautiful coeds. The bubbly owner, Mary Pritchard, a matronly woman in her late fifties who never married, had inherited the place from her father, along with his personality, and she made sure every patron was treated like royalty. She prided herself in the fact that she knew every client by name, their favorite drink, and all their secrets. If the walls or Mary could talk, there would be a lot of politicians who would have a lot of explaining to do.

Congressman Waters sat in a corner booth, a tall glass of Hennessy sitting in front of him and a young woman in her late twenties cuddled up close to him. She had wavy blonde hair, creamy white skin, and bright red lipstick that matched her neatly manicured nails. The low cut blue blouse she was wearing exposed her ample cleavage, and her exaggerated laughter could be heard around the intimate restaurant.

"Oh, Eugene," she gushed, "you are such a character. I can't believe all the things that go on behind the scenes in Washington. It's no wonder you're on so many select committees."

He picked up her hand delicately and kissed it, his eyes never leaving hers. "Oh, my dear, those are just a few of the stories I could tell you about Congress. Maybe when we have a lot of time I'll tell you some things about certain members that will make your jaw drop."

Giggling, she squeezed his hand. "Oh, I can't wait for that," she said, smiling. "I love nothing more than good gossip about public figures. It brings them down to a more personal level."

A vibration in his pocket made Waters let go of her hand. He pulled his phone out and checked the number, then quickly answered. "Please hold on a second." He looked at the woman as he put his hand over the mouthpiece. "I'm sorry, Pauline, but I've got to take this call. It's one of my constituents back in San Francisco. Order another drink and I'll be right back." He slid out of the booth and headed to the front door. Just before he reached it, he spoke into the phone. "I'm sorry, Mei, I had to move to a quieter spot. How are you doing today?"

"I'm well, thank you," she answered. "I'm concerned that our little operation might have been compromised. I've gotten some disturbing information from my people on the ground in Nevada."

"Really? I just talked to my connection in San Francisco," Waters said as he strode into the evening sunlight outside the restaurant. He pulled a pair of Gucci sunglasses out of his shirt pocket and put them on. "He confirmed that our second shipment made it through to its destination and everything went without a hitch. What did you hear that's got you worried?"

"The president of Soltech, Jason Ballard, showed up unannounced at our warehouse on a weekday night around midnight and started sniffing around. I don't know how much he saw before my people confronted him. One of the reasons I hired Jason was his attention to detail and the fact that his reputation was squeaky clean. I don't know how he would react if he figured out what we were doing,

221

but I was hoping he'd be onboard with us. I'm not sure he will be, though. He's too much of a straight shooter."

"Are you thinking he might go to the police?" Waters asked, his voice rising. A siren from a passing police car made him look to his left, and he followed it as it sped by him and continued down the street. This is great, he thought. A snoopy executive with a moral compass. I doubt he saw much. Mei's always looking for a conspiracy hiding behind every corner.

"I don't know, Congressman. I've got some of my people watching him and so far I haven't heard anything, but that doesn't mean he hasn't started talking. He was supposed to go to Shanghai to hold meetings at my solar panel facility, but he stopped in Hong Kong first. He didn't tell me he was going there first, as I thought he was headed to Shanghai, and I only found out he was there after the fact. That in itself isn't a big deal, as all my executives will sometimes travel through Hong Kong, but he might have gone there for other reasons."

"What other reasons would he go there, Mei?"

"I'm not at liberty to discuss that with you, Congressman," she answered curtly. "I may be completely wrong, but I don't like taking chances."

Hmmm, Waters thought. I wonder what other activities she might be involved in that she's worried about prying eyes. Maybe it's time to wrap this up while we're all ahead. "So, what do you suggest, Mei? What might I be able to do?"

"The one thing I know about Jason is he's incredibly loyal—to friends and particularly family. He's got a fifteen-year-old daughter and a girlfriend whom he's in love with. We might need to use them to make sure he doesn't do anything stupid. I want you to contact your friend who did the Andrew Dillon job and tell him we have another project for him."

Waters checked out a tall slender woman who was walking her small dog down the sidewalk. He smiled at her as she passed. So, she wants me to bring in Wo Sung, he thought. That's serious stuff. He's not cheap and he doesn't leave witnesses. I wonder if she knows what she's getting into. "You know, Mei, if I bring in my, uh, friend, it takes things to another level. He's an expensive professional who doesn't leave anything to chance. Are you sure this is the way you want to go?"

"Yes it is," she answered firmly. "My solar panel operation at Copper Mountain is making too much money and I don't want this little side business to mess anything up. There may be nothing going on and my people might have gotten to Jason before he saw anything. But somebody tipped him off, otherwise why would he be there in the middle of the night on a weeknight?"

Waters nodded as he thought about that. She's got a point there. It's better to be safe than sorry. "Okay, Mei, I'll make the call. Wo will need some information on the daughter and girlfriend. You know, pictures, addresses; the usual stuff. What would you like our professional to do with them?"

"I'll get that info for you in a day or so." She paused a second, then asked, "I want the daughter and girlfriend picked up and held at a safe house until I find out what Jason knows and what he plans to do next. If he doesn't cooperate with me, I'll want all of them eliminated." She let her words hang in the air, then asked calmly, "When is the next shipment scheduled to go out?"

"A week from tomorrow," he answered. "This one is going to be the biggest one so far. The payoff is going to be huge."

"Should we put it on hold until we're sure we're clear?" she asked, a note of concern in her voice.

Waters did some mental calculations. Thirteen million dollars each if this next one was successful. He smacked his lips and smiled. "No, let's continue with the plan, Mei, but let's be vigilant. If anything at all surfaces, we shut it down, no matter how small. Otherwise, we continue on."

"Okay, Congressman," she said. "I'll get the information you requested to you right away."

"That will work, Mei. I'll talk to you later." He stared at his phone for a second then looked over at the entrance to the restaurant. *I guess I shouldn't be rude and keep a beautiful woman waiting.* He chuckled to himself and headed toward the restaurant.

THIRTY-FOUR

The pounding on the door of Mei Chen's suite didn't stop until Jason, trying to be calm, walked over and opened it. Three armed men in uniforms of the Chinese army stood outside the entry, their fingers on their triggers. "Can I help you?" Jason asked, trying to sound casual.

The first two men brushed by him and rushed into the suite. The third stayed back, keeping an eye on Jason. They rushed from room to room, throwing back sheets and pulling out drawers. The first man made it to the kitchen and opened the refrigerator. Bending over, he looked around before focusing on the door. He pulled out the glass jar with the clear liquid and stuffed it into a pocket in his pants. He said something gruffly in Chinese, and the other two men moved quickly to the entrance of the suite, where they came to attention.

Jason had stood at the entry watching everything but not moving. The first man into the room finally came up to him and stood before him. "I think there might have been a mistake, sir," he said curtly. "We were told there might be a fugitive hiding here and were told to search the place. Obviously there isn't anyone else here."

Bowing slightly, Jason said to the man, "There are no worries, sir. I am glad you found everything in order. Madam Chen allows me to stay here when I'm in Hong Kong and I would not want her to think I have abused that privilege."

"It appears all is in order here. Again, we apologize for your inconvenience. We will be on our way. I hope you have a good day." He gave a quick salute and turned on his heel, the other two men following close behind. As Jason closed the door, he put his back to it, leaning on it for support. He looked up at the ceiling and took a big sigh. What was that all about? he wondered. Has Brian gotten out of the hospital already? I wonder if Agent Namath was going to use this place as a safe house.

Looking around the suite, he spotted his cellphone on an end table by the couch. He moved over to it and quickly dialed a number. The agent answered it after two rings. "Hello? Mark Namath here."

"Agent Namath, it's Jason Ballard." He stopped to catch his breath. "A group of Chinese military just left Mei Chen's suite at the Hyatt. They say they were looking for a fugitive and they damn near tore the place apart. Do you know what might be going on?"

After a pause, Mark answered. "Yeah, I'm sure they're looking for Brian Thompson. After we talked, I got a couple of colleagues in Hong Kong to help me get him out of that hospital. It went really smoothly until they were almost out of the place. A curious doctor confronted them. My friends had to make a noisy and hasty exit, and that might have alerted the authorities. Did they find anything during their search over there?"

"The only thing I saw them take was a jar of clear liquid out of the refrigerator." He ran his hand through his hair as he walked to the window looking out over the street below him. "I've got a sample of whatever was in that jar in my bag."

"I need to get that from you right away. I'll arrange for someone to meet you to do an exchange. Whatever's in there might give us an idea what's in Brian's system. He's in really bad shape."

"Where did you take him?" Jason asked. He pulled the curtain back from the window and peeked out. The same Chinese man who'd been watching him at the hospital was down on the street about half a block away, looking up at his window. Jason let go of the curtain and quickly stepped away.

"I can't tell you over the phone, but he's still in the country at a safe place," Namath answered. "We'll keep him there for a day to try to stabilize him before we fly him out. That is, if he survives. He's got a ways to go before he'll recover."

Why would Mei want Brian poisoned? Jason thought. There's only one reason and that is he must have turned down the bid for Copper Mountain and was going to give it to another company. I should leave Hong Kong before she gets suspicious of me. If she finds out I was behind Brian's being moved, she won't be very happy. "Well," he said to Agent Namath, "I'm going to fly out to Shanghai and do what I was supposed to be doing on this trip. I'll be in touch with you once I get on the ground there."

"That sounds good. I'll keep you posted on Brian's condition. We still haven't identified who the supplier of the guns stowed on Mei's planes is or where the guns are ending up. Keep vigilant and let me know if you find anything out. These people aren't stupid, and sooner or later they're going to figure out we're watching them."

Jason nodded. "Okay, I'll be careful and see what I can find out. The more I'm around this stuff, the scarier it gets." He hung up the phone and quickly gathered up his things. "I'd better help Mark put an end to Mei's charade before anyone else gets killed. I've got to play the part until Brian's out of this country and we figure out who's behind all this," he muttered to himself. "I hope this doesn't end up badly, but I can feel it going that way."

THIRTY-FIVE

A musical sound came from somewhere in the night. Groggily, Janine reached out with her left hand and felt around for her clock radio to turn it off. When she found it and the music continued, she leaned up on an elbow and reached for the light on the nightstand, turning it on. Her cellphone was ringing. As she reached for the phone to answer it, she noticed the time flashing on the clock: 2:30! *Who would be calling me at 2:30 on a Wednesday morning?* She shook her head to try to clear her thoughts. "Hello?" she asked sleepily.

A male voice came over the phone, "This is Officer Brannon of the Auburn Police Department." He cleared his throat and continued. "We have a female in her teens who was involved in a car accident on I-80 and when looking through her phone, your number came up with a 911 behind it. I thought I'd call you to possibly help identify her and get word to her parents."

Janine threw her legs over the bed and sat up, her nightie bunched up around her. *Oh my god, who could this officer be talking about? Where is Auburn?* "I'm sorry, officer," she stammered. "I'm confused. Where did the accident take place and who are you looking for?"

"The accident was just south of the city of Auburn, which is northeast of Sacramento. I'm trying to identify the girl so I can contact her family. She's been hurt badly."

Janine put her hand to her mouth, her mind in a whirl. "Oh no, what does she look like? What color is her hair? What was she wearing?"

"Hold on, ma'am, one question at a time. She's got long brown hair, she's white, and about five foot eight in height. She was wearing a pair of jeans and a light-colored blouse. We found an algebra textbook from Millennium High School in the back seat of the car. She was traveling with two other young males"

"Oh no, not Crystal!" Janine screamed. "Oh my god, that's my boyfriend's daughter." She tossed the covers off her and headed for her closet to get dressed. "How bad is she, officer? Is she going to survive? Oh my god, how am I going to get ahold of Jason?"

"Like I said, ma'am, she's in bad shape. When she was put in the ambulance, she wasn't conscious. I don't know how she's currently doing, but she's in good hands. Do you know how to contact her family and let them know what has happened?"

Janine cradled the phone between her neck and shoulder, pulled clothes off their hangers, and hastily dressed. "Yes, I can contact her family. What hospital did they take her to? I'm going to jump in my car and head there as soon as I can."

The officer answered in an even tone. "She's been taken to Kaiser Permanente Hospital in Roseville. It's not too far off the freeway. How long do you think it will take you to get there?"

"It'll take me a little over two and a half hours," she answered as she pulled her purse off a chair in her dining room. "I'm heading out my door right now."

"Okay, ma'am. Again, my name is Officer Brannon. I'll be at the hospital when you get there and I'll be able to fill you in on the details better by the time you arrive."

Janine was out of breath by the time she reached her car and opened it. "Thank you, officer, for all your help. I'll see you soon." She hung up and flung her phone on the passenger seat. *What is Crystal doing in Auburn? She's supposed to be staying at her friend's house. I shouldn't have told Jason I wouldn't watch her.* She pounded the steering wheel in frustration. *Why didn't I let her stay with me?* Tears stung her eyes as she steered her car through the quiet city streets until she made the onramp of the freeway. *Oh, Crystal, what were you thinking? Where were you going? Why didn't you call me?*

Her mind was spinning and she could barely concentrate on driving. *How do I get ahold of Jason? It's difficult to communicate with him when he's in China. He told me if there was ever an emergency, if I couldn't get him directly, to call his office staff and get them to track him down, but they're not going to arrive at work for another few hours. I hope she can hold on and pull out of this. I couldn't bear having to tell Jason his only daughter has died.*

She pounded the steering wheel as she blinked back tears. *Please, please hang in there, Crystal. You're a fighter; hang in there!*

♦

Two and a half hours later, she pulled up to the emergency entrance of the massive Kaiser Hospital facility in Roseville. She drove into the immense parking lot, found an open spot near the entrance, and then hurried inside. She sprinted to the elevator to get to the third floor, slowing down to walk once she spotted an officer standing outside a room about halfway down the corridor. He was tall, in his late thirties, and had a short military haircut. His cap was under his arm and he was in conversation with an orderly when Janine came up to him. "Officer Brannon?" she asked timidly. "I'm Janine Tully. We spoke over the phone about the girl in the accident, Crystal Ballard. Her father is my boyfriend and he's currently in China on business. I'm trying to track him down as we speak."

He shook her hand. "I'm sorry to meet you under these circumstances." He turned to the orderly. "Would you excuse me for a moment?"

"Of course," he answered. "We can go over this at a later time."

"Would you like to check in on Crystal?" the officer asked. "Not much has changed with her condition since we spoke."

"Yes," Janine said somberly. "I'd like to see her."

The officer pointed at the room one door down from where they stood. "She's in room 326. Go ahead. I'll wait here for you."

"Thanks." She softly opened the door and slid inside. As her eyes adjusted to the dimly lit room, she could see the outline of Crystal lying quietly on the bed. Her head was covered in a large white bandage and one of her eyes was blackened. Two different sets of tubes were coming out of her arms, with IVs hanging above her bed, methodically dripping medicine into her body. Janine moved over to the side of the bed and took Crystal's hand.

Crystal's breathing was shallow but steady. Janine ran her hand softly across her face, being careful not to touch the bruised cheekbone and her blackened left eye.

"You poor thing," she said to her softly. "I'm so sorry. Please get stronger. We need your smiling face." Janine looked down the bed at Crystal's legs. It doesn't look like there's anything broken or she would be in some kind of splint or something. I guess that's something. She sat down in the chair, put her head in her hands, and said a silent prayer. After a minute, she got up and left the room.

Officer Brannon was standing down the corridor talking to one of the nurses at the night watch station. When he saw her come out of the room, he came down to her.

"Why don't you take a seat and I'll tell you what I know. The doctor should be here in a few minutes and he can update you on Crystal's condition."

Janine nodded numbly and sat down where he indicated. "Okay, officer, I'm ready. Tell me what you know."

"Well, there were three kids in the car at the time of the accident. A male driver and another male who was in the back seat." He paused for a minute and took a deep breath. "Witnesses to the crash said the car veered into oncoming traffic then swerved hard to the right and smashed into the side of the hill alongside the highway. The kid in the backseat was thrown clear of the car." Officer Brannon cast his eyes downward and stared at the floor. "He didn't survive and was declared dead at the scene."

Janine took a deep breath, putting her hand to her mouth. "Oh no. That's awful. What about the driver? Is he okay?"

"He had a seatbelt on, as did Crystal, so he survived, but he hit the steering wheel hard and the front end of the car caved in, almost crushing him. He's got a punctured lung, two busted teeth, and some broken ribs. He also broke his left leg. The bottom line is he's going to survive." He lowered his voice and spoke softly. "We think alcohol was involved."

She looked up at him, shocked. "Was Crystal drinking? That's so unlike her."

"We don't know who was drinking, but there was a discernable smell of alcohol in the car and there was an almost-empty bottle of Jim Beam in the back seat." He stopped when he saw a short balding man come around the corner wearing a white smock and holding a clipboard. "Here's the doctor, Janine. You can ask him yourself about Crystal's condition."

Seeing the doctor, Janine rushed up to him and blurted out, "The girl in room 326, the one from the car accident, what's her condition?" She caught herself and said, "I'm so sorry, doctor. I'm Janine Tully. The girl in the room is my boyfriend's daughter. I just wanted to know her condition."

"I'm Doctor Winters, Janine," he said, his face anxious. "The young girl is in serious condition. She's got a severe concussion and some bruises on her face. We're keeping an eye on her to see if she sustained any internal injuries. Our initial diagnosis is she didn't, but we're being cautious."

"She should survive then, doctor?" Janine asked, pleading.

"I don't know yet since she's still in a coma. But the good thing is she's young and healthy. It's going to be a rough next few days and we'll know more when she wakes up. All we can do now is monitor her and wait." He looked up at the clock on the wall and then back. "I've got to make my rounds, Janine. There's nothing that can be done for her right now, so why don't you go down to the cafeteria and get yourself some coffee."

Janine nodded. "Thank you, doctor, I appreciate your help and kindness. I'm so tired I could fall asleep in this chair."

"Come with me, Janine," Officer Brannon said. "I'll walk you down to the cafeteria and have a cup of coffee with you. After that, I've got to get back to the office and turn in my report."

She followed along, her whole body feeling numb. He tried to make small talk, but she didn't hear much of what he said. When they got to the cafeteria, she slumped down in a chair.

"What would you like?" he asked. "I'm buying."

"Just a coffee would be great," she said as she looked up at him. "Thank you so much. You've been way too kind."

He smiled and bowed at her. "It's my pleasure." Then turned and headed toward the food area.

The cafeteria was white, stark, and almost deserted. A young couple, seated four tables away, sat in silence, both slowly nibbling on blueberry muffins. Food preparers shuffled behind the counters in slow motion, their hair covered in netting and plastic gloves on their hands. Every so often they would switch out a tray with freshly prepared food.

Janine sat in silence, watching as Officer Brannon fixed up two cups of coffee. He came back to the table and set hers in front of her, along with two packets of sugar and two small containers of cream.

"I didn't know what you put in your coffee, so I brought everything," he said as he slid into a chair. "Are you sure you're not hungry? The chicken they make here is pretty good."

She smiled weakly. "Thanks for the offer, but I'm not really hungry just yet." She looked down at her watch. "I've got to wait another hour before my boyfriend's colleagues show up for work."

"Why is that?" he asked. "Can't you just call him on the phone?"

Holding the coffee cup with both hands, she shook her head. "No, he's currently in China. I don't know how to contact him there. I have to wait until someone at his office shows up so I can get them to get him a message to call me." She looked at him as she sipped her coffee. "I don't relish that conversation at all. His daughter usually stays with me when he goes on trips, but this time she stayed with a friend's family."

"What was she doing over here in Auburn?" he asked. "This is a long way from Santa Clara. They were headed east on the freeway before the crash. Where were they going?"

"I have absolutely no idea," Janine answered. "I know her father wouldn't have let her take a trip like this. He's very protective of her." She stared up at the ceiling. "No, I think this was a trip Crystal planned on her own and she wasn't going to tell anyone about it." She looked at Officer Brannon. "I guess we won't know where she was going until we ask her after she wakes up."

THIRTY-SIX

Mei paced the floor of her kitchen, stopping every minute or two to stare at her cellphone, willing it to ring. The sound of piano music floated across the house as her daughter practiced a Beethoven piece for an upcoming concert. The fact that she had not nailed every note with one week remaining was a source of irritation for Mei, although that was not what was on her mind.

I knew I shouldn't have trusted Lin Ping for this job, she thought, her irritation growing the more she paced. All he had to do was make sure the cocktail I had made up was administered to Brian daily so when he died it would have looked like natural causes and no one would be suspicious. One more day and Brian would have been dead and forgotten. Now he's disappeared and who knows if he's gotten the medical attention to save him.

The phone rang and she rushed over to answer it. "Hello?" she said almost breathlessly.

She heard the familiar voice of Tan Wen, her chief of security. "Madam Chen, we have not located Mr. Thompson yet, but we have reason to believe he hasn't left Hong Kong. We have agents stationed at the airports to watch over who's leaving. If he tries to escape, we will find him."

"What about by boat?" she asked, irritated. "He could easily slip away on someone's yacht. There are too many ways for him to get away. You need to find him and find him quickly. What about Jason Ballard? Where is he?"

"He left Hong Kong yesterday and flew to Shanghai. He was headed to your factory there and is probably still there as we speak."

Mei opened the refrigerator and pulled out a bottled water. "I want him picked up and detained for questioning. This all happened once he showed up in Hong Kong. I don't think it was a coincidence. See if he will talk about Brian's disappearance. If he won't talk, let me know."

"I'll do that, Madam Chen." He paused then asked, "What are your plans for Mr. Wilson? We still have him locked up in jail, but he has not signed the papers you gave to me transferring ownership of the hotels to your company. He has many friends in high places who are making noise about his situation. I fear there will be problems if we keep him in jail too much longer."

Covering the phone with her hand, she yelled at her daughter, "Play that piece over from the beginning. A cat could walk across the keyboard and sound better than that!" She put the phone back to her ear. "Let him stay there a little longer, but start to use some coercion on him. It's time he saw the wisdom of divesting some of his hotel holdings. If he doesn't sign by next Wednesday, I'll forge his signature, and then I'll have to figure out what to do with him. But by all means keep him alive. That will be all, Tan."

Hanging up, she took a swig of water and sat down at the kitchen table. I should lock all of them up, everyone who has failed me. She smiled to herself. But all is not lost. Copper Mountain is moving along and the first payment for the panel shipment is due in one week. I'm going to be flush with money; money for green energy. Thank you, US government!

Her cellphone rang and she recognized the number. "Congressman Waters, how are you today?"

His deep male voice came over the phone. "I am well, Madam Chen. I thought I would report to you about a few of our business dealings. We're scheduled for a flight from the warehouse in Nevada to Mexico a week from tonight. It should go as smoothly as the last time and we should clear about thirteen million each. After that, I suggest we lay low for a few months."

"Are you as concerned as I am that someone is on to our little project?" she asked. "We are now moving the panels to the actual project, so everything should look legitimate."

He paused for a second, then answered, "I don't think we're being watched, if that's what you're referring to, but I think it might be prudent to take a break. We've cleaned up from the last two runs, so there's no sense getting greedy."

"Well, Congressman, if you think that's the way we should go, then I'll alert my people in Nevada to discontinue the trips to Mexico. I'm sure going to miss all the money we were making."

The Congressman laughed. "Don't worry. We can pick up where we left off at the drop of a hat." He coughed and cleared his throat. "Excuse me, I've got some bad allergies. You had asked me to get my friend Wo Sung to pick up your friend, Jason Ballard's, daughter and girlfriend, but there have been some developments there you might be interested in."

Mei raised her eyebrows. "Oh. What happened?"

"The daughter got into a bad accident last night. She's in a hospital in a town about two hours out of the bay area. The girlfriend is hanging out at the hospital keeping vigil. Wo couldn't get much information as to how long she might be kept there, but it would be a difficult place to extract them without making a big scene."

A shuffling sound behind her made Mei set the phone down and turn. Her daughter stood at the entrance to the kitchen, her hands folded in front of her and her head hanging down. "Mother, may I take a break? My hands are tired and my back is sore. I've been practicing for two hours straight."

Mei yelled at her, "Do you think that Korean girl, Wie, is taking a break? Chi, if you want to be the best, you have to sacrifice! That piece you're playing sounds awful and you'll get laughed off the stage and I'll be eternally humiliated." She pointed over her daughter's shoulder. "Get back on that piano and practice until I tell you it's okay to quit, and that won't be for a while!"

She watched as the girl spun around and left the room. Weakling, she thought, my daughter is a weakling. I refuse to let her grow up and be nothing.

Putting the phone back to her ear she said, "I'm sorry, Congressman, my daughter needed something from me. So, back to the daughter and girlfriend. You don't know how long she'll be in the hospital?"

"No, I don't," he answered. "It sounds like she was roughed up pretty good, so it might be awhile. What should I tell Wo to do?"

Mei sat at the table in silence. "Tell Wo to sit tight. He doesn't need to have his people hang around the hospital, just have them ready to move if the opportunity presents itself. Right now Jason is unaware we are after him, so I don't want to spook him yet. Let's wait until we have him in our clutches and see what he's willing to tell us. That will probably give us a few days to see how the daughter fares."

"Okay, Madam Chen, I'll have Wo stand down. I'll call you after the shipment arrives safely next week in Mexico."

"That will be good, Congressman Waters. I'll wait to hear from you then." She set the phone down and smiled. In the next three weeks, I will be one of the richest women in China. Even my weak-kneed husband will have to give me respect. She lifted her chin in a defiant manner. Madam Chen will be a name that will be feared and respected all over China.

THIRTY-SEVEN

Large cranes lifted a big wooden pallet of solar panels and placed them in the beds of a row of flatbed trucks lined up in a straight line, their engines spewing dirty diesel exhaust into the atmosphere. The drivers sat patiently in their cabs, smoking cigarettes and fiddling with radios and cell phones as their trucks were loaded.

Jason watched the activity through the glass of the second floor office in Shanghai. He still wasn't satisfied with the panel manufacturing in this plant, feeling it was still dangerous for the workers, but knew it was better than two months ago. A young woman came running up to him and tugged on his sleeve. "Mr. Ballard," she said in broken English. "There is a phone call for you from the United States. They say it is an emergency!"

Turning, he followed her down the narrow stairway to the main office and walked into the conference room, shutting the door behind him. He looked through the window to the office, and the girl held up three fingers. He pressed the third button on the phone. "This is Jason Ballard."

He recognized the voice of his operations officer from the San Jose office, Gary Jenkins, on the line. "Mr. Ballard, I'm sorry to have to tell you this, but your daughter has been in a car accident. She's currently in the intensive care unit at a hospital in Roseville."

Jason almost dropped the phone. "Intensive care?" he asked, his voice rising. He started firing off questions. "What hospital? Is she okay? What happened?"

"I don't have very much information, Mr. Ballard. Your girlfriend Janine called this morning and told us to track you down. She would be the person to talk to about your daughter's condition. She's with her at the hospital as we speak."

"Okay, thanks, Gary, I'll try to track Janine down. Thanks for calling me."

"Everyone here at Soltech is feeling horrible for you, sir. We hope she's okay."

"Tell everyone there I appreciate their concern," he said as he ran a hand through his hair. "I'll let you know how she is once I find out." Jason hung up and quickly redialed. As the phone rang, he said to himself, "Come on, Janine, pick up, pick up!" Finally after the fifth ring he heard her familiar voice.

"Oh, Jason, I'm so sorry," she said as she burst into tears. "I never meant for this to happen. I so wish I hadn't told you she couldn't stay with me."

Taking a deep breath, Jason spoke in a soothing tone, "Calm down, Janine. It's not your fault. Quit beating yourself up. How is she doing?"

Janine sniffed. "She's still in a coma, Jason, the same as she's been for the last day. Apparently she hit her head on the top of the car after it crashed into the embankment. She doesn't have any broken bones or any internal injuries."

"What do the doctors say about her chances? Is she going to be alright?"

"They don't know, Jason, they don't know. They've been all over her and have done the best they can. Her brain has some swelling, which they've tried to relieve, but now it's just a waiting game."

Jason looked up at the ceiling and let out a big sigh. "Do you know how this accident happened? Where was she? Who was she with?"

"I've only got bits and pieces, Jason. The kid who was driving was her friend, Steve. He survived but has a few broken bones. I talked to him for a few minutes and he told me she snuck out of the friend's house where she was staying while you were gone and they were driving to North Dakota to see her mother. Apparently Debbie knew nothing about it since it was going to be a surprise."

Rolling his eyes, Jason banged his fist into the wall, almost breaking through the sheetrock. "North Dakota? You've got to be kidding. How in the hell did she think she was going to pull that off?" He stopped for a moment. "Does Debbie know her daughter's been in an accident?"

There was a pause on the other line. "I didn't call her, Jason. I don't know her number. I also don't feel comfortable making that call."

"Don't worry about it. That will be my next call. Thank you for helping and staying with her, Janine. I really appreciate it. I'll make arrangements to grab the first plane out of here and head for home. It'll probably take me twenty hours or so, but I'll call you the first opportunity I get."

"Okay, Jason, be safe. I'll be here when you get here, and hopefully you'll return home to good news."

He hung up and stared at the phone for a second. He left the conference room and signaled to the young woman who had brought him the phone to come over. When she got there, he said to her, "Would you arrange for a car to be brought to the front with a driver who can take me to the airport? I need it done right away."

She bowed and hurried away.

Picking up the phone, he held it in his hand for a moment. This is not going to be a pleasant call. He took a deep breath and dialed. After a few rings he heard the familiar voice of his ex-wife. "Hello?"

"Debbie," he said, trying to keep his voice calm, "it's Jason." He paused for a second. "Crystal's been in a car accident. She's currently in a coma, and the doctors are doing the best they can for her."

A loud gasp came over the phone. "Oh no!" she screamed. "What have you done to my baby!?" She burst into tears and started yelling, "I can't believe you let her drive around! What kind of father are you? Oh my god, you've killed my baby!"

"Stop it, Debbie," he said firmly. "Get ahold of yourself. It was an accident. Yelling at me isn't going to accomplish anything. I only called to let you know what happened to Crystal. I thought you should know. I'm in China and I'm heading home."

"What are you doing in China? Why aren't you home taking care of Crystal? Did you leave her with that slut again?" She started wailing again into the phone so loud that Jason held it away from his ear.

"Look, I'm in China because of my job and she was staying with the family of one of her teammates and friends. I don't know more than that. Why don't you quit feeling sorry for yourself and make arrangements to get back to California so you can be with her? You could get there before I do."

"Oh sure, Jason, I'll just pull a plane ticket out of my ass and fly there. I'm not loaded with money like you are and you still haven't sent me the extra money you owe me from your new raise. I could afford to get there if you'd do what you're supposed to do."

Rubbing his eyes, he looked around the office through the glass windows of the conference room. Fifteen of his co-workers were sitting at their desks staring at him. He gave a half-hearted smile and a quick wave and turned his back to them. He saw the young woman he sent for the car wave at him and indicate the car was ready.

He nodded to her and turned his attention back to the phone. "Listen, Debbie, I've got to go. I suggest you ask Dave for a loan or take one out yourself and go check on your daughter. Your financial straits are not because of me. I send you plenty of money every month in child support and alimony, and I don't know nor do I care what you do with it. But don't try to lay any guilt trip on me if something happens. If you need money for a flight, book it and leave the payment information on my voicemail and I'll take care of it for you. I'll talk to you later." He hung up the phone and headed to the front entrance of the office.

Just before he got to the front of the office, a man came through the front door with a briefcase in his hand. He moved to Jason and stuck out his hand. "I'm here to pick up the package for Mark Namath. I know you're in a hurry, so if you can get it for me, I'll be on my way."

Jason waved him over. "Follow me. It's in my office and I'll get it for you." They moved through the main office until they reached Jason's office, and he closed the door quickly after the man stepped inside. Jason reached into a gym bag behind the door and handed the man a small container with clear liquid and a small envelope.

The man held the jar up to the light, then opened the briefcase and set it in a designated position along with the envelope. He shut the briefcase and shook Jason's hand. "Thanks. I'll be on my way."

Jason followed him out of the office and to the waiting car. As he opened the door, he noticed two military men sitting in a jeep across the street, parked in the same direction as his driver was. Once he got into the car, he turned around and looked through the rear window. As his driver pulled away, he noticed the jeep start up and follow at a distance.

I wonder what this is all about, he thought. It seems every time I turn around there's some type of military presence following me.

His cellphone rang and he answered it.

"Jason, it's Agent Namath. Thanks for all your cooperation. Do you know what your boss's relationship to Wo Sung is?"

Looking nervously through the back window at the jeep, which was still following him, Jason answered, "I've never heard of Wo Sung. Mei never mentioned him in my presence. Who is he?"

"That's what we're trying to figure out. If he's who we think he is, he may be the missing link to this whole gun-running operation. But one thing's for sure: Whoever he is, he's not someone to mess with. We'll be working on our end to figure out who he is, but you should keep an eye out and be careful."

"Listen, Mark," Jason said, "I'm trying to get out of China. My daughter has had an accident in the States. I may just be getting paranoid since everything that went down with Brian Thompson, but I have a feeling I'm being followed and that I'm not going to be allowed to leave the country. Is there anything you can do to help me?"

"How were you planning on getting out?"

"I was going to take one of Soltech's corporate jets, but I don't know that Mei would allow that," he answered. He noticed the jeep had dropped back a few hundred yards but continued to follow. "Do you have any other suggestions?"

"Yeah, go to the Malaysia Airlines counter and buy a flight to Thailand. Go through security and hang out in the waiting area for your flight. One of our agents will come get you and we'll fly you out of there on one of our government jets."

"How will I know if it's him?" Jason asked nervously.

"They'll ask you if you know the score of last Sunday's Dallas Cowboy's game. Don't talk to anyone while you're waiting and try to be inconspicuous."

"Okay," he said as he searched for the jeep behind him. It was nowhere to be seen.

THIRTY-EIGHT

The smell of body odor, urine, and vomit hung in the air of the tiny jail cell. The small straw bedding in the corner was chewed by rats and barely in one piece. The only light was a small amount that crept under the heavy metal door. David Wilson lay curled in a ball next to the mat, his white shirt stained with dirt and blood. His bare feet were raw from bite marks, and his lips were dry and cracked. He faded in and out of consciousness, waking up when he would hear a blood-curling scream come from another cell in the prison.

The clink of a key turning in the door woke him, and he tried to sit up. *What are they going to try to do to me this time? The last two beatings didn't get them what they wanted. Now are they going to kill me?* The door creaked open and he held his hand up to shield his eyes from the flashlight shining into his cell. He could barely make out the silhouettes of two men in the doorway.

One stepped forward and nudged him with a steel-toed boot. "Are you ready to come to you senses, Mr. Wilson?" he asked in a sarcastic voice. "There's no need for you to go through all this suffering. I only need a couple of signatures and we'll have you fixed up in no time. Fresh water, some good food—all will be good again. What do you say we put an end to all this nonsense?"

Still holding his hands to his eyes, David could see the man holding the light was the same army colonel who had visited him the last two times. "Why do you think I would change my mind?" he responded, his voice cracking. "I'm not giving half my hotels to Mei Chen or anyone else in the Chinese government. Not now or ever. I know what will happen next; she'll take total control and leave me with nothing. She'll probably leave me to rot in this jail!"

He felt a sharp pain in his side as the man kicked him in the ribs, lifting his body off the ground. He grabbed his side in agony and gasped for breath.

"I don't think you are understanding what I am saying, Mr. Wilson. I am not asking you to sign the papers; I am telling you to sign them. This is not Hong Kong as the British ruled it. It is Chinese Hong Kong, and in Chinese Hong Kong, the government runs the show. If the government tells you to do something, you do it." He leaned down on his haunches and put his face right up to David's. "Do you understand me now, Mr. Wilson?" He poked him in the ribs with his flashlight, causing David to yell out in pain.

Wincing, David stared back at him, his anger rising with every breath. Sadistic bastards, he thought. I'm not going to give you the pleasure of beating me into submission. I will never sign anything. He spit in the colonel's face, which brought the flashlight smashing into his nose.

The colonel stood up, wiping his face with his sleeve. He started kicking David in the side with his boots, angrily yelling at him, "You are a stupid, arrogant, capitalist pig. You think you can defy Madam Chen? You will never see your hotels or the outside of this cell again!" He stopped kicking and bent over, his hands on his knees to catch his breath. Turning, he waved his flashlight at his companion, who had stood at the doorway, his rifle at the ready. "Take over, comrade," he said, his breath labored. "Teach this fool a lesson about obeying orders."

The other man stepped into the cell and brought his rifle butt crashing into the side of David's head. Blood immediately started gushing from a large gash. The man brought the butt down again against David's face, smashing his nose.

David curled and tried to use his hands to fight off the blows, but they kept raining down. The pain seared through his body and he finally started to lose consciousness. The man continued beating him until he too ran out of breath.

"That's enough," the colonel said. "I must report to Tan Wen."

◆

The sleek Cessna Citation jet, with its white fuselage and red striping, sat idling on the runway at the Hong Kong Airport, awaiting clearance to take off. The pilots went through their preflight routing, glancing up to watch the Mitsubishi Commander jet that was ahead of them and lined up to take off. It started to move and gradually picked up speed as it raced down the runway.

One of the pilots pushed down on the throttle and the jet gently moved forward and turned, facing down the runway. After a minute, the co-pilot leaned across his seat and turned toward the back seat. "We're cleared for takeoff, Madam Chen. Please fasten your seat belt."

Without looking up from the stack of papers on her lap, Mei reached down, grabbed one section of seatbelt, and fastened it snuggly around her waist. She felt the momentum of the plane as it headed down the runway and felt it lift off into the bright, cloudless sky.

Holding one of the documents in her hand, she carefully re-read it. *Copper Mountain is ahead of schedule by two weeks. 100 megawatts of panels have been installed and accepted by Nevada Power.* She smiled to herself and looked out the window of the plane. This is such great news. Soltech gets paid thirty million for its solar panels and Inter-Power gets one point three million dollars per month

247

in energy sold back to Nevada power. The money is going to be gushing in.

The co-pilot leaned back again and announced, "You may power up your electronic devices and use them now."

Mei looked up and held the documents behind her. A uniformed man in his early forties sitting behind her reached up and took them from her hands.

"Put those in my briefcase," she commanded. "I'll want to look at them later." Reaching into her pink tote bag, she pulled out a cellphone and dialed a number. Her head of security answered.

"Madam Chen. I hope you're having a pleasant flight," Tan Wen said in a soothing voice.

"So far, it has been normal, which is good," she answered. "But I didn't call to discuss my flight. Give me your report on Mr. Wilson. Did you accomplish what I asked you to do?"

Tan cleared his throat before speaking. "Uh, unfortunately, Mr. Wilson has proven to be harder to convince then we thought. He refuses to sign your documents in spite of our repeated attempts to help him out. I don't understand his stubbornness, as what you offer to him is more than generous."

Frowning, Mei asked curtly, "Are you sure you're doing everything to convince him it's in his best interest to do as I ask? Does he understand that he could lose one hundred percent of his properties instead of only half?"

"Indeed, Madam Chen. My people have conveyed exactly that to Mr. Wilson, yet he refuses to budge. With your permission, I would like to push him harder. I think he will see the wisdom of cooperating with us soon."

Mei nodded. "Do as you see fit, Tan. But I want those signatures no later than the day after tomorrow, and I'm going to have to have him well enough and physically fit enough to come out and make a formal announcement of our new partnership. I'm tired of waiting around in limbo. I've got other things that need my attention and I don't want to keep getting bogged down with this. Remember, I need him healthy enough to be in public in a couple of months, so don't overdo it!"

"I will do my best to acquire the signatures within the timeframe you request, Madam Chen, and keep Mr. Wilson in good health, but neither will be easy tasks. He is a very determined man. He has not been easy to break."

"What's happening with Jason Ballard? Has he done anything unusual or been snooping around in places she shouldn't be?"

"No, he's been quiet. He spent the last day going over the operations at the Soltech plant in Shanghai. There's the personal issue with his daughter back in the States that he wants to attend to. He is currently trying to get back there, but my people are monitoring him."

"Don't let him out of your sight and don't let him leave Shanghai. I think he knows who took Brian Thompson out of the hospital and also knows where he is. I might need you to bring him in and find out what he knows before it's too late."

"I will do as you wish, Madam Chen. Is there anything else you need from me?"

Pausing for a second, she answered, "No, that will be all. Call me if there are any new developments."

"I will do that, Madam. Have a nice flight."

"Thank you, Tan." She hung up and stared out the window. *I don't understand why David is being so stubborn. I've given him a very fair proposal. And Jason, after all I've done for him, I hope he hasn't turned against me.* She sighed, shaking her head, and reached for another set of documents sitting next to her. *It's out of my hands if they won't cooperate, and they'll only have themselves to blame for whatever happens.*

THIRTY-NINE

The dark bar was almost deserted except for the lone bartender who tried to look busy by wiping the bar down from time after time. Wo Sung sat and the end of the bar with a clear view of the front door and sipped tequila. He rolled a dirty silver dollar coin back and forth through his fingers and over his knuckles.

Pulling out his cell, he studied the last text he had received. It said simply, *Payment received.* Wo smiled. His heroin peddler in North San Francisco, "Crawfish Mike," had come through after all. Good, he thought. I won't have him killed now. Quirky dude, but I kinda like the guy. I wonder if he really did work for the mob in New Orleans like he's always bragging about. I guess with that distinctive red tattoo of a crawfish on his arm, he has to have some connection to that area, otherwise why be so blatant? Oh well, he's got the three R's that I like in my guys: reliable, relentless and ruthless.

The front door opened and the figures of Congressman Waters and John Clayton appeared in the doorway. Wo nodded his head in recognition and motioned for the two of them to follow him to a booth in the corner of the bar.

Wo made it there first and slid in. The other two came over, and Waters extended his hand. "Always good to see you, Wo. I hope all is well."

Smiling, Wo shook his hand enthusiastically. "Eugene, it is always a pleasure." He shook John's hand and said to him, "John, it's good to see you too. Have a seat. Can I get either of you a drink?"

The congressman looked over at the bar, sizing up its contents. "Yeah, Wo, I'll have a Hennessy over ice." He turned to his aid. "John, do you want to imbibe with us?"

The young aide shook his head. "No, I still have some things to do at the office later. I'll just have a Coke and watch you guys and be jealous."

The congressman slapped him on the back playfully. "That's what I love about you, John. You're the only one with work ethic around here."

Wo signaled to the bartender, who quickly came around the bar and took their orders. He was back in a minute with all their drinks. Wo lifted his drink and made a toast. "Here's to our next shipment. Let it reach its destination without any issues."

John and the congressman lifted their glasses and touched Wo's. John said, "Here, here!"

Tossing back a full shot glass of tequila, Wo winced and hit his chest with his fist. "That's what I'm saying." He wiped his mouth off with the back of his hand. "So, Congressman, you want this shipment to be the last? Why are we stopping now? We've gotten all the bugs out of shipping these guns and getting them into Mexico. Why would Madam Chen want to stop now? There's so much more money to be made, it's scary."

Congressman Waters shrugged. "I know, but after talking it over with Mei, she and I both agree we should shut it down for a while, just to be safe. Neither she nor I want to get greedy and screw this up. Remember, we're using her government planes. That's one of the main components that make this operation successful. We need to be very careful, and if it means taking some time off from this operation, I'll do it. I'm thinking she's worried that this might have been compromised. I disagree with her, because we've been very careful and if there were any federal inquiries I would've heard about them through my contacts. So far, I haven't heard anything, so I think we've flown under the radar."

"Could we do this without her planes?" Wo asked as he signaled to the bartender to bring another round. "Don't you have some other contacts that could supply us with planes?"

"No way!" Waters answered emphatically. "That would be suicidal. We would get caught immediately. The only reason this has gone so smoothly is because we're using Chinese government planes. Be patient, Wo, we'll do this again. Especially if the shipment that goes out tonight gets there without a hitch. I guarantee Mei will want to try it again. She likes money too much to leave millions lying around. We'll just let the dust settle before we go at it again."

"Besides," John chimed in, "she's making a fortune on her solar projects. She owns both sides of the equation—the solar panel manufacturer and the actual solar farm out in Nevada. I hear it's coming in ahead of schedule and on budget."

Wo nodded. "Okay, I'll cool my heels. But I think it's a mistake to stop at this juncture. Now, let's go over Mei's request about Jason Ballard's daughter and girlfriend. Since things have changed due to the accident, what does she want me to do now? I hope she realizes there's no way I could barge in and kidnap them out of the hospital."

The bartender set them up with more drinks and retreated to attend to an elderly patron who had come in and sat at the bar.

The congressman sipped his drink, watching Wo carefully. "This is what she told me: She thinks Jason knows something about the disappearance of Brian Thompson. I believe he's the main principal of Inter-Power, the developer of the Copper Mountain solar farm. She wants to be in a position to use the two women as pawns to make Jason talk about what he knows if need be."

Wo listened intensely. "Okay, but what does she want me to do? First it was take them to a safe house and keep them. What is it now? Kill them?"

"I don't know the answers to those questions yet. I believe they're tracking Jason's movements now, and if Mr. Thompson, who is missing, doesn't show up within the next twenty-four hours, they're going to bring Jason in for a round of questioning. I'm sure after they grill him Mei will let you know what she wants to do with them."

"Do you have anyone checking on the daughter, Wo?" John asked. "Is there any chance she'll be released from the hospital soon? If she is, that would make your job easier."

"I have a man in Roseville as we speak," Wo answered. "He knows one of the nurses at the hospital, so she gives him updates. As far as I know, her condition hasn't changed. If Mei wants the daughter and girlfriend killed, it would be easier than trying to take them alive. And until she's moved out of the hospital, I can't do much. I hope you convey that to Mei."

Rubbing his chin, the congressman nodded, a serious look on his face. "I understand what you're up against, Wo. I'll make sure Mei understands that. But on the other hand, she's a powerful woman and doesn't like to be denied once she puts her mind on doing something. I would prepare for both scenarios and be ready."

Wo leaned back in the seat and took a deep breath. "I'll see what I can do, Congressman. Give me as much help as you can. Where will you be in the next twenty-four hours? I want to let you know once the shipment lands in Mexico."

Waters looked down at his watch. "I've got a ribbon-cutting in downtown tomorrow and then I'm scheduled to attend a fundraiser at Post Trio in the city tomorrow night."

Wo's eyes raised. "Post Trio? My, that's a fancy place for a fundraiser. I'm impressed."

The congressman laughed. "It's one of my constituent's functions. I just show up and start taking credit." He leaned in and

253

winked. "And of course accept campaign donations. But in answer to your question, I'll be around this area for the next two days, so call me anytime, and if I'm not available, leave a message. I'll get right back to you."

He tossed his drink down and stood up. "Come on, John, we need to get back to the office. I've got a couple of appointments I need to make." He tipped his hand to Wo. "Thanks for the drinks. Good luck tomorrow. I'll see you around again soon." He turned and left the bar, John following close behind.

Wo watched them for a minute before ordering another shot of tequila. I can't read Congressman Waters. I think he would sell out his mother for a hundred bucks, and if the pressure were put on him to give out names, he would sing like a canary. I need to be careful with him.

FORTY

The first thing Crystal heard was the sound of something pumping air around. Lifting her hand gingerly, she reached up and felt the bandage wrapped around her head. Her hand moved down to her right cheek and she felt a huge lump of puffy flesh around her eye. The other eye opened enough so that she could start making out images in the stark white room. Her temple throbbed. Every movement was painful, but she turned her head slightly to the side. Where am I? Slowly she started to piece together her last thoughts: Jimmy attacking her and Steve coming to her rescue, the car veering left then back right, the ground coming up at them. Where's Steve? Is he okay?

As her one eye adjusted, things in the room started to come into focus. Across from her bed she saw a person sitting quietly reading a book. Staring hard and trying to focus, it dawned on her who it was. Janine! What was she doing here? Running her tongue across her cracked lips, she whispered almost inaudibly, "Janine, is that you?"

Janine looked up from her book, her eyes wide with surprise. She leapt out of the chair and rushed to Crystal's bedside, reaching out and holding her hand. "Oh my god, Crystal!" she gushed, kissing her hand. "You're awake, you're awake." She reached over and pressed the nurse call button twice. "I'm so sorry, sweetie," she said, tears welling in her eyes. "I should have had you stay with me. I'm so sorry."

Crystal swallowed with difficulty then asked, "Is Steve alright?"

"Yes, he's okay. He suffered a couple of broken ribs, but he'll be okay." Janine continued to rub Crystal's hand. "Your dad is on his way home from China. He should be here later today. He's so concerned about you. We all have been."

"How long have I been out of it?" she asked, barely above a whisper.

Janine paused as she thought for a second. "You've been in a coma for a couple of days. The doctors weren't even sure if you'd come out of it. How are you feeling?"

Crystal shifted a little in the hospital bed. "I'm sore and my head hurts, but other than that I guess I feel alright. Where's my mom?" she asked. "She should be here, not you."

Janine stiffened but didn't move from the side of the bed. "I didn't talk to your mother, but your dad did and he told her about your accident. She didn't say if she would fly out here or not. She wanted your dad to pay for her ticket, but I don't know what happened after that."

"Why would my mom want my dad to pay for her plane ticket?" she asked irritably. "He pays her alimony and her boyfriend makes a lot of money. Why doesn't she come out here on her own and pay her own way?"

Shaking her head, Janine answered in a soft voice, "I don't know, Crystal, those are grownup questions you'll need to ask your dad. Were you and Steve really going to drive to North Dakota? Do you know a how far that is?"

"Steve told me it was a day's drive once we went through Reno. We planned on camping out at a campground along the way until we got there. It wasn't going to take that long."

Putting her hand to her mouth to contain a laugh, Janine said, "Oh my god, Crystal. Reno isn't even a quarter of the way to Fargo. It would have taken you five days and hundreds of dollars for gas, plus food and drinks. How were you going to pull that off?"

Crystal carefully pulled the top sheet up to her chest with both hands and answered sheepishly, "I don't know. I never looked at a map to see where we were going. I trusted he knew what he was doing." She looked at Janine, tears welling in her eyes. "I just wanted to surprise my mom. I haven't seen her in over a year."

A female nurse came into the room, immediately picked up Crystal's arm, and checked her blood pressure. She checked the bandages on her head, all while asking a few questions about how she was feeling. After a few minutes she stood back, folding her arms across her chest. "Well, this is really great. Your vital signs are good. You seem to be lucid. Welcome back. The doctor has been called and he should be here shortly to give you a more thorough exam."

The nurse bent down and spoke to Crystal. "You are a lucky young woman. There are a lot of people who love you and were praying for you." Pointing at Janine, she continued, "This woman has not left your side for more than a few moments the whole time you were in your coma. She obviously cares deeply for you. Count your blessings."

Crystal looked at Janine and smiled weakly. "Thank you. You didn't have to do that."

Janine wiped a tear out of her eye. "It was nothing, Crystal. I was just so worried about you. I'm so glad you're back with us."

The nurse picked up a chart at the end of the bed and started writing some notes. "There are some other friends of yours who have been by to check on you almost daily. They were very concerned about your condition."

Crystal turned her head to the side. "Really? Who was it?"

The nurse shook her head. "They didn't leave their names, but they were definitely older than you. Somewhere in their mid-twenties I'd guess." She partially shut the curtain covering the window. "I think we should let the young lady get some rest before the doctor gets here.

Why don't you go down to the cafeteria and get something to eat and let her rest for a little while?"

Janine stood up and patted Crystal's leg. "Of course, get some rest. I'll try to get ahold of your dad and tell him the good news. See you in a little while."

Watching her leave, Crystal felt a tear coming to her eye. Where is my mother? she thought. She's had a couple of days to get here, yet she's nowhere to be found. She's always bragging about how much money her boyfriend makes. Why can't she spend a few dollars to visit me? Was Dad telling the truth that the reason I couldn't go stay with her was because of her boyfriend? What else has she told me that isn't true?

She looked up and noticed two shady-looking young men peer into her room, take a glimpse of her, and then dart out. Who are those creeps? What are they looking in my room for? She fiddled with one of the IVs in her arm for a second. I wonder who's been by to see me. The nurse's description of them doesn't sound like anybody I know.

As she lay there, her eyelids grew heavy and she slowly drifted off to sleep.

FORTY-ONE

The counter at Malaysia Airlines was crowded as people jostled for position to determine what the statuses of their individual flights were. The electronic message board was reporting that the next flight had been delayed by an hour, and people were trying to figure out what the problem was from the harried workers behind the counter.

Jason leaned against a pillar near the waiting area and watched the commotion. Every twenty yards or so, Chinese soldiers with starched uniforms, shining pith helmets, and AR-15s strapped to their shoulders stood at rigid attention, their only movement being their eyes as they flicked left and right. Holding a Chinese newspaper at eye level, Jason would look over periodically, scanning the area to see if any of the soldiers were watching him or if anyone was approaching him. A voice behind him made him jump.

"Excuse me, do you happen to know who won the Cowboys' game?" the person asked nonchalantly.

Putting the paper down, Jason stared at a small man—about five-two with balding hair, wearing a pair of sweatpants and a tee-shirt—standing behind him. He answered, "I'm sorry, I don't know, but I heard they were leading going into the fourth quarter."

The man nodded and said in a low voice, "I'm Bret." He indicated with his head for Jason to follow him. He walked briskly past two gates and then came to a side door next to the men's restroom. Pulling out a keyring, he opened the door and stepped out as Jason followed. He led them down a long flight of stairs, and just before they hit the bottom, Jason heard the door behind them open and footsteps rushing down the stairs.

"Step it up," Bret said over his shoulder as he quickened his pace. "We need to get out of this terminal quickly." He flew down the rest of the stairs and came to another door. While he was fumbling with the keyring, Jason caught up with him and bent over, trying to catch his breath. He looked back at the stairway. Whoever was coming down the stairs was getting closer.

Bret found the right key and opened the door, which led to a tarmac, and tore off running. Shielding his eyes from the bright sunlight, Jason sprinted after him as they headed toward the awaiting jet. Bret bounded up the stairway and waited at the top for Jason to join him. Jason sprinted up, taking two steps at a time, and ducked into the jet as the pilot started to rev the engines. Behind them, a man emerged out of the airport door they had come from and sprinted toward the plane, waving a handgun. He was Chinese, young, dressed in a dark suit and dark glasses. Two military vehicles roared around the corner of the terminal building, their wheels squealing and smoke coming from the tires. Each jeep carried two soldiers. The soldiers aimed AR-15s at the plane. By the time the man in the suit reached the bottom of the jet's stairs, the jeeps had come up screeching to a halt.

Jason felt a tugging on his collar and was pulled into the jet's interior. Bret stepped around him then moved halfway down the stairway and started speaking rapidly in Chinese, gesturing wildly with his hands.

The man with the handgun waved it alternately at the plane then back at the man on the stairs. They each stood their ground, screaming at each other while the soldiers in the jeeps kept their AR-15s aimed at the jet.

Finally, another jeep pulled up with a man in a military uniform decorated with numerous medals on his chest. The soldiers in the jeeps immediately came to attention and saluted, as did the man in the suit at the bottom of the jet's stairs.

Leaning over a seat from the inside of the jet, Jason watched it all, his jaw open in amazement. What the hell's going on here? Are they going to let me get out of this country? His thoughts turned to his daughter. Hang in there, Crystal. I'll be home soon. I promise if I get out of this okay I won't leave you alone for so long. Things will change. I'll make sure of it.

The military man with the medals spoke briefly with Bret then turned and said something to the others, waving his arms wildly. The two jeeps backed up and turned around. The man with the gun jumped onto the back of one of the jeeps and they sped off.

Bret raced up the stairs, brushed past Jason, and stuck his head into the cockpit. "Get this bird in the air immediately!" he barked at the pilots. "We've got a real short window to get out of here!" He turned back and sat down in the seat outside the cockpit. He indicated to Jason to sit down. "Buckle up there, brother. This might be a wild ride."

As Jason fumbled with his seatbelt, he asked Bret, "What was all that about? I thought I was just going to take a civilian airline back to the States. I didn't realize I was causing an international incident."

Bret wiped his forehead with the back of his sleeve. He checked out of the plane's window, breathing heavily. He turned from the window and looked at Jason. "It seems you've created quite a stir. Your boss, Madam Chen, wants to keep you here in China. It's something to do with Brian Thompson's disappearance. I had to play the diplomatic immunity card out there. Fortunately for you, Agent Namath alerted us at the American Consulate and enlisted our help to get you out. You must be working on something big."

"If I am, it's news to me, Jason answered. I'm just trying to get back to the United States to my daughter. I know I've tripped over something the feds are interested in, but I'm not sure how it involves me." He felt a slight surge as the jet started moving.

"What about this Brian Thompson fellow?" Bret asked. "It seems I may have heard the name before."

"If you follow the solar energy or green energy movement, that's where you may have heard about him. He's a good friend of mine, and I helped him get out of the hospital in Hong Kong where they were keeping him. He told me he thinks Madan Chen was having him poisoned."

The jet's engines started to roar and Jason felt himself being pushed back in his seat by the thrust. The jet rumbled down the runway and lifted off, its nose pointed to the sky.

"I think you're going to join up with your friend Brian when we get to Japan and fly home with him back to the States. From what I heard, he's still in bad shape. So, what do you think?" Bret asked. "Is Madam Chen capable of murder?"

Looking out the window, Jason paused to ponder the question. Is she, he thought? She is ruthless and ambitious, and I'm beginning to believe she'll commit murder. He thought back on the events of the last few months. Andrew Dillon gets murdered, and since he owns Earth-Sun and is our only competitor for Copper Mountain, we get the job. Then when Brian Thompson expresses concern over Soltech's ability to perform, he gets sick and Mei Chen steps in. Now she's trying to keep me in China by force. Coincidence or nefarious? He looked back at Bret. "I don't know the answer to that, but I don't believe there is anything Mei Chen wouldn't do to get her way. Even murder!"

Bret unbuckled his seatbelt and sat up on the edge of his seat. "Well, we're not out of the woods yet. We're headed to Japan to re-fuel before we cross the ocean. The Chinese have some influence in Japan and they could make our lives difficult when we arrive." He stood. "We have a few hours to kill. Would you like a drink to ease the tension? I sure would."

"Yeah, a scotch sounds good right about now." He turned and stared out the window, looking down at the land slowly disappearing below him.

FORTY-TWO

The heavy jail door was pushed opened by a young soldier, and he stepped back to let the odor coming from the cell dissipate. The colonel standing next to him tapped another soldier on the shoulder. "Get Mr. Wilson on his feet. I want to see if he's finally changed his mind and is willing to sign the documents."

The young soldier bowed and entered the jail cell. His eyes adjusted to the light and he saw the form of a man lying curled up on the floor in the corner of the cell. Moving toward it, he kicked the man in the left side. Nothing happened so he kicked him again harder. The man didn't move. Bending down, the soldier fumbled around for the man's arm, squeezed his wrist for a second, and then tossed it away.

Jumping up, he bolted out of the cell, came to attention, and saluted. "Colonel, sir, I believe the prisoner has expired. I can't get a pulse and he feels stiff."

The colonel's face turned ashen and he hurried into the cell. He rolled the body over and placed two fingers on the man's jugular vein. He came back out of the cell, sweat pouring off his forehead. "How did this happen!?" he screamed, his face inches from the first soldier. "You were in charge of interrogating him, not killing him! You will be severely punished for this!" He screamed at another soldier standing at attention outside the cell. "Both of you, get him cleaned up and out of this cell!"

The two soldiers dropped their weapons and sprinted into the cell. Two minutes later they half-carried and half-dragged David Wilson's emaciated and bruised body out of the cell. The colonel paced back and forth in front of the cell, took his cigarette out of his mouth, and threw it on the floor. The soldiers stopped outside the cell and looked dazedly at him. "Where do you want us to take him?" one of them asked the colonel. "Should we take him to the prisoner's morgue?"

Stopping to light another cigarette, the colonel waved his arms excitedly. "Wait. Wait, let me think." He drew in a deep lungful of cigarette smoke and exhaled a thick, blue cloud. "No, don't take him there. Take him to the backroom of the infirmary, where the ambulances come to drop off patients. The members of the Party are going to want to keep this quiet." He turned and glared at the two soldiers. "No one is to be told about this. No one! If word gets out, you two will be shipped to the Mongolian front and will never be heard of again. Do you understand?"

Wide-eyed, both soldiers nodded. They bent down and grabbed David by his armpits and slowly carried him down the hallway. The colonel watched them for a moment then pulled out a cellphone from his pocket. He dialed a number and lit another cigarette while he waited for the other party to answer.

A male voice came on the phone. "Hello?"

The colonel cleared his throat before speaking. "Comrade Tan Wen, it's Colonel Zhang speaking."

"Ah, Colonel, good to hear from you. You are calling me with good news regarding our friend, Mr. Wilson? He has agreed to our terms for the hotel properties?"

The colonel lit another cigarette, his hands shaking as he held it. "Unfortunately, that is not what happened. Before we could get Mr. Wilson to agree to our terms and sign the necessary the papers, he passed away in his cell."

There was a long pause on the phone. The colonel took the cap off his head and wiped the sweat from his face. "You're telling me Mr. Wilson is dead?" Tan screamed into the phone. "You killed him?"

The colonel put his hand over his eyes and shifted uncomfortably. "Well, not exactly, Comrade. We didn't kill him purposely, but were trying to convince him to change his mind. We might have, uh, used some rough tactics to accomplish this, but we never left him in bad shape. I was with him yesterday and he was in great spirits." The colonel swallowed hard after he made that statement. When I saw him yesterday, he barely moved. I shouldn't have ordered that beating to be given to him, but how was I to know he was such a weakling? Chinese prisoners are beaten more severely every day and survive. It never occurred to me he might die.

"Well, Colonel, it seems you have created a very tenuous situation," Tan said in a stern voice. "Your instructions were to keep Mr. Wilson alive. He was a very visible member of Hong Kong society. Many people knew of his disappearance and many have suspected he might have been imprisoned, but for him to turn up dead at the hands of the Chinese government…this could turn into an ugly international event."

The inflection is Tan's voice told the colonel things were not going well with this conversation, and he knew what that meant for his future and it was not going to be good. Trying to keep his voice calm, he said, "I knew that would be the case, sir, so I instructed my soldiers to have the body taken to the infirmary. It can easily be moved from there to someplace where we can buy some time to come up with the appropriate story to explain the man's sudden demise. I didn't want anyone to know he was here in the prison the whole time."

Tan spoke firmly, without any emotion. "That was good thinking, Colonel. We're going to need to find a place to hide him and then come up with a believable explanation for finding him dead, wherever we leave him. I'll have to report this to Madam Chen. She will not be pleased."

The colonel winced at the mention of Madam Chen. Her status within the Party assured him that his career was probably over. "I understand, Comrade Wing. Let me know if there's anything else you want me to do with the body."

"For right now, leave it in the infirmary until further notice. You will hear from me as soon as I receive instructions."

♦

The scent of cherry blossoms from thousands of fruit trees left a pleasing scent in the air as the gentle breeze carried loose blossoms into the sky. A parade of dignitaries, all dressed in formal attire, meandered down the wide boulevard, cutting though the center of the immense orchard. The start of the summer festival was underway, and every high-ranking Party member was in attendance. Mei Chen and her husband, Ho, were at the forefront of the parade, waving half-heartedly to the throngs of people gathered on both sides of the street.

Mei had a fake smile planted on her face as she turned from one side to the other, pretending to be enjoying the spectacle. She heard her husband's hushed voice speaking to her as he leaned in next to her ear. "I have heard disconcerting rumors, my dear, about your recent activities," he whispered as they walked. "Many of the Party are very concerned about you. They are not looking favorably at what you are doing."

She turned slowly, her fake smile never wavering. "Why do you pay attention to such gibberish, husband? There are many jealous people in the Party who would like nothing better than to take over my position. They can't and they know it, so they try to make up gossip. It's beneath you to listen to that and take it seriously."

"Oh, but you are so wrong, my dear," he said softly as he bowed to the crowd. "True, there are jealous people in the Party, and there is

267

no doubt that some would like to replace us and take our positions. But new things have surfaced recently that have drawn unwanted attention shined on both you and me."

Mei raised her chin defiantly. "Really, and what might have happened recently that is causing such a fuss? I've been busy with my factory and haven't had time to do anything scandalous."

"Your friend, Mr. David Wilson, has been missing for about three weeks or so." They continued walking the same steady pace. "There's talk that you wanted to take over half of his properties and when he refused you put him in prison. Some of his friends and family contacted the British Embassy, and the embassy staff have been making inquiries. Uncomfortable inquiries. Scotland Yard has been alerted and they are also asking questions."

Turning to him, her face expressionless, she said in a firm voice, "Mr. Wilson is a big boy. He can handle himself. I did make him a proposition to buy half of his hotels and he was giving it some thought. He never turned me down." She turned back to the crowd and waved again. "Where he is right now, I couldn't say. I haven't talked to him or seen him in weeks. He's got interests all over the globe. More than likely he's with a women at one of his exotic resorts."

They turned a corner and headed down another street as the crowds excitedly waved and cheered when they came into sight. "Maybe you are correct and he is on holiday," Ho said quietly. "But I would hope you will take this matter seriously. If you have had anything to do with his disappearance, you must correct it immediately and let him go free. Stop interfering with ownership of businesses. This does not reflect well on the Party, and they are watching you. And if they are watching you, they are watching me. Don't think that I won't do what I need to do to protect myself, even if it's from you."

She stopped, glaring disdainfully at him. "Look at you, you fool," she hissed. "You wouldn't be near where you are without my pulling the strings." She felt her face heat up from anger and she stared straight ahead as she started walking again. "Don't even think of threatening me, as I will leave you in the dust so fast your head will swim."

"Always so confident, Mei," he said, his irritation growing. "You are not aware of the many people you have stepped on who are waiting patiently for the perfect moment to destroy you. Your family connections will not save you from your enemies, and you have many. There is talk in the Party that you might have committed treason of the State. You have been playing a very reckless game."

♦

Two hours later, the dignitaries had gathered in the main dining room of the Hong Kong Polo Club. Four long rows of tables sat parallel to each other, brimming with food set on silver platters. Servers in dark coats, starched white shirts and dark trousers, carried magnums of champagne and kept the patrons' glasses full. A string quartet played softly in the corner of the room and the air was filled with laughter and music.

Mei was chatting with another woman when she looked across the room to see Ho talking with Xi Ping, the Head of the Party. The conversation seemed to be intense from the look on the men's faces. What a pathetic creature Ho is, she thought. Who does he think he is, telling me what to do with my business? If he had half an ounce of sense, he would help me rather than hinder me. All he's interested in is being the next President, and he doesn't care whose ass he has to kiss to get there. What a joke. I would hope he realizes he's not going anywhere without my help!

Looking out as she sipped her champagne, she spotted Tan Wen standing near the wall at the entrance to the room. Their eyes locked and she could tell he needed to speak to her. She excused herself and followed him as he walked out of the room. He reached the main door to the club and held it for her as they stepped outside.

Pulling a pair of Gucci sunglasses out of her tiny purse, she slipped them on to buffer the bright sunlight. "Well, Tan, what an unexpected pleasure. What brings you to the Polo Club?"

"Let's take a walk, if you don't mind, Madam Chen," he said as he walked with her toward the garden area of the club, where a huge fountain sprayed water into the air in the center of a large pond. Colorful Mandarin ducks paddled aimlessly in the water, dipping their beaks down every so often to take a drink.

When they reached the edge of the pond, Tan stopped and looked back toward the clubhouse to see if there was anyone around them. Seeing no one, he put his hands behind his back and spoke in a serious tone. "We have a problem, Madam Chen. Mr. Wilson has died."

Her face never changed expression. "How did this happen? Your instructions were to get a signature from him, not kill him."

Tan put his head down and explained what had transpired. After he finished, he said in a lowered voice, "I am sorry we let you down, Madam. I will do whatever you ask to make this right."

She put her hands behind her back and paced in front of the pond. Tan followed at her side. "What are you going to do with the body? His body must never be found."

"I understand, Madam, and I will make sure it will not surface. I'm in the process of creating a fake itinerary for him to be out of the country as of two weeks ago. We will have witness statements saying he was in other parts of the country. It will look like he disappeared some place other than Hong Kong."

"What about Jason Ballard and Brian Thompson?" she asked, her face flush with anger. "Tell me at least that you have kept them in China."

Looking over her shoulder at another couple who had stepped outside the building, Tan shook his head. "No, we couldn't keep them. Someone alerted the US Embassy and they sent some personnel over to the airport and escorted them to a government jet. Without starting an international incident, there was nothing we could do to stop them."

Nodding, Mei stated, "It was good that you didn't interfere at the airport. Where are they going? We need to get to them. They both know too much and must be stopped. What do you suggest?"

"My sources tell me their flight plan was to Tokyo and then on to San Francisco. They also tell me that Brian Thompson is already in Tokyo and will join Jason for the flight to San Francisco. I don't think trying to mess with them in Japan would be a good idea. The Japanese are very touchy about us doing things in their country without their prior approval. We can get them easier when they land in the US. Once we get them, what do you want done with them?"

Mei started to walk slowly along on the edge of the lake, her hands folded across her waist. "What I want is for them to be permanently eliminated without repercussions. I don't want David Wilson's disappearance or this incident to touch me or anyone associated with me." She stopped and looked Tan in the eye. "You failed me last time with David Wilson. How can I be assured you won't fail in this also?"

Bowing slightly, Tan responded, his voice void of emotion, "With due respect, Madam Chen, you sent Mr. Wilson to jail, where he was tortured in order to comply with your demands. It was unfortunate the torture did not produce the results you desired, but torture is torture, and sometimes it gets out of hand. What you are asking is less complicated. We can take these two out without creating a scene and without drawing attention."

Still staring at him, she replied sharply, "Failure is not an option. If you need help, I have some sources in San Francisco who specialize in this sort of thing. If you want, I can place a call and maybe you can work together."

Tan bowed at her slightly. "I would be honored to work with any of your people in the US. I am sure these are competent people that you work with."

A majestic swan swam about a foot from the water's edge and started squawking loudly. Mei and Tan stepped back away from it.

"You don't happen to have any swan food with you, do you, Madam Chen?"

Looking at the swan she answered, "No, I don't, but that bird would look better coming out of an oven on a silver platter."

FORTY-THREE

The massage table sat in the middle of the room covered in clean white sheets. Soft music played from a Bose sound system located on a small dresser in the corner of the room. Cheap oil paintings of seascapes from San Francisco's coastline hung on the light-colored walls. A petite young woman, dressed in a white terrycloth robe, her dark hair pulled back in a ponytail, stood passively over the table, leaning into the brown body of Congressman Waters as he lay face down on the table, a small white cloth draped over his lower torso. She rubbed his shoulders with deft hands.

Smiling, he reached down and ran one of his hands up the back of the young woman's thigh as she massaged him. "I've been thinking about his all day, Kay," he said to her as he rubbed her up and down. "You do this so effortlessly, you put me in a trance."

Without moving his hand, she answered sweetly, "Eugene, you're a naughty boy. Every time I start to give you a massage, you want to rush right into hanky-panky. Relax and enjoy the music. We can get to that later."

Congressman Waters turned his head and looked up at her. "You mean we can get to that after I pay you in cash for the extra services. I know how you work, Kay."

Kay threw her head back and laughed. "Of course I negotiate and you pay up front. It's just smart business. If I wait to collect 'til after you're done, you won't be so anxious to pay up." She leaned down and whispered in his ear, "This way everyone is happy. You pay, you come, you go. It's all good."

"Indeed, it is." He continued rubbing her thigh. "You just have a way of making me want you badly."

The cellphone sitting on the table next to his car keys started to ring. Kay picked it up and handed it to him and he answered.

"Congressman Waters," Madam Chen said. "It's been a couple of weeks. How is everything?"

Sitting up, he waved at Kay to leave, and she turned and quietly left the room. "Madam Chen, it's good to hear your voice. Everything is grand. I assume you're calling to check on our final operation before we take a break in the action."

"That wasn't the purpose of my call, but since you mentioned it, fill me in."

The congressman reached for the glass of water sitting on the nightstand and took a sip. "We're scheduled to run the largest cargo to date tonight. Over fifteen hundred guns: AR-15s, pistols… You name it, it's in the shipment. Your plane will be flying out of Stead tonight at around eleven o'clock, and by 9:00 tomorrow morning everything should be unloaded and into the right hands."

"That's excellent, Congressman. There are no worries about anything?"

"No, Madam, we've been very cautious. No government agency has even heard of us or what we're doing. So far everything has worked out very cleanly." He curled his hand with his fingers and checked out his fingernails. "So, what was the real purpose of your call, Madam? How can I be of service to you?"

A pause greeted him over the phone and then she began to speak in a monotone. "Two men are arriving in San Francisco tonight from Tokyo on a specially chartered jet. Their names are Jason Ballard and

Brian Thompson. I want them taken care of immediately. Call your friend Wo Sung and see what he will charge for the job and then have him handle it."

The congressman's ears perked up. "Isn't Jason your president at Soltech and isn't Brian Thompson your partner at Inter-Power? My office was very instrumental in getting Inter-Power the BLM land lease for the Copper Mountain project. It would be very ugly if any of this was traced back to me."

"I understand, Congressman. That's why, when you speak to Wo, make sure he doesn't leave any traces. It's very important this job is carried out quickly and quietly."

The congressman scratched his thigh as he sat on the edge of the table. What is this all about? Why is she trying to get rid of two high-profile guys in the green industry? "Madam Chen, I'll call Wo right after we hang up, but I must caution you about being reckless. I don't know your motivation for this job, but I think you should give it some thought. These aren't just average people we're talking about."

"I appreciate your concern, Congressman, but trust me, you need these guys gone too. They know too much about a lot of things we're doing. I want to be on the safe side."

"What about Jason's daughter and the girlfriend? When we last talked, Wo was to have them picked up and held while you dealt with Jason. Wo hasn't been able to get the daughter since she's still in the hospital, but she should be getting out soon. Do you still want to proceed with that plan?"

"Yes, tell Wo I want him to finish that job also. It's too risky to try to hide them. I don't want to take any unnecessary chances."

The congressman laid back down on his stomach. This is getting convoluted, he thought. Four people getting murdered. This will be the last time I get involved with Mei Chen. The stakes are getting too high. He cleared his throat. "Okay, Madam Chen, I'll pass on your request to Wo. I'll call you tomorrow when the shipment is safely in Mexico."

"Thank you, Congressman Waters," she said passively. "I look forward to speaking with you tomorrow."

Waters studied the phone for a minute, then shrugged. He dialed a number and waited for Wo to pick up.

FORTY-FOUR

The moonless night was silent except for an occasional cricket. Millions of stars added some light, but overall it was pitch black. Agent Mark Namath, his face smeared with black face paint, stood in front of a camouflaged truck, his back up against its side. "ATF" was scrawled across the back of his jacket. He faced five other men and two women, all dressed in black uniforms with dark helmets and visors that were pulled up over their heads. They stood at attention, their arms cradling AR-15s as they waited for him to speak. The truck had been parked across the empty runway, and they could see over his shoulder the lights from a larger hangar in the distance. The silhouette of a cargo plane parked in front of the hangar could barely be made out.

"Okay, listen up," Agent Namath said in a hushed voice. "It's almost time to move. We're going to cross the runway and fan out around the C-47. Turn all electronic devices off now and communicate by hand signal. When you're all in position, I'll give the signal to rush the hangar." He paused for a second, looking into each of his team member's eyes. "No matter what happens, I want to take their leader, Quan, into custody alive. You've all studied his picture, so there should be no reason you don't recognize him. More than likely, there will be resistance, and you are authorized to use deadly force, but spare Quan. Are there any questions?"

No one raised a hand or called out, so Namath nodded to them. "Okay, let's roll." He turned and hunched down, walking briskly toward the lighted hangar. His heart started to beat quicker from the adrenaline rush he was feeling. He slid his index finger through the trigger hole and gently pressed down until he felt resistance. After moving one hundred yards, he signaled for the team to stop. He got down on one knee and relaxed his breathing.

So far, so good, he thought. He could hear the sound of a forklift engine coming from around the plane and another from inside the hangar. As his eyes adjusted to the light, he could see one man with an assault rifle standing just inside the hangar, his back to Namath and his team. There is a potential problem, Namath thought. He's going to be the first to go. He turned, held up one finger, and pointed to the corner of the hangar. He made a slashing motion across his throat. Each member of the team nodded.

Namath stood up and hunched over again, making his way steadily across the tarmac towards the plane. He could hear voices yelling back and forth at each other in Chinese as he reached the wingtip of the plane. He directed his team with hand signals, and they spread out in the dark around the plane, kneeling on one knee once they got into position.

Checking back at the man guarding the hangar, who still had his back to him, Namath held up his hand for his team to see. He looked left then right, checking to make sure everyone was in the right position. He dropped his hand and started sprinting the last twenty yards toward the hangar. He yelled at the top of his voice, "ATF! Freeze! Drop your weapons!"

Another agent yelled out, "FBI! Drop your weapons!"

The man at the entrance spun around and leveled his assault rifle at Namath. He squeezed off two rounds before five of Namath's team opened fire, the shots exploding around the hangar. The man

278

staggered as ten bullets found their mark and he fell backward, firing his weapon harmlessly in the air.

Two men at the back of the hangar raised up their hands in surrender. The team swooped into the hangar, their rifles sweeping left and right, looking for unseen threats.

Namath ran toward the forklift, which had stopped moving. He pointed his rifle at the driver's head. "Put your hands in the air! Where I can see them!" he screamed as he ran.

The man in the forklift slowly raised his hands. "I'm unarmed," he yelled. "Don't shoot!"

Reaching the forklift, Namath stopped, his heart racing. "Get down off the machine, Quan, and lie face down in front of me."

Quan, his hands over his head, stepped gingerly down to the ground. He turned to his companions and yelled something to them in Chinese. They both started laughing. He looked at Namath as he got down on his knees. "We'll be back here tomorrow night, Mr. Agent Man," he snarled. "All you are is a small inconvenience. My people will get us back to work in a few hours."

Standing over Quan, Namath relaxed a bit. Apparently our sting has caught these guys off guard, he thought. That's a good thing. He instructed one of the team members to handcuff Quan as he watched over him, his gun pointed at his shaven head. "I don't know about that, Quan. I'm guessing you might be out of business a little longer than that."

A camouflaged truck pulled up and stopped inside the hangar. The driver jumped out and opened the back, exposing a row of benches on both walls.

"Okay," Namath yelled as he waved his rifle over his head. "Read them their rights, load them up, and get them out of here." He stood and watched as the three men were helped to their feet and herded into the waiting truck. Tucking his rifle under his arm, he walked over to the plane and walked up the ramp to its entrance. Stacks of wooden crates lined the walls on both sides of the plane. He stood there in awe as he sized up the massive cargo.

A female team member came up to his side and stood next to him, her mouth open in amazement. "Are all of these boxes filled with guns?" she asked. "How many do you think there are here?"

"I don't have any idea, but my guess is thousands," he answered without taking his eyes off the boxes. "This was quite an operation they had going here. No wonder it had such high priority from the agency." He turned and smiled at the woman. "Well, let's get going. I think we did our job tonight. Now it's time for the justice system to run its course."

◆

A crashing sound from the other room brought Wo Sung out of his deep slumber. As he groggily groped for the pistol he kept on his nightstand, he heard voices yelling from inside his house. Remembering the thick lines of cocaine he'd snorted the night before, he wondered if he was dreaming.

Suddenly, bright lights flashed in his face and he heard men screaming. "Get your hands up! FBI! Get your hands away from the gun or we'll shoot! Do it now!"

Wo shielded his eyes with his left hand, and he slowly moved his right hand away from the gun and the nightstand. "Who are you? What do you want?" he pleaded, his voice gravelly. "I haven't done anything."

He felt a pair of hands reach under his armpit and someone yanked him to his feet. A uniformed man came within inches of his face. "Wo Sung, I presume?" he asked.

Wo answered nervously, "Yes, that's me. What do you want? Who are you?"

"I'm Agent Pete Clark, FBI. You're under arrest for illegal arms trading, heroin trafficking, and murder. You have the right to remain silent. Anything you say can and will be used against you."

The rest of the conversation was a blur as Wo was searched and moved into his living room, where he was let down onto his leather couch while agents combed his home. They had waved a search warrant in front of his face before they started, and all he could do was watch. I wonder who I should call first, he thought, my attorney or Congressman Waters. I hope he's covered his bases. I'm not taking the fall for that dumbass politician. These guys won't find anything here, but if they start following the money trail, there could be some bad repercussions. I need to take care of myself.

As he watched the agents catalog and box up his belongings, including the hard drive on his computer, Wo began to sweat. This is no small-time raid, he thought. These guys are looking for something or someone.

Agent Clark pulled up a chair sitting next to the couch. He produced a legal pad from under his arm and wrote some notes on it. "Any idea why we might be here, Mr. Sung? You've got to know by now this wasn't just a random search."

Wo raised his eyebrows and gave as innocent a look as he could muster. "I have no idea why you're here. I haven't done anything illegal. I don't know what you're taking with you in all those boxes, but you're not going to find anything incriminating."

Clark slapped him playfully on the thigh and smiled. "Oh, but you're wrong, Mr. Sung. We've uncovered a goldmine of information already. You probably hadn't heard this yet because we've got your man Quan in custody, but your gun-running operation hit a little snag."

Wo's breathing picked up. Oh crap, what did that weasel tell them? Quan likes to talk and feel important. I can imagine these guys feed his ego and he tells them everything. He swallowed hard, trying to stay calm. "Quan has worked for me in the past, but he's not currently doing anything for me now."

Clark cocked his head, his eyebrows raised. "Really? That's not what he told us when we caught him with that big shipment of guns you were about to fly to Mexico. He told us all about your little plans. Would you like to fill me in on who else might be behind this with you, or are you going to take the fall all by yourself?"

Wo took a look around his living room. Agents kept coming and going from various parts of his house, their arms loaded with boxes. He moved his neck to the left to ease up the sweat coming down the side of his head. What do I do here? Should I call my attorney? It could be a long time before I see the inside of this place again. He stared at Clark a second and then blurted out, "I know of an assassination that's being planned. What kind of deal will you give me if I tell you what's about to happen?"

Clark whistled to another agent, who hurried over. Speaking in a firm voice, he answered, "I'm not a judge nor can I promise you anything that happens in a court situation. But I can tell you if you withhold information that we could have used to save someone's life, the book will be thrown at you and the full weight of the federal government will be used against you."

He paused for a minute to let what he said sink in, then continued, "However, if you help us out and we end up saving people because of your cooperation, that will go a long way toward what we'll recommend to a judge. We're going to find out what you know eventually, so you might as well help yourself and help us now."

Wo looked at Clark and then at the other agent. This gig is up, he thought. I need to cover my own ass. He took a deep breath and started speaking. "There are teams looking to eliminate four people…"

By the time he was finished, Clark was on the phone to his superiors and sprinting out the door toward his car. "This is the information I have on these people. Two are possibly located at the Roseville Kaiser hospital in the intensive care unit. The other two have just arrived in San Francisco by jet from Japan, and one is possibly in route to the Roseville hospital. I need units rolling immediately!" He jumped into a car that had pulled up to the curb. "Head to the San Francisco Airport, fast! Turn on the siren!"

FORTY-FIVE

Jason leaned into the cockpit and watched as the plane taxied toward the far end of San Francisco Airport. In the distance he could see an ambulance waiting next to a small terminal that stood away by itself from the main terminals. He turned and moved back to the middle of the plane, where a hospital bed was strapped down. Brian Thompson, his eyes closed, lay quietly on the bed, two IVs of clear liquid flowing into his veins. A young male nurse sat next to Brian's bed, thumbing through a magazine. Jason came over to him and patted Brian's arm. "Hey, buddy. I think we made it. We've just landed in San Francisco and there's an ambulance waiting to take you to a real hospital. You're going to get better and help me finish the Copper Mountain project."

Brian opened one eye and gave a weary smile. "I wouldn't be alive without your help, Jason. I can't thank you enough. I really almost didn't believe I was being poisoned, but I knew it wasn't normal. What's going to happen to Mei Chen?"

Shaking his head, Jason answered, "I don't know, Brian. If she stays in China, probably nothing. But I've got to believe there will be enough to show she had a hand in trying to poison you. If that's the case, there would be a criminal complaint filed against her and she could be arrested if she comes back to Hong Kong. The British government still has a long reach there, so she'll probably stay away."

"I don't know, Jason. She's a powerful person with high-level contacts. I wouldn't put it past her to bribe her way back into this country just to get even with you and me." He pointed to a water bottle on a cabinet next to where Jason was standing. "Could you hand that to me?" he asked. "I'm thirsty."

Jason gave him the water and took it back after Brian had taken a few swigs. "I'm afraid you might be right. She does have friends in high places. If anyone could dodge legal problems, even attempted murder, it would be her."

The plane made an abrupt left turn and came to a stop. They heard the engines start to slow down and Jason got up to stretch. The pilot and copilot came out of the cockpit and opened up the door to the plane. A blast of sunlight came cascading into the fuselage, and Jason had to shield his eyes with his hand. "Great flight, fellas," he said to the pilots. "I barely felt we were in the air."

The pilot tipped his cap and then scrambled down the stairway. Two emergency personnel emerged from the ambulance and came into the plane, immediately checking on Brian. One of them toted a new plastic IV and quickly replaced the old one. They asked the nurse a series of questions while testing his blood pressure and checking his vital signs. After a few minutes, they strapped him down tight and lifted his bed, carrying him carefully down the stairs and off the plane.

Jason followed and hopped into the ambulance with Brian. The door was shut tight and the driver took off. Settling into a chair across from Brian and next to one of the EMTs, Jason took out his phone and made a call. He breathed easier when he heard Janine's soft voice on the other line.

"Janine," he said concernedly. "I'm back. I just landed a few minutes ago. I'm going to accompany Brian to the hospital, and then one of my employees has volunteered to let me use his car to drive to Roseville. How is Crystal?"

"Oh, it's so good to hear your voice, Jason," she answered, almost in tears. "She's doing much better. She woke up yesterday and seems to be getting stronger every minute. She'll be so excited to see you."

"I can't thank you enough for everything, Janine. I don't know what I would have done without you. I'll see you in a few hours."

"I can't wait to see you. Please be safe."

He hung up the phone, but before he could put it into his pocket, it rang again. Jason studied the number for a second then answered. "Hello?"

"It's Agent Mark Namath, Jason," the voice spoke in a steady voice. "Are you on the ground?"

"Yes, I just landed a few minutes ago. How is everything going?"

Namath's anxious voice filled him in. "We've found out that there's been a hit ordered on you and Brian, and also on your daughter and girlfriend. Do you know where they are at this minute?"

Jason glanced over at Brian lying on the bed. One of the paramedics was searching in his bag next to him. "Brian's in the ambulance with me right now and we're headed to St. Joseph's Hospital in San Francisco. My daughter and Janine are in Roseville at the Kaiser Hospital there. I just spoke to Janine before you called. What should we do?" He looked over at the paramedic who had pulled out a needle and was filling it with some kind of liquid.

"Right now, get Brian to the hospital and I'll have some of my agents there waiting. We can watch him from that point on. I'll also send a team to Roseville to watch over the two women there. Where will you be?"

Jason studied the paramedic as he fiddled with the needle. "I wanted to drive to Roseville to be with my daughter. Will that be okay?"

There was a pause on the other line. "Let me think," Namath said. "I believe one of my guys could drive with you, but let me check. When you get to the hospital to drop off Brian, stay there until I call you. It won't be long."

As Jason hung up, he looked harder at the paramedic. He was wearing tennis shoes and appeared to be wearing jeans under his uniform. Something isn't right about his guy. Why would he be giving Brian a shot?

The paramedic had rolled back the sheet covering Brian's arm and rubbed some antiseptic on it. He held the needle above the arm and started to bring it down. Jason reached over and grabbed his arm. "What are you injecting in my friend?" he asked. "Don't you think we should wait until we get to the hospital where a doctor can examine him?"

The paramedic glared at him, trying to shake loose from Jason's grip. "Let me do my job," he snarled. "You're not the one with the medical license."

Jason held firm. "Not until you tell me what you're putting in my friend's body. I think there's something wrong here."

The man smiled, reached down, pulled a Glock pistol out of his duffle bag, and pointed it at Jason's forehead. "You're right, Mr. Ballard. There is something wrong. I'm sitting here wasting my time listening to you babble when I can pull this trigger and be done with you."

Jason felt the hair on the back of his neck stand up. He stared into the barrel of the gun then into the paramedic's eyes. This is not good, he thought. Not good at all.

FORTY-SIX

Congressman Waters, his elbows on his desk and his chin resting on his folded hands, sat in rapt attention as he listened to Sheila Andrew, the young attorney representing a group called Victims of Gun Violence, walk him through the legislation he was going to introduce at the House of Representatives the following morning. A slender blonde with bright blue eyes, she was a striking figure in Washington D.C.

His eyes walked from her white blouse, which tastefully exposed a hint of her perky breasts, to her eyes and back. Man, what I won't do to party with you, he thought. Mmmm, what a dish. After I get this gun control bill to vote, I'm going to propose we go out and celebrate properly.

His thoughts were interrupted when she stopped and looked at him quizzically. "Is there something wrong, Congressman? Am I reading the bill too fast?"

Waters cleared his throat and rearranged some papers on his desk. He waved his arm at her. "Oh no, not at all. The legislation you've written is superb. When we're done, trying to buy an assault rifle in the US will be harder than buying heroin. Keep reading. It's music to my ears. The sooner we get those destructive weapons off the streets, the better the country will be."

She smiled sweetly at him and squirmed in her seat. "Well, Congressman, you don't know how much my clients appreciate your stance on gun control. You've been one of the most consistent voices on the Hill on this issue, and we'll reward you when it comes to contributing for your upcoming re-election campaign."

Waters grinned and waved at her dismissively. "It's a cause I feel strongly about, Sheila." And you're a cause I'd love to feel strongly about, he thought, smiling. "If I didn't believe this strongly about gun control, I wouldn't put my name on the legislation, but I do believe in it. I can't wait to get on the floor of the House tomorrow and introduce it." He snapped his fingers. "That reminds me, I need to make sure my assistant, John, sets up the news conference after the session. I need lots of cameras rolling." He leaned forward and said in a soft tone, "When you're in Congress, you can't get enough publicity. You've got to get a big bang for your buck." Winking at her, he threw his head back and laughed.

Biting the tip of her pen, Sheila laughed along. "Congressman Waters, you are one of a kind."

A sharp knock on the door made Sheila almost jump out of her seat. Waters had barely looked up from his desk when the door flew open and three men dressed in dark suits burst into the office, the first one holding up a badge at eye level. "Congressman, I'm agent Mark Namath with Alcohol, Firearms, and Tobacco. I'm placing you under arrest for the crime of illegal shipment of guns across state and country lines." He pointed at the agent next to him, a tall black man with a shiny, shaved head. "Willie here will read you your rights."

Sheila sprang up. "You've made a huge mistake!" she yelled. "Congressman Waters would never be involved in anything to do with guns. He hates them!"

Agent Namath ignored her and set a piece of paper in front of Waters. "This is a search warrant for your office, your home, and your office in San Francisco. I would appreciate you alerting your staff as to what's happening and encourage them to cooperate with us."

Waters's mouth hung open in disbelief. "I, uh, I," he stammered. "I don't know what you're talking about." He looked at Sheila innocently. "I don't know what's happening." Oh no, he thought. They caught Wo Sung with the guns. I need to get ahold of my lawyer and a good public relations firm. He stood there in handcuffs as agents scurried about his office, going through drawers and file cabinets.

Agent Namath grabbed him by the elbow and pushed him toward the door. "Come on, Congressman. I need to take you downtown to get booked."

As Waters stumbled forward and out of his office, his mind raced. Do they know about Mei Chen? What else do they know about Wo Sung? Can't everyone stay quiet?

FORTY-SEVEN

The kitchen counter was covered in legal documents. Mei scanned them one at a time. In her left hand she held a teacup filled with jasmine tea, its aroma floating around the kitchen. These documents will do the trick, she thought. My lawyer actually did what I told him for once and covered all the things I was worried about. Now, I need to take these to the proper authorities and I'll be the owner of all of David Wilson's hotels. At least Tan did a credible job at forging his signature. She held her teacup with both hands and took a sip, looking out through the French doors to her backyard. She squinted her eyes as she surveyed the lush gardens. David should have taken my offer. It was fair and he'd be alive and enjoying life right now. She sighed. This was all his choice.

A sound to her left made her turn to see her husband Ho standing at the kitchen's entrance, his arms folded and a concerned look on his face. "Did you know there is a formal inquiry, requested by the President, into your business dealings and the disappearance of a prominent British citizen, Mei?" he asked. "I've been summoned to the court to testify tomorrow. I have not been informed as to what they want to talk to me about, but I know they're going to demand to know about our finances and where our wealth came from."

Setting her cup on the counter, she stared at him, disgusted. Ho, you are such a wimp. Every time you get a hint of a whisper, you run off and hide in the corner. No one is going to challenge me. You're lucky you're married to me. "I don't listen to such garbage," she spat. "It's like a bunch of old ladies gossiping about nothing. I have better things to do than worry about what simple minds are talking about."

Ho walked up to her and pointed a finger in her face. "Let me tell you something, Mei. You think because your grandmother was a charter member of the Party with Chairman Mao that you are immune from following the rules." His voice rose. "You are mistaken. I know what you've been doing and I have a strong suspicion you were involved in the fate of Mr. Wilson. And if I know, so do other people in the Party. You've flaunted your wealth around when I told you not to, and you'd better hope it doesn't come back to haunt you. I will not take a fall for you. Do not look to me for help if your world comes crashing down!"

Mei threw her head back and laughed. "Me, need help from you? That's funny, Ho. I'm the one who has the connections in this family. If you are to become President of China, it will be because of my influence."

Ho's face turned red and he spoke in an angry voice. "You are not as influential as you think. Did you really believe the British government would sit by quietly and not pursue the cause of the death of David Wilson, a prominent citizen who died under mysterious circumstances here in China? Do you not think that there will be an investigation, and if it is proven your actions were behind the death it would be a huge embarrassment to China? That you would not be severely punished, possibly put to death?"

Mei walked past him and waved her arms dismissively. "You're wasting my time with your scare tactics, Ho. I've got to attend to my business. Go on and play with your ass-kissing Party members."

A loud banging on their front door stopped her in her tracks. She looked back at Ho. "What is that?" she asked in an irritated voice. The banging continued and voices could be heard shouting for the door to be opened.

Ho went to the door and hesitated before opening it up. Four men dressed in military fatigues and toting assault rifles rushed into the house, followed by an older man with a chest full of decorations on his uniform and a shiny silver helmet on his head. He had a riding crop under one arm as he strode up to Mei and pulled out a scrolled roll of paper. Rolling it out, he started reading out loud:

"By order of the Communist Party of China, Madam Mei Chen is to be arrested for murder, extortion, and other crimes against the State. She is immediately to be arrested and housed in the Beijing State Prison to await her trial. It is signed by President Xi." The man rolled the scroll back up and stuck it under his arm.

Mei stood in the foyer, her mouth wide open in horror. "There has to have been a mistake. I am Madam Mei Chen, daughter of Chi Hong and granddaughter of Tian Kung, the comrade of the great Mao Tse Tung! I am the face of the Party! You can't arrest me!"

The man with the medals motioned to the soldiers standing at attention, and they moved quickly to surround Mei. He walked up to her and put his face inches away from her nose. "I'm sorry, Madam, but I have my orders." He nodded to one of his men, and he grabbed Mei's wrists firmly and whipped them behind her back, cuffing them.

"You don't want to do this!" she screamed as the men pushed her out the door. "You will pay dearly for this insulting action. I am Madam Chen! Do you hear me! You will be sorry for this. Let me go!" She continued screaming as they led her to a waiting car out front and shoved her in unceremoniously. She turned her head and screamed to no one in particular. "When I get out of this mess, which I will get out of, there will be hell to pay! I will hunt down everyone who has any involvement in this action and they will be severely punished!" One of the soldiers pushed her back and slammed the door shut.

Ho watched the scene unfold but said nothing. After Mei had been placed in the car, the man with the medals came over to him and stood at attention, a soldier standing on each side of him. "Comrade Ho, you have been summoned to Party headquarters immediately. I will escort you there in my car. We need to leave here now."

Bowing his head, Ho nodded. "May I use the restroom before we leave?"

"If you hurry," the man said curtly. He nodded to one of the soldiers to follow him.

Ho walked steadily through the kitchen towards the bathroom next to it, stopped, and looked around. He went over to a line of drawers and quickly opened the first one on the left. Reaching in, he pulled out a long, stainless steel knife and held it close to his chest to shield it from the soldier who was standing a foot away. The soldier saw the knife and reached out to grab it, but Ho, with both hands, brought the blade down hard into his belly, pushing it to the hilt. The soldier struggled with Ho and yelled for his commander. Blood immediately gushed from Ho's mouth and the wound in his belly, and he wobbled on his feet a few steps before falling face first onto the floor, a pool of blood growing around him.

FORTY-EIGHT

A nurse came into the room where Crystal was lying, lifted her arm up, and took her blood pressure. She smiled as she let the arm down. "You seem to be getting better by the minute. How do you feel today?"

"I'm feeling better, thank you," she answered.

Sitting across from Crystal, Janine set the magazine she'd been reading on her lap. "Your dad should be here in about an hour. I know he's going to be so happy to see you."

As the nurse left the room, Crystal looked over at Janine, a concerned look on her face. "Do you think he's going to be mad at me for trying to drive to North Dakota, Janine? I didn't mean to cause all this trouble."

Janine got up from the chair and sat on the edge of the bed. "He might be upset that you took off without telling anyone, but he'll forgive you. Trust me, he's relieved that your injuries were not worse and you're getting better."

"Has my mom called since I've been here?" Crystal asked. "She knows what happened, doesn't she?"

Janine patted her hands and answered softly, "Your mom has a lot of things going on in her life, and I think she's just been really busy. She knows what happened and I'm sure she thinks about you all the time. You watch, she'll call soon and check on you."

Crystal looked down and stared at her folded hands. "I don't think she really cares. I'm a problem for her." She looked into Janine's eyes. "I'm sorry I've treated you so rotten, Janine. I was just angry at everything that's happened in the last few years. I wasn't happy my parents split up and I took out that anger on you. It wasn't fair."

Janine kept her eyes locked onto Crystal's and continued to rub her hands. "Don't apologize, Crystal. I know this has been hard on you and you coped with it the best way you could. I don't hold any grudges against you and I'm just happy you're doing better."

Two younger men entered the room, each wearing a white smock and a pair of stethoscopes hanging around their necks. Both had the same jet-black hair cut short and both had dark almond-shaped eyes. Janine stared at them as one of them examined a chart he had brought with him. These guys look too young to be doctors. Neither of them looks to be older than twenty-five. She noticed part of a bright red tattoo peeking out of the sleeve of the doctor with the chart. What is that, the tail of a lobster or a crawfish? I don't believe I've ever seen a doctor with a tattoo, she thought. I guess there's a first for everything.

The one with the chart spoke first in a cheery voice. "Good morning, Crystal. I'm Doctor Benson and this is Doctor Smith. We're here to get you out of this hospital and down to the UC Davis hospital so we can treat your head injury."

Doctor Smith stepped forward. "Your head injury needs attention and they don't have the right equipment here, so we're going to move you. It won't take too long."

Janine's stomach started to knot up. Something's not right here. There's no reason to be moving her. If the doctors thought she should have her head looked at, they would have done it days ago. As the two doctors positioned themselves at the front and back of Crystal's bed, Janine jumped up and put her hands on it to stop them.

Crystal clung to Janine, pointed at the doctor with the tattoo, and whispered to her, "Those were the creeps who've been hanging around my room while you were gone. They weren't wearing smocks before."

"Hold on here," Janine said, her voice quivering as she shielded Crystal from the doctors with her body. "Nobody's said anything about Crystal being moved. This is the first time it's been mentioned and nobody has discussed this with me. We don't know who you are or what your authority is to have this girl moved."

"Are you her legal guardian?" Doctor Benson asked. "If not, there would have been no reason to discuss this with you. We know what's best for her, so if you'll get out of the way and let us do our job, we'll be on our way. We would not be opposed if you would like to come with us for the trip."

Janine grabbed the frame of the bed and held on tight. "I want to see the doctor who's been caring for this young woman since she got here. No one has said anything about her moving to another hospital. She's not well enough to be moved." She looked Doctor Benson in the eyes and asked, "Who are you? Who sent you?"

He calmly started to reach inside his smock. "Do yourself a favor and let go of the bed. We have a job to do and you're interfering. One way or another, this girl is coming with us, so you can either join her or get out of the way."

The way he looked at Janine sent shivers down her spine. A mix of fear, anxiety, and dread filled her body. She shrank back on the bed and in a quivering voice yelled at the top of her lungs, "Nurse! I need some help here!"

"You shouldn't have done that," Doctor Benson said as he pulled a gun out of his coat. "You've only made my job harder, and I don't appreciate that."

◆

Special Agent Pete Clark turned from the off ramp of Interstate 80 onto Douglas Boulevard and reached the hospital entrance. He had driven the three hours from Santa Clara at the behest of his partner, Agent Namath. Pulling into the parking lot of the hospital, he was surprised to see how bucolic the scene was. A few dozen cars were parked in a lot that had room for a thousand. An ambulance sat at the entrance to the hospital with its back door open.

Strange, he thought, as he walked up to it. Why wouldn't it be parked at the emergency entrance on the other side of the hospital? Clark peered into the open back door. Bandage rolls and packages of pills were strewn about as if someone had ransacked the place. A couple of items of clothes were flung across the front seat area.

Clark looked from the back of the ambulance and over toward the hospital's entrance. He felt for the handgun strapped to his shoulder and headed through the automatic doors at the entrance. He stopped at the information counter and said to the nurse attending it, "Which room is Crystal Ballard in?"

Scanning her computer, the nurse typed some letters and said to him without looking up, "Room 326. The elevators are to your right. Are you family? I'm going to need some ID."

He yelled over his shoulder as he blew by her, "Sorry, this is an emergency." Moving quickly, he made it to the elevators just as the doors were closing. An elderly man in a Tommy Bahama shirt stuck his arm out to hold the door open and Clark stepped inside. "Thanks," he said as he nodded to the man. "Could you hit the third floor button for me?"

When the elevator opened at the third floor, Clark stepped cautiously outside. He looked to his left and then to his right. As he turned back, he heard a woman scream out in distress, "Nurse, I need some help here!" He ran toward the woman's voice and came to a sliding stop in front of room 326. As he stood in the doorway, he saw a woman clinging to a hospital bed while a doctor at the head and another doctor at the foot tried to wrestle it away from her grip.

The doctor at the foot of the bed pulled a gun from his coat. "You shouldn't have done that."

Clark didn't wait to hear what else the man said. He whipped his gun out and pointed it at the back of the doctor's head. "Drop the weapon! Drop it now!" He heard the woman scream and watched as the doctor spun around and ducked, pointing his gun at Clark.

As Clark backed up a step, he heard the gun go off and the bullet whiz by his head, spattering into the wall across the corridor. Clark methodically squeezed off three shots, hitting the doctor in the chest and forehead. The doctor's eyes flickered as he fell forward and slumped to the floor, blood pouring from his wounds.

Clark pointed the gun at the second doctor. "Put your hands up! You've got two seconds or I will fire!" Out of the corner of his eye he could see Crystal and Janine hugging each other on the bed, crying hysterically. He could hear running feet outside the room in the corridor as well as sounds of shouts and yelling.

The doctor raised his arms slowly, a bright red tattoo of a crawfish being exposed on his left arm. His lips turned up into an evil smile. "Move slowly toward me and away from the women!" Clark barked, his gun still trained on the man. By now chaos had ensued and there was more screaming and yelling coming from the corridor outside the room. Clark yelled over his shoulder to no one in particular, "Someone call 911! I need some backup." He maneuvered the second doctor out to the corridor and ordered him to lie face down. Pulling handcuffs from his belt, he cuffed the man and stood up, taking a deep breath.

A doctor and a nurse rushed by him to attend to the doctor who had been shot. He stepped around them and came up to Crystal and Janine, who were still in a tight embrace on the bed. "It's okay," he said softly. "You're going to be alright. Nobody is going to hurt you." He tapped Janine on the shoulder and said, "Help me get her into another room. There's going to be a lot of activity here and she should not be stressed watching it."

Looking up, Janine nodded. "Okay." She stood and cradled Crystal's head against her chest. "Come on, sweetie. Let's move you somewhere else."

"Janine," Crystal asked, her voice quivering. "Would you call my dad? I want to hear his voice right now."

FORTY-NINE

The black barrel of the Glock was pointed squarely at his chest. Jason looked the paramedic in the eye, only to see a steely look in return. The man had a malicious smile on his face, as if he were actually enjoying every second of making Jason sweat. Now what? Jason thought. His heart beat rapidly and his mind raced. There's no room to do anything in this cramped space.

Brian Thompson lay silent on his stretcher.

"You have upset my plans," the paramedic said as he held the gun on Jason. "I was going to finish off the patient first with a syringe of arsenic, but I don't mind going out of sequence."

The cellphone in Jason's pocket started ringing loudly. It startled the paramedic and he let the gun down. Jason charged at him, grabbed the hand holding the gun, causing the gun to discharge, the bullet grazing the side of Jason's head. The ear-splitting explosion and recoil from the gun caused the paramedic to fall against the back wall of the ambulance. Jason leapt forward and with his free hand reached for the man's windpipe. The man struggled to get free and fired the gun wildly a second time, the bullet ripping through the roof of the ambulance. Smoke and gunpowder filled the space, and Brian started to cough. Jason lost his grip and fell to the side of the man. The blood from the gunshot wound started to get into his eyes, blurring his vision. The paramedic's eyes rolled as he clutched his throat in agony. Jason hopped on his chest and pounded the man's face with his fists. After about five blows, the man rolled to his side and lay limp.

Jason leaned back against the side of the ambulance, trying to catch his breath. He suddenly felt it accelerate and swerve violently to the left. He reached out to touch the wall to steady himself when the ambulance swerved to the other side. Sirens wailed in the distance and Jason struggled to stand up and look out the back window. He could see three black and white highway patrol cars, their lights flashing, gaining ground on them. The ambulance continued to swerve left and right, weaving in and out of traffic, as if ignorant of the blaring horns and screeching tires behind it. Jason tried his best to keep his balance but was not succeeding.

One of the patrol cars pulled alongside the ambulance and prevented it from steering to the left. The ambulance veered right and cut across two lanes of traffic, driving off the highway and onto a dirt field. Jason and Brian bounced around in the back until the driver swerved once more and the ambulance tipped to its side, sliding viciously and throwing dirt and rocks into the air. It finally came to a stop in a cloud of dust after crashing up against a rock outcropping.

Brian hung helplessly in his gurney, still strapped in and hanging on his side. Jason felt blood running down his head, and he reached up to try to stop it. He heard noise coming out of the cab and then a door slam shut. Voices where yelling, "Freeze, put your hands up!" Two shots rang out and then there was a deadly silence.

The back door to the ambulance was sprung open and Jason stared at two uniformed highway patrol officers, their guns drawn as they swept them around the inside of the ambulance. "You guys arrived just in time," Jason said wearily as he struggled to stand. He moved over to where Brian hung sideways. "Help me get this poor guy out of this contraption. I think he's hung out here long enough."

"Are you guys alright?" the first officer asked. "Do we need another ambulance?"

Jason nodded, a smile coming across his face. "We're both fine, but an ambulance would be good for him. I'd just like a ride to Roseville to see my daughter." Suddenly, a hand grabbed his ankle and he looked down to see the paramedic raise his other hand, which was gripping a hyperemic needle coming down straight at his thigh. With all the force he could muster, Jason turned his hips, and the man's fist crashed into the metal floor, bending the needle backward. He kicked his foot straight out toward the foot of Brian's bed, crushing the arm holding his ankle, making his attacker yell out in pain and release his grip. Jason saw him reaching for the gun that had fallen to the floor and quickly grabbed the man's arm just as he picked up the weapon. His attacker tried to move the gun toward Jason's head as he fought to push it away.

Someone screamed behind him, "Move to your left so I can take a shot!" Jason looked into his attacker's eyes, hate and rage just behind his pupils. Jason, gripping the arm with the gun, trying desperately to twist it away. With his adrenaline rushing, Jason leaned forward with all his might and then jerked his body backward. He heard a shot explode behind his head, felt the whistle as the bullet flew by his shoulder, smashing into the attacker's forehead, spraying blood, flesh, and bone fragment around the ambulance. The attacker's eyes rolled into his head and he lay motionless, his hand releasing the gun.

Jason's body went limp as he lay against the ambulance wall catching his breath. The highway patrol officer climbed into the ambulance and checked the body for signs of life. Then he turned to Jason. "Are you okay?"

Jason heaved a big sigh, wiped some of the blood off his face, and then flashed a thumbs up sign. He gave him a weary smile and said, "I'm okay. Can you get us out of here?"

◆

Two hours later, a bandage over his left eye, Jason stepped into room 522 at the Roseville hospital. Crystal's eyes lit up and she sat up on the bed, holding her arms out. "Daddy!" she squealed in delight. "You finally made it."

Janine jumped up from her seat by the bed and hugged Jason as he hugged Crystal. "Oh, Jason, we're so glad you're here. It's been a crazy day." She pushed herself away and looked at the bandage wrapped around his head. "You've been injured. Are you okay?"

Squeezing them both tightly again, Jason said, "It's just a scratch and I'll be fine. Saying it's been a crazy day has to be the understatement of the year. I'm so happy you're both alright. Let's all go somewhere safe and try to put all this behind us."

FIFTY

The sun shone brightly through the full-sized window in the living room. Unopened cardboard boxes, each marked with its contents, were stacked in the corner of the room. A large leather couch sat in the middle of the room and a Persian throw rug covered the light-stained wood floor in front of it. A flat-screen TV hung on the wall facing the couch, and the Clemson-Georgia game was just getting under way. Jason leaned back on the couch, a cup of steaming coffee in his right hand and the front page of *The San Francisco Chronicle* in his left. His eyes flitted from the newspaper to the TV, depending on which had more action. His cellphone rang and he leapt up from the couch to retrieve it on the granite breakfast bar. "Hello?"

The familiar voice of Brian answered him. "Hey, bud, welcome back. How was China?"

"Hey, Brian," he answered, smiling. "It went very well. The new owners of Soltech want me to stay on as president and to continue to make improvements at the Shanghai factory. They're pleased at the progress we've made at Copper Mountain and are looking forward to being a contender for the Antelope Valley job." He paused and took a sip of his coffee. "How are you feeling? When I saw you three weeks ago you were looking stronger, and you sound much better."

"I'm getting better by the minute, Jason. I've been going to the office for a couple of hours a day for the last week and my strength is slowly building back up. It's been a long two months." He paused and then laughed. "In another month I'll be ready to take you out on the golf course and whip your ass."

Jason laughed along. "I'll be happy to concede a whippin' to you just this once due to your condition. But once you're one hundred percent, look out. I will show no mercy."

"Yeah, right, in your dreams. While you were in China, what did you hear about Mei Chen? There's been only a smidgen of information here in the States, and I'm curious to know what will happen to her. She's been mentioned as a co-conspirator with Congressman Waters in the gun-running scheme, and her name has popped up in the Copper Mountain investigation, but not much information has come out."

Filling up his coffee cup, Jason moved back to the couch and turned the TV down. Taking a deep breath, he said. "Madam Chen has taken a deep and embarrassing fall from grace. Scotland Yard handled the investigation of the disappearance of David Wilson and, after putting the squeeze on some low-ranking army officers, got them to point out where the body was hidden." He put his feet up on the coffee table and set his coffee cup next to his feet.

"Where did they find him?" Brian asked.

Jason reached down and took a sip from his coffee. "They found him in the bottom of a well in Quinghai Provence on a farm that Mei Chen owned. They fessed up about the torture and ultimate death of David and how it was all directly tied to Mei Chen and her ambition to take over his hotel chain." He changed the channel on the TV to Sportscenter and checked out the news at the bottom of the screen. "All the facts in the case were carefully laid out and presented to the Chinese government, and she's scheduled for trial in about a month. It doesn't look good for her, as she probably won't be executed but will be thrown into one of China's worst prisons for the rest of her life."

"What about her husband? Did anything happen to him?" Brian asked.

Jason nodded. "Ho committed suicide before he could be arrested. I don't think he could stand the humiliation."

Brian whistled softly. "Wow, that punishment was swift. What's going to happen to her daughter, Chi? I feel so sorry for her."

"Actually, she's going to doing better than her parents. She's such a violin prodigy she was accepted to the Juilliard Music Academy here in the US. She'll be staying with a Chinese family nearby, so I think she'll be in good hands."

"Well, that's good to hear," Brian said. "Were they going to do anything about Mei trying to poison me? Nobody in the government has talked to me about it at all."

"According to my sources, throwing your case into the mix would have been overkill. They had enough on Mei Chen to put her away and they felt they didn't need to complicate the case. I guess we'll see after her trial if they're right. I'm sure they can always come back and try your case if they need to." Jason stared at the TV and watched a replay of a Clemson touchdown, then asked, "You mentioned the Copper Mountain investigation and Congressman Waters. What's going on there?"

"Yeah, that's a bit of a mess," Brian answered. "I was unaware Mei Chen was working with Congressman Waters to make sure Inter-Power secured the lease with BLM for Copper Mountain." He paused for a second. "The feds are checking out if there were any illegal dealings with those two and who knew what. I don't think it will affect Inter-Power since I made sure everything we submitted to BLM was legitimate for the lease, but if Waters and Mei Chen were working the backroom, he's going to have more problems than he already has with the gun running and racketeering."

"I thought Congressman Waters was a stand-up guy and a real leader in Congress. What about him?" Jason asked.

Brian almost spit out his words. "What a piece of work the congressman was. Such a hypocrite. It's truly amazing to me that he would throw his career away being involved in an illegal operation like that."

"I completely agree," Jason said. "But he'll have time to reflect on the irony after he's shut up in prison for the rest of his life. How long do you think he'll keep collecting a paycheck from Congress?"

"Probably as long as he can," Brian answered. "So, how's Crystal doing? Is she getting along better with Janine? That had to be a pretty traumatic time for her with the accident and the mess at the hospital."

"Crystal's doing much better. She started her soccer practice for her high school and looks like she'll be starting at one of the forward positions. She seems to have recovered well from the concussion and doesn't show any ill effects. She's met with a counselor at the school numerous times and seems to be doing just fine."

He paused since he thought he heard a car pull into the driveway. He looked out the front window but couldn't see anything. "Janine is great as always, and we're getting along better than we ever have. Crystal seems to have a completely changed attitude toward her, and they're getting along well, thank god. Everything is good here."

"Well, that's great to hear, Jason. You and Janine are made for each other."

The doorbell rang and Jason stood up from the couch. "Listen, Brian, someone's at my door so I'll let you go. It's great to hear you're getting stronger and I'm looking forward to working together to finish Copper Mountain. Let's go out Monday night and have a beer."

"That sounds good to me. I'll catch up with you Monday and confirm. Take care."

Jason flipped the phone onto the couch and went to the door. He opened it to see Debbie standing on the porch, a suitcase at her side.

His breathing quickened and he tried to take a deep breath. "Debbie, what are you doing here?"

Debbie put her suitcase down and folded her arms across her chest. "Aren't you going to invite me in? What happened to your manners?"

"I'm sorry," he said defensively as he held the door wider. "Come inside."

Bending down, she grabbed her suitcase and stepped inside. She stepped into the family room and surveyed the house. "Looks like life has improved for you. This is a very impressive house." She turned to him. "I see you're doing well. I got this address from Crystal. I told her I wanted to send her something in the mail. May I sit down or do I have to stand all day?"

"Of course, have a seat. Would you like a cup of coffee? I made it a few minutes ago."

Sitting down on the couch, she tossed her hair over her shoulders. "No, I'm good." She folded her hands together on her lap and stared at him.

He looked at her for a second. This is the woman that I've carried a torch for so long, but all I see is someone who's after something. I don't know why she's here but I know she has an agenda. Clearing his throat, he asked. "You didn't answer as to what you are doing here in California. Is this a vacation? Where are you staying? I'm sure Crystal will be ecstatic to see you."

She took a deep breath without taking her eyes off his. She smiled thinly then said, "David kicked me out of the house last Saturday. He told me he was done with me and it was time to go our separate ways. I had nowhere else to go, so I came back home." She reached out, grabbed one of Jason's hands, and gave it a squeeze. "I knew that things were not going well with David and I really longed to be back here with you and Crystal. Do you think we could give it one more try to keep our family together?"

stared at her. I can't believe what I'm hearing, he thought.
After all this time she wants to get back together with me? He pulled
his hand back, went to the kitchen, and pulled out a cabinet drawer.
He fumbled around and picked up a business card. Walking toward
the front door, he opened it and stood next to it. "I'm sorry, Debbie,
but that window of opportunity was closed long ago. It's time for you
to move on with your life and leave me out of it. It's time for you to
leave. Please call Crystal and make an effort to see her. It would mean
a lot to her."

Debbie sat stunned but then slowly rose from the couch. She
picked up her suitcase and walked through the door, stopping on the
porch. Her face was flushed as she turned and faced Jason. "It's that
bitch girlfriend, isn't it?" she screamed. "The one that you couldn't
keep your hands off and broke up our marriage!"

Jason handed her the card. "Here, call this guy. Maybe he can
help you out."

Looking down at the card, she read it, a puzzled expression on
her face. "Dennis Watson," she said. "I haven't heard of him in years.
Why should I call him?"

"He's a psychologist and maybe he can help you out. Both of you
could hang out in the SVU."

Still holding the card she asked, her voice rising, "SVU? What's
an SVU?"

"It's the Special Victims Unit. You two could commiserate with
each other there and compare notes on how the world has done you
wrong."

Jason watched her face grow redder. She balled her fists and
waved them in front of his face. "We're not finished, Jason! I'm not
going to roll over and just give in. I'll drive that bitch out of your life
and…"

Before she could finish, Jason slammed the door shut and heard
some muffled sounds as she screamed through the door. She continued
for several minutes, and finally the screaming stopped. Jason heard a

310

car door slam and then screeching tires as she backed out of the driveway and sped away. He pulled a curtain back from the window to see the back end of her car disappear around the corner. Stepping back from window, he stared straight ahead until a smile came across his face. "Why did I wait so long to do that?"

FIFTY-ONE

The diner was half full since the lunchtime crowd had thinned out. A young server came up to the table and asked, "Is there anything else I can get you?"

Jason shook his head. "No, we're fine, thank you. If you could leave me the bill, I'll settle up with you."

The young man pulled a black folder out of his back pocket and set it on the table. "Here you go, sir. I'll take this whenever you're ready." He turned and headed toward the kitchen.

Janine, sitting to his left, said, "Thank you for lunch, Jason. That was really good."

Crystal, sitting on his other side, chimed in, "Yeah, thanks, Dad."

Pulling out his wallet, Jason picked out three twenties and placed them in the folder. "You're all welcome. So, Crystal, what do you think about Stanford? Coach Walker gave us a pretty thorough tour of the place, don't you think?"

Crystal beamed. "This place is awesome. I could easily see myself going to school here. I know I've been by the campus before, but I never imagined how gorgeous it was on the inside."

"That coach seemed really interested in you too," Janine said. "It sounds like, if you play as well this next year as you did last year, they're going to offer you a scholarship."

"How cool would that be, Crystal?" Jason asked. "I'm really proud of you. Not only have you got the grades to get into this university, but you've got the athleticism to play at a high level. Not many young people can do that."

Crystal's face flushed and she smiled shyly. "Thanks, both of you. I appreciate it."

Jason held up the folder for the server to see, and he nodded. "Just remember what the doctor said and take it easy for a few months. You'll be ready for the spring and will be as good as new."

"I'll be good, I promise." She took a sip of her iced tea. "Are you going to be traveling back and forth to China as much as before, Dad?"

Jason leaned back in his chair. "Well, now that the new ownership of Soltech has been solidified, they've given me a contract to stay on as president and continue to run the business. I'll still have to go over to check on the Shanghai plant, but I've been allowed to hire an operations person to help me so I won't have to travel as much. It's been a long and crazy couple of months. Up until two days ago, I wasn't even sure if they were even going to keep the company going, but apparently they saw the value in the Copper Mountain job."

"Speaking of Copper Mountain, how's Brian doing?" Janine asked.

"Brian's doing great. He's fully recovered and back working and is back to being his old self. In spite of all the chaos swirling around the ownership of Soltech, I managed to keep the production and delivery of the solar panels on schedule, and Copper Mountain is moving along well. Brian has been pleased with both our product and our service. It's been four months since we started the project and we're slightly ahead of schedule, which is a good thing."

Janine reached over and put her hand over Jason's. "Have you heard anything further about Mei Chen? What's going on with her?"

313

Jason shook his head. "I've heard nothing. It's like she fell into a black hole. Her name is never spoken and it's like she never existed. But I hope she never gets out and gets what's coming to her."

Crystal whistled softly. "Wow, that's brutal. They don't mess around in China do they?"

Jason looked at her and nodded. "No, they don't, especially when you embarrass the government and commit heinous crimes." He glanced down at his watch. "Hey, we better get moving if we're going to catch the movie."

As if choreographed, they all stood up at once and headed toward the restaurant's exit, with Jason in the middle, one arm around Janine and the other around Crystal.

Have you read Indecent Fortunes Trilogy?

PRAISE FOR *THE HOUSE'S MONEY*

**2013 Northern California Publishers and Authors
Book Award Winner**

"*The House's Money* is an exciting, riveting read for your general
fiction collection – highly recommended."
-The Midwest Book Review

The Indecent Fortunes Trilogy continues in book two with the fight for water rights in book two, *Liquid Gold*.

PRAISE FOR *LIQUID GOLD*

2014 Next Generation Indie Book Award Winner

"...A plot twisting journey through the hidden world of banking, water rights, greed and murder...It is hard to determine which is more terrifying – the body count or the banking practices."
- Wendy Shultz, Mountain Democrat

Delve into a cesspool of deceit as those who prey on the most vulnerable among us make a killing in the final novel, of the Indecent Fortunes Trilogy.

With a degree from USC's School of Business in Real Estate Finance and Marketing, Owen Sullivan has attacked almost every corner of the real estate industry for over 35 years. In 1987, he ventured off to start his own company, developing and selling in excess of $300 million in real estate ventures.

Owen is an avid football fan and enjoys playing and writing music, entertaining friends, and cooking. He lives in Orangevale, California with his wife, Genevieve. To learn more about Owen, visit: TheHousesMoney.com

www.ingramcontent.com/pod-product-compliance
Lightning Source LLC
Chambersburg PA
CBHW050553260626
47157CB00002B/547